Death is My BFF

KATARINA E. TONKS

DEATH IS MY BFF

BOOK 1 — THE DEATH CHRONICLES

wattpad books W

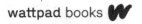

wattpad books

An imprint of Wattpad WEBTOON Book Group

Copyright © 2023 Katarina E. Tonks

Content warning: blood, violence, mention of death, swearing

Published in Canada by Wattpad WEBTOON Book Group, a division of Wattpad WEBTOON Studios, Inc.

36 Wellington Street E., Suite 200, Toronto, ON M5E 1C7 Canada

www.wattpad.com

First Wattpad Books edition: September 2023

ISBN 978-1-99025-999-9 (Trade Paper original)
ISBN 978-1-99885-427-1 (Hardcover original)
ISBN 978-1-99077-850-6 (eBook edition)

Library and Archives Canada Cataloguing in Publication information is available upon request.

Printed and bound in Canada

3 5 7 9 10 8 6 4 2

Cover design by Hillary Wilson
Interior Image © irham, ©sana_78 via Adobe Stock,
© cheeryshadow27 via Shutterstock

To Mom, Dad, and Christina: for always believing in my dream.

To my Wattpad readers: this one's for you, cupcakes.

PROLOGUE

Ten Years Ago . . . Pleasant Valley, New York

"I want to go home, Mommy."

Faith's mother, Lisa Williams, held the steering wheel precariously with one hand as she struggled to close the crammed glove compartment. One final slam shut the sucker for good, and she blew a strand of blond hair away from her face. "Why, baby? What's wrong?"

"My tummy hurts. Daddy made me toast, and it tasted like dirt."

"Not again," Lisa said. "Your father, the next Iron Chef. Mommy has a very long day at work tomorrow, so we have to go food shopping now. In and out, I promise. How about we get your favorite waffle mix? Do you want chocolate chip waffles for dinner?"

"Daddy said I'm not allowed to have sugar for dinner, or else all my teeth will fall out, like an old geezer's."

Her mother sighed. "Daddy also made you dirt toast for breakfast, so what does he know?"

Faith giggled. "Can we get bacon? Not the gross veggie bacon Aunt Sarah eats, please. It makes everyone fart."

"Normal bacon it is, princess." Lisa laughed. "Feeling a little better now?"

"Mm-hmm." Faith hugged Mr. Wiggles to her chest, extracting the comfort she needed from his soft body. Food shopping was her favorite activity to do with her mother and her stomachache was ruining it.

As they drove down a pothole-riddled road, Faith looked out the car window. Her little eight-year-old heart fluttered at the ghoulish clouds edging closer on the horizon. She unzipped her backpack, sliding out a folded picture of Mr. Wiggles. Turning the thick parchment paper over revealed another drawing she'd created, one she'd strangely forgotten. The picture was of a storm with an ominous black sky. At the center of the drawing stood a cloaked man with a tall, curved weapon. Shadows spread from his monstrous frame, like vicious snakes prepared to strike. There was a building behind him, a store of some sort, colored aggressively in red.

Glancing out the window again, Faith pressed the paper to the cold glass, lining up the sky of her drawing to the identical menacing clouds currently blanketing the horizon. With wide eyes, she stuffed the horrific sketch into her rainbow backpack and turned to tell her mother of her many drawings of the cloaked man. Instead, her attention switched to another wave of pain that shot through her stomach. She sat back and squeezed Mr. Wiggles to her tummy.

And once more, the illustration became a faded memory.

In the parking lot of the store, an eerie feeling came over Faith. She looked up at the sky, but her mother tugged her to the shopping cart and asked her to grip the metal cage on the sides as they walked. Hugging Mr. Wiggles under her arm, the pain in Faith's stomach mysteriously subsided.

The cart rolled forward. Faith and her mother approached the luminous store, unaware of the cloaked figure perched atop the building, watching them.

Lisa and Faith weaved in and out of the aisles and piled the cart high with waffle mix and other necessary sustenance for the week. At the register, Faith felt sick again and thought she might throw up.

The automatic doors of the market slid open, and three men charged into the building wearing ski masks and holding guns. Their voices thundered out commands as the leader of the pack stumbled out in front of the rest and loaded his shotgun in a clumsy manner. "Everybody get down and shut the fuck up!"

The men spread out across the store, grabbing items, breaking into cash registers.

Panicked, Lisa ripped Faith from the cart and dropped to the floor behind a cashier station. Faith whined against her mother's palm covering her mouth.

"I said, open the damn register!"

"Don't touch me!" a woman shouted. "Let me go!"

"Ow—fu—you bitch!"

Faith trembled as the woman darted into her line of sight, sprinting away from one of the armed men. A piercing shot went off, followed by a sickening crack. A heavy object smacked against the floor, followed by a moan. Another shot fired through the air. Faith's ears rang.

"Stay quiet," her mother whispered as she pulled Faith closer and struggled with her phone. Faith held Mr. Wiggles tight and whimpered.

As a thin stream of blood oozed down their checkout aisle and crept toward Faith, she began to scream. Her mother tried to suppress the cry with her hand again, but she was too late. A pair of boots lumbered closer, belonging to a man with a ski mask and twitching hands.

"Isn't she pretty?" His words slurred. He smelled rotten. With bloodshot eyes and decayed teeth, he grinned down at Faith. "Come here, little girl."

The man snatched Faith by the arm and yanked her to his side.

He was so frail his clothes sagged off his bones and gross sores poked through the gaps in his mask.

Faith choked out a sob.

"Take whatever you want! Take my whole purse!" Lisa threw her bag at the gunman's feet. "There's two hundred dollars in there. It's all I have. Please, don't hurt my daughter. Please."

"Two hundred dollars? Is that all your kid is worth?" The masked man laughed harshly, but his amusement terminated as his gaze dropped. Faith followed his stare and noticed her mother's phone was wedged between her legs. "Planning on calling the police?"

Lisa shook her head. "No, no, I wasn't! I swear!"

"Give me the phone now, or I'll shoot her!" A crazed look rolled over his bloodshot eyes. The coolness of metal paralyzed Faith as he pressed the barrel of the gun to her forehead. "Or maybe I'll shoot her anyway."

"No! No, please! She's just a child! I'll do anything you want!"

The intense pain in her stomach overcame Faith. Inhaling sharply, she let out a bloodcurdling scream.

"Why is she screaming like that?" the masked man demanded. "What's the matter with her?" He shoved Faith to the side, glaring at her with the gun clenched in his unsteady hand. "Shut up! Shut up, you little brat!"

Faith's mother jumped into action, emptying pepper spray into the gunman's face. They grappled for the gun.

"Faith! *Run!*"

Faith launched to her feet and ran toward the store entrance. But ahead, another masked gunman slinked out from a checkout aisle, blocking her way. At the crack of the bullet, Faith's ears roared, unable to hear her mother's shrieks. She felt neither the bullet enter her stomach nor the side of her head striking the tile floor.

Mr. Wiggles fell from her small hand. Her lips quivered. To her right lay the cashier who had been shot, a gaping hole in the center of her forehead. Faith wanted to scream, but her breath was short-lived; she stared at the ceiling with glazed eyes, drowning almost peacefully in a pool of crimson.

Above her, the harsh florescent lights warmed to a golden hue and spread out like heavenly wings. Calmed by the ethereal glow, she closed her eyes to sleep . . .

The store plunged to a bitter cold, awakening Faith with a sudden gasp for air. Her hands pressed into her stomach, finding no trace of blood or pain. The market was different, dimmer, drained of color. And there were no people. Regaining the ability to stand, she rose to her feet.

"You must be Faith."

She jumped at the melodic voice. A boy leaned against a shadowed wall behind her.

Faith analyzed the dulled surroundings in confusion, then narrowed in on the strange boy. Nearly blending in with the darkness, his features were concealed, except for a small grin.

"Who are you?" she asked.

He emerged from the shadows as if he were a part of them, threads of dark matter clinging to his body like fingers, before retreating back into the wall. He had the most frightening eyes. Otherworldly. Mismatched green with all the characteristics of a cat, including thin vertical pupils. A mean scar slashed from his eyebrow to his cheek enhanced his cruel appearance.

"Anyone I want to be," he replied at last.

She noted his strange accent as she watched him with rapt attention. He stood a good head taller than her, with a lean build that was by no means skinny. He was midnight, clad only in dark clothes, and around her age. A few years older, though, by Faith's guess.

"How do you know my name?"

"I know everyone's name, Faith."

"I don't understand."

"Of course, you don't." He looked her up and down. "What are you, five?"

"Eight."

"Five, eight. Same thing." He buried any sliver of pity behind a vacant expression.

"You don't look much older than me," Faith argued.

The boy snickered, as if he knew something she didn't. "Right, you got me there." He pushed off the wall and glided toward her. "I understand you've lost your way. I'm here to walk with you to the light."

When the boy moved closer, a black aura hovered around his body. His shadow on the wall was one of a man, not a boy. Faith tried to retreat backward, and panic struck her as she realized she couldn't move her feet. Her heart raced.

"No," Faith said firmly. "I'm not leaving my mom!"

"I'm not real big on sympathy, kid. It's time to come with me. Now, if you will. I have a busy schedule."

The boy reached to grab her hand, only the tips of his fingers brushing hers. He froze, surprise washing over his expression. Light filled the boy's vision in an instant, paralysis locking every bone in his frame. Memories. Memories buried long ago, crawled from the deep graves of his wicked mind and flashed before his eyes like broken film. His mother, smiling down at him, haloed by the sun behind her. A willow tree with a mirror embedded in its old bark. An arena with blood-stained compacted sand and a gladiator falling to his knees with a silent roar of despair.

Shadows curled around the boy's shoulders and tugged, jarring him to the present with the girl. It took him a moment to gather himself—those distant recollections promising to bury him alive alongside them.

Faith trembled with a small sob, their fingertips still touching. Her soft, innocent features had lost all color. And the boy knew. *He knew* she had somehow seen those glimpses into his past too. He felt weakened—vulnerable in a way he could never allow.

He lurched away from the girl as if he'd been struck by lightning. "What are you?" he hissed through tight teeth.

"What . . . what do you mean?"

The boy's darkness pooled across the floor. The inky tendrils veered around Faith's shoes, oil to water. His wicked gaze slowly lifted from this strange phenomenon, until he looked deep into her eyes. He regarded her curiously, as if just now noticing a peculiarity about her.

"Your soul. I have never encountered anything like it." The boy tilted his head to one side as his face and eyes hardened. He looked frightening then, a snake primed to strike. Faith wanted to run far, far away from this boy. "Do you wish to see your family again, *Faith*?"

Faith nodded like a bobblehead; her words wedged in her throat.

"You're in luck. I've got a deal for you." She stared into his catlike vertical pupils as they dilated ever so slightly. "If you haven't figured it out yet, you died. I will bring you back to life and to your mom, but I cannot do so without consequence. When you are eighteen, I will return to collect your soul. Ten years is a long time from now. Would you not agree?"

"Yes," she trembled out.

"Unless, of course," the boy continued, feigning concern, "you want me to take you away now?" He clasped his hands behind his back and stalked a slow circle around her. "If that's the case, you'll never see your family again. Do you want the deal?"

"The deal . . . I want the deal." Faith didn't think twice. She would have done anything to get away from the frightening boy as soon as possible. "Please, bring me back to my mom."

He stopped circling and stuck out his palm. Though he was wary of what would happen once they touched again, this could only be finalized one way. Faith looked down at his hand, hesitating, before clasping it fully with her own. He wasn't as cold as she'd expected.

Without warning, the boy's complexion changed. His hand clutched hers in a vise grip as his exposed skin developed intricate black markings. A shadowy matter expelled from his fingers, spiraling up Faith's arm in black coils. She tracked the mist with wide eyes before the blackness launched itself into her chest. She inhaled sharply, held motionless, as his power marked her soul with a kiss of death. The sunshine in her blond hair slowly drifted to midnight from the roots down.

"You will meet me again, Faith Williams." This time, when the boy grinned, he had a mouthful of fangs. "When your luck runs out."

Young Faith sat up in her bed with a jolt. A vague recollection of a nightmare left her heart hammering in her chest. A crash of thunder startled her. Her pink blinds weren't drawn all the way, and outside, torrential rain pelted down from malevolent clouds in deafening strikes against the windowpanes. Faith swung her small legs off her bed and jumped. She hurried out of her bedroom with Mr. Wiggles's little bear arm clutched in her hand, unaware of the shadows slinking up the hallway walls and clinging to the picture frames behind her. Within the frames, her golden-blond hair had darkened to a raven black.

She discovered her parents in the living room and sought their comfort. Their eyes were glued to the television screen. Climbing into her mother's lap, Faith watched the report on the television too. She recognized their local food store on the screen, surrounded by police, and her heart rapidly thumped, but she didn't know why.

The camera panned to a reporter, who announced a female

cashier was shot and killed in an armed robbery. The male suspects were all in police custody. In an ironic twist, all four suspects were rushed to the hospital with life-threatening injuries that could only be explained as a mauling from some sort of large wild animal.

"Oh, my goodness," her mother gasped, after the victim's face appeared on the screen. "I know her! That's Rachael Evans from down the street!"

"Christ, that's awful," her father said, his mouth gaping open. "And to think, you and Faith were supposed to go shopping there today."

I

DEATH

Present Day . . . Chicago, Illinois

Wisps of smoke dispersed as I manifested into the Pissing Cockroach. The place was just as low-rent as the name implied, a dingy biker bar with cigarette-stained pool tables and an unmistakable waif of urine in the air. Consumed by their cheap beer and full ashtrays, not a single cretin noticed my otherwise grand entrance.

I flagged down the young but hardened blond bartender with a raised gloved finger. Heavily applied makeup failed to conceal a nasty purple bruise swelling up the side of her face.

As Sugar—or so her name tag proclaimed—drew nearer, her anxious eyes clouded over and desire engulfed her body. Her mouth curved into a sultry smile as she drank me in.

"Hey there, stranger." She leaned forward, bracing herself on the worn bar rail. "What's your poison?"

"Whiskey, neat," I answered, indifferent to her advances. My attention was elsewhere, on the group of angry-looking bikers glaring from the opposite end of the bar.

"Sexy accent," she drawled. "Where ya in from?"

"Hell, and it's better than this place." I tapped the naked cocktail napkin in front of me. "I'm in a bit of a hurry."

"Aren't you the sweet talker."

As she turned to make my drink, a rather large biker rose from his stool and lumbered toward me.

I checked my watch. Five minutes.

"Are you flirting with my girl?" the enormous man bellowed.

"Earl, you think everyone's flirting with me," Sugar interjected with a nervous laugh, sliding my whiskey toward me. "He's not hurting anyone. Let him have his drink and be on his way."

"Stay out of this, Sugar, or you'll get more of what you got last night," Big Earl snarled.

Sugar cowered back a step, subconsciously touching her swollen cheek. Leather creaked as my fingers curled tight.

"Listen closely, you hooded freak," snarled Big Earl, invading my personal space. "The last person who hit on my girl has yet to come out of his coma."

His breath reeked, as if he'd dined on rotting animal carcass and washed it down with urine.

"What did you do?" I took a swig of my drink. "Breathe on him?"

A vein pulsed on Earl's broad forehead. "Who the hell do you think you are?"

His posse of bikers detached their sorry asses from their seats to surround my stool.

Taking another pull of my drink, I set the glass down with a clink. "I'm Death."

"I bet you're dumb too." Big Earl laughed. He leaned in over his giant stomach, "I SAID, WHO THE HELL DO YOU THINK YOU ARE, *FREAK*?"

I snatched Big Earl around his throat with one gloved hand. His eyes bulged and his sausage fingers clutched helplessly at my forearm as my vise grip tightened.

Rising to my towering height, I lifted Big Earl's body two feet off the ground. "I said, I'm *Death*. Not, *deaf*, you fucking moron."

Collective gasps filled the room. I cocked my head to the side, admiring his hopeless, sweaty face. "What's the matter, Earl? You look a little blue."

Big Earl's pulse jackhammered through his thick neck. I fantasized about smashing his skull into the bar, cracking it open like a chocolate Wonderball, when my watch went off with a series of beeps. *Damn it.* I needed to stay on schedule and keep my anger in check. My last "incident" with the humans had gotten a little too . . . messy.

Besides, I was at this bar for a different, delicious event.

Releasing a wry snarl, I flung Big Earl across the room, where he tumbled into his biker friends. I downed the rest of the whiskey, wiped the corners of my mouth with a napkin, and left a very traumatized Sugar a hefty tip. She quickly stuffed the cash into her bra and hightailed it through the kitchen door.

"Sorry, boys, I can't play tonight. I'm working." The entire club gawked, stunned by what had happened. I slid out a hand-rolled cigarette from inside my cloak. "Anybody got a light?"

On cue, the bottles of liquor along the back of the bar ignited one by one like fireworks, until the building itself exploded in a glorious apocalypse of flames. Howls of pure agony ripped from the dying mortals' throats. I raised my hand and, like a relentless infernal beast, the fire intensified, tearing viciously through the club, charring the humans to little remains.

I stood alone in the midst of death and glowing ash. From their demise came energy, moreish souls that swirled up into the air like ribbons of cerulean water.

Balancing the now lit cigarette between my lips, I approached what was left of Big Earl's twitching body.

"How do you like your private club now?" I slammed my boot into the seared flesh of his windpipe and crushed the remaining life out of him.

Fire licked at my cloak as I stalked around. I moved into the paths of the rest of the souls, consuming them. A wave of euphoria radiated through my body. Eating souls was a high unlike any other: a heightening of the senses, an intense pleasure that roused the insatiable beast within. Skimming over the ribbons of souls, I trimmed off the pieces Hell desired and devoured the rest.

I fed fast, left nothing behind. A single thought sent their essences straight to Hell.

All in a day's work.

Satiated, I barreled through the flaming remnants of the front door and prowled into the cool night air, embers of the incinerated Pissing Cockroach raining down around me. Across the street, I propped a shoulder against a telephone pole, a vicious grin plastered on my veiled face.

The rooftop neon cockroach sign crashed into the hellish depths of the burning bar. I took a drag of my cherry cigarette. "Nothing like a good smoke after a tasty meal."

My break was short-lived.

Thunder cracked the barriers of the night sky, drawing my eyes upward as the silhouette of black wings plunged to the ground. My talons twitched against my gloves at the sensation that someone was now directly behind me.

"There he is—the cat that ate the canary. Barbecue and I wasn't invited?"

Grinning, I turned and faced a figure in a bloodred cloak, a regal garment, fashioned from luxurious fabric that framed the lethal creature beneath.

"Yet here you are anyway." I exhaled and snuffed out my roll-up. "Big Earl and his big mouth turned a simple boiler explosion job into a whole thing. I got a little carried away. Doesn't matter, thirty-two were dying tonight, one way or the other."

"Don't you mean thirty-one?"

I followed his gaze down the road. In the far distance, Sugar stumbled as she ran away clumsily in a total panic.

"No wonder I didn't get a 'thank you, come again.'" I raised my gloved hand to smite her down when she tripped and fell face-first into a puddle of mud. I had to laugh. "Now, that's funny. You know, good bartenders *are* hard to find . . . "

Even Lucifer smiled. I let her live.

"Local bar explosion kills thirty-one," Lucifer quipped. "Details at eleven."

"Why are you here, old man?"

"You're being assigned, kid."

"Assigned?" I poked at a serrated tooth with the tip of my tongue. "To what?"

"To *whom*," he clarified. "The girl you spared ten years ago." My face fell faster than a mortal at my touch. "It's time to carry out the plan."

"Is her soul as powerful as the prophecy claims?"

"Unknown," Lucifer said cryptically. "Not according to the tabs we've kept on her, at least. If she is the one, she remains dormant. But I wouldn't take any chances, she could be of great use to us." He paused as the wail of police sirens undulated in the distance. "No funny business. Under no circumstances is she to be consumed, eaten, or otherwise harmed."

"You're making me hungry. Is she meaty?"

"Death," Lucifer snarled.

"Kidding." *Partially*. Biting back another vile smirk, I bowed my head. "Your wish is my eternal command, Your Majesty."

Lucifer made his flaming exit. The fire trucks rolled up and it was time for me to leave as well. I faded into the night with a single thought: *this is going to be fun.*

II

FAITH

Present Day . . . Pleasant Valley, New York

" . . . Happy birthday to . . . *YOUUU!*"

Marcy Delgado, my best friend since kindergarten, hit an unrestrained, opera-style final note that cost half my hearing.

We stood in the middle of my dim bedroom. In one hand, Marcy balanced a plate of eighteen strawberry-frosted cupcakes with eighteen black candles. In the other, she held my phone, where a video chat with my parents illuminated the screen. We'd had a big celebration last weekend as a family before they left for their vacation. I kept assuring them it didn't matter when or if we even celebrated. In fact, I would have preferred that we hadn't at all.

Because tonight, October 20, on my actual birthday, those eighteen candles kindled with the promise that everything would change. Soon it would be time to grow up and grow out of Pleasant Valley. I was not ready. Not when I didn't feel confident in my own skin. Not when I didn't know where I fit in, or even who I was, no matter how hard I tried to figure it out. My mood wilted a little at these melancholy thoughts.

"Make a wish already, you old fart!" Dad shouted through the phone.

My smile sprang up and we all laughed. I shut my eyes, inhaled, and plunged the room into darkness with one wish: *I want to know who I am.*

The lights came back up and I spent the next few minutes catching up with my parents. They were away on a once-in-a-lifetime trip that I'd had to push them into taking. My mother had been determined to stay home for my birthday, but I'd really wanted them to go. I loved that they were able to get away, just the two of them, for the first time since their honeymoon twenty-two years ago. I'd have many more birthdays.

After the call, Marcy continued to get ready for the Halloween party while I did some finishing touches on a painting. Even though my parents were cool about most things, they had a strict rule of no drinking or going to parties where alcohol would be served. Normally, I was the goody-two-shoes child that they never had to worry about. Tonight *had* to be different. Hey, I would only turn eighteen once.

Marcy turned in the mirror to look at her backside in her go-go dancer costume. "Be honest, how does my butt look?"

I set down my paintbrush and reached for a cupcake on the nightstand beside me. "Pancake," I replied jokingly and licked the strawberry frosting.

"Pancake? Now, that's just rude." Marcy came rushing out of the bathroom to rant further about her butt, but I couldn't rip my attention away from the painting in front of me. "Earth to Faith? My ass is flat, this is an emergency! Fix my pancake!"

A pair of almond-shaped mismatched green eyes glared scathingly from the canvas. Their pupils shimmered with catlike vertical slits. Smoke draped upward like the candles I blew out moments ago.

Marcy scrutinized the painting. "Hot," she quipped. "I wish I could paint like you, I've always been jealous. I'm also jealous of your butt . . . okay, now back to me. Do you think I'd add mass to my glutes if I ate another cupcake?" She padded across the floor and started unwrapping one of my birthday cupcakes with her pink gel nails. "I mean, you eat these all the time, and you're skinny *and* have a big booty. It's totally unfair . . . "

In my head, a lightbulb came on. I swapped my paintbrush for a pencil and began to trace a cupcake on the canvas I'd been working on. My hand moved in another direction on its own, transforming the cupcake into an eye. I battled my right hand with my left, trying to regain control. I couldn't. I could never stop my hand from completing these paintings.

Finally, the pencil stopped, and I tossed it backward over my shoulder. Good thing Marcy was bending down to pick up the cupcake wrapper, or the pencil would have speared her in the head.

"Oh my God!" I shouted.

Marcy jumped up with a shriek, covering her ass with both hands. "What? Is my butt really that bad?"

"No, not *that*." I rubbed at my temples, glancing shamefully at the stack of canvases in the corner of the room. Identical unfinished portraits of violent mismatched eyes and various paintings of the same willow tree.

Standing up, I tossed my paint-splattered apron over my most recent creation and spun the easel around, nearly knocking it over.

Marcy touched my shoulder. "You good?"

"Slap me," I demanded, grabbing Marcy's manicured hand. "Don't hold back. Slap me as hard as you can."

Marcy shrank back. "I'm not going to slap you!"

"Slap me, dang it, I'm losing it!"

"Oh, I agree," Marcy said, crossing her arms. "Whose eyes are those? This is the third time I've watched you paint them." A sly smirk lined her glossy lips as her concern melted away. "Faith Williams, is there a new *man* you haven't told me about?"

There was no possible way I could tell her the truth without sounding like a lunatic. Heck, I couldn't logically explain it myself. "No, no, it's . . . a character I created. I'm sorry, I'm acting like a total weirdo. I've been so stressed out lately." *To put it mildly.*

"Do you want to talk about it?"

"Nah, it's no big deal." I shook my head. "I should start getting ready."

What I loved most about Marcy was she knew when not to press. As I started to clean up my paints, she took another peek at the painting from under the apron. I caught sight of those eyes again, and an unnerving sensation inched its way down my spine. I hurried to the bathroom to splash water on my face and clear my head.

"Whoever you keep trying to paint, he's looking pretty sexy," Marcy called from the bedroom. I turned the water on low enough to hear her appraisal. "I love his stare. It repels, yet allures."

"Repels, yet allures? You okay out there, Jane Austen?"

"Jane who? And those man-lashes are killer. Yep, those eyes could definitely do some damage. He's going to rip out your soul."

I shut the water off. Heart racing, I poked my head back into the room. "What did you say?"

Marcy turned over her shoulder with a curling iron in her hair. "I said those eyes could do some damage. You sure you're okay?"

I questioned my sanity for the umpteenth time that day. "I'm fine."

"Maybe you shouldn't go to this costume party after all, Faith."

The black lace dress on my bed sat there taunting me. I picked it up, holding it against my body as I stood in front of the full-length mirror. My inner introvert wanted nothing more than to stay home tonight, but this was my senior year, and my birthday. I didn't want to graduate an antisocial loser.

"I need to go out and get my mind off things," I decided.

Marcy observed me like a science experiment.

"Pretty sure something's going on with you," she said. "I won't ask, eventually you'll spill the jelly beans." She applied a finishing touch to her mascara in front of my vanity. "What's with Hottie's different-colored eyes? One eye's an electric lime color and the other is a forest-y green. It's some sort of genetic thing, right? Oh, we learned about it in that class!" She started snapping as if it would help her recall. "You know the class where I copied your answers on the quizzes?"

"That's every class we've taken together, Marcy."

"Have I mentioned how beautiful, talented, and intelligent you are?" She reached out to me with her mascara wand. "Love me?"

I forced a laugh the best I could. Thinking about those eyes took away my sense of humor.

"The condition is called complete heterochromia," I said, drifting off again. "The mismatched-eyes thing. Sometimes it's genetic, sometimes it's caused by injury. It's very rare." I distanced myself from the canvases and moved in front of the vanity.

"Ah, right. We learned that in bone class with Mr. Garcia. The sexiest teacher in school." Her hazel eyes went dreamy.

Smiling, I brushed out my long, straight jet-black hair, and then whipped out my makeup bag to do my eye shadow. On my bed behind me, the black lace dress mocked me. Jeans and a T-shirt with a few costume accessories seemed fine to wear to the party. Who the hell did I need to impress?

"Anatomy," I said, zipping up my makeup bag. "The class is called anatomy. Maybe if you paid attention in school, you'd at least get the names of the courses right."

Marcy shot me a look. "Cranky much? It's hard to focus on any-thing in class when I'm busy staring at *Garcia's* anatomy. You should try it sometime, instead of reading ahead of the homework every week like a chronic dweeb."

"Remind me not to let you copy my answers ever again."

"Hey, it's not my fault insults are our second most fluent language."

I snapped my fingers and pointed them at her with finger guns. "Right below sarcasm."

"Trueee," Marcy said. "Rumor has it there might be a hot shot celebrity at Thomas's house, so we should probably get going soon. Parking could get annoying."

A celebrity in Pleasant Valley meant the whole town probably knew about it already. Thomas's dad knew a ton of A-list celebrities, so it didn't come as too much of a shock. "Who's the celebrity?" I asked.

"No clue," Marcy said. "All I heard is he's around our age and taking a gap year before college."

Driving into the rich part of town with my beat-up car was bad enough; now there was a mystery celebrity making an appearance, likely in a fancy limo to further humiliate my ride.

Picking up the skimpy black lace dress, I huffed out an annoyed breath. I looked down at my typical everyday outfit of ripped black skinny jeans and a band T-shirt and compared it to Marcy's costume. She wore an electric pink dress with long bell-shaped sleeves and high-knee white leather boots. The bright material of the dress clung to her lean, powerful volleyball player frame, and her push-up bra accentuated her cleavage. Marcy lived on the divide between the elite and the aver-age family households of Pleasant Valley, but since her grandfather was filthy rich, she got an invite to parties with lower-listed celebrities all the time. But an *A-lister*? This was all totally out of my comfort zone.

"What's wrong with what I have on again?" I asked.

"Nothing's wrong with what you have on. You're beautiful. To me. Your best friend. Who's a girl. Guys are a species driven by visuals. If you don't show enough skin, you're practically invisible." Marcy crossed the room, faux leather squeaking with each stride as she disappeared into my closet. "Your legs are one of your best assets, and they need to be *unleashed*!" She threw a pair of heels at me that I had forgotten I'd bought. "Also, I say this constructively. Tone it down with the gothic makeup tonight. Makes you look mean."

Marcy had long balayage brown hair and a beautiful caramel skin tone. Compared to her sun goddess perfection, I was a cave-dwelling vampire. I didn't consider myself "gothic," but my wardrobe was basically all black, and I did have a pale complexion. My recent obsession with dark lipsticks, smoky eyes, and occult symbols didn't help diffuse any goth labels at school.

"I'm dressing up as an evil witch," I said. "I'm supposed to look mean."

Marcy sighed. "Fine. Live the rest of your life with twenty cats, just like old lady Kravitz next door!"

I reached over and flicked her arm. "Hey! Ms. Kravitz is a sweetheart! Those cats were all strays!"

Marcy cackled. "The truth hurts."

Seething, I dug through my makeup bag for my eyeliner. "I'm not changing who I am because you're convinced it'll get me a hookup. You know I hate this 'dress up for a guy' stuff."

"It's a Halloween party, Faith," Marcy deadpanned. "Everyone is someone else tonight."

"You know what I mean. If a guy is into me strictly because of my legs, boobs, or butt, then he's not the guy for me. What happened to chivalry anyway?"

"It's dead. Listen, I get what you're saying but that mentality won't get you laid."

"Marcy!"

"Hey, I'm being honest. You're great with school, and I'm great with guys. Now, do you want to make out with a hot guy tonight or what?" When I didn't reply she repeated, "Or what, girl?"

The embarrassment of not having been kissed weighed on me. I know, melodramatic, sue me. Losing my V card to a stranger or a boy I barely knew was totally out of the question. An innocent kiss, however, that was achievable, even though I'd always wanted to make sure it was right for me. At this point, I wanted to get it over with. Marcy was right. Men did find me intimidating and deep down, that made me insecure.

This was my senior year, damn it. I could push my pride and morals aside for one night.

"Fine, you win."

Hissing jokingly at Marcy, I stomped off into the bathroom with the dress—a sexy number with a 1950s edge to it. The bodice was lacy, the waist pinched close to my ribs, and the skirt was short and fanned out without being too puffy like a prom dress. If I bent over, my underwear would show. Not that I was going to be doing any bending over. The heels Marcy selected were modest, leather, and only two inches off the ground, just the way I liked them.

Securing my witch hat, I looked up at myself in the mirror and sighed.

It was official. Halloween had shifted from an innocent contest of who could collect the most candy in their pillowcase by midnight to who could wear the sexiest, skimpiest costume.

And I was winning.

Marcy cupped her hands over her mouth to hype me up. "Okay, legs for days! Aren't you a snack and a half? You look hot!"

"You think so? How does my butt look?" I shook myself. "Never mind. Tonight, I leave my first kiss to fate. If it happens, it happens. Don't try and hook me up, and don't try getting me drunk because I'm driving home. Last week's incident proved you can't be trusted. I still can't believe you drove wasted to get a greasy cheeseburger at three in the morning."

"It was one time!"

"One time is all it takes. It's not the first time you've done something stupid because of Tommy." As soon as it came tumbling out, I regretted it. Pain pooled in Marcy's eyes at the mention of her ex-boyfriend, Thomas Gregory. Who, by the way, was the host of the party we were attending. With his deep-blue eyes, blond hair, swimmer's body, and charismatic personality, the whole school swooned over him. As for me, he had a permanent spot reserved at the top of my shit list.

"I didn't mean to—" I started.

"Yes, you did," Marcy snapped and stormed out of my room.

She was silent the entire car ride over. I pulled up quite a few houses behind the Gregory mansion, shocked by the number of cars already here. I gave the parking brake of my old car a ridiculous heave upward to click it into place and turned to face Marcy.

"Listen, I'm sorry. I know you're upset about how it ended with Thomas. I would be too. But showing up at one of his bangers, again, determined to make him jealous . . . this isn't going to make things better." I let out a frustrated sigh, knowing I was not getting through to her. Lately, nothing got through to Marcy about him. "Thomas is a jerk, all he cares about is himself and his rep at school."

"I am moving on, Faith," Marcy said. Funny, she never seemed to believe herself. "I know this sounds stupid, but I just need to show him I'm moving on. He has to see how much better I'm doing without him."

"That's not healthy, and you know it," I said. "You're trying to win him over again through jealousy." Her reddening face meant she was about to flip on me. It was the reality check she needed. Marcy got her heart broken by Thomas, and I was sick and tired of her finding ways to win him back. "Believe in the amazing catch that you are and forget him. If you keep trying to get his attention by sleeping with his friends, you're never going to heal."

She glared out her passenger window.

I wrung my hands on the steering wheel. "Look at all these cars. It's going to be insane in there. Why don't we get some pizza and have a Friday movie night like old times? We haven't had one of those in a while. Who needs to grind against sweaty guys with beer breath when we can watch *Buffy* and eat junk food until we fall into a stupor?"

"Sleeping with his friends?" She turned to me, unleashing her anger as it finally boiled over. "Who the hell would have told *you* that?"

Her choice of words stung, as if I had nobody else but her as a friend. Which was true. Marcy was my only friend. Unless my cat counted.

"You and Tyler. I overheard someone in the school bathroom," I admitted. Marcy's face slowly drained to a pallid color and hurt entered her eyes again. "He's Thomas's best friend, Marcy. It's all right you didn't tell me, I get it—"

Marcy held up her hand to stop me. "That's the thing, Faith, you *don't* get it. I didn't tell you because I thought you would judge me. And you did." Reaching for her purse, Marcy rushed to exit the car. She followed a group of giggling girls on the sidewalk toward the mansion with the pounding music.

I twisted the keys out of the ignition and jumped out of the car. "Marcy!" I shouted and jogged to her. "Wait! Come on, don't do this!"

She turned sharply around, stopping me with a terrifying glare. "You only came to this party to prevent me from seeing him, didn't you?"

"Marcy . . . "

She shook her head with a bitter smile. "This has been a wonderful conversation. Truly. It's nice to know my best friend thinks I'm a desperate slut." She turned her back to me again, stomping up the stone steps leading up to the mansion.

As I chased Marcy up into Thomas's house, a wave of nostalgia hit me hard. The three of us grew up together. Throughout our childhood, Thomas had a crush on Marcy, and in middle school, he finally acted on it. Thankfully, I was never a third wheel, so our trio never died. Until, of course, Thomas grew apart from both of us and became captain of the swim team. He joined the popular crowd and, according to the high school food chain, Marcy and I were well below the apex predators.

Thomas continued to play games with Marcy, hooking up with her from time to time, never putting a label on it. Real Prince Charming material. Despite my distaste of their toxic relationship, they became an item junior year, when Marcy started to party more. Their relationship ended the summer before senior year, when she found out he'd cheated on her. Well, technically, they'd been on a break, and it was a drunken kiss he'd regretted, but Marcy loved him so much, *too much* for him to not get his shit together and step up. So, in my mind, he might as well have been a cheater.

Marcy had changed a lot over the past two years, ever since her mom died. She was in a dark place for a while and never wanted to hang out. Since her father was sheriff and worked often, she'd relied on Thomas for comfort. For a distraction. And when that security blanket was gone, a part of her never recovered. She was right—I felt obligated to help her get over Thomas. Marcy wasn't just a best friend to me. She was my sister.

The silhouettes of jocks ran out of the home and onto the lawn. They shouted drunken slurs, laughed, and wrestled each other over a blow-up Halloween decoration.

I caught up to Marcy and grabbed her by the arm. "We haven't fought like this since the first grade, when you threatened to pull my hair out if I didn't trade my chocolate chip cookies for your carrot sticks." Marcy almost laughed at the corniness. "You aren't hopeless, Marcy. Come on, this party is going to be lame anyway. Let's pick up some Chinese food and ditch this Popsicle stand."

She hesitated for a second and then ripped her arm out of my grasp. "You're not my guardian angel, Faith. I don't want your help with my love life. Besides, how can you help me when you have *no* experience?"

Marcy hurried up the steps to the front door before I could formulate a response.

I followed her into the house, only to discover this party was claustrophobic anarchy. Inside the Gregory mansion, drunken teens and college students were crammed in together. Trying to move through them felt like running through trenches of thick mud wearing a parka.

I peered into every room on the first floor, calling out Marcy's name. The music and chaos swallowed up my voice.

The air was thick, hot, heavy. People moved sensually to the music, grinding and grappling bodies. I tore free from a throng of people and came across a girl standing in the middle of the grand staircase. She ranted in strange tongues, laughing maniacally to herself. I looked above her, grossed out by the sight of a couple half-naked on the stairs, and decided it was best to check the rest of the ground floor.

I walked past the indoor pool house to the billiard room. Nostalgia washed over me again as I took in the tall bookshelves and the crimson-red pool table to the left of the room. I'd hidden in here once during a game of hide-and-seek, when Thomas, Marcy, and I were kids.

Leaning against the pool table was a guy wearing a gray Henley long-sleeve and dark denim jeans. Three cheerleaders, dressed as Charlie's Angels, hovered by the fancy mini bar behind him, their glossy eyes eager. He had his back to me and bowed over the table with a lazy fluidity. His arm, lean with strong muscle, snapped back in a dexterous movement to strike the cue ball and make an impressive bank shot.

I headed toward the three cheerleaders. Marcy was loosely friends with them, since the varsity volleyball team was invited to all the cool parties. "Hey, have you seen Marcy by any chance?"

The girls laughed like there was a joke I missed, their nasty stares crawling over my skin. The middle one, Nicole Hawkins, captain of the cheerleading squad, stepped up to me. "Why don't you check under the bleachers, goth girl?"

My face grew hot. My friendly ambiance slipped away, and I wanted to defend Marcy and myself, but I bit my tongue. These girls weren't worth it. They were boring, copy-and-paste stereotypes with no discernible qualities that made them stand out enough to insult. I actually felt a little bad for them.

"Need help looking for your friend?" The billiards guy was racking up another shot. He had taken off a pair of mirrored aviators and hung them on the collar of his shirt. I recognized him instantly and froze.

David Star.

The Stars, Devin and his only son, David, had surpassed the Kardashians in fame. Charming and an innovative genius, Devin Star had taken the advertisement industry by storm, quickly expanding his interests into multiple successful companies, including the infamous D&S Tower in New York City. David, the alleged child protégé, would soon follow in his father's footsteps, but I found that awfully hard to believe. I'd heard all about David Star's partying escapades through Europe during his gap year before Harvard. I only knew this because my mom was subscribed to every gossip magazine known to man and had a life-size cardboard standup of Devin Star in the basement.

David Star was the primary enemy of proper brain development in all the girls at my high school. *The pastiche of God's finest creations, a proud, lucrative product of an even hand*, or so the tabloids said last summer.

Give me a break.

David sauntered around the pool table to me and leaned against his pool stick. Thick chestnut-colored hair with subtle blond highlights styled away from a handsome, angular face, and gorgeous brown eyes that speared mine with an unflinching, assertive confidence. Everything about David Star repelled me, especially his vain beauty, but now that he was here, *in person*, like a 3D printout of the perfect man, and I was starstruck.

"Well?" That lollipop stick wedged between his teeth shifted to the other side of his mouth, those full lips curving into a slow fox grin. "We gonna hunt for your friend or what?"

Get a grip, girl. My brain chugged back into gear, slow as molasses. "No offense," I said, "but guys with reputations like yours are the reason I'm worried about her."

David raised a supercilious brow and stared down at me like he couldn't fully process the rejection. He clutched his heart in mock hurt. "Ouch. If she's with a guy like me, then wouldn't I be the perfect person to know where to find her?"

He had me there, but why did he even want to help me? I looked over at the three pretty cheerleaders. They giggled and whispered behind their coveted hands as they watched us interact. My gut feeling had been right. He was messing with me.

"I wouldn't want to keep you from your groupies," I said.

I turned away before I could see David's reaction, but I did see my words had impacted those three mean girls. They fumed with disdain as I left the room.

Music blared in the hallway as I ventured to the center of the mansion again. My skin felt slick with adrenaline, my mind still reeling over my conversation with David Star. Talking to him had certainly been the last interaction I'd expected that night. I'd *dissed* him too. Wait until Marcy got a load of that story. If, of course, I ever found her . . .

In the Gregorys' crowded living room, I became lost at the center of a bouquet of strobe lights and realized everyone had stopped dancing to stare at me. At first, I thought it was my dress. But the dress was fine. I thought there was a spectacle behind me, so I turned around. There wasn't. All at once, their distorted faces looked away from me and everything went back to normal.

I frowned. 'Kay . . .

This night was about to go from bad to worse. I could feel it in my gut like a sixth sense, and at the back of my neck, where small hairs stood on end.

Time's up.

It was an almost imperceptible whisper in my skull, layered over the pounding music.

My mouse in a maze. Come to me.

I turned sharply around, meeting an empty spot across the room. Someone had been standing there, watching me.

And somehow, I knew they were also the voice in my head.

Panic climbed my throat. Squeezing through a grinding couple, I passed a girl in a crayon costume throwing up and slid into the kitchen. I was elbowed into a counter, where I knocked over a line of colorful rum drinks onto a girl's white sequined top.

"Watch it!" she seethed, her bloodshot, glossy gaze sliding up and down my lace dress. Another snobbish student from the rich side of Pleasant Valley. "Nice costume, gothic freak—"

All of a sudden, the girl gasped, her eyes rolling back. She foamed at the mouth. I began to yell for help, when her hand shot out and clutched my arm in a crushing grip. When she spoke again, her words were choked out and guttural. "He wants your soul . . . " Her eyes flipped back down. "The pool," she wheezed. She gripped me by the wrists, a smile peeling back her lips. "He's waiting for you there."

I ripped free of her grasp.

"Go to him!" Voices shouted at me from all directions, cascading one after another. Their faces contorted, bone leaking beneath their skin like painted skeleton faces. "He wants your flesh . . . blood . . . " There was a sharp, clenching feeling in my stomach and terror hit me like a truck. "Go to the pool!"

"What the hell is happening?" Shoving away the partiers, I ran. People followed me close behind, chasing me with sinister grins. I slipped on the liquor-stained floor, crashed into a wall, and took off again.

Shoving through heavy doors, I rushed to lock them behind me and hunkered down inside the dark room. My heart was an orchestra at crescendo. Chlorine filled my nostrils and paranoia set in.

The pool house. I was in the *pool* house. Great, I was exactly the type of person I despised in horror movies. I blindly patted the wall for a light switch with a shaking hand. Lights flicked on row by row, revealing the crystal blue water of the indoor pool.

A cold sensation spread through me, licking up my spine. I clutched my stomach against the sharp sting of a phantom wound, which spread like a coverlet over my skin.

And that's when I saw him.

A cloaked man stood at the other end of the pool, leaning against the ladder of the high diving board. In his right gloved hand, he flicked a lighter on and off. And in his left, he held a scythe with a blade at least the size of my body. It almost looked real too.

No, thank you.

It was time to hide elsewhere. Spinning around, I strained to open the pool door, but the lock wouldn't budge.

The lights dimmed with a hiss. Cursing, I peeked over my shoulder. The guy in the Grim Reaper costume was gone.

"Of course," I muttered under my breath.

I tried the door again and slammed my open palm against it. A sweet aroma hovered in the air, mixed with a trace of leather and cologne. Goose bumps pebbled my arms. Every muscle stiffened. The heat of another body radiated behind me.

"Boo."

"Jesus Christ!"

I craned my neck up to meet the shadowed face of the cloaked man. My jaw slackened. He was massive, easily two heads taller than me, and his silhouette rippled with menacing muscle.

"Wrong."

I was at a loss for words. Partially because of his size, but also because of his hypnotic voice. Deep and husky, yet velvety smooth.

"Grim Reaper, right?"

"What gave it away? The cloak or the scythe?"

There was a lilt to his words, an accent I couldn't pinpoint. It was enchanting, magnetic, and maybe that was why I was fighting the urge to lean into him.

A timorous laugh escaped my mouth.

"The costume is great, I'll give you that." I moved around him, my eyes sliding down the blade of the enormous scythe. He didn't turn around, as if he were allowing me to view him. "Your scythe looks legit."

He remained silent, unnerving me further. His cloak moved slightly at the hem, as if there was a draft. There wasn't one.

"It's not a costume," he seethed. "I'm here to collect."

With each word he spoke, he carried a confidence that he was in full control of this conversation, and it was intimidating, to say the least.

"Collect what?" I asked, playing along. This had to be a prank. I was thoroughly impressed with the joke too. "Who are you?"

"You don't remember. Try harder, Faith."

He knew my name.

Marcy must have put everyone up to this. Yeah, that had to be it. But my body wasn't so convinced. My chest felt so tight, I could only muster enough breath to say, "Okay, I'm leaving now. Good luck with your reaping."

I turned to desperately try the door one more time, but it had disappeared. My eyes widened at the glass wall now in its place. "Where'd the door go?"

"Does it matter?" he snickered. "You couldn't open it anyway."

As I slowly looked back at him, the gravity of the situation struck me. No matter how hard I strained to see his face, a shadow curtained his features. The dark void was endless. As I stared into the hypnotic abyss, his head tilted slightly. For a moment, he seemed familiar. Not a good familiar either.

My heart plummeted to the pit of my stomach.

I took off running, but the cloaked man materialized in front of me. A black mist expelled from his body as he solidified. Trying to stop quickly in heels, I nearly slid right into him. "Oh, shit!"

"I'm not done with you," he growled.

Only a small sound scratched its way out of my throat. I looked over my shoulder, where the cloaked man once stood. Back at him. Back at the place where he once stood.

"You—you just . . . " I clutched at my chest in shock, unable to finish the rest.

"I know. I'm breathtaking."

"You're not real!"

"Yeah, and you're not annoying." He brought a rolled, unfiltered cigarette to his shadowed face and lit up. "Aren't you tired of painting me over and over again?" Sweet, scented smoke expelled from his mouth. Cherry. "And those *awful* nightmares. Every. Single. Night." A feigned pity dripped from his cultured voice. "If only you could remember them."

Reality fell away as I imagined those mismatched green eyes.

"Marcy told you about me." It was the most reasonable explanation I could think of, even though she was completely in the dark about the nightmares.

"I don't give a fuck about Marcy." He took a hard pull from the cigarette. "The sooner you accept I'm real, the sooner your memories will come back to you. We need to be on the same page. I'm here, in the flesh, for you. You know exactly who I am."

"I can't be awake." I fought the urge to slug this psycho in the face and take off again. "This is impossible—"

"Or it's a nightmare with your eyes wide open. Call me Death." Blood drained from my face, and I could *feel* him grinning beneath his hood. "Breathe. If I wanted you dead, you would be. I've gotten pretty good at that."

He snuffed out his cigarette with the heel of his boot and advanced toward me with long, calculated strides. I backpedaled.

"I won't repeat myself," said *Death*, as he continued forward.

"Through our deal, I saved your life. Now you're mine. You need to come with me."

I'm his? My back hit a glass window. There was something about his sureness that smothered my fear. "*So* not happening."

He stopped in his tracks. "Oh, really."

I rolled my fingers into fists to prevent them from shaking. "There is no way I'm going anywhere with you, psycho."

Silence.

He threw back his head and barked out a laugh. "Cute," he purred. "As if you have a choice."

"I must have a choice, otherwise you wouldn't be trying to convince me I don't," I insisted. "To put it in a way you might understand, the chances of me leaving with you are *grim*."

Death's hidden stare now felt lethal and piercing, like a predator stalking its prey. "I'd be very careful how you speak to me." He leaned down close. "I have a short temper. You have no idea what I'm capable of."

The terror of the moment broke as a ringtone version of "Hell's Bells" blared from underneath his cloak. He straightened and clenched his fist. I detected his embarrassment of the timing of the call.

Death growled, put up a gloved finger, then parted his thick cloak. I caught a glimpse of black leather pants. He slipped a cell phone out from his back pocket, read the screen, and snarled, "I'll deal with you later."

His body evaporated into a black mist.

I was alone.

Something shattered within me. I nearly fell to my knees, locking them before I did. My throat tightened. I choked back a sob and moved mindlessly toward another exit in the pool room, which led to the backyard. The more I thought about *him*, the more the line between reality and insanity blurred. Nothing felt real. How could it? *The Grim Reaper is after me. Me!*

My witch hat flew off into the dark abyss as I ran around the Gregory mansion following a stone path with shrubbery and walkway lights on either side. The night air was cool, while my blood boiled with adrenaline. The wind and moonlight twisted the shadows of trees, transforming them into writhing creatures slinking closer. Several dark figures appeared ahead. To my relief, they were actual people. Without warning, two of them stumbled into my path, one of them giggling.

"Marcy?" I asked incredulously.

I recognized her electric pink dress and the blond curls of the boy she was pressed against. Thomas Gregory.

"Oh no, here comes the witch," Marcy slurred, staggering away from Thomas. "I thought you'd be home by now."

"Long time no see, Faith," Thomas said, noticeably more sober than Marcy. He was wearing his usual varsity jacket and designer jeans. *He must be dressed up as a douchebag for Halloween.* "Enjoying the par-tay?"

Ignoring him, I grabbed Marcy by the arm. "We have to go. We have to leave. Now!"

She was sober enough to catch the fear in my voice because, by some miracle, she didn't argue. I rushed her to my car, poured her in, and peeled away as if the monster was still on my tail.

Which maybe wasn't too far off.

III

Death. He'd introduced himself as Death.

The Grim Reaper was a mythical being, not a nutjob I met at a Halloween party.

Yeah, a nutjob who knows my name. Knows my paintings. My *nightmares*. How was any of this possible?

Marcy stared ahead in a stupor, leaning her head on the passenger window. Frantic, I reached over and shook her shoulder. "Hey, snap out of it. Did you tell anyone else about the paintings?"

She lifted her head lethargically, hair splaying over her smudged makeup. "Huh?"

Headlights flashed behind us. A car appeared in my rearview mirror right on our tail. It swerved back and forth, flashing its headlights. Clearly, the driver wanted me to pull over.

"The cherry on top of my night."

Suddenly, a deafening bang rang out from underneath my car, as if I ran over a speed bump and bottomed out, and I slammed on the brakes. Spoiler alert: they didn't work.

Terror seized my heart and squeezed.

"Marcy, put your seat belt on! The brakes aren't working!" She sobered up. Marginally. "What? My seat belt is on!" She turned over her shoulder to peer out the back windshield. "Pull over! Pull over!"

"I can't! There's no shoulder and no brakes!" Not to mention, my car was speeding up on its own. I chose not to disclose *that* information to her.

"E brake! E brake!" Marcy attempted to yank up the emergency break and the handle came off. "It snapped off! It snapped off!"

"I can *see* that!" I scanned the bushes on the side of the road, contemplating where to pull over and slow this car down. "I refuse to let us die in this stupid hunk of metal! Hold on to something!"

The car behind us had strangely backed off.

"Watch out!" Marcy cried.

This time, when I slammed on the brakes, they worked. My eyes closed involuntarily as a huge mass struck my car with a blood-curdling crash, shattering part of the windshield. Screams ripped from both our throats, even after the car finally stopped. Though we were wearing seat belts, both our heads went sharply forward. Airbags blew up into our faces at the wrong moment, knocking my head back into the seat.

It wasn't over. A red Lamborghini maneuvered to the left of my car, scraping the driver side with a sickening screech as it sideswiped past. The vehicle fishtailed ahead and blocked my path.

My airbag deflated as a hand smacked it down. "Faith!" Marcy reached over the center console, screaming in hysterics. "Faith! Are you okay?"

I cut the ignition. My car hissed. I was fleetingly aware of blood in my mouth from biting down on my lip, and there were large spiderwebs of fissures in my windshield. Clicking out of my seat belt, I threw myself from the vehicle, fell to the asphalt, and collapsed, bile rising in my throat.

"Oh, my gosh!" The shrill, distant voice of a woman sliced through the ringing in my ears. A perfectly manicured hand tried to lift me up. "Oh, my gosh! Are you, like, dead?"

"No, I'm not dead! Let go of me!" I said, shaking off her bony hand. When I tried to stand, the road tilted on its side. My back hit the ground, glass scraping against my bare legs. Wincing, I rolled over and was slow to get to my feet. The woman with the bleach-blond hair reached for me again with her scrawny hands.

"I said don't touch me."

"We hit a deer!" Marcy cried from the opposite side of the car. "We hit a poor, helpless deer! Oh my God . . . " She braced a hand on the roof and heaved.

"Help the passenger, Meghan," a deep, melodious voice projected behind me. "Make sure she doesn't choke on her vomit."

A man stepped into my line of vision. Once again, I could not believe the surreal night I was having. It was David Star's father, *Devin Star*, president of the D&S Tower, aka the most prestigious advertising agency in the world.

"Are you all right?"

Despite my aversion to the Stars, my brain short-circuited. Devin's eyes were as electric and intense as in all those magazines my mother cherished. But here, under the streetlight, they dimmed to an arcane ocean blue. His features were sharp, lethal, perfect. Money expertly concealed any wrinkles from his skin, making it hard to believe he was forty-five.

"No." I took a deep breath and exhaled. "I am not all right."

"Let's get you off this broken glass." He guided me by the elbow to his vehicle. My legs threatened to give out as I rested on the hood of his car. "Take deep breaths. Everything is okay." His voice was level, reassuring.

"Why were you tailgating me?" I asked. "It distracted me, or else none of this would've happened."

"Your muffler was scraping the ground and sparking," he explained. "I was just trying to get you to pull over, before your gas tank caught on fire." We both looked over my mangled car. I visualized my tombstone: *Here lies Faith, murdered by her own parents for destroying an already shitty car. R.I.P.*

"You stopped so suddenly," Devin said, "and it seemed like you hit something. You're lucky I didn't rear end you."

I gripped my temples with both hands. "I am *so* screwed."

"Please, let me take care of any medical expenses and repairs to your vehicle." Concern pooled in his crisp blue eyes. "All I ask is that you don't talk to the press about this accident." He smoothly slid a business card from his breast pocket and held it out to me. "I'm Devin Star, owner of the D&S Tower."

"I know who you are," I said. *I just met your entitled son.*

Devin straightened and withdrew his card, bewilderment flickering over his perfect face. How arrogant do you have to be to expect people to fangirl over you the moment you drop your name?

"Listen, I understand you don't need any more negative press"—*on top the money laundering scandal you'll magically make disappear*—"but you were driving like a maniac and hit my car. We could have been killed, so I'm not making any promises. Not until I talk to my parents. If you'll excuse me, I have to check on my best friend—"

"Twenty thousand dollars, cash," he offered. "That's a lot of money for a young girl."

I let out a short laugh. "Mr. Star, you have some nerve."

He cocked his head in confusion, squinting his icy eyes. "How so?"

"*How so?* You're trying to negotiate a deal to protect yourself, five minutes after I was almost killed in a car crash. Because of *your* obnoxious driving. That's how so."

He was perplexed for a second time. "What's your name?"

"Faith."

"Do you paint, Faith?"

"How does everybody know I paint?" I said, exasperated.

Devin pointed at my hand with a raised eyebrow, drawing my attention down to my paint-stained fingertips. "You're creative. Headstrong. Ambitious, I bet."

I looked up, held by those sapphire eyes. "What does that have to do with anything?"

He scanned my features. "How old are you?"

My mind immediately jumped to thinking Devin Star was hitting on me. *You read way too many books and watch way too much TV.* "Eighteen."

"Are you currently unemployed?"

"Technically, yes . . . I babysit and sign up for my town's fairs. We have a lot of them in Pleasant Valley." *Why am I telling him all this?*

"My son and I run an inner-city art program," Devin explained. "We're always looking for young aspiring artists to counsel the kids. Twenty-five dollars an hour. If, of course, you can get past the interview and an overview of your portfolio."

"Did you say twenty-five dollars an hour?"

"Art school is expensive, is it not?"

"I never said I was applying to art schools—"

"Aren't you?"

"Well, yes, I—"

"Wonderful, then it's settled," Devin said, flashing his famed smile. "I'll have an associate retrieve your car to be fixed free of charge, and I'll call a chauffeur to pick you up to ensure you both get home safely."

I had no intention of doing any interviews or seeing David Star ever again, but his offer rendered me speechless.

"I hope we didn't hit a deer! I love deer!" Marcy wailed. "They're so cute! They don't do anything but eat grass and be cute! I'm never drinking again! Not even root beer!"

As soon as she started belting out a melancholy rendition of "Rudolph the Red-Nosed Reindeer," I turned away.

After the strangest night of my life and with Marcy's drunken state, I needed to get us both home safe.

"Do you want me to stay until my driver comes?" Devin inquired.

"We'll take an Uber," I answered. "Thank you though. We'll be fine."

"Do I have your word you won't mention my name or this accident to anyone?"

I shrugged passively. "Sure, whatever. I won't tell anyone."

"Call or come by the office Monday morning. If you don't want the job, we'll figure something else out to make it up to you." Devin stuck out his hand, and I clasped it in a daze. "I'm sorry we had to meet under these circumstances."

"Same here . . . "

He turned his beautiful face to the side. "Meghan." Like a trained dog, the supermodel left my best friend and hurried in the direction of the red Lamborghini. Devin Star retreated to his car. I peered down at my hand and realized he'd slipped his business card into my palm.

"Wait!" I called out, and he turned around. "Smile!" Like a professional photographer, I shot rapid photos of him by himself, a selfie with him beside me, photos of his car and license plate, and then another with both our cars in the frame, for evidence. "Evidence. In case you screw me over. Ya know?"

His eyes crinkled from a broad grin. "Completely understand."

"What are you doing picking up David in the suburbs anyway? Don't you live in the city?"

"To think I got the impression you weren't a fan."

"I'm not. My mom is."

He laughed, a pleasant sound. "Since you're so inquisitive, me and my lady friend were at a wedding today in Albany and she lives by here. Figured I'd drop her off and scoop David up before he calls a driver home. It was great meeting you, Faith. Think about that job offer."

Devin ducked into his vehicle and shut the door. As his Lambo took off in a roar, my eyebrows scrunched together. *What just happened?*

Scrolling through my phone with frozen, shaking fingers, I tracked a nearby Uber. I stuffed the business card into my bra and took a few more pictures of my car, before I walked back to Marcy. She sat in the grass on the side of the road, wrapped in the blanket I thankfully kept in my trunk. I stood next to her, embracing the cold.

"I can't believe that was *Devin Star*," Marcy groaned. "Any other night I would have asked him to sign my boobs. So sexy." She giggled. "I own all of his modeling calendars."

"Yes, I know." Softer, I added, "So does my mom."

"Now what?" she asked, her voice reduced to a whisper. "I'm going to have such a bad hangover tomorrow." Her bloodshot eyes widened as she exclaimed, "Oh, God, wait! Did you call the police? My dad will flip—"

"I'm not calling the police. Mr. Star is handling the car, I hope. I called an Uber to pick us up." I peered into the dark woods behind us and hugged my body tighter. "I hope that deer is alive, so I can come back tomorrow and shoot it."

"Faith!"

"Kidding." I stifled a dark laugh. "My parents are going to kill me because of that stupid deer."

We were quiet for a long stretch of time. I wanted to tell Marcy what happened at the party, but she was too smashed to comprehend. Even sober, the story was so outrageous, I struggled to comprehend it myself.

Marcy had paled significantly.

"What's wrong?"

"I know this is going to sound crazy, since I'm totally shitfaced . . . " She let out a shaky breath. "Now that I'm thinking about it, I don't . . . I don't think we hit a deer. I could have sworn it was a person."

"Don't be silly, it was a deer. What would a person be doing way out here in the woods?"

She wiped at a stray tear. "You're right. It couldn't have been a person."

Unable to sit still, I fished through my car and cleared out any valuable items between the seats and in the glove compartment. My hands were pretty much empty at the end, besides a few vehicle documents and some spare change. After, I stood in front of my car and inspected the windshield.

There was no blood, which amazed me, considering the extent of the damage. The animal had been hit hard and ran off like a champ. Inspecting the ground around the car with the flashlight on my phone, I found skid marks and retraced them twenty or thirty feet back, where I pictured hitting the deer.

The flashlight danced over an object on the road, and I froze. Blood pulsed in my ears as I crouched down to pick up the stub of a hand-rolled cigarette. Cherry.

Cold washed down the back of my neck. I sensed his stare before I saw him. Across the road was the cloaked man, Death. He stood motionless in front of the backdrop of the woods, a mere silhouette outlined by the light of the moon. Time slowed.

I put two and two together. Marcy had claimed there'd been a figure in the road, and she was correct. It was Death. But why? *To prove how fragile your life is, to give you a glimpse of what he's capable of.*

As if agreeing with my thoughts, Death pulled back from the moonlight and faded into the night. At that point, I was too exhausted and confused to be afraid.

A car appeared at the end of the road. I checked my app and saw it was our driver.

"If the driver asks any questions, let me do the talking," I said to Marcy.

She gave me an unenthusiastic salute.

The car rolled to a stop in front of us. Why wasn't our car getting towed yet? Where were the police? I began to script my answers for the driver's possible questions. Fortunately, for once in my life, our Uber driver didn't care for conversation and focused only on his driving.

He dropped Marcy off first. She turned down my offer to sleep over and wanted to be home in her own bed. I had a feeling she was still hurt about our fight, and so was I, more than I could let on.

Despite her intoxication and heels, Marcy climbed the old tree outside her bedroom window and hoisted herself inside like a pro. This wasn't her first prison break.

When the car pulled into my driveway, I wished my parents were home and not in Hawaii. But they deserved the time off and the last thing I wanted was to get in the middle of their "second-honeymoon activities." Ick.

I bolted toward the house. After a brief struggle with my keys, I threw open my front door and scrambled to lock it. Pressing my back against the cool wood, I sighed in relief.

Flicking on all the lights, I closed all the blinds. I paced the kitchen barefoot and sipped a root beer, reeling over what'd happened at the pool and the car accident. I pinched myself. Stomped my feet dinosaur-style into the cool tile floor, as if it would somehow ground my reality. Okay, I was awake. This was happening.

What was I supposed to do now? At some point, I'd have to tell someone about this Death character. Who *could* handle this alone? And did Devin Star actually want me to work for him? Or was it a clever ruse to buy my silence? I needed answers.

Placing Devin's card on the counter, I considered my options. His office was closed for the weekend. I needed my car back ASAP to get groceries. If I didn't call him Monday morning, for all I knew, he'd pull a fast one and junk my car and blow me off. No, I had to see him in person.

I scribbled a Post-it reminder and stuck it to my bedroom door. It was settled. Monday morning, I would wake up early, head to Devin's office, and force myself into a meeting.

"So let it be written, so let it be done."

I peeled off the never-to-be-worn-*again* black lace dress, showered, and slipped into a T-shirt with sweatpants. My bed was a cloud of blankets. I hit the mattress with a bounce, clutching my old teddy bear, Mr. Wiggles, to my chest. Only then could I breathe again.

Happy birthday to me.

IV

The weekend crawled by with nonstop schoolwork, which helped to keep my mind occupied. Monday was staff development day, and the students were off, so midmorning I took the train into the city.

All the D&S Tower needed was Batman perched on top of it to complete the menacing matte-black steel superstructure. The modern skyscraper was one of the most visited buildings in the city, gaining popularity from the Star family and their iconic advertisements.

After I pulled open heavy glass doors, the building swallowed me into the enormous lobby. Suspended from the high ceiling was an ornate chandelier, which dangled elegantly between massive trees. There were freaking *trees* in here.

Obscured by their large trunks were two escalators with cascading wall fountains on either side. Black marble with flecks of gold covered the walls and floors. I stood there in awe far longer than I should have. Attractive men and women strutted along the lobby with purpose, carrying designer briefcases and purses, laughing, smiling. Their beautiful, tanned faces never looked in my direction, as if I were invisible to them.

Even when I stand out like a sore thumb, I'm still invisible.

I thought I'd dressed appropriately for the meeting, until I saw everyone *else's* sumptuous business attire. The plain black slacks that I discovered in the dusty corner of my mother's closet had a teeny tiny hole in the crotch. Marcy's bloodred American Apparel blouse fit snugly on my chest, the button right above my cleavage threatening to burst any moment. Paired with last night's black heels, matching jewelry, and a reserved amount of eyeliner and lipstick, I feigned an important role among the gorgeous, graceful, *qualified* workers at the D&S Tower.

Crossing the lobby, I entered an elevator. There was *nothing* I hated more than elevators. And of course, Devin's office was the penthouse suite, the eighty-eighth floor of the enormous building. Gripping the steel hand bar behind me, I shut my eyes, concentrating on the eerie elevator music. *Claustrophobic box from hell.*

The doors opened and I all but threw myself out. A pleasant autumn scent of freshly cut green apples and cinnamon welcomed me to a modernized yet cozy reception area.

A beautiful redheaded woman was perched behind a raised wraparound desk. As I approached her, she peered at me for a moment and continued to type away. Her metal name plate read *Tiara Reid.*

"Hi, I'm here for Devin Star?"

Typing.

"I'm here for an appointment with Mr. Star," I spoke louder. "Are you his secretary?"

More typing.

I cleared my throat. "Hello?"

She hit one last key with her talonlike red nails, swinging her cold eyes to me. "I'm Mr. Star's *receptionist.*" Hostility saturated her voice, as if I was aggravating her by my mere presence. "Name."

I was taken aback by her snippiness but held my own. "Williams. Faith Williams." I cringed inwardly at my accidental 007 reference.

Tiara reached under her desk and smacked a small pack of D&S Tower tissues in front of me. "These are for you." She smiled. It didn't reach her eyes. "May I offer you a complimentary glass of D&S Tower Detox Water?"

"No, thank you. Wait, why the tissues—"

"Please, have a seat," she cut in. "He'll be with you shortly."

A loud crash, followed by a girlish cry, jolted me into awareness. My attention darted to the source, yet another thick glass door next to Tiara's desk. Devin's office, I assumed. The blinds were drawn tight.

"You'll need the tissues soon." Tiara's tight-lipped smirk was so nasty it made my skin crawl. Neatly getting up, she slid her hands down her tiny waist and smoothed her maroon skirt.

My tight blouse seemed to restrict my nervous inhale. "Is he ready to see me?"

"Are *you* ready to see *him*?" Another cold smile. Tiara opened the door into Devin's office, right as a woman with smudged makeup and puffy eyes rushed out, sobbing. The sniffling woman fumbled with a pack of D&S Tower tissues in her hands and muttered incoherently as she flew past me to escape.

"Oookay, then." I scratched the back of my neck, stunned by that woman's clear distress in her swift exit. I reminded myself why I was here in the first place. Sure, I had my portfolio and my resume but my sole intention was to ensure my car was getting fixed.

Tiara shut the office door and snickered.

"That would be the sixth applicant for the art counselor position," she said with a vile gleam in her smile. "Definitely less emotional than the girl before her." Despite the sour look in her eyes, I didn't shrink back as she strutted toward me. "Little advice, darling.

Turn around and go back to whatever poorhouse you came from. I know what money looks like, and honey, you aren't it."

"Are you always this caring or is this just for me?"

She scoffed. "This is an elite corporate building—"

"Maybe I should leave, then." Once Tiara seemed convinced, I burst out laughing. "Psych. I couldn't care less about your assumptions of me. Now get your fake ass out of my way and step aside, I don't want to be late to my appointment."

I started to move around her, when Tiara curled her talon nails into my arm and yanked me back.

"How dare you talk to me like that? I can ruin your life, and believe me, you'll regret—" Tiara retracted her hand and stepped back. Before she could finish her threat, the door to Devin's office had swung open, and out came an unexpected face. His son.

David Star.

When he moved, he carried his height with confidence and dispersed fresh, clean cologne into the room. Strong shoulders filled out his pressed white Armani shirt. Thick chestnut-brown hair with natural highlights was styled casually from his face. He was clean-shaven, emphasizing a prominent jawline and full lips.

All he needed was a fan blowing on him, and he'd be fully equipped for a photo shoot.

David scrolled through his phone and stepped up to me. Without looking up, he spoke. "There's broken glass in my office. Clean it up." *Oh, hell no!* He sauntered past me to Tiara. "Tia, I'm going out. Cancel any other job applicants today. Tell them I have the stomach virus that's going around. Yeah, I have it bad. If they get pushy, say I shit myself or something."

"Excuse me," I interjected irritably. "I'm not your maid."

David looked sharply in my direction. His eyes were mesmerizing, a deceiving soft milk chocolate, considering their hard cruelty as they raked my frame once. You know that savage look people give you when they're judging you instantly?

Yep.

His stare pierced mine with every long-swaggered stride he took in my direction. He was the storm after the calm, and I was in the eye of it. I feared this man's awareness of me, especially once he got closer.

"Wait a minute, I know you . . . " His deep, slightly husky voice crooned over his words with an effortless charm. My brain typed out a prompt reminder that the Star family annoyed the shit out of me. My hormones never received the memo. "You're the cute goth girl who hates my guts."

My face blistered with embarrassment, a small laugh tumbling out. "We may have gotten off on the wrong foot."

To that, David said nothing, his head tilted down to the portfolio clutched under my arm. "Don't tell me you're the art girl too? Small world."

"Apparently," I replied warily.

David flashed a grin that held no genuine kindness. It wasn't quite as heartless as Tiara's at least. He turned and glided to his door to hold it open for me. "Please, come in."

"There's been a misunderstanding," I said. "I'm scheduled to see your father, not you. To discuss the situation with my car."

For a second, David appeared to be biting back a laugh. Did I forget to wax my upper lip? The weight of the world lifted off me as his eyes fell away from mine and dropped to the portfolio again. "Then why did you bring your portfolio?"

"Oh, I—"

He snatched it out of my grasp. "Fantastic, I'll have a look. Unfortunately, my father took a jet to Australia this morning for the company. I'm the one currently interviewing for the art counselor positions. We can discuss your car situation as well."

He motioned me inside, and I had no other argument to make. As I walked past David into his office, Tiara shot envious daggers down at me from atop her perch.

Receptionist, my butt. More like gargoyle.

"My father said I would like you," David said, once we were alone. "I guess you didn't tell him how we've already met."

"No, I didn't," I said. "Listen, I was having a bad night—"

"Then let's go back to the beginning," David said with that deep, appealing voice. He held out his hand. "David Star."

"Faith Williams," I said and returned his firm handshake. David's eyes drilled mine as his index finger rested against my wrist for a prolonged moment. It was as if this man was purposely trying to make me squirm.

"Welcome to D&S Enterprises, Faith."

Heat crawled up my neck under his intense stare. He was still holding my hand. Was he checking my pulse?

He let me go. "Have a seat."

My wrist buzzed where his index finger had been. I sat in the black leather chair across from his desk. Seeing David now, dressed as an astute businessman rather than the normal nineteen-year-old I'd met Friday night, was surprising, to say the least. He embodied the mature role like a chameleon adapting to his surroundings, and I couldn't help but feel like I'd underestimated his intelligence. Looked like Playboy Junior was the genius protégé the world claimed, after all.

The office was spacious with lush gray carpeting and black leather furniture scattered sparingly. A few fake leafy potted plants sat by his desk. His computer setup had dual monitors and a fancy ergonomic keyboard with the latest state-of-the-art technology. On the opposite side of the room, a galaxy-wide flat-screen hung above a collection of black-and-white shots of the city.

Massive floor-to-ceiling panels overlooked the skyline of New York City. Heavily tinted, each panel limited the amount of light in the room, creating the illusion of night.

Despite all the impressive decor and peculiar window choice, what really caught my attention was the shattered glass coffee table I'd passed on my way to my seat, and his unbelievably cluttered desk.

"This is *your* office?" I asked.

David sat down in the leather chair behind his desk, his hand hovering over the messy surface as he searched for an item. "Has my name on it."

"But you're . . . "

"Too young?" David offered. He slid a pack of gum from beneath a pile of debris and popped a piece into his mouth. "I'm nowhere near my father's level of responsibilities, but he did start showing me the ropes from the moment I could say *call to action.*"

I thumbed over my shoulder. "What's with the coffee table?"

"It broke."

"I hate when that happens . . . " *You sarcastic jerk.* "All these beautiful windows, and yet it's so dark in here."

"I had them heavily tinted. Got jabbed in the eye when I was little, and now I'm sensitive to light. Have to wear sunglasses even when it's cloudy."

"You have photophobia?"

His head tilted to one side. "You have a firm grasp of the obvious."

"I took an anatomy class, so I knew the term." *I really hate this guy.* I flattened out a small wrinkle in my slacks with my palm. My inner neat freak was screaming at the debacle of papers and garbage scattered along David's beautiful mahogany desk. Or at least, I imagined it was a beautiful mahogany desk. It was hard to tell what was under all the debris.

How could a man so flawless be so messy? Tragic.

Discreetly, as David fiddled with my resume, I plucked an old french fry off his desk and threw it into the garbage can. Three-pointer.

"Miss Williams."

Caught.

He set my resume down and folded his hands together. "You should know, Rudolph was my favorite reindeer."

It took me a second to get it. The car accident. Devin must have told him I'd hit a deer. Trepidation clutched at my chest, as I recalled discovering Death's cigarette on the ground by my car. I shook myself from my thoughts and focused on the celebrity before me.

"Ha-ha, very funny. I didn't hit the deer on purpose, you know."

"That's what they all say." Amusement lit up his face. "Believe me, you would know if I was trying to be funny. I was trying to be cute."

Was he flirting?

"Damn things are overpopulating anyway," he continued. "Consider it your good deed for the month."

I accidentally snorted at his dark humor. I should have just let out a hog noise after that humiliating sound. "About my car," I began.

"We'll get to your car. Relax. You're making *me* nervous." He stood to pour himself a drink of what I assumed was whiskey on the rocks. "Here. For any stress."

"I don't drink."

"Have a sip."

"No, thank you."

"I *insist.*"

His voice held an element of control, which intimidated me. Despite my complete aversion to alcohol, I brought the drink to my lips and sipped. I expected the whiskey to burn hotly down my throat. Instead, I tasted sugar. "Is this . . . iced tea?"

He raised his glass in a salute. "Peach."

"You keep peach iced tea in a whiskey bottle?"

"You should be a detective."

"Why'd you make me think it was alcohol?"

He half shrugged. "Just testing something." On that strangely enigmatic note, David lifted his drink to his mouth, watching me over the rim. "Tell me more about the accident last Friday."

"I was driving home from a party—"

"Drunk?" He placed the bottle of "whiskey" on his desk with a clink. He watched my reaction carefully, which was unnerving. I had a feeling that was his intention. This was one weird interview.

"I wasn't drunk," I answered.

"Ever been?"

"No, it's not my thing." I looked down at my glass and frowned. *Then why did you try this, assuming it was alcohol?* "Anyway, I was the designated driver for my friend. Your dad tried to signal me that my muffler was sparking. That's when I noticed my brakes weren't working, and we hit the deer." I politely left out the part about his Fast and Furious father shredding the side of my car like a block of cheese with his Lamborghini.

"Sounds like you're lucky to be alive," David said.

A lump rose in my throat. All I could do was nod. He had no idea.

David smoothed his tie with a hand. "You're at the top of the food chain right now. Working at the D&S Tower would be a life-changing opportunity for anyone. We have top-notch internship programs and surefire scholarships for all our young practicums. Devin must have seen some remarkable traits in you."

The way he'd called his father by his first name was unexpected. "I appreciate the compliment and I'm grateful for the opportunity your father offered me. But I came here because—"

"Or maybe he hit his head on the steering wheel," David joked. "Do you want to know why the last girl ran crying out of my office? I'm sure you're dying to know."

I set my glass on a coaster. "Low self-esteem?"

"No, she lied to me. She wasn't here for a counseling position. She was trying to dig up some dirt on me to sell to the tabloids. Unfortunately for her, it was pretty easy to figure out, so I made her a promise. One phone call, and she'd never work a press job in this city again."

"You're not really going to do that, are you?"

"I have to, I promised her. Always keep your promises, Faith, and never lie." A slow, provocative grin broke through his serious expression. "Speaking of lies, let's have a look at your qualifications."

For the next two minutes, I watched him flip through the various scanned copies of my art. I'd only shown my family and my art teacher my personal paintings.

David flipped another page and my stomach fell. The willow tree from my dreams. It filled a plastic divider, and I didn't remember putting it in there.

David sat in silence, analyzing the painting in what appeared to be admiration. "Beautiful. Do you have any other landscapes?"

"Not in my portfolio, no. I-I don't normally paint landscapes."

"You should." David turned the page, and we both seemed to cease any movement. There, in the next two plastic dividers of the binder, were identical drawings of the mismatched green eyes. When he turned the page, there were two more scans of the eyes. I thought I might have a heart attack or hurl up my lunch.

"Um," David said. "This your boyfriend or something?"

I fought the urge to lunge over the desk and slam the portfolio shut. "I'm—I'm sorry, I must have made a mistake and grabbed the wrong portfolio."

"No worries, it happens." He set the portfolio aside. "Well, I'm impressed, Faith. You're talented."

"Thank you—"

"Which is a pleasant surprise, considering the only reason I gave you the time of day today is because you have a hot rack." He wrote a comment down on his notepad, snickering.

Was this guy out of his mind? I dug my fingers into the armrests of my chair, engraving my nails into the leather. "*Excuse* me?"

"You seem confused. Isn't that what *guys with reputations like mine* go around saying to girls?"

He'd held a grudge after all.

David rolled up the sleeves of his shirt, drawing attention to his biceps and the way the fabric strained against his wide chest. As I noticed the black Rolex on his wrist, I was reminded that we were from two different worlds. This was his territory and we both knew it.

"Now, here's how this is going to go," David said, his eyes now gleaming with devilry. "If you want your car back, of course. My version of the game Twenty Questions and a list of your positive and negative attributes. I have two columns drawn on this piece of paper."

David held up a piece of printer paper with scribbles on it. All I could make out was a tiny doodle of boobs in the positive column next to *nice tits*. "One side is negative, the other side is positive," he explained, indicating to each side with his pen. "As of now, you have several attributes listed under negatives and only one attribute listed under positives."

Any other time, I would have walked right out of that room after his degrading remark, but I couldn't move. "Is this some sort of joke?"

"I said you would know when I'm joking. I'm not joking." David jotted down more remarks on the paper. "Doesn't take me seriously. Negative. Damn it, hold on, I'm writing in the wrong column." He slipped on a pair of glasses, which made him look even more hand-some, if that was even possible—*not that it mattered*—and resumed writing on the paper again. After, he smirked up at me. "Wow. Eleven negatives in the first ten minutes? A record. You're going to have to seriously impress me at this point."

"Eleven negatives?" I leaned forward in my chair. "You didn't even write that many times!"

"You've struck me as competitive," David said, pointing the pen at me. "I like it."

"Let me see the paper!" I sprang out of my seat to see what he'd written, but he tugged the paper out of my line of vision.

"Uh, uh, uh, Miss Williams." He shook a finger at me. I imag-ined chopping that finger into little pieces and throwing it back at him like confetti. "Let's keep this professional."

"*Please.* As if any of this has been professional or mature!" I lurched out of my chair, a ballistic explosion in the midst. "How dare you talk to me like I'm—I'm—"

"Beautiful?"

My eyes clashed with his, expecting mockery within them, but instead, I found honesty, and that left me a little breathless despite my better judgment. "I want an update on my car," I said. "And I want it in my driveway by tomorrow at twelve p.m. Or else I'll leak to the press how your father tried to shut me up last night."

David slowly rose to his full height and strode around the cluttered desk. Intimidating good looks hovered over mine like a challenge that could end in condemnation, his body language self-assured and dom-inant with the anticipation of a victory that he never received. I stood my ground. David leaned away to sit on the edge of his desk, the gravity in the room shifting back to normal as our height evened out.

"If you leave, you don't get the job," he said, at last.

"I don't *want* the job—"

"And you *lose*." He reached back on his desk and held up the list of positives and negatives. My focus shifted to the positive listed on the paper.

Doesn't like to lose.

"You'll have to admit defeat and walk out of this building knowing you gave up." David pushed off his desk and walked around it again. You'll see my name everywhere and remember the smug look I had on my face when I defeated you." He poured himself another "whiskey" and snatched it off the desk. Then he stood in front of the windows overlooking the city and sipped his drink with a theatrical "Ah."

I headed toward the door. "Try your reverse psychology on yourself."

"*Stop,*" he commanded, and I turned back. David burrowed through me with his steely brown eyes, and through a dreamlike haze, I obeyed.

"Don't you at least want to know if you're qualified?" he asked. "Metaphorically, of course."

This man had been playing a game with me from the moment we met. And he was right. I didn't like to lose. It was a curse. Or maybe I was entranced by him. Either way, I felt like a madwoman for even considering staying. This wasn't me.

"Come on, Faith," he said around a broad grin. "Humor me."

This was sick. Stinging, I made my way back to my seat with the intention of putting this jerk in his place.

David strode to his desk without breaking eye contact and sat down. "Let's get serious. Tell me about your previous jobs."

"I've worked as a waitress for half a year. They weren't giving me enough hours and favoring other employees, so I quit. I also babysit, tutor, and volunteer in my spare time."

"Bor-ring," he sang under his breath.

"Serious doesn't last with you, does it? I would pay to see *you* try to wait tables."

He quirked an eyebrow. "As one of our counselors, you would have to commute here a few times a week after school. Would that be overwhelming?"

"Metaphorically, no. Like you said, working at the D&S Tower is a once-in-a-lifetime opportunity and art is my passion. When I'm passionate about something, I'm dedicated to my responsibilities and willing to learn. No matter what obstacles are thrown in my way, I don't give up. Ever."

"Ever?"

"You already know I don't like to lose. I'd push forward and get any task you'd need done. I'd do it efficiently too. That's how I am. I've always been that way."

"You live in Pleasant Valley, correct? In Thomas's neighborhood?"

"No, I live on the opposite side of town." The part that didn't have gated-in homes and fifty-thousand-dollar pools in every backyard.

He scribbled something else in the cons side of the paper. "All right, so that's a pretty long commute here. How old are you?"

"Eighteen. How old are *you*?"

His pen paused, before moving again. "Who's the one being interviewed here?"

"It was just a question. It's not like I asked you where you live or what time you get home after work."

"Are you asking me out?" he quipped.

I snorted. "When pigs fly."

"At-ti-tude!" David rested the cap of his pen against his bottom lip. "Would that be a negative or positive attribute?"

I gave him a flat look.

"You asked how old I am." He leaned forward on his elbows, a piece of hair falling out of its perfectly styled position and onto his forehead. He was so sexy that it hurt to look at him. It hurt even more to admit to myself I *still* found this disgusting jerk attractive. "Take your best guess."

As I analyzed his features, I recalled every article I'd read about the Star family and took a stab from memory. "Nineteen."

David whistled lowly. "So close. A fan would have known my age."

"A fan would have cared too."

He inclined his head to the side. "Ouch. See, I knew you never liked me."

"Not much gets past you."

A muscle pulsed in his jaw. He bridged his fingers together in a steeple position. "What is your opinion of me? Be honest. Take as long as you want. This is your chance to tear me to pieces."

"That's easy, David, because you're a cliché." I lazed back in the chair. "You are an arrogant, womanizing elitist, and you think you can have anything you want with a snap of your fingers because you're rich and famous. But no matter how many hot models you surround yourself with, and no matter how many expensive cars you drive, the only luxury you'll truly have in this life is the luxury of being alone, watching everyone else around you lead a normal life."

"And my heart is an endless void, which must be filled with love by the stroke of midnight, or else my Bugatti will turn into a pumpkin?" David added with a haughty grin, spinning around in his chair. "You live in a fantasy world. I have everything I want."

"You asked me a question and I answered it honestly," I reminded him. "The unhappiness part was an observation."

"What could I possibly need in my life to make me happier?"

"I'm not your psychologist."

He curled his lips into a thin line. "Smart-ass. That would be a negative."

"Did you expect me to kiss your feet and tell you you're perfect in every way, shape, and form? Sorry, not sorry."

David burst into a fit of laughter. "I *like* you." He wrote again on his pros and cons list. "You have guts coming in here and telling me off. Especially after my being so rude. You're exactly what I'm looking for."

I uncrossed and recrossed my legs. "If only this wasn't a metaphorical interview."

David stared at me for a long stretch of time. Jaw clenched, he picked up my portfolio and plopped it to the side of his desk. "Have you really never had a boyfriend?"

"What?"

"A boyfriend," David repeated. "A boy, who's a friend. Except the two of you—" He started to make lewd hand gestures, at which point I cut him off.

"I know what a boyfriend is, bozo."

"So the answer is no, you haven't," David said, his grin wolfish. "You're a virgin too. Saving yourself for a special guy?"

Geez, is it that obvious I'm a virgin? "That is none of your damn business."

"Touchy." His expression was a hybrid of wicked and amused. Like he'd found a new way to tamper with his favorite toy. "I bet . . . you've never seen a guy naked."

"I have," I lied, semi-choking it out. *How the hell could he possibly know that?* Had the room raised a few degrees or had I imagined it? I was hyperaware of every pore in my body sweating too. Recently, on the front cover of *Rolling Stone* magazine, David had appeared naked with both hands in front of his privates. It was all over the news. Now it was all I could see. Once more, David was purposely trying to rouse a reaction out of me, and it was working. "I have seen a guy naked, but once again, that's none of your business."

"It was health class, wasn't it? You saw your first and only in health class?"

There was no possible way he was asking if I'd ever seen a . . .

"You know, the Love Muscle? Mr. Happy? I personally like to call mine: 'The Anaconda.'" Then he moved his hand around like a snake. "Sssssss."

"I'm four hundred percent done with this interview."

"Sssss."

I launched from my seat to stand. "You're *sick*!"

"You have no idea." He propped his feet up onto his desk. "Out of the goodness of my heart, I must inform you that the top button of your blouse popped off about ten minutes ago. Must have been those D cups breaking free."

I snatched my purse and bolted. "Good-bye, David."

"I always win." He'd only muttered it under his breath, but I'd heard him clear as day.

I stopped dead in my tracks and pivoted at the door.

"You're a sad excuse for a man," I said, and his cocky grin faltered. "You're wrong too. You lost by losing me, and I won by losing you." I yanked open the office door and tossed him my complimentary D&S Tower tissues, which he caught smoothly with one hand. His features had molded into granite, his mouth a tight, thin line.

For once, David Star had nothing to say.

When I got home, I sulked around the rest of the afternoon and cured my tribulations with cheddar popcorn and reruns of *Buffy the Vampire Slayer*.

I tossed a kernel of popcorn at the TV. "Come on, Buff! Make out with Spike already!"

The lock to the front door jangled, before a frazzled version of Aunt Sarah entered my home with an eccentric neon-purple tote bag. Sarah was my mom's little sister by twelve years. She lived close by, and with my parents gone, she'd been charged with checking in on me. Inside the doorway, she wrestled her umbrella closed with hilarious aggravated noises.

"Sup," I managed around a mouthful of food.

She whirled around with her hand to her chest. "Jesus! Are you trying to give me a heart attack?"

"You're the one breaking into my house unannounced," I pointed out.

"I was in the area, missy. And I have a key, which means you can't throw any alcohol-infested partizzles while the folks are away." She dangled the key smugly.

"You have to have friends to throw a *partizzle*, Aunt Sarah. What's in the Mary Poppins bag?"

"Vegetarian lasagna."

"Bleh!"

"Oh, I'm sorry, would you like scurvy for dinner instead? We both know you haven't eaten a vegetable in days."

I fluttered my eyelashes innocently. "In what world is Count Chocula not a vegetable?"

"Exactly." Tossing her raincoat haphazardly onto the rack by the front door, my aunt stepped into the kitchen to put my dinner in the fridge. Then she wandered into the living room and slumped onto the couch beside me.

"What's up with the business outfit?" she asked. My heart ticked up a notch. I was still wearing the clothes from my failed appointment at the D&S Tower, and she couldn't know that I'd visited New York

City by myself. That was 100 percent off-limits when my parents were around and 110 percent off-limits when they weren't even in the same state. My parents made it clear I couldn't leave town while they were away and that they would ground me if I did.

"Apparently, ripped jeans and band T-shirts aren't suitable for yearbook pictures anymore. Pleasant Valley likes to torture its students by making them come in on a staff development day."

"Hmm." She didn't seem entirely convinced. "And where the heck is your car?"

Dad had turned half our garage into a gym and the other half was where my mom parked her car, which meant Aunt Sarah had noticed my car wasn't parked its usual spot next to my dad's truck in the driveway. The gig was up.

"I drove Marcy to get our photos done this morning," I said. "She asked to borrow my car afterward to see this guy and said she'd drop it off later."

Damn that was good. I'm pretty amazing at this whole lying thing.

"Doesn't Marcy have her own car?"

"Mr. Delgado isn't letting her drive for a while. Long story short, a few weeks ago, Marcy drove tipsy to get fast food. Her dad happened to be on duty that night and pulled her over. Now she's on an unofficial license suspension."

Sheriff Delgado was one of the most well-respected men in Pleasant Valley. Although I loved him like a second father, his overprotectiveness was mostly responsible for Marcy's rebellious behavior. Since Mrs. Delgado's passing, it was no secret that Marcy and her dad had a rocky relationship. Revoking her license to teach her a lesson is something he would actually do, and Marcy had driven drunk to get a burger before, so the blatant lie to my aunt wasn't *too* far-fetched.

"Her dad thinks she'll behave better without a car," I continued. "But you know Marcy."

"Always finds a way to get what she wants," Aunt Sarah said. "And apparently, you're her accomplice."

"It was a onetime thing, I swear." I passed the bowl of cheddar popcorn, swiftly changing the subject. "How was your week?"

"Adulting sucks." She shoved a handful of popcorn into her mouth. "I'm trying to organize all these local bookstore events to help get some new customers and it's a major drag. I wish I could hire another employee full-time, but nobody wants to work anymore."

"True dat. Is Ruby still there? I miss Ruby. She always has hard candy in her pocket."

"I love Ruby to death, but she's a thousand years old, and she keeps telling customers as they leave not to take any wooden nickels."

"Harsh."

"Never grow up, my beautiful niece. Life can make you bitter." On that cheerful note, she slapped her hands on her legs and brightened. "Anyhoo! What else have you been up to?"

"I drank two cases of root beer?"

"Wow, so eventful." She scrutinized my cocoon of blankets and the undeniable dark circles under my eyes as if she knew there had to be more gossip. "Now that you've reached the big one-eight, how's that *woe is me* teen angst?"

"Let's see." I settled back into the couch. "I have one friend, I repel the opposite sex like water repels a cat, and I have no idea what I want to do with my life. I plan on camping on this couch, on this exact cushion, until my butt forever imprints this sofa."

"Dang. That bad, huh? Wanna talk about it?"

"Nope."

Glancing up at *Buffy* on the TV, Aunt Sarah smiled to herself and reached into her purple tote. "Then it's a good thing I brought something to cheer you up."

I looked down at the book in her hand and gasped. She sometimes brought me a new book and this one was too fitting. *"Encyclopedia of Vampires*! No way!"* I smiled uncontrollably, cracking open the bad boy. "This is awesome. You know me way too well."

"This is a good one," Aunt Sarah said, pointing to Angel on the TV. We binged a few classic episodes together—shouting and throwing popcorn at the TV at the exact right moments. Family. Sometimes they just *get* you.

After Aunt Sarah left to meet a friend for dinner, I leafed through the vampire book and read a few passages about the mythical origin of vampires, when the paranormal aspect of it all suddenly reminded me of a certain cloaked hallucination.

Nope. I decided to save the read for later.

As the next episode of *Buffy* queued, I messaged my parents to ask them how their trip was going.

Mom sent me a picture of Dad's sunburn and then a picture of a lobster. She wrote how excited she was about a beach concert later. Shortly after, Dad sent me a picture of Mom asleep in a beach chair with her mouth wide open. Jokingly, he wrote he'd rather shoot himself in the leg than go to the beach concert. I burst out laughing and sent them a picture of my pale arm and Buffy on the TV screen.

The doorbell rang a few times, interrupting my final text.

When I peered through the peephole, wavy balayage hair and hazel eyes greeted me.

"Peace offering?" Marcy asked, presenting a plate of slutty brownies. Her eyes were sunken in and her skin was washed out like she hadn't slept well in days. "They're extra slutty."

Despite our argument on my birthday and the fact that I'd ignored her calls, I couldn't help but feel so happy to see her. Before

I could let her in, words came tumbling out of her mouth. "I tried to stop by all weekend. My grandparents came to visit, and then Dad wouldn't let me leave the house. I'm sorry for everything I said Friday. I didn't mean a single word of it. I'm so, so, so—"

"Girl, get in here." I ushered her inside and pulled her into the kitchen to set the brownies down. "I'm sorry too. I shouldn't have criticized you, I just get worried and have no filter."

"I know, but the no filter is why I love you. Dude, I *ruined* your birthday."

"Dude, no you didn't," I said. "I celebrated it twice, remember?"

If anything, a certain hooded figure had ruined it.

"I'll make it up to you, I swear." Marcy's voice broke off as her eyes flooded with tears, and then it all came tumbling out again. "When my mom died, I turned to Thomas for help, instead of you. I put him in that gaping hole in my heart because I thought I needed the distraction. You're the most reliable person in my life, Faith. You have the kindest heart of anybody I know, and I was angry with you Friday because you were right about everything."

The break in her voice brought tears to my own eyes. It broke my heart when she cried, but this was the breakthrough I'd been waiting for—Marcy couldn't move on until she dealt with her emotions.

"If I promise to be better and not some self-absorbed, ex-boyfriend-crazed lunatic, will you be my best friend again?" Marcy mumbled into my shirt.

"You're not a lunatic." This made us both laugh and I held her at arm's length by the shoulders. "I'll never stop being your friend. Thomas is a dick. You'll find someone who deserves you."

"Thanks, Faith." Marcy glanced down at my outfit and grimaced, the touching moment fleeing. "Hold on. What are you *wearing*? Is that my blouse? And—oh my fashion catastrophe—tell me those are not hand-me-down slacks?"

"Funny story. I went to the D&S Tower today to get an update on my car from Devin Star."

Marcy gasped. "You went to the D&S Tower? To see Devin?" She jumped once. Twice. A third time. "Eeep! What are you waiting for? A role call? Tell me everything!"

"Unfortunately, there's nothing wonderful to tell. I never met with Devin, I ended up meeting with his son instead."

"You met . . . *David* Star?" She emitted a high-pitched scream. "No. Freaking. Way!"

"Well, actually, I met David at Thomas's party."

"*What?* I knew David was the A-lister after the whole car crash thing with his dad, but I thought we both missed him at the party!" Marcy grabbed the plate of brownies, seized my arm, dragged me into the living room, and threw me down onto the couch. She hopped onto the cushion next to me. "Spill. Now."

"It couldn't have been much worse. All I wanted was to get more info on my car, but David interviewed me instead and played all these mind games. The whole thing was so aggravating and degrading."

"What do you mean, degrading?" She bit into a brownie and chewed fast, as if she were watching a suspenseful film. "What did he do?"

At the memory of the whole ordeal, I had a rush of energy and stood up to pace the length of the room. I rehashed every aspect of the interview.

She glanced at my chest. "You do have great boobs."

"Marcy."

"I mean, ugh, the nerve! Did you make out?"

"Marcy!"

She wiggled her eyebrows. "Did he cop a feel of your bazookas?"

"Marcy! Stop it!"

"What? David Star is *the* hottest man to ever grace this planet. Not to mention, he is worth billions. He is every girl's fantasy."

"Sure, but did you hear anything I just said? The man is an arrogant, sexist pig."

"Didn't he just donate twenty million dollars to a children's hospital and help build a bunch of houses in some third world country?"

I glared. "Whose side are you on?"

"Yours!" She looked unsure for a moment. "Definitely yours!" She held out her palms in front of me. "Let me just spell something out for you. Star is H-O-T, and you are R-E-A-L-L-Y S-I-N-G-L-E. As your best friend and wingwoman, it is my duty to look at this from every possible angle. That way, you don't blow a potential once-in-a-lifetime opportunity to do the nasty with David Star!"

On the inside, I was about to self-destruct. On the outside, I wore a calm, detached expression. "I need a new wingwoman."

"I'm not taking his side, Faith," she insisted. "It sounds like the conversation between you two was a little more playful than you think. Is it possible he was kidding around with you? Maybe flirting? Off topic, how'd he smell? I heard he smells like a dream and radiates BDE."

I jokingly pinched her arm and she winced. "Will you cut it out? He wasn't flirting! He was being an asshole! It was the most humiliating moment of my life. Period. Believe me, I could go on, but my head is pounding with rage."

"How'd you end it with him?"

"Told him he was a sad excuse for a man and left."

Her mouth fell open and bits of brownie fell out. "Oh, hell yeah! You go, girl!"

I smirked with pride. "You should have seen his face!"

"I wish I did!" We high-fived, and Marcy's enthusiasm died out. "Wait, you got his number though, right?"

V

The following afternoon, I had to work a booth for charity at my local town carnival. A big-shot billionaire had sponsored various carnivals this year to keep them open for the entire month of October, all to encourage donations. The Pleasant Valley Community Outreach Committee required a certain amount of hours to remain a member, so I let them rope me into the job last minute. Normally I'd be okay with this sort of thing. I loved volunteering my time—when I didn't have a Mount Everest pile of homework stacked on my bed.

When they mentioned all volunteers got let out of school early, a free T-shirt, and a jumbo bag of popcorn, I caved.

Everyone and their mother was at this carnival today, except for poor Marcy, who had to attend tutoring and then babysit her neighbor's conniving Dennis the Menace brat of a kid.

I worked the dorky drink booth, shaped like a neon-purple lemonade cup with a straw hanging out of it. Between tending to customers, there was controlled chaos around me. Loud upbeat music accompanied by the occasional happy scream piercing the air. Bright neon colors, swirling rides, a rainbow of prizes. And the best part: the yummy aroma of funnel cake, kettle corn, pizza, and hot dogs that filled the air.

Suddenly, a large black bird landed on the counter in front of me, snapping me away from people-watching. The crow, or whatever it was, sat there cawing in its deep, raspy voice. When shooing it didn't work, I whipped the towel off my shoulder and swatted at the counter with a smack, which spooked it into flying away.

A sharp wind kicked up my ponytail.

"One large lemonade. Seven sugars." My head snapped up at the deep voice, meeting the black aviators of the devil himself.

We spoke at the same time.

"Are you stalking me?"

"Not a bird lover I see."

David Star chuckled.

I shot him a long, dry look. "Really?" I made a show of aggressively grabbing a stack of plastic containers from a cardboard box and slammed them down on the counter to refill the cup holder. "What are you doing here, David?"

His mouth curved into a wry smile. "I'm thirsty."

I adjusted my baseball cap and wiped down a tiny spill on the counter with my towel. It was all I could do to hide my total shock at seeing him. "There are plenty of other drink stands here," I pointed out.

"But I want a lemonade." When he saw I wasn't making a move to start his drink, David crossed his tanned arms, inspecting me with an amused expression. My eyes drew to his broad chest as the fabric of his shirt stretched over his muscles. We both happened to be wearing baseball caps, but where he looked alluring with his plain white T-shirt and ripped medium wash jeans, I felt reclusive with my all-black funeral ensemble.

Lord, if you're listening, please smite this gorgeous man with a monster pimple.

"Have I come to the wrong place?" David inquired, interrupting my ogling and spiteful thoughts.

I crossed my arms, mirroring his position. "You drove all the way out here because you wanted a lemonade?"

"I'm here on a date."

I couldn't ignore the small flick of jealousy within me. "How much did you pay her?"

"Shots fired." David tracked me like a hawk as I moved across the counter to crush the ice for his drink.

"Volunteering?" he asked. "Or is this your new career?"

"Volunteering." I narrowed my eyes. "All proceeds from this stand go toward finding a cure for Alzheimer's." I set his drink on the counter, not at all apologetic when it sloshed a little onto his hand. "That'll be ten bucks, Mr. Star. Five, if you're taking it to go."

He pointed. "Sign says three dollars."

"Oh, you mean this chalkboard?" I took a piece of chalk out of my apron, erased the current price with the back of my hand, and wrote in *fifteen dollars*. "It says fifteen, actually."

David bit back a smile and produced a fifty-dollar bill from his wallet.

"Why are you here, David?"

He placed the money on the counter. "I came to apologize."

"What a waste of gas."

"I have to disagree." He leaned on the counter, closer to me. "Even if you don't forgive me, seeing you in person was well worth the drive."

"How'd you know where I was?" I asked. "Did you plant a GPS on me?"

"My father and I are sponsoring the carnival. For business

reasons, I had to give the directors my email. Now I'm getting spammed with emails listing volunteers and employees. I happened to open one of the emails this morning and noticed your name at the bottom. Guess it was fate."

"Ill-fated," I mused as I shoved the fifty into the register and started to count change.

"Keep it, Faith, it's for charity," he said, rubbing the back of his neck. "Listen, I was a jerk yesterday. You were a fighter, and I wanted to see if you could go the distance. I'll admit I was having a little too much fun teasing you."

David reached over and shut the register drawer I was distracting myself with, forcing my eyes to meet his black sunglasses. "Faith, I want you to know I'm . . . " His face screwed up, as if the words physically pained him. "I want you to know I'm . . . "

"You're?" I egged him on, finding this utterly pathetic. *"Sorry?"*

He exhaled. "Yes. Exactly."

"Let me get this straight. You drove thirty miles to make sure I knew you were sorry? A phrase, which, you can't even say?"

"I also wanted to update you on your car. It's in the shop." He scratched his jaw, although there was no stubble there. "Listen, are you free after your shift? I was hoping we could walk around, maybe grab a bite to eat."

Seconds ticked by. Out of the goodness of my heart, I held back my laughter. "You're asking me out now? You said you were here on a date!"

"I am, she just hasn't said yes yet." David's grin was playful. "It doesn't need to be a date. We could just talk."

I imagined if my eyebrows scaled any higher up my forehead they'd disappear into my hairline like a cartoon. David Star, the celebrity, Greek god, and asshat, had asked *me* out on a date.

"And you're . . . serious?"

"Absolutely."

All I wanted to do was tell this man to go pound salt, but he sounded genuine, and it threw me off.

Sigh. I'd have to restrain my inner bitch and let him down easy.

"I don't think a date is a good idea, David."

He cocked his head. "Why not?"

Why not! He has to be messing with you again. Gritting my teeth together, I chose my next words carefully. "I appreciate you coming all this way to apologize, but the things you said to me were unacceptable. Sorry or no sorry."

I started to busy myself, hoping David would get the hint, when he reached out and caught my hand in his. I froze. "You're right, my behavior was unacceptable. It annoyed me how you blew me off at the party, and I let my ego get in the way. I went too far. But I'm not a bad guy. Let me prove it to you. We'll grab something to eat, and if you feel uncomfortable at any moment, I'll leave, and you'll never have to see me again."

My pulse rebounded faster and faster off his palm. "Why are you being so persistent?"

"I have a feeling you're worth it."

Despite my pride, I'll admit a *small* part of me felt flattered, and my skin warmed.

The evil bird from earlier flew up to my face and hovered there with outstretched wings. Jumping back with a high-pitched scream, I knocked over a container of straws, and then hit the ground with my hands over my head.

"Whoa!" David swung his long legs over the counter and the booth became ten times smaller. "I got it. Stay down."

After a few failed attempts to swat it away, David grabbed my clipboard and hit the bird square on. It darted out of the booth and flew away seemingly unharmed.

Our eyes connected.

"You okay?" he asked.

"What the hell is wrong with that bird?"

"No clue, that thing was out for blood." A stack of cups tumbled over in the booth. Startled, David armed himself again with the clipboard, as if he expected a swarm of birds to follow, and I lost it. I convulsed in laughter. As he watched, he lowered his arms and his stare intensified behind his sunglasses.

Standing this close, heat radiated from his clothes. I was painfully aware of how delicious he smelled too. I wanted to lean into him and press my nose into his chest . . . *WTF? Stop it. Bad.* Flustered, I drew my fingers away from his and retreated, bending down to pick up the straws.

David crouched down to help. His heat. His scent. He was so close. Nervousness crashed into my chest and rattled my heart.

"Thanks for saving me from the crow," I muttered, as we stuffed the final few wrapped straws into the container.

"Raven," David said. "At least, I think it was a raven. They're larger than crows. And anytime." He grabbed the container and we rose to our feet together.

"Should I wait around until your shift is over?" he asked.

I looked up at his aviators, wishing I could see the expression in his eyes. For a split second, I wondered if he liked me after all, which led to more conflict. Everyone knew David Star only dated supermodels, and I was no supermodel.

"Is this all about the car accident?" I queried, in a final attempt to get any ill intentions out into the open. "Did your father tell you to apologize to me so I wouldn't leak to the press?"

"No, I came here on my own." He held his arms out, exposing himself to me. "Listen, if you want to beat me up instead of hanging out, I understand. You might hurt your hands on my muscles, though . . . " He stretched his arms wider, grinning ear to ear. "Hit me!" Now he'd earned the concerned stares of people walking by.

I wiped a hand across my own mouth to hide my amusement. My morals must have been on intermission because I couldn't say no to him anymore. Reaching out, I pushed his arms down to his sides. "You're ridiculous, and I get off at five."

His smile was now warm and infectious. "Five it is. You won't regret this, I promise."

"Always keep your promises, David." I repeated his own words at the D&S Tower.

He bent down, and for a split second, I thought he might kiss me. Instead, his lips brushed against the shell of my ear as he whispered, "And never lie." Then he turned and vaulted over the counter before melting into the crowd.

VI

The final two hours of my shift felt like the countdown to my nervous breakdown.

This date was a disaster waiting to happen. What if he was playing another game with me? What if this was all a joke being recorded for a TV prank show? What if, what if, what if.

After all, David Star wasn't simply attractive; he was the glowing porch light, and everyone, and I mean *everyone*, were the little bugs launching themselves at him. He could have any girl he wanted, and yet here I was, cherry-picked from the bunch. *Why me?* I kept circling back to that one thought as my insecurities reared their ugly heads.

I texted Marcy.

What do you do when a guy is a total d-bag to you and then asks you on a date?

Her text bubble popped up.

OMG!! This is it. This is the moment I've been waiting for. WHO IS HE? DOES HE GO TO PLEASANT VALLEY? IS IT STAR?

Me: Can't say.

Marcy: Nooooooo!!!!

Me: Help, plz! Hurry!

Marcy: Guys who are mean to girls 10/10 times are in to them. Or he has severe anger issues . . . Either way, YES, PAPI!

Four fifty-nine. The next volunteer showed up for her shift and started flirting with the boy in the funnel cake booth beside us. My hands trembled as I reached under the counter to pack up my bag to leave. "Snap out of it," I told myself. "You can do this. It's only a date."

"Hey, gorgeous," said a hoarse voice.

I popped my head up over the counter and came face-to-face with a clown. "Ahhh!" I screamed and recoiled. "David! Don't ever do that again!"

Laughing hysterically, David peeled the clown mask up over his forehead, his expression reflecting a child's delight. "I won it in a game. Are you ready to go?"

"I'm going to kill you," I growled.

"Cool," he beamed. "I'll meet you around back."

Leaving the booth, my stomach performed a series of happy cartwheels. David waited for me right outside, posed like a magazine ad come to life. With a backdrop of a Ferris wheel and other colorful rides, he stood relaxed with his hands in his pockets. The clown mask was replaced by his baseball cap, tufts of chestnut-brown hair poking out along the sides. As I examined him like an art appraiser, his lips curved into a slow smile.

"Hungry?"

Hungry for your abs. "What?"

"Do you want to get something to eat?" he reiterated, grinning now.

"Oh." *Snap out of it!* "I'm kinda suffering from a major sugar rush from the lemonade. Could we eat a little later?"

"Sure, whatever you want to do." He filled the silence expertly as we began to walk. "I hope you're feeling better about the car accident. I've been in a few fender benders myself. They can really shake you up."

"It's been okay." I blew a flyaway strand of hair from my forehead and tucked it under my baseball cap. "My friend and I weren't injured or anything, just a few minor bumps and bruises."

"That's great to hear. You guys got lucky." He placed his hand on my back as he steered us out of the way of a group of kids fighting over a bag of ride tickets. I felt the heat of his fingers through my clothing, even after he removed them. "Tell me more about you. What are your plans after high school?"

My brain was static, an old television with a broken antenna. "Um . . ."

"Are you applying to art school?"

"I've considered it, but the cost . . ."

"It's outrageous, I know."

Thinking about college always began a domino effect of stressful thoughts. My parents maintained they'd help pay off most of my loans, but I knew they couldn't afford any of my top schools without major scholarships, and I didn't want to burden them.

"You couldn't possibly understand," I murmured.

"I understand very few people follow their dreams because of one excuse or another. It could be money, time, or the fear of failing. Most will regret not doing so the rest of their life. If your passion is art, you should chase it. Even if you fail, it's better than looking back at your life and knowing you didn't even try."

His words resonated with me deeper than he could know. After my haunting interaction with David at the interview, this side of him pleasantly surprised me. I looked down at our shoes as we walked.

"To be completely honest with you, I have no idea what I want to do with my life. I have a few ideas of where I want to go to art school, but I have no idea what I'm going to do with my degree after I've earned it. I feel rushed to figure everything out, you know?"

David chuckled. "You say that as if it's a bad thing. You have plenty of time to figure that out. People go to college to be a history teacher and wind up becoming a lawyer, or a business owner. Fate has a funny way of putting you right where you belong."

"Spoken like an old soul," I said.

"More like a guy with time to think while procrastinating in a gap year." The sun peered out from behind a cloud and a halo of light slanted over David, stretching a golden glow across his features. Suddenly, David stopped in his tracks. He winced, squeezing his eyes shut and unclasping his aviators from the neck of his cotton T-shirt.

"You all right?" I brushed his arm with my fingertips, and he flinched.

"Yeah, I'm fine." He gaped at me a moment and rubbed his arm where I'd touched him before his mouth stretched into a dazzling smile. "The sun went in. I figured I was good for the rest of the day. Let's keep walking." He touched the back of my shirt, guiding me forward again.

"That photophobia thing must suck."

"I'm used to it."

"How did you injure your eye, again?"

"When I was a kid, I was at the playground with Dad. I tried to see how fast I could run through the jungle gym to impress him and went down the slide the wrong way. I fell off the side of it into the mulch. A piece of a wood chip stabbed me right in the eye. Wound up in the hospital with a broken wrist and a permanently damaged cornea. No vision loss, thankfully."

"Sheesh, that's awful for a child to go through! I'm so sorry."

He seemed uncomfortable talking about it, so I figured I should change the topic. "We were discussing passions, right? What are you passionate about?"

His pause suspended in the air, as if he were still reeling over my previous question. We passed a fire juggler, contortionist, and various dancers with Hula-Hoops performing sideshow acts. David bent down to put cash in a tip box by the fire juggler, earning a seductive wave from the upside-down contortionist.

"Humanitarianism," he said, once we continued on.

"Humanitarianism?"

"That's my passion. I have an impulse to help others."

The night before, Marcy mentioned the Stars donating a ton of money to children's hospitals. "How do you help others?"

"I don't want to bore you with the details." He cleared his throat. "I'm curious, do you still have any interest at all in the art counseling position for our program? Or maybe an advertising or public relations direction with your creativity? I'd be more than happy to find you an internship at the D&S Tower."

I fidgeted with the cross at my neck, withdrawing from the conversation. There was a sinking feeling in my stomach after he dodged another question in his direction. I was noticing David didn't want to tell me anything about himself, which heightened my theory that this wasn't a date after all but some kind of self-serving ruse to make himself feel better.

David glanced down at me as we walked further. "You're upset."

"A little."

His smile was lazy and sexy. "Because I tried to make a job connection for you? I'm only trying to help."

"There are people much more worse off than I am. I don't need your pity."

Grabbing the sleeve of my shirt, David jerked me to a stop.

"Hold on, I don't *pity* you, Faith," he said in an earnest voice. "I'm just trying to get to know you—"

"I want to know more about *you* first."

David opened his mouth, perhaps to defend himself, but held his tongue. "Fair enough. I guess I figured you knew everything about me from the media. Down to the supposed freckle on my right ass cheek, if you read *Cosmopolitan*'s latest article."

He had my full attention. "They did *not* write a whole article about a freckle on your butt?"

"That's the thing, it wasn't my ass. During a trip to Aruba, paparazzi snapped a photo of me on the balcony of my hotel and photoshopped another person's ass and legs over my bathing suit. To make it seem like I got work done." He snickered. "Submitted a photo of my actual ass to show my real one is fine just the way it is, but *Cosmo* ignored it. So now I'm being ass-shamed under totally false pretenses."

I peered around him. "Dumpy is *certainly* fine just the way it is . . . "

"Dumpy?" David realized I was checking him out and jumped, covering his jean-clad bottom with both hands. *"Hey!"*

I burst into laughter, borderline cackling at his reaction. David watched me try to compose myself with his mouth quirked up. "I'm in trouble."

"Why's that?"

"I really like your laugh."

Heat swiftly dispersed throughout my face.

"Did Miss Competitive bring her A-game?" he asked, nodding to the game booths lined beside us. "Because I'm not leaving here without winning a giant stuffed animal from one of these vendors. I'm not messing around."

I cracked a smile. "I always bring my A-game. Just don't challenge me to Frog Bog because you'll lose miserably."

He leaned into me. "You don't understand. I *have* to play Frog Bog, it's the only reason I came here."

"A-ha!" I said and pointed accusingly at his chest. "Now the long drive makes perfect sense. You're a fellow Bogger addict trying to get his fix!"

"Something about smashing a hammer into that little platform and catapulting rubber frogs onto lily pads brings out the inner sadistic child in me. If I start battle crying or pull my shirt up over my head, do me a favor and just walk away."

At Frog Bog, the various dramatic stances David attempted to get the frogs in the lily pads had me in actual tears. He'd restrained his reactions to winning until the very end, when he'd finally accumulated enough points to win the largest prize.

David punched his fist in the air and gunned his muscular arm into his side with a bellowing, "Boo-ya! That's the money shot, baby!" He then proceeded to yank his shirt up over his head like a soccer player and sprint around the area, blessing my regular townspeople with glorious washboard abs.

And no, I didn't walk away.

After the heated events at Frog Bog, we decided to cool down with a classic game of Gone Fishing. A private smile tugged at my mouth at the sight of David crouching down to help guide a little girl's fishing pole toward a magnetic duck, and I could feel myself dangerously warming up to this man.

Basketball was next. David executed swishes like he was a power forward in the NBA. My skills took over once we threw darts at balloons. I was in the zone, winning David a goofy pair of blue sunglasses and a mini stuffed toy while he stepped away to take a work call.

Soon, it was night. We wandered to the arcade to play Skee-Ball. A bet was placed. Loser with the lowest score had to get a surprise temporary airbrushed tattoo of the winner's choice. I beat him by a hair with the nagging feeling he'd let me win.

"Any good at Disco Rebel?" David asked, as we strolled to the back of the arcade. He shook his jean pocket, jingling a few tokens.

"Oh, please, no. I'm a terrible dancer." Now that was a total lie.

"No kidding?" He flicked the mini toy pinwheel I'd won at darts so that it fanned my face. "Now we *have* to play."

Marcy and I were Disco Rebel queens. We'd beaten all the game packs on my game console at home. Needless to say, David was screwed. He crouched to put our tokens in and then stood beside me as the two large television screens lit up.

"Good luck," David said with a wink. "You're gonna need it."

I flashed a fake smile and spun my baseball cap backward. "Try to keep up, freckle-butt."

Turns out, I was the one who was screwed. David was a phenomenal Disco Rebel player. It was in his stance. The second he slipped on the sensory gloves and got into formation, I knew he'd nail every instruction on the screen. Our characters awakened and sidestepped across the screens, raising their arms over their head and hitting each beat to the disco music. Our scores deadlocked. David melted into his groove, smooth and confident. On my side of the game, sweat poured down my neck. We stomped and rocked to the same rhythm, the madness to win reflecting back at us through the colorful lit screen. He was nailing *every* move!

David peeled his focus off the screen, noticed my frustration, and grinned. Then he did the unthinkable and went off the rails, tossing in his own sexy pelvic movements and iconic dance moves in between steps. An off-rail distraction!

"Ever play switch, Twinkle Toes?" David taunted.

He sidestepped toward me. I anticipated this move and we sinuously switched spots, our character's jumping across the screen to mirror us. Thrown off balance by being on a different side now, I missed a cluster of movements and David got farther ahead. *Cheater.* I would see hippie neon game characters with afros boogying in my head every time I shut my eyes before I lost to him now.

"You cheated!" I shouted.

"No, sweetheart, that was flirting. If I wanted to cheat, I'd do this."

We switched places again. As David slid past, he gripped my waist and spun me around so our bodies were flush together. In one fast movement, he wedged his shoe behind my heel and leaned his weight into me, arching me backward like putty in his hands. He caught me in a perfect dip and posed with a disco finger to the sky. The crowd cheered.

A crowd?

David picked me up in a smooth tug, and my heart pounded uncontrollably as he leaned in to kiss my cheek.

Electric. Our eyes connected. He twisted back into his game and picked up right where he left off, barely missing a beat.

Warmth migrated up my neck. Off-kilter, I stumbled off the small stage, giving David an insurmountable lead. He ended with another *Saturday Night Fever* finger to the sky as the screen declared him: "WINNER!" The crowd of women flooded into his space, begging for autographs and taking pictures of him. They must have recognized him underneath his disguise. My mind was inactive as I continued to stare at David's profile. He chatted with a group of fans and uncapped a marker with his teeth.

My fingertips lifted to my cheek, where his lips had seared my skin like a branding mark.

I went outside to cool down, and sometime later, David found me.

"There you are," he said, resting his arms on the railing beside

me. I was leaning against the outer barrier of the carousel, watching
the horses glide up and down. He must have warded off his fans with
selfies and autographs because he came alone. "I was looking all over
for you in the arcade. What are you doing out here? Wallowing in
despair over your brutal loss?"

I playfully nudged him away. "I wanted fresh air."

"You a hippie now?"

I laughed, despite my best efforts to hold it in.

"Seriously, why the long face?" he asked.

"Thinking."

"About?"

"I'm sorry," I blurted. "For my remark in your office."

"Ah . . . " He leaned back, sliding his hands into his pockets.
"You mean the savage remark about my womanizing tendencies and
superiority complex proving I've become completely detached from
ordinary life?"

"That's the one." I tucked a stray piece of hair underneath my
baseball cap and pulled the ends of my flannel sleeves to my palms.
"Listen . . . I tend to make a lot of judgments about people. I always
thought it was because I make better decisions than them, but lately,
I'm realizing it's because I'm jealous. I mean, I rarely go out, I never
take risks, I don't warm up quickly to new people. I'm kind of a huge
stick-in-the-mud." *And I'm a nobody.* "I guess what I'm saying is, I
don't know you well enough to make global statements about your
life."

David angled himself toward me, having listened intently to my
rant without any interruption. "Want to know what I think?"

"Sure," I said with a casual shrug. Although on the inside, I felt
like I was having a major identity crisis at a super untimely moment.

"I think you should stop apologizing for being yourself." The
lights of the carousel raced over his black aviators. "You have a

remarkable authentic quality about you, Faith. You're honest. Honesty might disguise itself as a monster when people don't want to receive it, but for people like me—we need the truth to remember who we are."

After watching the carousel unload, David and I headed back to the game booths to play Soda Pop Toss. The vendor plopped down two green plastic buckets with pink plastic rings. Empty soda bottles were lined in neat row after row on a raised platform. At first, David and I were back in our competitive zones and aiming for the gold bottle, but at some point, I gave up, flinging them blindly into the pit of bottles. Then there was a catastrophe. One of my rings ricocheted off the bottle and nailed me right in the boob. David stood behind me and jokingly showed me the "correct" way to toss the rings.

I swear it should have been an Olympic sport to pull all my focus onto his instructions, rather than the press of his strong hand around my waist or his sinful lips a breath away from my ear.

"Tension is thick in the air," David said, rolling a baseball around in his fingers at the baseball toss. "Two outs, bottom of the ninth, bases loaded and up one run."

I pinched his shoulders, pretending to massage. "What's the count?"

"Full count. This is the payoff pitch. If I knock down the tower, you get that stuffed penguin you keep eyeballing."

"Woop-woop! Get that penguin!"

He smirked for a second and then fixated on the stack of blocks ahead of him. "Watch and learn, grasshopper."

He adjusted his baseball cap and wound up like a professional pitcher. The muscles in his back tightened at release as the baseball flew through the air in a blur. It knocked off two out of three of the blocks, before slamming into the backboard with a thud. The last block spun a few times, teetering precariously over the edge of the

platform, before finally tumbling off with the others, as if scripted
for maximum suspense. A buzzer went off.

David pivoted, surprise all over his face. He threw out his arms
in triumph. "PENGUIN!"

"PENGUIN!" I echoed.

I jumped into his embrace without a second thought. Our bodies
molded together, and his chiseled arms swept me off the ground in
a spin. When he set me down, our smiles fell away. His gaze lowered
to my lips and the tender heat of attraction blooming within me
sparked to a fierce magnetism. *Whoa.*

"I have a great idea," David said in a calm, unhurried voice.
"Earlier, you said you wanted to know more about me. Why don't
we discuss me over food and make this date official?"

I hesitated. Of course, I did. This night was bizarre, yet perfect
and too good to be true.

"I'd like that," I whispered, "although I think you're forgetting
something . . . "

"How bad is it?" David asked for the third time. The terms of my
Skee-Ball victory were he had to get a temporary tat of my choosing.
"There better not be any pink. I'm not kidding, Faith."

The tattoo artist handed him a mirror. He got a look-see at the
sparkly pink butterfly on his tan cheek and lunged out of the chair
to chase me.

Luckily, the line went fast at the food court because I was starving. David took my order of one slice of pepperoni pizza, cheese
fries, and an ice-cold root beer and got in line at a concession stand.

Searching for a place for us to eat, I scoped out a red picnic table
away from everyone else and sat down with my penguin. Sometime

later, David came over with our trays of food and sat down across from me. My mouth fell open at the smorgasbord he'd ordered for himself: four hot dogs, two large cheese fries, onion rings, *and* funnel cake.

"Holy crap!" I laughed out. "Do you have ten stomachs?"

"Why yes, yes I do." He patted his flat stomach, and I imagined the six-pack abs beneath.

His white cotton T-shirt left little to the imagination. For the thousandth time that night, I immersed myself in the sight of his hard biceps, wide shoulders, and the tight ridges of his abdominals.

"I was going to get a double cheeseburger, too, but I didn't want to gross you out. You're welcome."

"You're such a dork."

He waggled his eyebrows. "What'd you name your penguin?"

"Maddox," I said.

"Maddox? Does he carry a switchblade around his penguin cankle?"

"No, but if you make fun of Maddox's cankles, you'll get the flipper." I lifted the penguin's arm and swatted the air for emphasis.

"He's crazy." David tore the wrapper off his straw. "So what do you want to know about me?"

"Hmm." I picked at my cheese fries with a cute little plastic fork. "In one word, how would you describe yourself?"

"Extremelysexy."

I rolled my eyes and we both fell into a fit of laughter. "And humble."

"What's your favorite food?" David asked, before biting into a hot dog.

"Tie between mac and cheese and tacos." I was going to say cupcakes, although that was more of a dessert, at least to "normals."

"I respect that."

"What about you? You look like a steak and potatoes kind of guy."

"Great," David replied sarcastically, "I'm supposed to give off the lobster and chardonnay vibe."

"Maybe from a distance. I don't like lobster, do you?"

"Nah, they scream way too loud when you kill them."

I stifled a laugh at his dark humor. "It's awful. My grandpa used to cook bunches of live lobster in this huge stockpot at his house for family parties. Totally traumatizing."

David shuddered. "If my grandfather had a lobster Jacuzzi in his house it would freak me out too." He finished off his current hot dog and wiped his mouth with a napkin as he contemplated. "Back to your question though, steak and potatoes are great and all, but I have a major sweet tooth. Is it weird to say my favorite food is frosting? If it is, then I'll lie and say my favorite food is cake."

"Frosting is the best creation since sliced bread!"

A slow, lazy grin. "Easily the hottest thing a girl has ever said to me."

"Morning person or night owl?" I asked.

"Night owl." His head inclined. "It's when I get the most work done. You?"

"I'm the same way. We've now reached the point of the date where you have to tell me your zodiac sign before we can take this any further."

Now he rolled his eyes. It was criminally hot. "Sagittarius."

"I'm a Libra." I formed an angel halo over my head with my fingers. "The most gentle and cooperative of the signs."

He snorted. "Gentle, maybe, but cooperative?"

I chucked a dry french fry at his chest, which he caught and happily ate.

"How serious are you about astrology?" David inquired, leaning his forearms onto the table as he sipped his soda through a straw.

"I like to believe it holds some truth. I've always loved anything celestial. Look at the complexity of planet Earth alone and the endless universe our little world is surrounded by. We must have *some* connection to the stars, to other galaxies, to each other. Don't you think?"

"I think I can get on board with some of it. The concept of the zodiac is as old as Babylonian times. Ever hear about Ptolemaic astrology?"

"Of course! He's a famous Greek astrologist. I have this huge astrology book in my room that has Ptolemy in it. My aunt owns a bookstore and gave it to me for Christmas a few years ago. I used to read it late at night with a flashlight under my comforter and take notes." Heat crept up to my face. "I'm rambling, sorry. That all sounded a lot less geeky in my head . . . "

"I'll have to show you my consciousness and determinism book collection one day. You'll quickly reconsider who's the bigger nerd between us."

I smiled a little at the thought of him wanting to see me again. "Now I know for sure I'm in good company. Shall we return to simplistic discussion before we get in a heated debate over whether or not fate and free will exist?"

"Yes, let us go back to unsophistication," David agreed, matching my jokingly haughty tone. "A debate might end with one of us marked by another pink airbrushed tattoo."

Gazing at his cheek, I tucked my lips inward to repress my amusement. "Oh . . . " I unzipped my bag. "Before I forget, I won these bad boys while you were on the phone." I handed him the blue sunglasses from the dart game. There was a change in his demeanor that flickered by so fast I almost missed it. "I figured you could always use a spare. They're too cool, I know . . . "

David flashed his famous Star smile and swapped his sunglasses for mine. "I feel pretty. Do they go with my tattoo?"

"It's meant to be. Now get ready for the extra-special surprise." My teeth tugged at my bottom lip as I presented the tiny stuffed frog in a dramatic display. "Ta-da! Your very own bog frog!"

David's mouth drew into a straight line.

Wasn't exactly the reaction I'd expected.

"You don't like it?" I asked.

He scratched the back of his head. "No, no I like it, but I think you should take him home instead. You love stuffed animals."

"Oh, okay." I slipped the frog back into my bag, wondering if I'd done something wrong. I felt a little pathetic for feeling hurt. It was just a stupid stuffed frog.

"I didn't mean to hurt your feelings," he said carefully.

"No, no it's totally fine. I have a perfect spot for him." I picked at another fry and strained a little to smile.

Neither of us talked for an uncomfortable minute.

"You must have more questions," David urged, and I was convinced he'd mastered the art of lithely changing topics.

I rubbed at my arms. "Have any weird fears?"

"I'm not afraid of anything."

"Oh, come on."

He smirked, although it was a little forced. "I get afraid on occasion. But fears? No. I always prove them to be nonsensical."

"You're getting all macho on me."

He shrugged a broad shoulder. "I can tell you something that makes me a little nervous though."

"What?"

He stared unflinchingly at me. "You."

"Me?" A flush swarmed to my cheeks as a smile lifted the corners of my mouth. "How do I make you nervous?"

"You're a total knockout, for starters. Exceptionally beautiful."

Even though my heart did skip a beat, I burst out laughing at the corny line. However, when David's expression dipped down a little, I realized he was serious, and covered my mouth.

"Thank you," I said, as heat crept up my neck.

David stared at me for a prolonged amount of time. His mouth hung open slightly, midword. I couldn't tell if he was looking at me or something behind me, because of his sunglasses, so I turned around.

Blood pulsed in my ears.

To my horror, everything and everyone was frozen in time. Unmoving, as if someone had pressed Pause on a remote. It was dead silent too. I turned back to David in disbelief and waved my hand in front of his face. I leaned across the table, slid off his glasses, and stared him in the eyes, desperately hoping that this was a prank.

"David?" I dashed around the table and tried to shake his shoulders, but he wouldn't budge out of his locked position. "David, what's going on?"

As my chest constricted with each sharp intake of oxygen, I took in my surroundings. The people, the bright lights, and the numerous rides—they were all motionless.

There was a shift in the air. I wished I hadn't noticed because now I could feel *them*. The eyes at the back of my head.

Finding the will within, I turned around. A shudder rang through me like a metal nail grating down my spine. Advancing toward me was a boy with eyes so familiar I instinctively lurched away from them.

He had *those* eyes. Those violent, otherworldly eyes trapped somewhere between a cat's and a serpent's. The ones I drew over and over on my canvases. A thick, jagged scar slashed horizontally through his one eyebrow, directly over the lighter chromatic green eye. He couldn't have been older than thirteen, yet he had the aura of an adult. His back was perfectly aligned, his strides calculated, his stare sinister.

The boy neared and fear engulfed my brain, clouding out all other thoughts. He strode past me, indicating with a subtle movement of his head to follow him.

I obeyed.

VII

As the captivating boy guided me across the carnival, I was bewitched, stripped of any voluntary movement. Whatever spell he'd put on me dulled my will to fight him. My mind was no longer my own.

We approached the entrance to a fun house the size of three large trailers, containing whimsical colors, textures, and quirky, motorized animals. Colorfully painted cartoons with exaggerated expressions covered the exterior walls, and by the entrance stood a creepy motorized clown. It shifted side to side, waving.

The boy stopped, eerily facing the shadowy doorway. He turned faintly in my direction and scrutinized me with those hypnotic mismatched green eyes. His cold features sharpened into a callous, almost hostile expression that slanted his lips into a cruel grin, before he withdrew into the darkness of the building.

Come to me.

Helpless to resist, I followed. I stepped through the threshold and let the darkness consume me.

A door slammed and the spell shattered. The awareness of where I was threw me into a panic. Grappling for the door, I couldn't regulate my breathing. There were no handles on the shadowy metal walls. No escape.

My thoughts crowded together into a hectic tangle. I couldn't believe how stupid I'd been to enter this fun house alone. *No. The boy.* The boy compelled me to this point. I needed to find a way out and get far, far away from that hypnotic creature.

The sensation of being watched pricked the back of my neck. I moved too quickly, too fearfully, stumbling over the uneven floor. My hands desperately traced the sides of a hallway as guidance. The loud, quirky music playing stuttered, then shut off completely. I could now only hear the sound of my heavy breathing and the faint buzz and clicking of mechanics.

Menacing laughter thundered through the silence. Startled, I flattened myself against a wall and held my breath. That laugh was far too husky and masculine to be the boy's. Boots lumbered closer. The relentless sensation of fear settled deep into my gut, threatening to hurl up my dinner.

Pushing off the wall, I tumbled into another room that was so humid and dusty, it was hard to get enough oxygen. A single lightbulb swung from the ceiling, forming the ominous shadow of the boy along the wall. I watched in horror as he morphed from darkness to corporeal, shadows peeling away from his young yet eerie, sinister face.

I was held motionless.

A distant memory unfurled itself from a cobwebbed corner of my subconscious. It was then that I looked at the boy differently. "Who are you?" I demanded.

The boy tilted his head up. A gloved hand darted out from the darkness to snatch the chain attached to the lightbulb and yank it down with a click. My eyes widened as light slanted over a bone-chilling clown standing behind the little boy. Soulless obsidian eyes bore into mine, heavy layers of makeup exaggerating a vile smirk, as its lips slowly stretched upward.

"Let's play," the clown hissed.

An enormous force pitched into my body, knocking me backward. I lost my footing, stumbled into thick curtains, and fell a great distance. My head hit the ground. Hard.

I wrenched awake in an awkward position on the floor, having evidently lost consciousness. As my vision swam, a room with crooked floors and buzzing, flickering neon lights spread out before me. The room was freezing. Each breath smoked the air; my skin burst into gooseflesh. Disoriented, I peered at the mirrored walls, which were rotating slowly, like a carousel.

What is happening?

I couldn't remember how I'd entered this room or how much time had passed. My thoughts jumped to the boy first as I hurried myself up to my feet in a dizzy panic. Where was he?

David. I recalled him sitting at the picnic table, unable to move. Was he okay? I remembered falling and tilted my head up at the closed ceiling above me. Had I hurt myself and dreamt it all? My hand pressed against the back of my head and there was no trace of blood.

Whimsical music erupted in crackles from cheap speakers and the tilted, crooked floor violently shook. As I fell into a wider stance, I glanced up at a piece of metal in front of me. There, in the reflective surface, the clown stood over my shoulder.

A grin stretched across his mouth, baring a mouthful of bloody fangs.

My heart exploded in my chest.

I took off, hurtling through rockets of compressed air into

another disorienting room. Everything was black and white; strobe lights flashed across the walls and floor.

Suddenly the clown appeared out of nowhere and leapt into my space. I shrieked. The frightening figure towered over me, backing me into a wall. He wore a black-and-white checkered outfit with a bell dangling around his neck.

As I stood frozen, trembling, trapped, taking in the dreadful sight of one of my worst fears, a snakelike tongue lolled out of the clown's wicked mouth, grazing at my cheek. "I can taste your fear," he whispered.

This time, when he grinned, I noticed how all his teeth were sharp, and how his black-and-white makeup altered, lining up differently, like a skeleton.

Death.

A moment of bravery overcame my body as I shoved him away and hightailed it toward an exit. Entering a hallway with optical illusions on the floor, the walls grew tighter, closing in as adrenaline propelled me faster. I came to an impossibly small opening at the end and panicked. I was terrified of tight spaces, to the point where I always kept my bedroom door cracked open at night. With no other way out, I stole a look over my shoulder. The wicked clown stood at the end of the hallway with outstretched arms, white-gloved hands pressed against either wall, watching his prey with no escape.

I turned sideways and shuffled against the tightening space ahead, casting one last look over my shoulder. The clown was rapidly approaching now, his gloved fingers dragging against the walls, his feet no longer touching the ground. His head tilted down with a menacing grin, humming like a psychopath to the screwy carnival music.

"Don't you want to play, Faith?" the clown purred.

"Stay away from me!" I stumbled back as his hand reached out, my back hitting the end of the hall. This was it. With no way out, I closed my eyes tight and pushed my back against the wall, which gave way behind me. A small dark opening had appeared in the wall, too small for the huge clown to follow. I dove into it and crawled fast against polished hardwood, the ground growing slick with some sort of warm liquid. I lost my grip as the ground tilted forward. My throat unleashed a shriek. Rapidly sliding face-first down a long tunnel, my limbs crashed and slammed into crooked turns before I was dumped into a ball pit.

I clutched my head as I rose from the rainbow assortment of plastic balls, the room dizzying with flashing lights. When I looked down at my hands, they were stained red with blood. Before I could register if it was mine or someone else's, something touched my ankle in the ball pit. Screaming and sobbing at this point, I hurried from the ball pit and hoisted myself onto a ledge, stumbling toward a neon-red sign over a door that read EXIT.

Bursting through the doorway, a labyrinth of mirrors stretched out and the whimsical music intensified. The sound of feet pounding against the ground reverberated off the walls, as if I was being pursued from all directions, forcing me through a certain route with more constricted passageways and distorted mirrors. After what seemed like an eternity of cruel pandemonium, I came to a dead end. I turned my head and caught my reflection in multiple glass panes.

There was no visible pathway, and the way I came from had closed up as if it were never there. I frantically paced the perimeter of the room, feeling around for another hidden door. My fingers climbed up to my throat as I backpedaled to the center of the room.

"Wake up," I pleaded. "Please, wake up. Just wake up!"

"Happy belated."

I whirled around and there he was. *Death*. Fear trapped me in a little cage. He wore the same obsidian riding cloak with a draping hood concealing his features. He was much larger than I remembered—if that was even possible—built like a linebacker. I was left with no room to run. No room to scream. No room to breathe.

"I said I would deal with you later." The deep rumble of his voice was as silky as luxurious velveteen, lilted with that rich, unmarked accent. "It's later."

"Why are you doing this?"

"You're not that bright, are you?" He loomed over me, as if he were about to whoosh me away. The faint smell of cherries fanned my face. "I'm here to collect."

Swallowing hard, I shrank back, which drew my attention to the cold silver chain that shifted at my throat. *My cross.*

"Burn, asshole!" I unclasped my necklace and held it out between us. "The power of Christ compels you!"

Death's hooded head dipped down to my hand. The tiny space between us shrank down to nothing. "The power of Christ bores me."

In one last attempt at freedom, I threw the cross at him. It anticlimactically smacked against his broad chest and clattered to the ground. *Cringe.*

"Oh," the words came out flat, "the agony." He cut his concealed glare to me and kicked the cross to the side. "That was pathetic."

"Not as pathetic as your cliché Grim Reaper costume," I snapped, before I could stop myself.

He moved in an instant, pinning me against a mirror with a single gloved finger. I knew he could have easily drilled that finger straight through my flesh and bone.

"Even when Faith was scared shitless, she still had a mouth on her." Death snickered in a low, sinister way. "Sounds like a great obituary."

"If you were going to kill me," I said, deliberately echoing his words, "you would have done it already."

He tilted his head to one side. "Accidents happen."

Terror swirled sickly in my stomach as he bent closer, but I wouldn't allow any fear to show on my face. As long as he didn't get the pleasure of seeing my fear, I didn't feel so helpless. His veiled features lingered right in front of me like an infinite black hole. As I fell into his mesmerizing darkness, I knew I was staring into the masked eyes of a creature several levels above me on the food chain.

Which made me wonder what he ate.

"You won't like the answer," Death said.

He drew away from me, circling the small space of mirrors. His frame was crammed with layers of thick, bulging muscle, which shifted beneath his cloak. Nevertheless, he carried himself gracefully, gliding across the floor like a jaguar. His hooded head angled in my direction as the gloved fingers of his right hand dragged along the glass surfaces of the mirrors. The reflective faces stirred, transforming into some sort of metallic liquid that rippled to life.

"My purpose here is to jog your memory." His voice boomed off the walls of the tiny reflective room. "Only then can we discuss your future."

"Why is she screaming like that?"

My eyes cut to the mirror next to me. My image dissolved as the scene spread along the reflective surface like a television screen. A masked man held a little girl tightly by the arms. As she thrashed around, I recognized the blond girl as my younger self, and I recognized the market too. Pressure pinched at the front of my skull, but I couldn't tear myself away from this.

"How about a front-row seat?" Death rasped at my ear, and then shoved me forward. I fell through the mirror as if it were a silver pool.

My back hit cold tile. Terror struck. I was now in the food market, witnessing firsthand what had been in the mirror.

Little Faith ran toward me, her golden-blond hair tossing in waves over her tiny shoulders. Unease shimmied down my spine as I watched my mother grapple for the gunman's weapon while another masked robber slinked out of a checkout aisle to block Little Faith's path. He raised his gun. The crack of a bullet rang through my ears, an explosion of pain ensuing in my stomach. I staggered a little in shock, before falling to my knees. As I hit the ground, Little Faith did too.

Heat seared through my abdomen like a branding iron. With a sharp intake of breath, I tilted my head down and pressed my hand against my belly. There was no wound. The pain dissipated. *What the* . . . Tilting my head up, I watched as my younger self bled out on the floor. Time stopped within the store, just like it had stopped in the carnival.

Little Faith and I were now alone in the market. Everything changed. Color drained from the darkening store as if we were in an alternate reality. The temperature plummeted to the raw, arctic chill of a meat locker.

"You must be Faith."

My eyes darted to the voice. The boy with the mismatched eyes. He was here, bewitching my younger self. The more I analyzed him, the more he became distorted, as if he were a trick, an illusion. He kept his hands clasped casually behind his back. To hide his hands, I concluded, since his fingers ended in black talons at the fingertips. When he moved closer to Little Faith, he had the stride of a predator. A shadow stretched out on the wall behind him, revealing a full-grown man instead of a boy.

"When you are eighteen, I will return to collect your soul," the boy said. "Ten years is a long time from now. Would you not agree?"

"No." I stepped back from the scene, shaking my head. "No . . . "

He grasped her delicate hand with his deadly one. Instantaneously, the boy transformed. His facial features sharpened into something exotic, animalistic. Intricate markings emerged from beneath his skin. Little Faith's eyes rolled back into her head, and her golden hair altered into a midnight shade, matching his. I touched my own dark hair with a tremulous hand.

"You'll remember me one day, Faith Williams."

When your luck runs out. The scene cleared in a whirl of colors.

And once again, I stood in the room of mirrors.

Death was no longer here. Stifling a sob, I stared wide-eyed at my petrified reflection. A chill ripped through me as more fragments of my lost memory collided with my conscious and stained my vision.

I'd lived my life with blinders, unable to see anything else but the false safety of what I thought my life would be. Now the lost parts of my memory were back, and reality cracked its heartless whip across my face. My life was an out-of-control roller coaster without a lap bar and it was only going downhill from here.

I remembered the day I struck the deal with the boy with mismatched green eyes. But he wasn't a boy. He was a trick, a façade the real monster wore that fateful day. He was Death. And he was *real*. God help me, he was real.

The Grim Reaper had spared my life because of his cryptic interest in my soul. Which only begged the question: What would happen to me if I didn't go with him?

"Take a wild guess," Death hissed down the back of my neck, *"cupcake."*

There was a loud rushing in my ears, the roar of a storm. Consciousness was gradual at first with the uncertainty of awakening from a deep sleep. Voices entered my ears like distant radio signals.

My eyes flipped open.

Stunned, my reality slowly sank in. I was now standing by the picnic tables in front of the food vendors, where I'd been earlier when everything had frozen around me. My attention slid to a man who had his back to me. He wore a worn-out baseball cap and held out a cell phone with a glittery purple case. Tapping the screen, he snapped a flash-on selfie with four giggling girls.

"I can't believe you're here!" the one girl gushed. She happened to be wearing a T-shirt with David's face on it, which explained how she was able to see through his poor camouflage of sunglasses and a hat. "I love you, I love you, I love you!"

I cautiously rounded the crowded table.

"David?"

He looked up from signing the fan's T-shirt, and his eyebrows scrunched together for a second. "Back already? Was the line too long for fried Oreos?"

A lump wedged in my throat.

This could not be happening. I'd been in the fun house. I knew I'd been in the fun house. It'd been too real. The boy. The demonic clown. Death. When I reached back and touched the back of my skull, I winced. It was slightly tender from where I fell.

For the umpteenth time, I contemplated whether or not I was losing my freaking mind. At this point, it was a hard pill to swallow.

I need to get out of here. I snatched my cell phone off the table and—

A hand touched my arm.

I almost jumped out of my skin.

"Easy," David said, showing his palms. "Are you okay?"

"I'm fine." Shaking, I started to walk away. "I have to go. I'm sorry."

"Hey, wait!" With Maddox the Penguin tucked under his arm, David caught up with me and blocked my way. "What do you mean, you have to go? I thought we were having a good time."

"It's a personal issue," I said, desperately trying to calm myself.

He took a cautious step closer. "Want me to drive you home?"

"I'll walk. I live right around the corner."

David's posture fell a little in defeat, and his lips pressed tight. He handed me Maddox.

"Did I do something wrong?"

"No, not at all." *I'm such a piece of crap for leaving him like this.* "You're not being shot down, I swear. I just don't feel well. It must be something I ate."

"Maybe it's that stomach bug going around."

I managed a small laugh, recalling his dramatic stomach bug excuse for canceling the rest of his interviewees the day before. "Thank you, David. I had a lot of fun."

"So did I." He smiled. It didn't quite reach his eyes. I could tell he was hurt by my quick retreat. Without another word, I maneuvered around him and headed home.

VIII

Skittles, my white Ragdoll cat, purred loudly in my ear, and I knew I'd slept in past her breakfast. She was my go-to cuddle buddy, although lately, all I saw when gazing into her big chlorine eyes was the catlike boy with mismatched eyes. After a groggy stretch in bed, I sat up and stared at the stack of covered canvases in the corner of the room. The disturbing memories from the carnival three nights before resurfaced for another nerve-wracking day.

Dragging myself from the covers, I slogged over to the bathroom to toss cold water onto my face. In the mirror above the sink stood a ghost, a frightened girl I couldn't recognize.

"You're stronger than this."

I stormed back into the bedroom, ripped the blanket off the stack of canvases, and launched into cleanup mode. By the time I was done, the garbage was overflowing with frames. Outside, I flung them into a big trash can at the end of our driveway and threw up a middle finger.

Ha.

Despite the container of melatonin and bedtime tea next to my bed, I was starting to accept that sleeping at night in general was no longer a possibility. When I would fall asleep, the abysmal nightmares I'd had for weeks worsened, to the point where I now woke up screaming, drenched in sweat with my limbs twisted in my sheets. Lying absolutely still, I'd retrace the events of the nightmare but could never remember all the contents. Only the shadowy mass that would consume me, trapping me between awake and asleep in a cocoon of smoke. Faded went the dream with a kiss. Wicked lips caressing mine like silken trickery, marking my brain with one unforgettable name. *Death.*

School that day went by in a blur. To avoid dreaming, I made up for my sleepless night by snoozing away in patchy cycles during my classes.

David had texted me Wednesday, the morning after the carnival, to make sure I was feeling better. I hadn't texted back, and he'd called and left a voicemail yesterday. I assumed he'd gotten my number from my portfolio. Several times my finger itched to push the Redial button to call him back. I never did.

I was afraid to get close to him. For obvious reasons.

I wanted to tell David the truth about what'd happened at the carnival, but who would believe such an absurd story? Hell, I was having trouble believing it myself. None of what happened in the fun house made any logical sense, so unless I wanted a cool new bedroom with white padded walls, David, Marcy, and even my family all had to be left in the dark.

When I entered my house again, Skittles weaved between my feet, and I carried her like a baby into the kitchen to set her down on the hardwood floor.

"Sorry about that, princess. You just want your meow-meow

food, don't you?" I scooped a cup of food into her bowl, wondering when I'd eaten last. "If I'm going crazy, at least I have you to keep me company. Right?"

Skittles continued to eat her food.

"Good talk."

Sighing, I chose a stool at the kitchen counter and scrolled through the notifications on my phone. Marcy had texted me several times. She knew something was up the past two days at school, especially when I dismissed any conversation about "the guy who asked me out," but like I said, she wasn't one to press, and I didn't want to talk about it. Maybe it'd make me feel better to tell her a tall tale version of why I left David alone at the carnival. At least then, I could tackle a fraction of my current problems.

Dodging Marcy was like dodging a boomerang. She always came right back.

My phone alerted me about a text message. I thought it would be Marcy or my parents, but it was an unknown number. My heart picked up as I read the first line.

> I've been thinking about you. I had fun on our date. More fun than I've had in a while, honestly. I feel like I did something wrong and scared you off. I'm worried about you. At least text me back and let me know you're okay.

I set down my phone, torn. David complicated things, but I'd had fun on our date too.

I invited Marcy over.

"And you *left* him!" Marcy cried, after I rehashed a drastically edited version of the time I spent with David. We were sitting on stools at the breakfast counter in my kitchen. I excluded anything having to do with

Death and the fun house, of course. "Rewind. You went on a *whole date* with David Star. A whole date and you didn't give me a *crumb* of information about it all week? No, you let me dangle from a cliffhanger of delicious mystery! You are an evil, evil woman . . . "

"You should be in theater."

"I can't believe this. What am I lately, chopped liver?" She inhaled sharply and pressed a hand to her chest. "Am I *olive loaf*?"

"What's so bad about olive loaf?" I pursed my lips and gave a little shrug. "I like olive loaf."

She gagged and held up her palm. "Girl, I'm going to pretend you didn't just say that."

"I didn't tell you because I knew you'd freak out. I had no idea how the date would go, and I was so nervous." Technically the nervous part wasn't a lie. It was no walk in the park to converse with a guy who could probably toast marshmallows on his own blistering hot abs. "The entire night, I could literally *feel* the droplets of sweat amalgamating into one big swimming pool of anxiety in my bra," I told her.

"Amalga-*huh*? Babe, what language do you speak? To hell with your nerves! Have you seen his lips? They're luscious. You should have grabbed him by his hunky shoulders and tongued that beautiful model mouth!"

I grimaced a little at the "tongued" part, although David's lips *were* the Bermuda Triangle of kisses. I'd felt his lips on my cheek, soft and enticing. One could get lost kissing lips like those . . .

Shaking myself from my thoughts, I seized Marcy's empty cereal bowl and placed it in the dishwasher. *Damn you, raging hormones. This would be so much easier if you'd stop swooning over David and loathe him again!*

"I need a moment to process," Marcy said, slumping miserably on her stool. "I can't believe we ditched David Star."

"We?"

"I'm dating him vicariously through you," she explained.

"We're not dating, Marcy." With a roll of my eyes, I drew open the double doors to the food pantry. Cue the angel's chorus. I marveled at the rainbowesque display of cereal boxes and junk food crowding the shelves Mom had stocked before flying to Hawaii with Dad. Too bad I couldn't stomach anything all week. I felt so weak and restless; maybe eating would make me feel better.

Resurrecting my lack of appetite required sugar. I thought about the strawberry frosted cupcakes Marcy made for my birthday and strode across the kitchen to open the freezer. *Take a wild guess, cupcake.*

I slammed the freezer door shut.

"Yeah," I said, dragging in an unsteady breath. "No more cupcakes for a while."

I twisted around and there was Marcy, eyeing me like I was batshit crazy.

"Maybe it's better I don't contact David," I said, as I rubbed the back of my neck. "I've got a lot of stress with applying to college and an AP Chem test next week . . . "

"I love you, but you're overreacting. Honestly, it sounds like you had a great time." She wiggled her eyebrows. "I think you liiike him."

Spending time with David had changed my perception of him, and now I knew he was so much more than what the tabloids claimed—funny, playful, and hardworking. He was a great listener, too, and drank in every word I said. If it was all an act, I'd almost bought it hook, line, and sinker.

However . . .

Although David's unusual behavior during the interview was forgiven, it was not forgotten. A part of me still didn't understand his interest in me either. A rich celebrity who liked me? Come on.

Call it paranoia, call it intuition—whatever it was, I had a feeling my rejection at Thomas's party and then again at the interview was what drove David to the carnival. I didn't have the energy for some two-faced megalomaniac who was toying with me to see if he could get into my pants.

"I have an idea," Marcy said. "It's an hour train ride, right? Why don't you visit David at the D&S Tower and talk with him in person?"

"And what, show the broad-shouldered brooder with ego issues that my love is his redemption? This isn't a romance novel."

"Broad-shouldered brooder with ego issues? Yummy."

"You are on another level, sister. I hardly know the guy, and I'm going to show up at his office again? It's too late in the day, plus it's Friday and my parents get back from their trip at nine tonight."

"If you get dressed, I can drive you to the train station and you'll be at the tower by five. You can totally be back by eight. His father is a workaholic, he probably keeps David there past five anyway."

"Even if I wanted to go, I don't have enough money for a train ticket."

"I'll spot you!"

"Marcy, no—"

"It's totally fine, babe. This is bothering you, and I'm not the one who will make you feel better or find closure." She was doing that creepy best friend thing and reading my mind. "You need to go talk to the broad-shouldered brooder with mommy issues."

I stifled a laugh. "Thank you for offering your help, but I can't. I have enough going on already. I'm not going to get myself tangled in a messy tryst, when I should be figuring out what I want to do with my life."

A tiny, crumbled piece of paper hit my face. Marcy was riffling through her purse, tossing various pieces of trash and gum wrappers over her shoulder, while she sang an off-key song under her breath.

"A-ha!" She thrust a handful of bills at me. "Bam."

I backed away with a glare. Marcy followed with an outstretched fistful of cash, raising an eyebrow at me in challenge. "You need this, and you know it. I see right through your insults of him. You *like* David."

Her words rang true in my head. What she didn't know was that she gave me a ticket out, not in. I needed to figure out if I was cuckoo for Cocoa Puffs with all these head trips to Paranormal Land before I could even begin to consider a relationship with David or anyone else.

The tip of the D&S Tower impaled the violent blackened sky as rain pelted the pedestrians on the sidewalk with icy droplets. Mouth breathing like I'd run a marathon (I practically had), I took refuge in the lobby. I glowered from under my hood at the beautiful and *dry* businessmen and businesswomen sauntering around the lobby and discreetly wrung out the ends of my hair like a mop into a potted plant.

Partly cloudy with a chance of an afternoon shower, my butt.

My impromptu outfit of a graphic T-shirt, jeans, and Converse was completely waterlogged, so I considered turning back and taking a taxi home. But I'd come too far now. Tugging the zipper of my drenched hoodie up to my neck, I wrapped my arms around myself and trudged through the lobby.

At the security area, I pulled down my hood to show my face to the guard. Although I looked like some punk teenager who was about to spray paint the nearest bare wall, he let me pass without any questions. Security had done the same thing the first time I was here. When I turned back over my shoulder, one of the guards stopped a woman dressed considerably nicer than me and asked for her name. I wondered if David or Devin had shown them a picture of me or something. *Weird.*

Trepidation slid down my spine as I glided into an elevator with four other people. I felt jittery and wired, and not just because of the nervousness of seeing David again. This whole building was intimidating. I walked down the hallway to his office with squeaky sneakers.

A woman wearing a stunning lace blouse strutted past, glancing down at me over her thin nose. What the hell had I been thinking wearing my *turd* of an outfit? Sure, David and I had seen each other in casual clothes, but were we at casual turd outfit level yet? I guess I'd find out . . .

I heaved in a deep breath and yanked open the doors to an empty waiting room. Tiara, David's witch of a receptionist, wasn't perched behind her desk. Heart in my throat, I crossed the waiting room and lifted my hand to knock on David's door, when I noticed it was slightly ajar.

I nudged the door open. "David? It's me, Faith." When he didn't respond, I peeked through the crack in the door, the faint light of the shadowy room haloing the outline of his large mahogany desk.

"Yo, anybody home?" I pushed the door open farther and took a guarded step forward. The room appeared significantly different than the last time I'd been in it. It was colder, darker. Everything fell to a hush as I took another step inside.

Untouched, opulent furniture was scattered around the room with the potent smell of new leather, like the couches were brand-new. The carpets were indented in certain places, indicating furniture had recently been rearranged. The damaged coffee table was gone, replaced with another sleek glass table. There was not a trace of anyone ever inhabiting the office, not even a single food wrapper from David's desk. Everything was spotless.

Snooping around, I picked up the remote to the television and tried the power button. The television didn't work. I studied the wall next to the TV, and my head tilted. The black-and-white photographs of New York hanging there were cardboard demo photos the frames came with. Now that I was thinking about it, there were no photographs of him or his dad anywhere in here.

This is weird. There must have been a reasonable explanation. Maybe it was a new office for him, and he was still decorating.

I crossed a pocket of air where I could smell the ghost of David's cologne and hesitated walking any farther. This was wrong. I was trespassing. Coming to my senses, I began to exit the room. As my hand touched the door handle, it occurred to me to look back over my shoulder, and I saw something gleam like a wink under the lamp on his desk.

I checked to see if the coast was clear in the waiting room and left a crack between the door and the frame. Striding toward his desk, I searched for the sparkle that had caught my eye.

Various papers were stacked neatly on his desk, my portfolio included. Clipped to it, the pros and cons list with a scribbled-out drawing of boobs. I noticed he'd written a lot less cons than I assumed. *Cons: Killed Rudolph. Doesn't drink (Narc?). Sassy. Uptight. Wore slacks . . .*

Now I was disgusted with myself for giving David another chance, until I read the pros list.

Pros: Punctual. Organized. Funny and quirky. Hardworking. Dedicated. Intelligent. Bold. Self-motivated. Honest. Reliable. Creative. Listener. Perceptive. Opinionated. Courageous. Vibrant. Doesn't like to lose, will surrender if her pride is at risk. Will not fangirl over you under any circumstance.

I set the loose-leaf down and a small smile edged my lips. He'd gotten all that by being in a room with me for less than thirty minutes?

Rummaging through the crowd of papers on his desk, I tried to find the source of the sparkle again. Wedged between files lay the end of a dainty silver chain. I began to tug on it when the dim room flashed with light. Through the massive tinted windowpanes, a purple lightning bolt zigzagged across the sky, followed by a muted crash of thunder.

"Faith?"

Startled, I honed in on the figure standing in the office doorway. Droplets of water cascaded down David's straight nose and full lips. Sopping wet, his white dress shirt clung deliciously to the hard muscles of his arms and the deep ridges of his abdominals. As I gawked at his physique, he raked his fingers through his chestnut hair, combing it back. My mouth went bone dry.

"What are you doing in here?"

He's talking to you! Say something, idiot!

"Hey . . . you," I said.

David checked his watch as he leaned against the doorway. "Did you come here straight from your classes?"

"No, I was home first. Seniors get out at two fifteen. I was hoping to catch you before you left work. I was just, um—"

"Snooping through my office?"

"No, I—well—" I lifted my arms and then let them slap to my sides. "Yes."

The harsh panels of his face softened. "Find anything juicy?"

"I wish. It's pretty boring in here. I take it you're not a fan of livening up the place?"

"Hey, I just moved into this office. Give me time." He crossed his arms over his chest. "If you're so disappointed, you should try the bottom left drawer. You will find my stash of Twinkies and a remarkable bag of spicy Funyuns."

"Is this a test?"

"Possibly."

"For the record, I didn't read any papers on your desk, except the pros and cons list. Didn't open any drawers, or anything. You can dust for prints."

He simpered. "Faith, it's fine. I believe you. I'm really glad you're here. I was starting to think you were ghosting me."

Heat climbed up my neck. "I should have texted you before I came by. Now you probably think I'm nuts." *Way to let that cat out of the bag.*

"Please, I already thought that. I've seen the way you Frog Bog." He flashed another warm, attractive grin. But like the previous one, it didn't quite reach his eyes.

I offered a timid smile in return and wiped my clammy hands on my leggings. Not the finest solution, considering the leggings were damp from the rain.

"It's brutal out there." He cast his eyes to the charcoal sky outside. "You should stay here for a while, until the storm clears."

"You don't have to tell me twice." I plucked at my sodden sweatshirt. "Looks like we both got assaulted by rain, huh?"

As if now getting permission, David raked my frame once. His eyes intensified, but he hid his satisfaction almost impeccably. "You're shivering. I'll get you dry clothes."

I wished I could blurt out an apology and clear the air with a joke, but I felt too shy. It wasn't in my nature to attack emotional situations so directly. The fact that I had mustered up the courage to travel to the D&S Tower again to see David in person was a big step for me.

Crossing the opposite side of the room in a few strides, David pressed a touch panel in the wall, revealing a hidden door. He disappeared into the doorway and emerged with a stack of clothes. As he neared again, my heart picked up. *Apologize already!*

"Sweatpants shouldn't be too big, I purchased the wrong size a while back," he said absently. "This jersey is the only shirt here that won't be a dress on you."

David handed me the stack of clothes and our fingers brushed. A jolt. My nerve endings resuscitated. Our eyes locked, and there was an ineffable exchange between us.

He jerked his hand away. I rocked back with the clothes like a total klutz.

David rubbed the back of his neck. "I should probably get changed too." The corners of his mouth twisted in an evanescent smirk. "Would you like to get dressed in here? In that case, I'll leave the room. Or you can use the bathroom?"

"I'll use the bathroom, thanks." Had he felt that weird shock when we'd touched too? With downcast eyes, I speed-walked out of the room like a determined soccer mom with weights.

How had I managed to have an entire conversation with David last weekend, when now I was a gawping mess in front of him? Not to mention the charged tension in the room and his bizarre mood. What had changed between us?

I'd totally forgotten my purpose of being at the D&S Tower. I peeled off my damp clothing, my bra and underwear soaked through with rain. Eyeballing the convenient electric hand dryer on the wall, I crouched down and aimed the hot air at my chest.

Now was not the time to be dating, especially when I was skeptical of David's objective with me. The more I reeled over my thoughts, the harder it became to return to the office and face that beautiful man and his chocolate puppy dog eyes.

The sweatpants he'd given me were soft cotton with the D&S Tower logo on the upper thigh. The waistband had to be rolled over three times with the drawstrings pulled as tight as possible so they wouldn't sag off my hips. I slipped the Chicago Bears jersey over my head, dried my hair a little bit with paper towels, applied some watermelon lip gloss from the pocket of my discarded wet jeans, and gathered up all my bravery to enter his office again.

David was resting against the edge of his desk and peering out into the thunderstorm. He had his cell phone to his ear, and although his back was to me, I could tell he'd styled his damp hair away from his face with a comb. He'd also exchanged his waterlogged clothes for another Armani number.

"Your phone is breaking up," David susurrated. "Tell me again what happened. Slower."

A pause.

"No," he said firmly. "Do not show up here. I'm unavailable."

He cracked his neck to the side as he listened to whoever was on the other line. *Well, shit.*

"I'm not mad." The displeasure in his body language and the leisurely way he drew out each word said otherwise. He adjusted his position on the desk, his fist tightening against his thigh. "Enough. We'll discuss this later."

He hung up.

"Sorry about that," he said, without turning around. My sneakers must have been squeakier than I thought. "One of the creative directors has been testing me all day."

"About?"

"An external conflict in the agency he hasn't resolved yet." He gave a half shrug as he pushed off the desk, pivoting toward me. His expression closed off any visible emotion. "I don't want to bore you with the details."

I pressed my lips together. *Now, there's a line he replays like a broken record.*

"Do you need anything? Water? Food?" He scratched his jaw. "I can head down to the refectory and get you a sandwich and chips?"

"I'm good, thank you." I ran my hands down the sides of his jersey a few times. "So Chicago Bears?" In the bathroom, it'd been my decided-upon transition into a conversation. Now it was my saving grace to assuage the tension in the room. "Not a Giants or Jets fan?"

He crossed his arms. "Nah, Chicago's my team. Through thick and thin, I stick with Da Bears."

"I don't know why you torture yourself," I said in a teasing way. "The Bears haven't won a Super Bowl since the eighties."

David blinked a few times, taken aback. "You follow football?"

I couldn't help but smile. "I watch football and hockey with my dad. Football is religion on my dad's side of the family. He has five brothers, and they're each loyal to different teams. I can't tell you how many times a sports argument has ruined a holiday family dinner."

"You're into sports." His disposition transformed as a slow, radiant grin stretched across his mouth. This man had me wrapped around his finger. "How do you not have a boyfriend?"

I gave a mirthless laugh, reciting the only answer I knew. "I'm intimidating."

He cocked his head with a quizzical look.

"The way I dress at school, the makeup I wear." He stared at me so intensely as I spoke that a flush crept up my neck. "I've been told I'm intimidating."

A muscle in his jaw ticked. "Who told you that?"

Myself. I tucked a strand of my hair behind my ear. "It's not a big deal."

"Faith, there is not a single intimidating bone in your body," David said with conviction.

"Not even one?"

He closed the distance between us. "At least not any unattractive ones."

"If I didn't know any better, I'd say you're attracted to my bones."

His eyes smoldered with mischief. Leaning in close, as if to tell me a secret, he whispered, "You know, it's not what's on the outside that counts, but I have to think a girl as outwardly mesmerizing as you would have one sexy fibula on the inside."

"*Mesmerizing*, huh?" I teased. "You're making me sound like an enchantress."

David's lips arched, his fingers grazing the sides of my jersey. "It would explain the effect you have on me." My heart raced as our eyes connected in a warm, meaningful moment. His smile fell a little as he slid his hand to the narrow of my waist. My stomach fluttered and I waited with bated breath for him to kiss me.

A phone buzzed on David's desk, directing his thoughts elsewhere. His expression darkened. Coming around the desk, he read the lit-up screen and enclosed his big hand around the device to turn it off.

He obviously wasn't taking the call because I was in the room, which made me feel like I was getting in the way of an issue that was troubling him. If I was going to say my piece, it had to be now. I had to remember what was at stake, the danger I could place him in with Death on my tail.

"I want to apologize," I began, messing with my fingers as I strolled to the front of his desk. "About leaving so suddenly at the carnival and not texting you back."

"There's nothing to apologize for." He bowed his head a little and leered at me from across the desk, his brown eyes two dreamy elixirs tempting me closer. "Unless you've come here to deepen my wounded pride?"

Actually, yes! I came here to tell you I want to be friends!

"David, I need you to know—"

"How's your head anyway?" he asked at the same time.

My eyes widened. "My head?"

David turned a paper over on his desk to read it. "You said something about your head hurting before you left the carnival?"

"I did? I thought I told you I was nauseous?"

"You were nauseous?"

"Yes," I said, with a shallow inhale. "I told you I was nauseous."

How would he know about my head?

"Oh, right." He picked at a button on the cuff of his dress shirt. "You were touching your head before you left. I thought you might have a migraine. I get them occasionally."

I vaguely remembered touching my head in his presence, but it wasn't enough to shake the awful feeling brewing inside of me. Flattening his palms against his desk, David parted his mouth to speak, when suddenly, his head slanted to the side, like an animal hearing a sharp noise. His eyes narrowed as he darted his gaze to the right, to the massive windows.

"You have got to be kidding me," he said.

He moved too fast for me to comprehend. One moment, there was a desk between him and me, and the next, David had me pinned to the floor, shielding me with his body.

There was a deafening explosion of glass as an enormous mass crashed through the windows.

IX

The protective shield above me vanished as David got up. Dazed, I stared blankly up at the ceiling, then lifted myself from the floor to find the source of the crash.

My mind shut down. Everything shut down.

Regaining my senses, I focused on the back of David's Armani shirt as I tentatively approached him and the *thing* he was crouched over. Rain slanted through the gaping hole where a window had been, saturating us. Waves of shifting winds engulfed a small potted plant, which had miraculously survived on the sill, and hurled it into the city below.

My legs gave out from under me. Sprawled across the floor amongst shards of bloodied glass lay an angelic-looking creature with frayed ivory wings. The wings beat once, then twice; the feathers cut clean through the couch beside me like a knife through butter and nicked my leg. I shrieked. The creature now lay still, its head slowly turned to face me. Terror climbed up my throat. Its eyes had been freshly gouged out, blood dripping from the remains of flesh in the sockets and half of its humanlike features mauled to a shredded pulp. There was so much blood. So much blood.

The angelic creature jerked into alertness, throwing an outstretched hand toward David with foreign words. David's features strained with pain, and he recoiled from the being. The tendons in his neck bulged as if he were fighting an invisible force. Regaining composure, David oddly laughed. Then his head snapped back, heavenward, and he gurgled out a curse. He dropped down to one knee, then the other, locked in a rigid position.

Switching its attention from David to me, the angelic creature stood on unstable legs, staggering forward. It reared larger than life, bladelike wings unable to fully extend against the walls of the otherwise huge office. Reaching for me with long fingers, it hooked into David's Bears jersey and yanked me closer.

"You are *her*," it said, blood trickling from its mouth. "A great evil is coming. Soon, they will *all* come for you!"

I turned my head away from its nightmarish face with a sob, frantically trying to get free.

A blurred arm shot out between the creature and me as David gripped the angel around the throat and flung it against the wall with a great force. He moved impossibly fast, pinning the angelic creature with one hand. It thrashed about, wings twitching, crying out in a foreign tongue.

I stood there, held by the numbing horror of it all.

A shadow cast across the room, drawing my attention outside through the cavernous gap in the massive windows. Through the pelting rain, a horde of birds ascended into the sky with shrill, unnerving croaks. They greased any light from the city with their coal feathers, before rocketing toward us like piranhas smelling blood.

David whipped his head over his shoulder. "Faith! *Run!*"

He didn't have to tell me twice.

Adrenaline took the baton. I sprinted through the waiting room, my feet striking marble as a thousand throaty croaks chased me like an orchestra of doom. I punched down the long hallway, made a sharp turn, and slid, catching myself with one hand as my heel gripped the floor again. Kicking off, I flung myself inside the elevator and slammed my fingers frantically into the buttons. The doors closed just in time, birds spearing into the polished metal like bullets.

Bland elevator music played.

"The *fuck?*"

Plastered against the back wall of the cubical contraption, I fought with every fiber of my being to catch my breath. My hands patted around the pockets of David's sweatpants.

My phone. I'd left it in his office.

"This can't be happening. This can't be happening."

The bottom floor didn't come fast enough. I made haste through the lobby, shoving my whole weight into the colossal glass doors of the entrance into the D&S Tower, only to be ensnared by a surge of rain and wind outside. There were scarcely any pedestrians or cars. This was New York City, and the streets were *bare.*

I ran in any direction.

Rawk! Rawk! Rawk!

My heart nose-dived into my stomach. Ahead of me, on the sidewalk, a group of the birds spiraled together into an inky mass, forming two terrifying-looking men with jet-black clothes. Porcelain skin, stark black eyes. Hollow cheekbones with lean bodies and bony fingers leading to nails like scalpels at the ends.

Screaming, I came to a quick halt, slipping once more in the process. The one creature tried to grab me, but the rubber of my cheap Converse thankfully gripped the wet sidewalk again, and I launched onward to my only escape: a dark, spine-chilling alleyway beside the D&S Tower.

Alleyways always work out well in the movies!

At the end of the passageway, more demonic-looking men had formed, until I was surrounded by ten of these creatures. Twelve. Fifteen. Panic rose up my throat and trapped my voice, leaving me mute—although I had a feeling no one would hear my desperate cries anyway.

"Hello, *girl*," said the skinniest one, his voice thick with phlegm. "Don't be afraid."

"Comforting," I clipped sarcastically.

"She smells tasty," said another with a Scottish accent. He was the ugliest of them all. As he glided closer, pale lips peeled back from ugly, sharp fangs and an unpleasant inky liquid dripped from his gums. "Kin we git a taste afore master arrives?"

Fear trickled down my spine and my teeth chattered from the cold droplets above. Glaring the creature in the face, I stood my ground. "Don't. Touch. Me." This made it pause, analyzing my lesser frame. He faced the other demons, threw his head backward, and cachinnated.

"What a scary wee lassie!"

The rest of them laughed, too, until the Scottish creature turned back around and saw my withdrawn fist, which fired and connected with his grisly face. His head snapped rearward from the impact, inky spittle flying out of his mouth. White-hot pain pulsated around my knuckles, and within seconds, the creature recovered, although his appearance had transformed—unpleasant features mutating until they were petrifying.

Suddenly the other creatures were on him, holding the Scottish creature back, and I was paralyzed against the wall. He was the largest of the men and dragged them in my direction. A violent grin framed his venomous mouth. "You *bitch*!"

He uncoiled his arm and lashed out. Out of reflex, I raised my arm to protect myself and scalpel nails sliced into my forearm, ripping straight to the bone. Springing forward, he shunted me to the ground.

My howl resounded down the passageway as the lacerations on my arm heated up like a welding torch had been pressed into the wounds. Tormenting pain surged through my veins, terminating any thought except instinct. I clamped my hand over the wound to stop the bleeding.

"You idiot!" one of the pale men seethed at my attacker. "Malphas will kill us all now!"

"No, he won't," purred a deep, disembodied voice. "But I will."

A dark mass shadowed the ground overhead as my attacker was snatched up into the obscurity of the alleyway in one fell swoop. His cries were cut off short. A decapitated head dropped to the middle of the demons and rolled, as a deep, menacing laugh bellowed through the rain.

From above came a curtain of obsidian as a cloaked figure dropped soundlessly to the pavement behind another demon. He stood to his full skyscraper height and gripped the creature by the back of the neck, lifting him off the ground. The demon's porcelain skin became riddled with black veins as his skin grayed and his eyes bulged with suffocation.

The cloaked man tossed him to the side as if he weighed nothing. "This is the part where you run," Death said.

Instead, the demons snapped into action, unleashing weapons and charging at him. Death waited patiently, as motionless as a statue. In the blink of an eye, his enormous scythe appeared from nothing at his side, and his cloak pressed tightly against his body, outlining an intimidating physique. Another blade shot out of the end of his weapon as he launched into action, cleaving through the demons. He maneuvered with the elegance of an assassin, rotating his scythe dexterously around his frame in between each strike and vaulting his heavy body into the air in various flips and twists. It was a frightening dance to watch, and he was well practiced.

Death evaded each blow as if it were too easy, eviscerating everything in his line of vision. I thought he stomped out every last one of them, when shadows of more creatures crawled down the sides of the alleyway and leapt into the passage.

I watched in horror as the creatures zigzagged closer to him, catching him off guard from multiple directions. He deflected as much as he could, but he was quickly outnumbered. Soon, they clung to him like parasites, jabbing him with their claws. He staggered back but wouldn't fall. They barraged him with bullets and other weapons—bit him with their fangs.

I thought he was done for—until he began to *grow*, his height extending even farther from the ground until he dominated all the lesser creatures like an impending doom. Bones cracked and joints popped. Breathing raggedly, Death snapped to an egregious height again and unleashed a monstrous, animalistic roar that shook me to the core. One by one, the creatures dropped dead around him. Their eyes bulged out of their heads, skin graying, vacuuming against their bones as they gasped for air.

His first strike as a newly formed monster was to snatch a dying raven creature by the scalp and rip out its throat with his hidden teeth. Each demon was dismembered, mutilated, until every inch of that alleyway was speckled with blood and shining with gore.

With his back to me, Death tore off his tattered gloves and flexed his hands at his sides. Those frightening black talons retracted back into his fingers. He began to wither down to his normal height.

I let out a stifled noise.

Death's veiled face snapped at the sound. He came at me like a bullet. His cloak loosened and spread out as he moved, no longer flush against his body like spandex. His prowling steps halted as he loomed over me, and my eyes glued to that massive bloodstained scythe. I recoiled back against the dumpster, curling my knees into my chest.

"Stay away!" I shrieked. "You're a monster!"

"And you're a brat. A simple thank-you would have sufficed." He dug into the lapels of his cloak and swapped his torn leather gloves with new ones. As he discarded the shredded material, I gaped at the intricate black designs covering the exposed skin of his hands. When he spoke next, his accent had thickened with rage. "You're coming with me."

"Like hell I am!"

"It wasn't a question." Death clamped down on my good arm and hauled me off the ground. I was so light-headed that I rocked backward. Cocking his head, he caught my other arm and examined the wound there. He elicited a foul curse in a foreign language.

The grotesque claw marks on my arm had stopped bleeding. It didn't seem like the best scenario, considering the skin around the wound blackened to a rot, and I'd lost complete feeling in my fingers. Five Deaths also swam in my vision.

I tore my arm out of his grasp. "What's happening to me?"

"Your body is accepting the demon's mark. You're going to turn unless you trust me."

"Turn? Into one of those *things*?"

"Amputation might be the most viable option."

I looked up at him with wide eyes. "Say what?"

"You still have time." Blackness dispersed from his shoulders. He stiffened, rolled his wide shoulders. Freed another venomous swear word. "Or not—a spell is preventing me from dematerializing. I'll have to carry you."

I flattened against the wall. "Don't you put your hands on me!" This was happening too fast, and I was in unbearable pain, but I had enough moxie to put up a fight. "I need to go to a hospital! I need a doctor!"

"They won't be able to save you," Death growled and reached for me again. Shadows stretched over the pavement. We craned our necks up at the same time. To my utter horror, birds piled into the alleyway from all directions.

"Stay down!" Death ducked and brought me into the lapels of his cloak as debris tore up from the ground. My legs abruptly gave out from beneath me as I doubled over in pain, but Death caught me with a strong arm. *"Cruentas!"* He signaled to the end of the alleyway, shadows expelling from his gloved hand. A thick, eerie fog leaked out from the crevices of the ground from where he gestured. What was a terrifying experience without fog?

The sound of a horse galloped in the distance, hooves clacking against wet pavement. Beyond any doubt, I was hallucinating through the sheeting pain. Or maybe I was already dead. Out of the fog and shadow came a monstrous, handsome black stallion at full gallop, untouched by the pelting rain, the birds, and thunder from above. The muscles on the animal's body were enormous and sinewy, and its eyes were abnormally red, like two ferocious rubies burning beneath the sun.

The beast charged at the birds, flames shelling out from its nostrils right before it collided with them. As the fire hit the animals, they burst into ashes and then disappeared altogether. The stallion stood up on hind legs and knocked more birds away from us, smashing them with its hooves until there was enough space for a getaway.

Death bent down and threw me over his shoulder. He darted through that gap and leapt, straddling the beast from behind me. I slipped into a new wave of disorienting pain. Spots dotted my vision. I slumped forward, unable to keep myself upright. Death hooked a strong arm across my midsection and grabbed the reins with one gloved hand.

Thousands of birds circled the pavement, forming a vortex of obsidian feathers. For whatever reason, this grand display had caught Death's interest enough that we weren't moving. The beast whined, hooves scraping against the ground. It tried to resist the strong pull of the vortex as we were on the verge of getting sucked in.

Just then, the pull gave way all at once and the birds combined in a clumped mass. Death's muscles tightened around me like a vise and the stallion regained its footing.

"It's been far too long," proclaimed a gravelly voice, "Death."

I peered around Death's arm to see what had formed from the birds. Or, more specifically, *who* had formed.

It wore no clothing, only feathers layered over the most intimate part of its body. It had long talons as hands, endless obsidian onyx eyes, and a misshapen face contorted in such a way that the bottom half resembled a beak. Upon its head lay thick black feathers in the shape of hair.

The creature forcefully beat its wings and they began to gain a fleshy color, transforming into well-shaped male arms. His beak-like mouth modified to a narrow Roman nose and a man's lips. He was clean-shaven, slightly hallowed in the cheeks, with skin so gray it bordered silver. He cracked his head from side to side and lowered his arms in a graceful movement. The feathers upon his head cascaded down into Viking braids and long, silky rivulets that matched the color of the ravens.

He took two gliding steps forward and silk pants curtained down his long, powerful legs. As I stared at him, those blistering coal eyes burned back.

"What's the matter?" He shifted those unblinking, soulless eyes to Death. "You look like you've seen a ghost."

"More like swine," Death grated out.

The demon released a hiss, treading toward us. Death returned the hiss like a wild animal. The horse beneath us went up on his hind legs and shot at the demon with blistering tendrils of fire. The flames made the demon withdraw to his original spot.

"Aren't you going to introduce me to your little friend?" The demon turned his head to me and bared his fanged teeth in a grin that must have been charming once upon a time.

"She has nothing to do with our vendetta, Malphas," Death snarled. This version of his voice brought chills down my spine.

"Oh, but she does." The demon's mouth twisted into a malicious grin and Death gripped me so hard I thought he was going to crack a rib. "You've never brought a mortal back to life. Did you think nobody would notice?"

"Stay away from the girl." Death's scythe blazed down the staff, glowing with symbols and patterns. Lightning zigzagged across the sky, trailed by an earsplitting clap of thunder.

"It's too late now," Malphas said. "What are you waiting for? Go on, boy! Run off and play nurse to your pet. Once that venom gets to her heart, you know the effects will be impossible to reverse."

The raven demon vanished. Bullets of rain poured down for one final assault and aggravated the lacerations along my forearm. I wilted into unconsciousness, succumbing to the storm.

X

Water dripped down my face as I came to. I blinked past a thick haze, a headache stabbing at my temples. Moving in slow motion my brain struggled to register what my eyes captured. Shadows fell from crates and packing materials stacked all the way up to an immense factory ceiling with glass windows painted black to block out the light.

Wind echoed through the cavernous space, hitting my bare skin like ice.

A dark mass shifted to my right, and I flinched, breathing raggedly. I was tied to a workbench, my arms and legs strapped tight with rope. My head was a boulder as I lifted it up. Blood. There was blood all over me, streaking my jersey. Bile climbed up my throat at the sight of my right forearm, the gruesome aftermath of a shark bite, torn muscle and bone sticking out. The sweatpants David had given me were absent, exposing the cheeky lilac panties I'd worn underneath. My right leg was mauled by two deep slashes. Panic drove me into a frenzy, and I tugged at the restraints, releasing a cry.

Two massive hands pressed my shoulders back down.

"I wouldn't move if I were you." Death's hooded head bent over me. Nothing could hide the pure wrath in his voice. He was pissed. "You've been poisoned. I slowed it temporarily from entering your heart, but you won't last much longer if you flail around. I have to remove the rest of the venom." He stuffed a wad of cloth between my lips. "This will hurt. Stay awake."

His head lowered over the wound on my arm. Horrified, I understood what was next and let out a strangled scream against the gag. His teeth were like razor blades piercing into my skin as his hot mouth clamped down onto my flesh. Breathing raggedly through my nose, I tried to sit up, but his powerful arm splayed across my chest and gripped the edge of the table. He drank hard and fast. The pain throughout my body was indescribable, knives picking me apart. I longed for it to end, begged to be put out of my misery as the torment peaked and unleashed its fury.

Something warm and wet ran across my wound. His tongue. The pain that demanded to be felt faded to a dull ache. Through half-opened eyes, I watched my forearm stitch itself together, leaving only a small trace of blood behind. Drained of energy, my head thumped back against the workbench. Dizziness hit me like a baseball to the face and everything spun into splotchy, distorted images, like the carousel from the carnival, except with creeping shadows closing in to consume the horses. Life ebbed away with the promise of peace, only to flood back in with a sharp shake into awareness.

"Hey! *Hey!*" As if Death's thunderous voice wasn't enough, his hands were shaking my shoulders. "Wake up!" He grasped both sides of my skull. "Open your eyes, Faith. Open them now. Come back to me."

Just five more minutes.

"No, not five more minutes! It is not time to sleep!" Death

barked, as frantic as a creature with so much control in his voice could sound. "Faith, listen to me. You need to stay awake. You're *not* dying on me, stupid human. Not tonight."

He gave my jaw one last firm shake and yanked the cloth out of my mouth. I managed to pry my eyes open.

"You came for me," I croaked.

Liquid fire dripped onto my cold lips. Blood. His wrist bled profusely, blood as black as the demon's. He pushed his skin against my mouth, but I clamped my lips shut and thrashed my head to the side.

"You're drinking it. All of it. You've lost too much blood." He pried my jaw open with his gloved fingers, forcing the liquid down my dry throat until I choked it down. It wasn't coppery like normal blood, but instead thin, and it tasted almost . . . sweet, the perfect candy. Suddenly, I needed more. I drank vigorously, fighting back a moan as the taste of his blood transformed into a charge of heat that licked down my spine. I could feel myself becoming stronger. My mouth filled with one more swallow, when he pulled his wrist sharply away. Realizing what I'd been doing, I tried to spit out the remains of the black substance, but he clamped his hand over my mouth, holding me against his steel frame.

"Swallow it, or you'll die," Death snarled. Then he muttered the unthinkable, "Please, Faith."

The blood slid down my throat like warm sugar.

Death released me and shifted a step back, as if I were about to explode. Shadows crawled over me as invisible hands undid the rope knotted at my wrists and feet.

I swung my bare legs over the edge of the table, adrenaline rushing in my veins. My senses were tremendously intensified, and I struggled to adjust to the new world around me. Blood, dust, and mold overpowered the air. Rain struck the roof of the warehouse, louder and louder, hammers striking the inside of my skull with each pattering drop. Pressing my palms against my ears, I suctioned out the noise with a wince.

"Is the rain extremely loud or is it just me?"

"You're shouting." I couldn't see him, but I knew he hung back in the darkness somewhere behind me.

An uncomfortable amount of energy buzzed through me, and I could no longer stay in one place. Taking off in a hurtling sprint, I raced around the warehouse, the world blurring around me. I leapt over wooden crates, weaved between construction material, and smashed my fists into a sheet of metal, denting it without any pain.

I soared up a spiral of stairs to the high platform above and braced myself on a railing at the top, looking down at the hooded man below. He stood in the same spot like a statue.

"Holy crud, this is *awesome*!" I exclaimed. "Are you seeing how fast I'm running? I'm like a cheetah!"

"Get back down here!" Death barked, the fury in his voice startling enough to form goose bumps all over my arms. "You are *high*, not invincible. If you hurt yourself, I will not heal you again."

I shimmied my shoulders to the music in my head, giggling. "Somebody's grouchy!"

"I'm warning you, Faith."

"If you want me," I purred with a smile, bracing my hands on the rusted railing, "you'll have to catch me—" My stomach floated up into my throat as the railing broke and gave way. I tumbled over the side of the platform with a scream. The cement floor zoomed in, and I braced for a deadly impact that never occurred. Death had moved across the warehouse in a blink of an eye, cradling my fall with his arms before I hit the ground. I stared up at him in shock, hard muscles surrounding me like steel.

"I knew you liked me," I said and bit down on my lip to suppress another delirious giggle.

Death set me down with a foreign curse, crowding my space with his intimidating size. I could feel the effects of his blood wearing off as the euphoric humor of the situation slipped away. I finally had the good sense to try to put distance between me and him and took a step back, when Death's large paw of a hand shot out, gripping the fabric of my jersey, and plucking me a foot off the ground. My gaze leveled with his veiled eyes, and I stiffened.

"Do you have any idea," Death grated in his thickened accent, "how close you came to getting yourself killed tonight?" His usual velvet tone had yet to show up, replaced by that feral growl that carried through the storehouse with ease. "All because you provoked that demon. And now you have the gall to try and provoke *me*?"

I struggled to focus on what he was saying since his scent was so intoxicating it engulfed my senses. Leather, cherries, a yummy cologne with traces of—

Yummy? Sobering up, I tried to tear myself free from his fingers. "Get your hands off me. Would you have rather seen them take me away?"

"You are a *fool*!" he roared. "A little monstrosity in emo clothes! Things could have ended much worse for you in that alleyway!"

"I won't apologize for defending myself."

He dropped me to the ground, and I landed awkwardly on my butt. "Put your pants back on."

A single step forward. That's all he had to do to put me on edge. His body language was lethal, a raging force of nature aimed to fire. I crab-walked a few inches back, cold concrete rubbing against my bare legs. I scrambled to my soggy socked feet and backpedaled into the workbench, snatching my discarded sweatpants from the floor, while also making sure the Chicago Bears jersey didn't ride up and expose my ass cheeks more than it already had. The sweatpants were torn at the leg and saturated with rain and blood.

My brain suddenly revisited the alleyway, when Death splattered my world red. He didn't have to use weapons. With only his mind and his talons, he could have slain all of *those* creatures. He'd chosen to use a blade because it was messier, because it was in his nature to destroy. *He could effortlessly rip me to pieces.*

Leaning back against a row of shelves, I shimmied the cold wet fabric up my legs the best I could and tightened the drawstring at my waist. The effects of his blood had faded, replaced by fatigue and fear.

"You saved my life," I trembled out. It was all I could manage to say with the blistering sensation of Death's hidden gaze.

"Saved?" His laughter was low, sinister. "What a polite way to put what I did. I slaughtered every last one of those demons. Tore and cut them to pieces." Tendrils of darkness curled outward from his massive frame, as if they wanted to attach to the shadows behind him, or maybe, I feared, attach to me. "You're not much better off than you were in that alleyway. Now you're alone. With me."

My knees wobbled at the hunger laced in his cryptic words. "What *are* you?" I asked. "A vampire? A werewolf? Demon?"

"A nightmare."

He slunk closer, taking his sweet time. Behind my back, my hand fanned for a weapon—anything I could get my hands on. I gripped something cold and heavy. A pipe of some sort. It immediately vanished from my hand.

"Too slow, cheetah," he mused dryly.

We were in a blocked-off area in the warehouse. I had nowhere to run. Nobody would hear my screams. Death crowded my vision, claiming my space like night suffocating day, until I was overcome by his toxic presence. Heat shelled off his enormous frame; the sweet aroma of cherries fragranced the air like a lure.

"The creature I conversed with," he said gruffly. "The raven demigod. Have you seen him before?"

"No," I choked out. Just thinking about that thing made my skin crawl. "Thankfully."

"Have you painted him? Seen him in a dream? Think hard."

"I've never seen him before in my life."

Death's hooded face peered down at me. I fidgeted under his gaze, sweating like a whore in church.

"Who is he to you?" I asked when the silence became too painful. "I sensed a bit of hostility."

Leather creaked as he clenched his hands. "That's none of your goddamn business."

Touchy. "Silly me, I thought we were having a conversation."

"You were wrong."

I maneuvered away from the table, distancing myself from him. Sucking in through my teeth, I said, "You're right, it is none of my goddamn business. That demon didn't show any interest in me at all."

Death's body remained static, a cobra in the grass about to strike. I didn't even think he was breathing, which was incredibly unnerving. *Watch your fucking tone,* he didn't have to say.

You won't do shit, I didn't respond.

His spine straightened. Had he heard me?

Death took a few unhurried strides, circling me like a predator. I rotated my body, never giving him my back. He feigned a lunge, causing me to screech. Booming laughter reverberated off the warehouse as he moved in a blur, emerging from an aura of shadows to my left.

"Who's the male?" Death asked, the words rasped at the back of his throat.

I blinked a few times and tried to come down from the heart attack he almost gave me. "I don't know what you're talking about."

"The male you were at the carnival with." More circling. *He's toying with you.* This time, I let him stalk somewhere behind me.

A mistake, I realized, when his hot breath tickled my ear. "The boyfriend."

I imagined those hidden fangs ripping into my neck and whirled around. He'd already straightened to his full height. "My private life is none of your business. Besides, you won't answer any of my questions. Why should I answer yours?"

"Me-ow," he purred, circling again. He didn't walk. He glided with a pantherine grace. "You're rather bold, for a human."

The way he said *human* settled uneasily in my stomach. It confirmed my assumption that he was playing with his food. He flipped my hair with a gloved finger, and I released a shaky breath.

"I'll be more careful next time," I said. "Please, can you take me home? I need to be home."

"No."

"No?"

"Yes," he said, cocking his head like an animal as he often did. *"No."*

It was time to change the subject. Fast.

"What—what are you going to do with me?" I stammered, as he corralled me backward. *Wow, brilliant subject change.* "I don't have much meat on me. I rarely eat vegetables and junk food is my favorite food group, so I definitely don't taste good—"

Death pinned me to a row of steel shelves with a single finger to my chest. A deliberate gesture of dominance, a movement he clearly enjoyed making, but something had changed since the last time. My fear took a step to the side as I ignited beneath his touch. I was attuned to the sinewy muscle rippling the edges of his silhouette—the leather of his right pant leg grazing my bare skin through a hole in my sweatpants, and the glowering burn of his veiled stare fueling the anticipation of his next calculated move.

"If I were you," he purred out slowly, intensifying the sweep of heat down my front, "I wouldn't mention your taste again, *cupcake*. And I wouldn't fuck with me."

Message received. I must have looked like a pop-eyed toy.

He held that gloved finger on my chest a moment longer, before removing it.

"You didn't have to save me," I said softly.

He threw off heat like blazing coals. "My, my, your heart is racing."

My breath hitched. With a cool expression, I stared into the endless shadow of Death's face. "Did you expect anything different?"

"Of course not," he said rather silkily. "Though, I know it's not entirely from fear." His laugh was low and seductive as sin. "You mortal women and your strange fetishes for mysterious, psychopathic men. It's sick, really."

A shameful blush warmed my cheeks. Couldn't defend myself there.

"I'll tell you a secret, Faith." He leaned in, and I battled with the urge to move away. "I always get what I want."

"Not this time," I snapped.

"We'll see about that."

Although he was practically purring again with that deliciously velvet voice, there was a lethal undertone to his words, which I couldn't overlook.

"From the memory I saw in the fun house," I began, "I am going to assume you want my soul because it's special."

"Correct." It was obvious he'd held back a snarky remark.

"I'm going to take a wild guess and say you don't plan on telling me why you want it."

"Get to your point."

"You're doing a pretty shitty job of convincing me to trust you," I said, fighting the slight tremble in my words. "That's what you want me to do, right? Trust you, so that you can do whatever it is you want to do with me?"

He flexed his fingers at his side, as if wanting to unleash his claws.

"You can't make me come with you, can you?" I challenged. "You can't force me."

I could *feel* his glare. "It's in your best interest to come with me."

"And that best interest is?"

He clasped his hands behind his back. "You ask far too many questions."

"Because you're vague and speak in riddles! This is the longest conversation I've had with you, and you don't even want to have it!"

"Do you want what happened tonight to happen again?" Death inquired, in a dangerously calm voice. "Because that's exactly what will happen without my protection. Once rumor spreads of your existence, monsters you couldn't conjure up in your worst night-mares will come after you. They're drawn to your soul."

"Like you?"

Silence.

"Why me? What's so special about my soul?"

"I won't convince you to trust me," he said, disregarding the rest. "I'm your only option."

"I don't know who you are! I don't know what you are!"

"Deal with it."

My jaw tightened. "You saved my life to strike a deal with a little girl. You took advantage of me, and for what? What kind of person takes advantage of a child's fear?" I was breathing hard, burning with fury. "Or hides his face beneath a hood!"

A low growl vibrated his throat and rolled out like a roar. "You owe me your soul, regardless of my character. This is a dangerous game you're playing, Faith. I will not play nice forever."

"Oh, great, this is you being 'nice'!" My arms rose and slumped to my sides. "Well, what's the plan now? Why are we talking if you're not going to give me any answers?"

"Good point." He jabbed a finger at the workbench. "Stay. I'll be back, eventually."

"Eventually! You're just going to leave me in here? Did you not see those things in the alleyway?"

"This warehouse is a safe haven for you." At that, Death stalked away with long, powerful strides. I struggled to keep up. "I made sure of it."

"Wait! *Wait!*"

He blended into the shadows, waning away. I lunged forward and gripped the thick material of his cloak. The fabric filled with heat and shadows lurched from him like hands trying to grab me. I tore my hand free from the cloak, the tendrils of darkness surrounding Death still snapping at me like snakes.

In a blur, Death's gloved hand shot out and clutched my throat in a vise grip. His massive frame resurfaced from the shadows, and the snakes evaporated. *"You stupid girl!"* he snarled in a merciless hiss, fingers crushing into my neck. "Never touch me!"

But I couldn't process a single thought, except the instinct to stay alive. I grabbed onto his wrist to free myself and touched a gap of his uncovered skin.

A sharp jolt of energy went through me. Grief hit me in a cruel wave. The loss, it was endless. I was *him*. Pain. Crushing, suffocating pain. Everything in my body compacting together, constricting in raw torment and wrathful hunger . . .

Then there was light, beams of sun spreading out in front of my fastened eyelids. The pungent smell of manure and aged straw permeated the humid air. Flowery weeds brushed my cheek as I peeled my eyes open. I sat up and blood drained from my face.

A farm. I was on a farm, but it wasn't a farm from my century. The fields were manned by men who wore outdated beige tunics, baggy shirts, and worn-out trousers. They plowed into the dirt as if it was all they knew, melting beneath the sweltering heat of the sun. Past rows and rows of olive trees stood a proud Romanesque villa built of stone, surrounded by various leafy fruit trees, flowers, and shrubbery. Fountains rippled in an exquisite, enchanting garden straight out of a storybook.

Movement in my peripheral vision caught my attention. My eyes darted to a boy sitting a mere ten paces away from me. He was squatting under the shade of a blooming tree, which draped over us both with its long, emerald green arms. The boy wore a baggy toga tied at his waist that exposed tan skin. His athletic build suggested he was older at first, though his profile was soft, childlike, marking him around twelve or thirteen. Curly golden ringlets of hair fell into his eyes, concealing them in shade. As I noticed the blade the boy held in his hand, he suddenly turned his head over his shoulder in my direction, those mud-streaked locks curtaining over his features.

Could he see me?

A smooth, feminine voice spoke out in a foreign language from behind me. A young woman looked right through me with gentle emerald eyes, and only then did I know for sure I was invisible in this world. She was around my Aunt Sarah's age and the most beautiful woman I'd ever seen. Soft features cradled by unblemished olive-toned skin and mermaid liquid-gold waves cascading to a narrow waist.

This time, when she spoke, I oddly understood her. "I was picking olives for a snack, when I saw you racing down the rows like the farm dogs were nipping at your bottom."

I twisted around for the strange boy's response and leapt back. The boy! It was *him*! Death! Or, at least, the trick he'd used to approach me as a child. I'd know those mismatched green eyes anywhere. Except this version of him was different, which made me question exactly where I was. His hair, for starters, wasn't black. His expression wasn't cold and void of emotion. He'd yet to show any terrifying animalistic characteristics or flash any fangs. And although he scared the crap out of me at first, I currently didn't have the overwhelming urge to hurl myself behind the woman and use her as a human shield.

His features were boyish, soft, undeveloped, and yet a haunting maturity hardened his expression. Sun damage freckles splattered a Roman nose, and the large vertical scar that slashed across his lighter green eye was pinker than the boy's scar in the fun house, as if the wound had only recently transpired and mended together to form a permanent mark.

The woman walked through me like a ghost. My mind raced as their conversation continued, pieces to a puzzle falling into place. I'd been here before. *I'd seen this before.* But how?

The boy took off toward the woods. "Alexandru," his mother yelled, "Not too late!"

Alexandru . . .

I'd been so absorbed in the scene I'd forgotten I was standing here. Then again, everything about this strange place made me feel detached. Compelled to follow, I dashed after the boy with the mismatched eyes.

We came to an opening near a stream with flat moss, where a massive, enchanting willow tree anchored its roots beneath a haloing light. Long weeping branches with oval leaves curved over the ground like wings of an archangel, swaying in the gentle wind.

Alexandru grabbed a cluster of vines at the trunk of the willow and wrenched free a blanket of camouflage. This revealed an aging mirror made of silver instead of glass. It blended into the bark of the trunk as though they were merged into one. The mirror had a chipped frame, the silver scarred with imperfections and growths on the surface.

What transpired next between the boy and the willow tree unfolded like the beginning of a dark, twisted tale, etching into my soul. I would never forget it.

With a sudden jolt of pain, I warped back into the warehouse. Death breathed raggedly, his strong hand wrapped around my throat like a vise. The air was so cold my rapid breaths clung to it.

"Get out of my head!" Death barked. He clutched my throat tighter. *"Get out!"*

I wanted to delve further into this world, feel more from this tainted heart, but our connection was fragmenting bit by bit. I couldn't let go; I didn't know *how*. A phantom hand reached into my chest and squeezed as a great weight pressed against my lungs. His power vibrated through me, released from my eyes in a torrent of tears.

The link severed. And the black veil fell.

XI

DEATH

Wind and rain whipped around my cloak, a nightmarish storm wreaking havoc on precious Pleasant Valley.

This girl was getting on my last nerve.

From the sidewalk across the street, I watched Faith pace the length of her bedroom, absorbed in the little piece of paper I'd written on. My scowl deepened. She had collapsed in the warehouse, folding into my arms like a doll. I'd taken her home, but I didn't plan on sticking around to chat once she awakened.

I'd let my guard down. She'd touched me again. Delving into my most private domain and leaving me helpless to a power she couldn't even control. She'd torn through a barrier between us, paralyzing me, implanting her consciousness into mine like a viper injecting venom into its prey. Now, in the wake of what she'd done, my control wavered. A dent embedded in a cage door that imprisoned the monster on the other side.

I could hear its sinister whispers, leaking into my thoughts.

A cruel, malicious voice, so akin to mine I could hardly tell the difference anymore. *End this all*, it purred. *You know she would be tasty.*

My neck rolled, a groan tumbling out. I should have snapped her skinny neck in the warehouse. Snatched the light from her eyes and saved myself from the constant burden of keeping tabs on her. A simple thought, a slight movement of my fingers—dead.

The longer I reeled over our interaction, the darker my thoughts dimmed, and the more I wished I had indeed ended this charade once and for all. *Tempting* was not the word for the effect her nearness had on me. Interacting with a human was always a dangerous game when I was depleted of energy, but over two thousand years of experience and adapting to my cravings had not prepared me for *her* and that sharp tongue.

It didn't help that her hair products, skin cream, and perfume combined created the aroma of a goddamn dessert. Why couldn't she reek of body odor and stale french fries, like the other mortals at her high school?

I'd known from the day she took the deal that a power dwelled in her soul. An energy, which made her aura glow like a lantern. I never thought it'd develop into such a pain in the ass.

Faith's thoughts after she'd entered my conscious were too chaotic to decipher. Half the time, I couldn't hear her thoughts at all, and when I could, they were often in broken-up fragments, like a poor radio signal. However, this time I'd plucked enough from her brain to know exactly where she'd landed in my head.

I squeezed my eyes shut, willing myself to keep it together. Facing what I'd buried long ago was inevitable. Memory is the true curse of immortality and forgetting is a forgiveness the wicked are not spared. The night pulsed to the pounding of my undead heart, the roar of my past smothering out the howling winds.

I was around ten or eleven years old, perched below the canopy of the mulberry tree. Rooted at the peak of a grassy hill, it overlooked our entire vineyard with proud emerald arms. Every early afternoon, I would take my meal from the servants to go in my satchel and race through the endless rows of the olive trees to feast beneath its blooming branches. Now the blooms were turning to fruit—deep red berries. I'd pluck them straight off the branches, my mouth stained crimson from their juice.

I dropped down to a lower branch, then another, before landing in the pillowing grass. Ringlets of golden hair fell into my eyes as I pushed aside a worn-out log and dug into the dirt below it with a flat stone. My bare feet were grimed with dirt, and my play tunic, draping off my one shoulder from where it was torn, bore a few stains from adventuring in the woods.

Displayed on a linen cloth to my right were a few rocks, a snake's skin, and various-sized pieces of wood I would chisel into figurines. What stood out amongst the rest was an odd-shaped blade, which I picked up and caressed my small fingers over. It reminded me of a jagged crescent moon, with intricate symbols along the blade and hilt. This weapon was my most prized possession and my greatest secret. Uncovering it had led me to something so otherworldly and precious that I felt it was my responsibility to protect it. Which was why I was burying it here, under my mulberry tree, where it would be safe, and my father would never find it.

"Alexandru!"

A hot wind surged against my face as I shot a frantic look over my shoulder. I twirled the weapon around my fingers in a dance of skill, before stuffing it into the hole I'd dug. Shoving dirt with my forearm, buring it in seconds.

"Alexandru!" the woman's voice grew louder

I cupped my hands around my mouth. "Over here!"

The woman trudged up the grassy hill to meet me at the mulberry tree. Her soft, feminine features were cradled by unblemished olive-toned skin and wavy curls cascading down her back like liquid gold. My mother, Phoebe Cruscellio, renowned for her broad knowledge in herbal medicine and her deep care for the deprived of Rome. Townspeople flocked to her for affordable medical services. Little did they know what she truly was. How her late mother, my grandmother, had taught her magic since she was a little girl, and now she was the most powerful witch in her inner circle.

Giving commoners medical advice, while keeping her powers hidden, left my mother with a dangerous employment. Nobody could ever discover the eccentricities of our family. We'd risk exposure, or worse, executions, as my father constantly reminded us. Father could not see the hypocrisy in his own words, how he was entrenched in mortal society and risking our lives more than any of us. No, he would never see the whole truth, like I did. Mother went to great lengths to save others because she could never find the courage to save herself from him.

"There you are, my naughty child," Mother said, slightly panting as she hiked up the satchel slung over her shoulder. "I was picking olives for a snack, when I saw you racing down the rows like the farm dogs were nipping at your bottom." A small smile curved her lips as she approached the mulberry tree, her hand pressing against the bark as she looked up into the canopy blooms. "The Fates work in mysterious ways . . . "

"What do you mean?" I asked, watching Mama pluck a berry to taste it. Her lips puckered as the berry was not ripe yet.

"I too used to climb up here to be alone," Mama explained. "I would sing to you under this very tree. You were only a small swell in my belly then, and I came down with a great sickness while you grew. Your father would climb up here to collect the mulberry leaves and its fruit to aid in a healthful pregnancy. These berries were my only cure." She touched her flat stomach with a reminiscent smile and laid a kiss on my forehead. "Have you fed your animals, my sweet?"

"I fed the dogs and the sheep," I said, plopping down in front of the dirt pile so she would not question it. I fiddled with my wooden figurine of a lion and made it pounce on top of a rock.

Mother bent down to pluck a twig out of my hair. Her fingers wiped dirt off my cheek, too, the scar on my face tingling before I flinched away. The large vertical mark slashed through my lighter green eye was a cruel reminder of the trauma I'd suffered a year ago. My face had been torn by a wild cat during a combat exercise, jagged flesh mending together to form a grueling permanent mark. It was still pink from poor healing, but I did not mind the appearance as much as Mama did. I only wished it wouldn't ward off other children my age. Since I was homeschooled, I rarely had any social interaction with others.

"And the horses?" Mama asked, drawing my attention back to her. "Have you fed the horses? Cruentas needs a wash, my love." Her nose scrunched up. "As do you."

"Father told me not to visit Cruentas today. I hurt my arm . . . sparring."

I trained daily with my father. The harrowing lessons with him were the worst parts of my day.

My mother looked down at me for a prolonged length of time. "You lie to me. I can hear it in your voice." Before I could move away from her grasp, she reached down and tugged up the sleeve of my toga, exposing a darkening purple bruise on my upper arm.

Her eyes widened, and she gasped. "Did your father do this?" I didn't want to instigate another fight between them, so I began to draw in the dirt again. Her voice only amplified. "Answer me, Alexandru!"

"I went out in the forest early this morning," I said, stabbing a broken branch into the ground and snapping it in two. "Father went looking for me, though he was not concerned with my safety as I am sure he will tell you. He was angry because I was late. His only concern is my training."

Mama stood and hugged her arms to her chest. "I have tried to get through to your father, but he is so stubborn, and he only wants what is best for you. There are many dangerous animals, hunters, even drunk men that wander about the forest. He worries for your safety when you run outside our land all alone."

I shook my head at my mother's naivety, laughing bitterly. "I only wanted to show the town boys my new secret spot in the woods. They are allowed to play in the morning, and it is not fair. I am forced to spar with Father until midday break, and if I disobey him, I am treated like an animal. And you . . . " I tried to hide my seething tone from my mother and failed. "You do nothing about it."

My mother slid a hand over her mouth, her eyes pooling with emotion. "If I could, I would take you far away from here."

"Then why not try?"

"It is complicated, Alexandru," she murmured. I'd heard that vague answer a thousand times before and had grown numb to it. "Do you wish I was not your mother?"

"Never." Absentmindedly, I dug in the ground beside me for the blade I had buried. "I wish for a friend. A true friend."

Mama was heartbroken by this, and it made me feel worse. I didn't talk to her often about feelings because I knew she had her own issues with my father.

"*I* am your friend," she said, and then she hugged me to her chest. We sat in silence, her fingers combing absently through my hair.

"What is this?" she inquired, poking the toe of her sandal against the hill of dirt where I'd buried the blade—buried it too shallow. The hilt of the weapon lifted up from the dirt, and I lurched to the ground to cover it.

"Nothing." I buried it again and shot a nervous glance at my mother, my heart racing in my ribs. "An old treasure I found in the fields."

"That is not *nothing.*" Mama nudged me to the side as she knelt to the ground, digging up the weapon and brushing it off. Anger filled her emerald gaze, and for a sliver of a moment, I visualized my father's rage, and my leg muscles tightened to run. "This is a weapon! Alexandru, you have lied to me again. Where did you find this?" Her fingertips traced the inky symbols lining the weapon. "Black magic is engraved into its blade, words not even I can translate. Perhaps it is from the Helm of Darkness!"

"It is not a dagger of Hades," I said, snatching it from her. I tucked it into my pants and stood up. "I made sure it was not enchanted, like you taught me. I found it, and so it is mine."

"Alex—"

"May I go play? I want to sift for rocks in the stream. I will be back well before dusk."

She gaped at me as if I had two heads. I had skillfully dismissed the subject of the weapon, and she didn't have the time to question it further. She was leaving today to attend to her clients in the city. "Your father will not be pleased."

I smiled mischievously. "Only if he finds out."

"You will not go anywhere until you promise me this: you will get rid of that blade and be back long before the sun falls. *Promise* me, Alexandru."

"I promise."

She kissed me good-bye, and I took off toward the woods.

"Alexandru," she yelled after me, "not too late!"

I ran through the woods until I arrived at an empty dirt road. Kneeling in the bushes, I waited. A rider on a tan horse trotted down the dirt path. When he neared my hiding spot, I threw myself into the middle of the road and landed on all fours. The man brought his beast to an abrupt halt. As he was distracted by the reins, I bared my teeth at the horse and released a hiss. The horse's nostrils went wide. It kicked up its hooves, dancing restlessly in place as if I were a snake.

"What are you doing, boy?" The rider calmed his horse and glared down at me. "I could have killed you!"

"I need your help!" I wept, feigning fear. "My friend, he's dying! He's in the forest!" I thrust my finger toward the opposite side of the road, where the ominous trees swayed. "You have to help him, *please!*"

The rider tied up his anxious horse and followed me through the woods. We ran for a long time, when the man urgently asked, "Where is your trapped friend?"

"Right here, follow me!"

We came to an opening near a body of water and flat moss, where an old willow tree stood. My hands gripped a cluster of vines at the base of the tree trunk, and I tugged my arms to the side, wrenching free the blanket of camouflage I'd laid there. This revealed an aging mirror made of silver, since it was created before mirrors were glass.

"My friend . . . he is inside the mirror," I said. "He says I am different, because I can communicate to lost spirits such as his. The souls lost to the shadows between here and . . . elsewhere. That is where he is, and he is scared. Trapped."

"What's your name, boy?"

"Alexandru."

"I'm Bastien." He scrutinized me up and down with his eyebrows drawn inward. "You have an unusual imagination, Alex . . . "

"I am telling you the truth. He has been imprisoned in this mirror for a long time. My friend, he was punished for stealing food for his sick wife. The evil man who trapped him, the man who my friend stole from, practiced the dark elements, and now my friend suffers. If we do not help him soon, he will be encased in his own nightmares and memories for all eternity. My friend says I can help him create a bridge to cross worlds because I am half-human. I could save him, but I need your assistance. You are a good man, I can tell. You have a kind heart, and you are exactly the person I need."

Bastien roared with boisterous laughter, and my shoulders crippled inward a little in defeat. He didn't believe me.

"Do you have a family, son?" Bastien said, wiping at a tear as he composed himself. "They must miss you. Go to them. Stop playing pretend and be a man. Soon it will be dark, and these parts of the woods are filled with wild cats and other creatures of the night. It is not safe for children." He began to walk away. "Come with me, I will lead you back to my horse."

"Wait!" I took out the curved dagger I had buried in the sand, clenching it at my side. "I have proof. I will call to my friend with this blade, and you can meet him yourself."

The rider glanced over his shoulder, his attention snagging on the weapon. "You will put that knife away, child. I do not want to play your game—"

"*Ahrimad!*" I shouted, pivoting, and straightening my arm to point the dagger toward the mirror. "*Ahrimad*, I summon you!"

A great wind kicked up, knocking leaves off the trees, and spreading the rest of the vines, growth, and thorns away from the ancient mirror. The reflective surface rippled like silvery water and a low whistle pierced the air, making Bastien cover his ears.

"He is here!" I said, smiling as I moved closer to the mirror. "Ahrimad, can you hear me? I told you I would find a good man.

This is Bastien!" I grabbed Bastien by the arm, ushering the stunned man forward. "Bastien will help us, so you can finally be freed, I know he will!"

Bastien looked up at the darkening clouds above the willow and took a step away from me. "What is wrong with the sky?" he demanded, his voice wavering. "I hear . . . whispering. Where are those voices coming from?"

"My friend has returned," I explained. "Do not be afraid. Ahrimad is funny and clever. He is kind too."

Evidently mystified by the mirror's waving surface, Bastien allowed me to lead the dagger to the mirror.

"Come closer, Bastien," whispered a voice. Startled, Bastien looked down at me, and I gave him a reassuring smile.

"It's all right, Ahrimad will not hurt you." I ushered Bastien closer and placed the weapon into his hand. "He said the man with a pure heart must point the hilt of the blade toward the mirror, and this will unlock his prison. Like this."

I guided Bastien's trembling hand with the base of the dagger pointed toward the mirror. As the hilt of the weapon hit the surface, the mirror stilled and the whistle in the air amplified. I winced at the unexpected reaction and clamped my hands over my ears.

"What witchery is this?" Bastien cried, and my eyes widened as I saw that blood trickled from his ears. "What have you lead me into!" Bastian let out a howling scream and tried to pull back from the mirror, but his hand and the dagger had fused with the surface. A burst of energy suddenly exploded from the mirror in a sonic boom, knocking me back to the ground and pinning me down.

Two silvery, wet hands flew out from the mirror and gripped Bastien's arms. They seized the dagger out of his hand and stabbed him repeatedly in the heart. Blood sprayed the ground and Bastien's face as he roared in agony. I gaped at the scene in horror, tears filling my eyes. My screams lodged in my throat as I watched the rider get brutally knifed to death.

Bastien's limp frame was heaved forward by those silvery hands and pulled into the mirror, until there were no remains of his body.

The mirror's surface cracked into a million pieces and exploded into shards. I threw an arm over my face to shield myself as bloody glass rained down to the earth.

An amorphous figure glided forward from the willow tree and took shape, bending and twisting, until it converted to the silhouette of a man with a draping obsidian cloak. With his face concealed, the creature tilted his head down at me, and I went cold as ice.

"Ahrimad?" I whispered.

"Hello, my friend." He drew his sword in one fluid motion. Through widened eyes, I saw it was engraved with the same intricate designs as the dagger I had discovered. "Whatever creature you are, reveal yourself to me now, or I will have to destroy you."

"I-I am only mortal."

"You dare lie to *me*!" My eyes widened as he thrust his sword out and dug the tip of it into my throat to pin me to the ground. "*No one* can touch my blade. Not without turning to ash."

"Perhaps it is because my father's blood runs in my veins. He is a demigod."

The hooded creature stilled. "A demigod . . . " Two vicious eyes glowed with a wrathful amber yellow beneath the creature's hood. "Ah, I know of your father. The young demigod general has a son?"

All I could do was nod, tears flooding my eyes. "I don't understand what is happening. Where is Bastien?"

"Bastien is dead. One soul, gone, for another freed."

I choked on a sob. "You promised you wouldn't hurt him!"

"All gods are tricksters." Ahrimad laughed under his breath. "Your father, he deprives you of your greatness. He forces you to lie about your uniqueness. Such a shame." His head angled as he analyzed me. "Tell me, how did you get that scar on your face, child?"

"A large wild cat. Father made me fight it for my training."

"It almost killed you. Yes, I sense you were close to death indeed. What has become of your damaged eye?"

"Nothing," I said quickly.

The hooded creature released a chilling growl. "The truth, or I will twist your little neck."

I trembled from head to toe, sweat soaking my underclothes. "The truth is . . . I am a monster," I whispered. "Mama, when she healed my injured eye with black magic, it came with a dark consequence. I do not tell her of the pain I have carried. How I can see the evil parts in people, the twisted secrets they hide inside. I see the wrongs they have committed. Other times, I will see the light parts, the good."

"It appears your power failed you this time," Ahrimad noted, drawing his sword tighter to my throat. "Wipe your tears, boy. I want to know more of this uniqueness."

I lifted my chin against the blade, willing my tears to stop.

"I am different than other children my age," I said. "I learn fast, and what I learn, I never forget. I am faster than a man in his prime and I am strong. Strong enough to lift a horse. Father says these gifts will only get stronger. Because his blood runs through my veins. So when I enter gladiator school, and when I fight, I will win. This will satisfy our king as I will become Rome's champion gladiator."

"You do not want this fate," said Ahrimad. "It will be challenging for you to hurt others, to kill, when you are able to see what makes every mortal an innocent. Your father is using you to gain political power."

"Yes," I breathed, relieved someone understood. "I dread my future at all times."

Ahrimad harnessed his sword to his side. "You have saved me

from a world of torment. I must offer you a gift in equivalence to my life. Do you understand this?"

I took a labored breath. I thought of Bastien and how quickly Ahrimad had taken his life, and I knew I had no other choice. "Yes, I understand."

"No one, including your father or mother, can know I have escaped this prison. You are a child. Children do not keep secrets well. I will make you forget me, forget this day, for now."

Panic laced my voice. "Please, I beg of you not to touch my memory. I would never tell a soul about you. I have nobody to tell!"

Ahrimad knelt to the ground beside me. My words fell away as I stared in horror at the darkness underneath his hood, where a face should have been.

"One day, not far from now," Ahrimad began in a mighty voice, "you will fight who you hate the most inside the gladiator arena. With your gift, you will see both the dark and the light within their soul, and you will make a choice. Whether they live, or whether they die. If you should decide to kill them, then from that day forward, you will have a piece of my soul. You will cross into the shadows and evolve into the immortal creature I am. You will have all my power."

"I don't understand," I whispered. "Why are you giving me these choices?"

"You freed me, and now I must give you a gift in equivalence. This is how good and evil coexist, Alexandru. At a balance." Ahrimad rose to his full height. "Nevertheless, I will not offer my power to a weak soul, which is why you must prove you are worthy. Creatures before me have ruled entire realms with my abilities. You could be a god."

"A god," I echoed in consternation. "Would I be loved?"

"Foolish child, you would be far greater than *loved*. You would be feared. Feared by all."

With a sharp jerk of my head, I wrenched myself back to the present. Faith's silhouette stood in her bedroom window. She peered out into the night, the glow of a desk light haloing the slight curve to her feminine waist as she leaned forward to slam her window shut and close the blinds.

A mere mortal, invading *my* mind, was not only humiliating, but potentially catastrophic for my reputation in Hell. I needed to know if she'd seen more. Maybe she had information against me now; maybe she'd seen the truth about my intentions. If she knew my true name . . .

I reached into my cloak for a rolled cigarette. If it were up to me, she'd be punished for what she'd done. Oh, yes, I'd have fun with her. But no, Lucifer had full authority over this one. He wanted the girl safe and unscathed, both mentally and physically. Yawn.

Flicking my lighter, I lit the cig. One whole pack in three hours told me I was already building a tolerance to the most recent blend of herbs supplied to me by a witch. Her blends suppressed my hunger, at least for a little while, but as I exhaled, I knew I'd already ventured past the point of no return.

The migraine landed like a sledgehammer to the skull. I snuffed out my now useless cigarette, preparing for what was next. A painful churn of my stomach sent me nearly doubling over. Fangs gnashing together, muscles cramping up, a trickle of panic slid down my spine that this would be worse than usual. *Not here. Not here.* I cast all thoughts of the girl and my appetite aside and concentrated on the waning gibbous moon carved into the night. The sensations slowly rolled over, decelerating my heartbeat until it grew still. A low growl rolled out from the back of my throat as the rest of my organs shut off.

"Control yourself," I seethed.

Easier said than done, when all I wanted was to hunt and chase and feast on this whole neighborhood. I rolled my neck, easing a crick, and forced an intentional inhale again as the sensations faded away. The next hunger episode wouldn't be pretty. I needed to collect at a much faster rate.

Lately, I hadn't been focused enough on souls. I'd been too burdened with keeping Faith alive. How could I get someone as stubborn and headstrong as her to trust me before it was too late? The Elders, aka the original goody two-shoes head honcho angels in the realm of Heaven, had recently created a garbage law that humans could only give their souls to Hell if they consented to it. Which meant the mortals had to verbally agree to, or physically sign over, their souls to Hell. Despite the headache of getting creative with our ploys, Lucifer and I had yet to have too many problems tricking the humans into selling their souls.

Then there was Faith.

Faith didn't trust me as far as her skinny emo arms could throw me. Smart. But what she didn't know was that she had a deadline. If she didn't verbally agree to my protection and give her soul to me soon, well, let's just say her life wouldn't burst at the seams with sunshine and happiness.

I didn't want to admit it, but I required counseling on this. Faith tested my control in ways that clouded my judgment, and apparently, I didn't have the best people skills. Especially when I was hungry and said people looked like dinner.

Glaring down at my phone, I debated whether to dial Lucifer or just track him down in Hell. Cell phones were so delicate and irritating, and they could never fit in my leather pants. Whenever I steered away from the new advances in Hell and Earth, I felt like an old man with his khakis pulled up to his nipples. I might have existed for two thousand years, give or take, but I was physically imprisoned in time and cursed for all eternity as a young adult. Still had the great hair, overconfidence, random spurts of insane horniness, and late-night cravings for anything-cheesy sauce to prove it.

"My lord," trembled a voice. Glenn, my kick around demon, emerged from the shadow of the tree to my left. Thirtysomething years old when he died, Glenn was short and wiry in stature with outdated rivet spectacles that balanced on his nose. "I apologize for the interruption, but you didn't answer your phone. I have news from Hell. It's not good news, I'm afraid."

I fisted my hands until leather creaked and nodded once. I enjoyed my moments of peace and quiet. Everyone annoyed the shit out of me.

Especially Glenn.

"My lord," Glenn spoke up again, edging closer with a clipboard in hand. "Does the nod mean I have permission to speak? Or, does the nod mean to 'go eff myself'? I only want to make sure—"

"Glenn," I snarled.

"Never mind, forget I even asked! My apologies, my lord." Glenn cleared his throat, shuffling in front of my view and adjusting his spectacles on the bridge of his nose. As if it were broad daylight, I could see the crisp bleach white of his shirt, and the sheen of wetness bubbling across his pale forehead. Glenn focused on his clipboard and read off a script, as he often did the past two hundred years. "Hello, sir! You look exceptionally evil and menacing tonight!" His gaze darted frantically between me and the clipboard. "I have all the information you wanted to acquire. According to Hell's records, there have been three documented eliminations of guardian angels within the span of three weeks."

Darkness crawled from my body, concealing the ground with howling shadows. "Where?"

Glenn turned faintly green. He kept his eyes glued to the script. "All w-within New York City, my lord." The bubbling sweat turned to a stream. "All with their eyes pecked out. The corpses were not too far apart."

I combed through Glenn's anarchic thoughts as a single drop of sweat rolled down his nose and prompted him, "There's more."

"Yes, my lord." Terror overtook Glenn's face, and he clutched his clipboard to his frail chest as if it were a shield. "About your own Fallen, I'm afraid."

"Well?" When he was hesitant to respond, my fangs lengthened in my mouth. "Spit it out!"

Glenn jerked back half a step, fumbling with his clipboard as he turned a page too fast and tore it in half. "In the past three days, there have been seven recorded attacks on our Fallen outside of Hell. Five casualties within *twenty-four* hours."

"Five casualties." I cracked my neck to the side. "Within twenty-four hours."

All color emptied from Glenn's face. "Correct, my lord."

"And when, exactly," I grated out, a venomous outburst brewing beneath my façade, "did you learn this information?"

"Today. Precisely, a few hours ago, my lord." His expression twisted, as if anticipating a wrecking ball to the face. "I couldn't reach you . . ."

I flexed my fingers, willing my talons to stay in place. Had I known of these attacks sooner, I would have kept Faith far, far away from me. I would have known it was Malphas, and I could have stopped the events in the alleyway from ever happening.

Suddenly my control slipped, and an upheaval of anger swelled within me. The porch lamp of the property nearby shuttered on and off. Soon the entire block's lights were flickering and buzzing, the trees violently swinging.

My rage hit Glenn like a laser and his clipboard went flying into the street. I unleashed a guttural roar. *"You idiot!"*

Perhaps the suburbs were not the best place to release my nasty temper; however, we were camouflaged by my power, and I didn't have the patience to teleport elsewhere to discipline this inbred fool.

Lifting my lip in a snarl, I honed back in on Glenn. Stalking forward, I seized the pitiful little demon by the shirt and hoisted him to my lofty height. "*Five* of my Fallen have been killed within twenty-four hours," I roared in a thundering voice, "and you didn't *tell* me? You have one job, Glenn. One job! To do as I say. You were supposed to tell me everything you obtained immediately. What if it had been one of the Seven? Don't you know what the death of a reaper would cost me? We have objectives to reach!"

"Believe me, I understand I have failed you," Glenn squeaked out, shuddering from head to toe. "It was an honest mistake, I swear. Electronic communication is difficult for a demon my age. You understand, don't you? Please, spare me! I beg you, my lord!"

"Your whiny voice grates my ears," I hissed waspishly, as my features shifted beneath my hood to a creature more animalistic and exotic. I threw Glenn down and willed tendrils of darkness to curl around his feet like snakes. "I know how to shut you up."

Heat blasted outward from my frame, crashing into Glenn's chest and knocking him flat. Serpent shadows lunged for his small frame, fastening his thrashing body to the ground.

"Please, Your Highness!" he gasped out. "I tried to provide the information to you, I tried! You were with the human, and then your phone kept going straight to voicemail! It'll never happen again!"

Capturing Glenn's jaw, I forced his eyes to meet mine. "You're damn right it'll never happen again." A smirk peeled away from my enormous fangs. "You won't be able to do much of anything with your spine separated from your skull."

"You said not to expose ourselves to the girl!" he wept. "I couldn't get the message to you while she was with you! Please, have mercy! Don't send me down to the pits of Hell, they give me awful anxiety!"

Horror collected in Glenn's eyes as I struck, trapping the organ between his teeth with two fingers. A sharp tug ripped his tongue, and his cry of distress, clean out. The wind hurled around us, as the wicked creature inside me purred in delight from this gory scene.

Rationally, I knew the lack of communication between Glenn and I had *somewhat* been my fault. I had been with the girl when he called, and my ringtone hadn't been on. Nevertheless, the primal part of me was itching to rip this demon limb from limb for not finding another way to warn me about Malphas's attack, which could have certainly ended with Faith dead, had I arrived a moment later.

My black soul valued Glenn's life as much as I valued the life of an ant I could crush beneath my boot. Zilch. Still, Glenn *had* survived under my employment far longer than the rest, and the whole awkward nerdy virgin thing he had going on *was* hilarious . . .

Above all, I enjoyed screwing with him.

"You'll heal," I said, wiping my bloodstained gloves on Glenn's once perfectly pressed white shirt. I backed off the thrashing demon and rose to my full towering height. "Never withhold information from me again."

Choking out a sob, Glenn dragged himself to the shadows then evaporated.

Maybe I was too harsh, I supposed, and then shrugged it off. *Nah.*

"Hell's Bells" blared from my pocket.

I slid my cell out and answered. "Vegan Delights. How can we help you?"

"*You idiot!*" Lucifer roared.

I yanked the phone away from my ear and held it at arm's length as he cursed me out in several languages. This was the last thing I needed tonight.

"I am done cleaning up your messes," Lucifer snarled. "There were witnesses to your massacre earlier today. Next time you flex your powers in front of the girl, pay a little more mind to the elementary school loading off a bus for a class trip twenty feet away!"

I ground my fangs together. "You try having four hundred underling demons simultaneously pecking at your dick and see if you're mindful of your environment."

"You have not only risked our exposure and harming the girl, again, but you have also put my ass on the line. I've let you get away with a lot over the years, but these trails of dead Fallen and Guardians you're leaving are the last straw. Now I have to sit in on a council meeting in Hell. The board is *not* happy about this."

"You think I've been killing Guardians and our own Fallen?" A catlike grin lined my mouth, and for a moment, I was able to disregard my ravenous appetite. "I am flattered, but it was not me. I'm neat with my extracurricular activities."

"*Neat!*" There was a crash on the other line. He'd thrown something heavy. "Two months ago, you left four human bodies with their throats cut, hanging from their intestines in the middle of McDonald's. And let's not leave out the Guadalajara incident last year. Or the poisonous snakes on the plane? Real fucking original."

"Burger King," I corrected, a muscle in my jaw ticking. "It was at Burger King. They were all going to die anyway, and I was having a sugar low and the line was too long. You have to admit, leaving those cardboard crowns on their corpses was pure comedy."

"A nice touch," Lucifer seethed.

I scratched the stubble on my jaw. "You want to know who's going on an angel-murdering spree in New York City? I'll tell you."

Tensing, I accidentally crushed my phone a little. "But you're not going to like it."

"Elaborate."

"Malphas." Just saying that name made my blood curl. "He's alive."

Lucifer was silent for a long stretch of time. *"How?"*

"Your guess is as good as mine. Is it too much to ask for all my nemeses to take a permanent dirt nap for once?" Another migraine threatened to surface, and I massaged my temple. "I had a feeling I was being shadowed by someone last weekend. Thought I was being paranoid. Malphas knew about Faith, even before he met her. There must be rumors in Underworld of her soul being spared."

"Shadow her with more of our Fallen."

"Already on it." On cue, four dark forms made themselves known on Faith's roof. They perched on each corner of the house, monitoring their surroundings.

"Malphas's underlings nearly took her away from me." There was roaring in my ears at the memory, and my talons itched to be free. Another small wave of hunger overtook me, and this time I smashed a frustrated palm into my throbbing temple. "One of his newborns marked her. I had to suck the venom out, so she didn't turn. She clocked a demon in the nose, if you can imagine it."

"She was able to see the demons even before they died," Lucifer noted.

"Yes, although she hasn't seen through any of my illusions yet. I wouldn't put that ability past her either though. Her soul is transforming." I ran a hand absently over my jaw. "I put up a nasty ward around her house and charmed her backpack. If anything supernatural tries to weasel its way into her home, or steps within an acre of that backpack, I'll be notified."

The other line went quiet again.

"Sounds like you're going all out, kid."

I tried to ignore the usual mocking *kid* moniker but failed this time. "Of course, I am. The girl was almost taken."

He didn't press further. "We're running out of time, Death. *You're* running out of time. My patience runs thin. Hurt her, torture her into complacency. Whatever it takes, get the job done."

"You said you didn't want me to harm her." I couldn't believe I was defending her safety.

"You have had plenty of opportunities to do this the humane way," Lucifer said. "Do not disappoint me, or you're grounded."

"What?"

"That's right, I'll *ground* you. Like a child. I'll take away your ability to fly."

I scratched at my stubble. "You can do that?"

He hung up.

Fuck. If Malphas somehow got his hands on Faith before Hell did, she was as good as dead. I knew what he was capable of more than anyone. But the thought of physically harming Faith or her family to get what I wanted was a line I felt conflicted about crossing. Hunger clawed at my gut and the monster freed another menacing growl from my throat.

There had to be another way.

I could try being nice to her.

Pass. I would rather gouge my own eyes out than resort to pleasantries.

Standing on the curb, I sorted through my limited options, when the perfect idea suddenly hit me. A slow, wicked grin framed my mouth. "Bingo."

I signaled to the Fallen on the roof of Faith's house. They bowed their heads in unison. She was safe, for now, so it was time to sate my never-ending craving.

As I stepped into the road, I flexed my arms outward and enormous wings unfurled from my back. I cast one last look at her bedroom window before launching into the night.

XII

FAITH

A nudge to my arm woke me. I was nestled on the living room couch, wrapped in a plush blanket. The heaviness of a deep sleep fluttered away from my vision, revealing a face I'd missed far too much.

"Mom?"

"Hey, sleepyhead." She knelt at my side with a tan glow from the island sun. Mom had thick straight blond hair, layered just above her shoulders, and cerulean blue eyes. The comforting, familiar scent of her favorite lavender lotion enveloped me.

"You looked so peaceful, I didn't want to wake you. Dad and I brought you—"

I pulled her into a constricted hug.

"Aw, my baby. Is everything okay?"

Not even a little bit. "I missed you." I hid the unease in my voice as I pulled away from her. "You look great, Mom. I must look like a bottle of Wite-Out compared to you." I did a quick visual sweep of the room. "Where's Dad?"

"Oh, you know your father. He insisted on unpacking the whole car in one trip." She scanned my features. "We missed you, baby. I tried to call you when we arrived at the airport, but your phone kept going straight to voicemail." She beamed. "Which reminds me! Don't you have a secret to tell me?"

My heartbeat picked up. "A secret?"

"As we were waiting for our flight, I saw this magazine," she started chirpily, until her eyes widened and clung to a spot on my arm. "What happened here?"

A fading pink line ran down my forearm. It wasn't raised enough to be a scar and appeared to be more like a graze. My thoughts circled back to the demon that attacked me in the alleyway, the memory of its scalpel-like talon slicing through my flesh. "Oh, that," I said with a hard swallow. "I, um, went for a hike."

Mom looked at me as if I had three heads. "Since when do you like nature?"

"I was in a car accident last week," I blurted. *Idiot, idiot, idiot!* "I've been meaning to tell you."

Her eyes nearly popped out of her skull. Before she exploded, I rambled on, "But it wasn't my fault, and the other driver offered to fix it. It's all being taken care of."

"Did you exchange insurance information? Why on earth didn't you call us?"

On cue, a lobster version of my dad entered the house. He wore a bright-green Hawaiian shirt and held a cluster of bags. Dad was a few inches taller than Mom and me, with dark-auburn hair and a lean build from cycling. He flipped up his square sunglasses onto his head without using his hands, revealing an awful tan line around his eyes. "Aloha, sweetheart! TGIF!"

"Aloha, Dad. Are you good? You look a little . . . "

"Sun poisoned? Probably. Sunscreen is for sissies." He raised the huge load of bags on his arms. "Look, one trip! I still got it!" He caught Mom's expression and lowered the luggage, wincing as the straps rolled down his pink arms. "What's the matter, honey?"

"Our daughter was in a car accident."

Dad tucked his sunglasses into his shirt pocket with a frown. "Really? Her car looks fine to me."

I sat up straighter. "Wait, my car is in the driveway?"

"Should it not be?" Dad asked. "You left your interior lights on, by the way."

Blood rushed to my ears. I hadn't seen my car since the accident with Devin Star a week ago, and now it was in the driveway? I got up and hurried to the window, parting the blinds. Sure enough, my car was there. But it wasn't in my habitual parking spot and faced away from the house, which brought me a little relief, because that meant someone else had parked it. Maybe I wasn't as crazy as I thought.

"I'm confused," Mom said.

"So am I," Dad agreed.

"I can explain." I tried to make up another lie and hide the hysteria in my voice. "It was Marcy's car, not mine."

Mom cupped a hand over her mouth. "Is Marcy okay? Is she hurt?" She patted the pockets of her jeans, frantically searching for her cell. "I should call her father. Where's my dang phone . . . ?"

"No, please, you really don't have to do that." Marcy hadn't told her father about the accident or the party we attended that night. The last thing I needed was for Marcy to be grounded for a month again without her grandpa's gold card to go shopping. Marcy was scary without her gold card.

"Marcy is perfectly fine. We're both fine. Just a few bumps and scratches. With all my honor's work for school and," *supernatural events and/or possible nightmares involving a murderous yet sexy Grim*

Reaper and venomous demons, "other minor stressors," I decided to say instead, "I totally forgot to text you about it. I'm so sorry."

Mom looked visibly relieved. "Okay, I'm glad both of you girls are all right . . . "

"I'm not surprised Marcy got in an accident," Dad said. "That girl has never been good at steering things. Remember her infamous scooter accident a few years back? Cost us an arm and a leg to get the garage door fixed."

"Henry," Mom scolded. "Marcy got a terrible concussion from that."

"Hey, I never said she deserved it. She didn't, but neither did my door. Why don't we unpack and show Faith all the presents we brought her?"

"You guys didn't need to get me anything," I muttered.

Mom rubbed my shoulder. "Of course, we did, sweetie. Next time we go to Hawaii, you're coming with us. We missed you way too much!" She tucked her hair behind one ear with a coy smile. "Now, don't you have something to tell me? Something that maybe happened while we were away?"

"Nope." I looked to the side. "Nothing at all."

"We heard you went on a date," she cooed. "With *David Star.*"

"Oh."

"Why didn't you tell me?" Right before my eyes, a teenage fangirl possessed my mother. "Remember when your father waited in line for eight hours to get Devin Star to sign his modeling calendar for my birthday?"

Dad stared into the oblivion, as if reliving the traumatic experience.

"I didn't tell you because I knew you'd do this," I said, gesturing at her giddy self with my hand for emphasis.

"And impulsively buy Skittles another Devin Star catnip mouse toy," Dad chimed in.

Mom narrowed her eyes at Dad. "That cat toy was high-quality material, Henry."

"It was polyester."

"*Entertaining* is what it was. Skittles loves that toy!"

"Skittles would love a paperclip if you attached it to a piece of string and snaked it around the carpet," Dad argued.

"Yoo-hoo," I said, snapping my fingers and directing their attention back to me. "Yes, hello. Your only child is standing here and would rather not hear your bickering. If you must know, I didn't exactly plan on going out with David."

Mom's shaped eyebrows scrunched together. "How did you two even meet?"

"How did you know we went on a date?" I countered.

"There was a delay at the airport, so I picked up a magazine to read." Mom leafed through her purse, bouncing a little on her feet with glee. "Imagine my surprise when I found these!"

She held out glossy copies of three popular magazines. On the cover of each magazine were various shots of David and I walking, smiling, laughing. David looked like a sex god strutting down the runway in his baseball cap, leather jacket, white T-shirt, and medium wash jeans, whereas I looked like an angsty buffoon in hand-me-down clothing. He was amused in a relaxed way, whereas I was mid–ugly laugh with my eyes squeezed shut. As if it couldn't get any worse, there was a little photo of me shoving a hot dog down my face in the corner of one of the issues.

"Oh, no, no, no, *no!*" I grabbed the various magazines and read the headlines beneath each cover photo, horrified.

David Star: The secret love life of New York's finest bachelor. Who IS she?

David Star: America's hottest celebrity meets cute goth girl next door. And she loves hot dogs. Is Jr. Star down for that?

David Star: "I can be myself when I'm with her."

"He was quoted!" I yelled.

"They called you cute," Mom gushed, as I furiously flipped to the article from the last magazine. She grabbed one of the weeklies and frowned at the photo of me engulfing half a hot dog. "Hmm. Well, that one's a little inappropriate."

I honed in on the article, then quickly snapped the gossip magazine shut. David was quoted, which meant he knew these pictures were leaked and hadn't told me. It also meant he was feeding into this stuff by not denying we were dating.

"Have you kissed?" Mom asked.

"Lisa." My father grimaced, but Mom corralled me with questions.

"What was the date like? Did he pay? Was he well-mannered? Is he funny? I have to call Aunt Sarah, she'll be so excited to hear you have a *celebrity* boyfriend! Unless you told her already?"

"Mom, he's *not* my boyfriend."

"If he breaks your heart, I'll kill him," Dad said, scowling at the magazine over my shoulder. "I don't care how famous or pretty he is. Say the word and I'll make him disappear, pumpkin."

Mom glared. "Henry!"

"What? I'm obviously kidding." Dad kissed the top of my head and whispered, "Just say the word, I know a guy."

"What if a student from your high school leaks your name and paparazzi come to the house?" Mom paced the living room back and forth. "The house is not in any condition to be filmed in for an interview—*oh*!" She spun toward us and plastered her hands on either side of her face. "What if David comes over for dinner? What if he invites his father? What if they see our unfinished bathroom, Henry? Henry, the *unfinished bathroom*."

As my mother went on, I crept out of the living room and locked myself in my room. At least I knew my date with David had been real. Honestly, I felt so uncomfortable that he had fed into this gossip. I got wrapped up in his charming smile and hadn't considered how his chaotic celebrity life could affect me after that carnival date. Now not only were demonic creatures after me, so were the paparazzi.

I think I prefer the demons over the paparazzi.

I probed the pink scratch on my forearm. The gash on my arm, the slashes on my leg from the angel's wings had disappeared. My fingers drifted to my neck, where Death's monstrous gloved hand once clutched my throat. There was no trace of the events at the D&S Tower and the warehouse. Had it all been a nightmare?

Decompressing the whirlwind of thoughts racing through my mind was like trying to hit off a broken tennis ball machine on rapid fire.

David's Chicago Bears jersey was nowhere to be seen, and I now wore an oversized nightshirt, which I couldn't remember putting on. Pulling it up revealed the same bra and underwear I'd worn to David's office. They were still a little damp from the rain too. I lifted the nightshirt to my nose and inhaled.

The faintest scent of cherries.

"Oh my God."

Death had staged my sleeping spot on the couch!

Which meant he'd wiped the blood off me. I hurried into my bathroom and flipped on the light. The noxious scent of bleach hit my nostrils as I approached the tub. Suddenly there were phantom hands washing away the blood and grime on my bare skin, rolling a fresh shirt over my head. A shudder rippled through me. I remembered Death's silken voice in my ear, strangely asking me to invite him into my house, and my weak response, *yes*. Why did he care to cover up the tracks of this night?

My cheeks pinked in the mirror at the embarrassing thought

that the Grim Reaper had seen me in my bra and underwear. Up close and personal. *Better than having to explain a gallon of blood splattered on someone else's clothes to my parents.*

I wandered back into my room and peered around, soaking in the bedroom as if I were Death seeing it for the first time. Stuffed animals and old pictures from my childhood lined the top shelf beside my bed, trophies from softball and a few art competitions. What did the seven-foot-tall Grinch in a cloak think of my band posters, my fluffy body pillow, or my old teddy bear, Mr. Wiggles? Not to mention, my latest additions to the family: Boggy the Froggy and Maddox the Penguin. Did he analyze my paintings lining the walls, or did he overlook it all?

Why did I care what Death thought of me? I had nothing to prove to him. He wasn't exactly shooting trust vibes out of his deadly pores, and the guy had wiped out an entire species of bird in five seconds. The Grim Reaper didn't care about my little universe. Especially after what happened in the warehouse.

Removing the rest of my clothes, I stepped under the hot spray of the shower and lathered my skin with my favorite watermelon and blue raspberry body washes.

The angel crashing through the office, the alleyway, the raven demigod, and the warehouse were real. So was the vision with the boy with the mismatched eyes and the willow tree, where that deceptive creature, Ahrimad, had tricked young Death.

. . . you would be far greater than loved. You would be feared. Feared by all.

Ahrimad had been forced to offer Alexandru an equal exchange to saving his life, an opportunity to have all his dark power. Because of a balance. A balance between good and evil.

All of the fantastical happenings in my life were turning out to not be so fantastical, after all.

And I still had to go to school on Monday.

My shower thoughts jumped to David. Everything seemed to circle back to him in my mind. The last time I'd seen him, he'd been restraining that angel in his office and told me to run. An angel, which David hadn't even seemed that surprised to see!

Then, a little too conveniently, Death showed up to save me. I drew comparisons between David and Death. The way they stood. Their personalities. Their mannerisms. They were so different. Where David's voice was deep and masculine, like a normal human man's, Death's was deep and masculine in a profoundly enchanting inhuman way. In an instant, his voice had the ability to switch from a menacing growl to a velvety purr.

Based on the apparent younger Death I'd seen glimpses of the two men had vastly different appearances too.

The water ran cold. Quickly washing the rest of my body, I slipped on another oversized cotton shirt and anxiously reorganized my makeup on my vanity. I wished I had my phone to text David. I couldn't shake his interest in me, and I was starting to think it wasn't just poor self-esteem. How had he restrained that angel in his office without breaking a sweat? He always dodged every personal question about himself and didn't have one picture of his family in his office.

There was no way in hell I was going to get any sleep. I decided to write down my thoughts, so I wouldn't forget them, which I hadn't done since freshman year of high school. I slid out an untouched journal from under my bed that my grandma had given me for Christmas and armed myself with a purple gel pen.

I began to write, staining the pages in hectic sentences, when I felt eyes at the back of my head. Skittles jumped up onto the vanity and hissed at something behind me. I caught a large shadow in the mirror and whirled around with a gasp. Empty. The room was empty, but a trace of *him* remained. Cherries.

My cell phone. My cell phone was now on my bed. It had suffered further damage. Prying my feet from the ground, I crossed the room and picked up the device with a trembling hand. Beneath it was a note.

Tick-tock.

—D

A cold breeze turned my blood to ice. The window was open. I hurried to yank the panel down, staring out into the night with a thrashing heart.

I felt it stare back.

XIII

The angel that had crashed through David's office wasn't in the news.

Wouldn't an angel and a horde of demonic birds at least make the *New York Times*? That's what I told myself, as I refreshed multiple news websites all weekend long, hoping to get some assurance that I wasn't insane.

Now it was Monday morning, and David still hadn't responded to my texts and calls. I had no idea what had happened to him Friday, after the horde of birds chased me through the D&S Tower, but at least I knew he was alive. If one of the Stars died, *that* would at least reach the news.

He'd protected me. David had moved in a blur to throw his body on top of mine, moments before the angel came crashing through the window. He'd effortlessly restrained the creature against his office wall. I'd be an idiot to assume David was human now. The question was: What *was* he?

I couldn't stop thinking about how Death had saved me in the alleyway. Ever since the carnival date with David, Death always seemed to appear right after him and vice versa. I had my suspicions that it was no coincidence either. If I assumed David was Death, the next obvious question was *why*? Why gain my attention with two different personas? Why go on a date with me? Why become one of America's most iconic celebrities? It didn't make any sense.

A headache throbbed at the center of my forehead as I scrolled through my phone. Imagine my surprise when the first thing I saw on social media was more tabloid stories of me and David from the carnival. *And* a new video. It was dated Sunday, yesterday morning too. My heart pounded uncontrollably as I clicked on a mini clip of David Star getting bamboozled by paparazzi. They fired questions at him about "Mystery Girl" from the carnival, but he ignored all of them, shielding his eyes from the flashing cameras as he entered what appeared to be a coffee shop.

Had David not reported the angel accident?

Approaching the first panic attack of the day, I paced the floor of my bedroom, having no idea what to do at this point.

What if another deranged angel fell out of the sky, or a bunch of venomous demon birds tried to tear me apart again? Was I supposed to move on without any contact from David, like the most terrifying day of my life had not just occurred?

My parents. They were probably already suspecting something was wrong, and the last thing I wanted was for them to think I was going nuts. I couldn't just skip school and hide out in my room for the rest of my existence. Besides, schoolwork kept my mind occupied. All I had to do was get through classes, and then I would track down David after school and figure out what the hell was going on. I could do this.

Slinging my backpack over my shoulder as I headed out of my room, my eyes snagged on the little piece of paper I'd left on my vanity.

Death's tenderhearted "tick-tock" note. Perhaps the only proof of what had occurred yesterday. The whole situation with Death was the cherry that capped off my crappy ice cream sundae life. Where did I even begin with that guy?

In an attempt to remain incognito, I wore my dad's navy bucket hat and sunglasses to school. Paired with an old gray sweatshirt and leggings, my style had leveled up, bearing in mind last week's *I'm dead on the inside*, day-to-day black ensemble.

"Love the bucket hat, *chica*," Marcy said, stepping in sync with me as I shuffled with my head down through the hallway.

I tugged the strings of my sweatshirt until just my mouth and nose showed. "How'd you recognize me?"

"Magic."

I shielded my face as we passed a group of varsity football jocks to stop at her locker. I had to be careful. It had only been eighteen hours, forty-two minutes, and ten seconds since the release of the viral articles about my date with David Star.

"I'll assume you saw the articles," I muttered.

"I texted you about it a bajillion times."

"Sorry I missed your texts, my phone is acting up again."

Marcy glossed her lips with a glittery wand. "I didn't even get an update on Friday about you going into the city to see David. It's fine, I like to be neglected."

I gave an apologetic smile. "I'm not neglecting you. I'll tell you more about David later, it's kind of complicated."

I wanted tell Marcy the truth about Friday, but between what had happened in David's office, being mauled by freaking raven demons, and yet another bizarre exchange between me and the *Grim Reaper*, who would believe me? Heck, I was having trouble believing it myself. Nothing about the past few weeks made any logical sense. Marcy, and even my parents, all had to be left in the dark.

"If it makes you feel any better, my weekend was pretty uneventful," I continued with a sigh. "Mom forced me to watch recorded footage from a six-hour luau they went to. It was brutally long." I was getting better at lying because even I felt a little convinced by the tall tale. "Believe it or not, Mom's the one who told me about the articles. There were magazines covered with our faces all over the airport."

Marcy capped her lip gloss and tucked it into her backpack. "Has David talked to you about it?"

"Nope." I couldn't hide the anger in my voice. "He even had a quote in one of the magazines."

I should have assumed wherever David Star went cameras followed, but he could have at least warned me. In all honesty, though, I was mostly angry because David had the nerve to ghost me after the attack in his office. He could have at least let me know he was okay. Instead, he'd stirred up more drama with the paparazzi and practically encouraged them to hunt me down, when I was already walking around like a cat on hot bricks with monsters popping up left and right in my life.

"Now I have David's rabid fans to worry about," I said. "It was nice knowing you, Marcy. You've been the world's okayest best friend."

Marcy nudged me in the rib with her elbow and we both laughed. "Dude, you are such a diva today. David is a celebrity, what did you expect? Nobody would ever find out about you two?"

"I sure didn't expect *this*. I'm a blender, Marcy. I blend. I never stand out. Blending is my forte, damn it. It's why my incognito outfit is on point."

"You do realize you have your last name on the back of your sweatshirt, right?"

"What?" Panicked, I gripped the back of my sweatshirt and

practically broke my neck to get a peek. Sure enough, in gigantic black lettering was the last name *Williams*. I was wearing my old soccer sweatshirt from middle school. "Oh, come on!" I flattened my back against the lockers as a group of students passed by. "Marcy, what am I going to do? His fans are going to eat me alive!"

"Ah, it'll blow over. I'll find you a remote island where you can start a new life."

"And befriend a volleyball named Wilson?"

"Exactly. Faith, babe, you know I'm the last person who should be telling you this, but you're totally overreacting. It's only an article. I haven't heard a single student talk about it."

As if the universe was plotting against me, Nicole Hawkins, the most popular girl at school, and her two clones approached us, pointing at a magazine with my face plastered on the cover. Marcy and I tracked them with our eyes as they walked by.

"She looks kind of familiar," one of the girls was saying. "Her hair is so long and silky. I wonder what deep conditioner she uses."

"I bet those are extensions," hissed Nicole Hawkins. "I hope she gets run over by a tractor. What a dumb bitch!"

Marcy snatched a hair dryer from her locker. "Fake a fever at the nurse and go home early?" she offered.

"Yup," I said, grabbing the hair dryer.

About an hour later, I peeled out of the senior parking lot and headed home. The article and the ignored calls weren't the worst issues I had with David Star. I needed to know what had happened in his office, and whether he was involved in all of this. It was the only way I'd get any sleep tonight.

The nurse had to get a hold of my mom to send me home, but since Dad had a long commute home and Mom had an important presentation scheduled at her office, I'd insisted they should both stay at work and let me go to the doctor by myself. Mom put money on my debit card to get medicine and whatever else I needed at the pharmacy. Now I had an excuse for coming home a little late for dinner and money to head into the city again.

Wow, I was getting good at this "rotten daughter who constantly lies to her parents" stuff.

There were two options here. Either I could let life beat me down and toss me whichever way it wanted, or I could grab it by its reins and take control of my fate. I chose the latter.

Sliding out my beat-up phone, I texted David.

We need to talk. Today.

Armed with one pathetic canister of pepper spray in the pocket of my hoodie, I entered the D&S Tower. Assaulted by the unexpected shrill shrieks of enthusiastic fangirls in the overcrowded lobby, I stood at the entrance in an introvert stupor before refocusing on my purpose.

Holy cow.

Good thing at home I'd swapped my previous hoodie for a Nike sweatshirt without my name on it. I drew the hood over my head and shoved through the obstacle course of flailing arms and girls snapping pictures, until I knew exactly what the commotion was about. An interview David had participated in that morning replayed on a massive drop-down flat-screen. I caught a snippet of it earlier before school but paused to rewatch it now.

"Good morning, I'm Stacy O'Casey, and you're watching *NYC A-S-A-P*," announced the blond woman on the screen. "I'm here with megastar celebrity and heartthrob David Star. David, we've all heard the big news from your father, Devin. Can you tell us a little about the launch of your new art program?"

David leaned down to the microphone and locked onto the

camera, brown eyes striking under the various studio lights pointed at him. "The goal of the program is to give underprivileged children of New York City an outlet and a safe space to be creative. We believe art is an imperative tool for kids to express themselves and cope with any negative emotions or mental health concerns they may be facing. My team has been working tirelessly on this project to build the perfect team of dedicated artists and therapists to guide the children. We consider this the first step to securing the future of all of New York's children and improving the communities of our great city for generations. This project has been a very rewarding process, to say the least. I'm confident those who attend our premiere tomorrow evening, at the D&S Tower Halloween ball, will feel just as passionate about our cause as we do. All proceeds are going to deteriorating areas of New York that need your help the most."

"How wonderful! You must be so proud of your accomplishments, young man." She laid her hand on the swell of his bicep. She squeezed it a little too. *Real subtle*, I thought bitterly. "Modeling, acting, philanthropy, and all your responsibilities at the D&S Tower. How the heck do you find the energy?"

"I have a secret weapon, Stacy. Due to my input in designing the most recent Sonic Nerve energy drink campaign, they gave me a ton of samples of their new beverage flavors. I've been downing these like they're water. As they say, I'm not just a spokesperson, I'm a customer. We're selling this flavor exclusively from D&S Enterprises for the next two days. If you scan the code on the back of the can with your phone, you'll enter a sweepstakes, with the chance to attend the D&S Tower ball. As my date."

He flashed his famous dazzling smile at the camera. The horde of fans in the lobby erupted into girlish screams, holding up their energy drink containers with David's face on them that the merchandise sellers were giving out.

As the show cut to commercial, a short clip of David and Devin modeling in suits transitioned onto the screen. Time to get the heck out of there before the interview came back and the reporter asked anything about "Mystery Girl."

I headed through security at the end of the lobby, took an elevator with five other people, and tensely watched them exit the claustrophobic space one by one. As I approached the top floor alone, the empty feeling in the pit of my stomach worsened. The memory of last Friday's impossible events fired into me like war flashbacks, and I struggled to keep my breathing even. *You can do this. You need answers. Did all of that really happen, or are you losing it?* Adjusting the strings of my hoodie, I rubbed my clammy hands down my leggings and stepped off the elevator.

My vision tunneled as I neared David's waiting room. Taking a deep breath, I shoved through thick glass doors to be greeted by an unwelcoming glare. Tiara, David's receptionist, sat perched like a gargoyle behind her elevated circular desk. She wore a bright-red business suit that accentuated her ballerina waist, and her makeup sharpened her thin, chiseled features. I hated that she was perfect. I also hated that I loved her outfit.

"Look what the cat dragged in," Tiara said, peeling back her painted lips into a wry smile. "David's unavailable."

"Can you tell me when he will be?"

"Do you have an appointment?"

"No, but I—"

"Mr. Star is a very busy man, Miss Williams. You'll have to make an appointment. He may have something available next week." She skimmed her computer screen far too fast to have read anything. "Gosh, he's absolutely booked this month. Can you come in four weeks from now?" Her expression soured. "That may give you time to upgrade your wardrobe."

I inhaled slowly. "Listen, Tina—"

"Tiara."

"Whatever, I know you dislike me," I said, adrenaline shaking my entire body, "but I'm *not* in the mood for this shit. I'm functioning on zero hours of sleep, there's a viral picture of me stuffing a hot dog down my gullet all over the world, my grades are tanking, and I need to see David to find out if I'm losing my mind or not. Either call David and tell him I'm here to speak to him, or I'm picking up that stupid D&S Tower Detox water cooler over there, breaking down his door, and causing a scene that will make what happened Friday seem like a namaste meditation oasis!"

Tiara gaped for a long moment, then plucked at her desk phone with her long fingernails. She pressed a button. "Faith Williams is here to see you." She fidgeted with the ends of her hair. "Yes, I told her you were otherwise engaged, but she's refusing to leave. She says it's urgent." Her expression fell a little in defeat. "Oh. Of course, my apologies. I'll tell her now." She hung up and switched to receptionist mode, centering her attention on her computer screen. "You may go in."

The windows of the office looked exactly the way they did before the angel crashed through them. How was it possible? It had only been three days. David Star stood behind his desk, posed like a sculpture. He radiated authority, impeccably dressed in a dark-gray business suit that matured him. Chameleon mode: on.

"Have a seat, Miss Williams," David said without looking at me.

"I'll stand, thank you," I snapped, matching his rude tone.

"You shouldn't have come here."

My chest tightened. This was unexpected, to say the least. "Why's that?"

His head lifted, once familiar brown eyes so dark with disdain they were nearly black. He wore a cruel expression, impenetrable cold marble, and gazed at me like I was an unwelcome stranger. "We could have had this discussion over the phone. Would have saved you the time and money traveling."

"I can afford traveling here." I'd lied with an insecure need to defend myself. *What's up with him?* "I called and texted multiple times. You could've at least texted me back."

David leaned his hands on his desk and skimmed over a sheet of paper. "What do you want, Faith? I have an important meeting in ten minutes."

"What do I *want?*" I couldn't help it. I laughed. "I want to know what's going on!"

"I'm not sure what you mean."

"Why are you acting this way? What's happened to *you?*"

His head flinched back slightly. "What happened to me? What happened to you?" He ran his fingers across his jaw. "Last Friday, you came here and made it very clear you never wanted to see me again. Now you're here again, and you're asking me what happened to *me?*" His laughter had an edge to it. "Are you serious?"

Blood rushed to my head. "No . . . " I took an uneven step back, glancing at the once shattered window to my left. Everything, and I mean everything in that office, was exactly as it was before the angel crashed through it. I considered three possibilities here: Death had reset the room and wiped David's memories clean, David was lying to me, or I had lost my mind and none of what I remembered ever happened.

I looked David dead in the eye. "The last time I saw you, an angel with a wingspan the size of a bus crashed through that window." I pointed an unsteady finger to it. "You restrained the creature in seconds, as if it were just another day at the office. As if that wasn't traumatizing enough, a bunch of horrifying bird demons manifested and tried to kill me in the alleyway outside *your* building!"

He scratched the back of his head. "Um, *what?*"

"This isn't funny, David!" My heart thrashed wildly against its cage, and I fought to take a deep breath. "You were there with me! It *happened!*"

"I don't understand what your goal is here, but I don't find this funny, and I don't have time for games." He picked up his desk phone.

"Don't you dare call security on me! Ever since I met you and your father, all of this crazy shit started happening!" I pinched my temples as a migraine began to pound. "Either you're lying to me and you have something to do with all of this, or your memories have been erased. That last one would really suck right now!"

David's eyes hardened as a vein pulsed in his forehead. "You need to leave, Faith."

A part of me thought if I kept talking about what happened, David's memory would come back to him, but it only pissed him off. Which I couldn't blame him for if he was brainwashed into thinking I'd told him off the day before. But what if he was lying? I crossed my arms over my chest to hold myself together. There wasn't an ounce of uncertainty in his voice, and he was showing no signs of lying that I could glean. How could I get the answers I wanted from him without getting thrown out by security?

I refused to believe I was going off the deep end. "Are you lying to me?"

"What reason do I have to lie to you?"

I took a few tentative steps closer to him. "What happened Friday was real, whether you can remember it or not, and your mind being wiped clean is an easy way of getting out of this conversation."

"And what exactly is the point of this conversation?"

"To get answers." *Something Death hates more than anything.* "To help you remember."

I looked down at David's hands, which gripped the ledge of his desk. The last time I'd touched Death, I'd seen things from his past that I shouldn't have. If I tried to touch David now, his reaction could be very telling.

"I think what you need is closure," David said, and my heart skipped a beat at his callous tone. "Your personal problems no longer concern me. This was never going anywhere, Faith."

It was my way out. An end to this charade, so I didn't get wrapped up in David's world on top of all the other chaos in my life. I never expected his cruel words to cut so deep.

David's shadowy eyes flicked up to mine. His jaw set. Seeing that I was on the verge of crying, he shifted from one foot to the other, finally exhibiting an emotion outside of anger through his cold mask. "I'll call my driver to take you home."

"I'm fine to take the train," I managed to get out evenly.

He stared straight at the door, evading eye contact. "Then I'll escort you to the lobby."

Never in a million years would I have predicted myself allowing this man, this *stranger* I hardly knew, to hurt me like this. But he had, and I was a fool. *Pull yourself together.* My shoulders hunched. I was fighting so hard to hold back the waterworks that I knew if I opened my mouth, I would lose control, so I forced a pathetic nod.

In the elevator, I switched to Autopilot. Detached. Numb. David stood facing away from me, his hands clasped behind his back. His long fingers were fiddling with a rolled-up gum wrapper.

"If you ever need that pepper spray, make sure it's not locked," David said. "Point it away from you before you spray."

I stared at the back of his suit jacket for seven floors. "How'd you know I'm carrying pepper spray?"

"You keep touching a lump in your sweatshirt pocket. There should be a knob or a switch to make sure the canister isn't locked."

"Heard you the first time." *I'm not yours to protect,* had almost slipped out childishly too. I yanked up the hood of my sweatshirt, remembering the chaos from all the fangirls in the lobby.

A hard rock riff blasted through the awkward tension. David took his phone out from his back pocket, silencing the noise.

The doors slid open. Neither of us moved. I could not breathe.

Prying my Converse off the ground, I forced myself to exit the elevator and hurried past him into the mayhem. Everything moved in slow motion, my mind whirling. By the time I looked back at the elevator, the doors were closed.

He had Death's ringtone.

XIV

After seeing David, I took the train back to Pleasant Valley and met Marcy at our favorite Mexican restaurant for dinner. Manuel's was a hole-in-the-wall taco joint ten minutes from my house. If there were ever a cure for heartbreak, it was the guac at this restaurant.

The last thing I wanted was to be alone with all the emotional turmoil inside me. I explained that after I'd faked sick from school, I'd gone to the D&S Tower to talk to David again, and he'd broken things off.

"You protected me through all the stuff with Thomas, and now it's time to return the favor," Marcy said, as she fixed her makeup in a compact mirror. "If David D-bag Star has the audacity to cross paths with you again, he's done for. Pretty Boy won't know what hit him." She shut the compact with a vicious snap and traded it for her wallet in her bright-orange Coach tote. "Think of me as the chastity belt between his little burrito and your taco. See what I did there?"

"Marcy, please," I laughed out. "We're in public."

"Ugh, guys are slime," she grumbled and fished for a twenty-dollar bill. "I'm sorry I keep yapping about this, but I'm just *so* mad! My sweet best friend is hurting. If you ask me, David is the last man on this planet who deserves his last name. The only astronomical thing about him was his big bubbly ass in the tabloids a while back, and we all know how *that* ended up. A Photoshop sham."

"Have I ever told you how much I love you?"

"Plenty of times, although I love myself enough for the both of us." She shrugged self-importantly but in a joking way. "It's a curse."

Holding back another laugh, I stepped toward the girl behind the glass dome of toppings to create my order: three beef tacos with lettuce, tomato, cheese, sour cream, salsa, and a side of Manuel's homemade chips and guac.

"I'll have you know," Marcy continued, once she was done placing her order, "I'm writing David a *terrible* review on my fashion blog for his new men's clothing line!" She took out her phone and viciously typed. "Aaand Send. Ha! Come on, girl, time to eat our feelings. Then we'll kick it at your place and binge watch the rest of season three of *Buffy*."

I managed a smile. Sounded like a plan to me. Together, we walked to the soda station. I put some ice into my large cup and filled it to the brim with a little of each colorful soda. I called this creation the Sugar Splurge. Marcy made a face.

"What?" I asked, sipping the drink.

"I can't believe you're still doing that, loser." We walked to our usual table. "Your metabolism is so unfair. If I drank these, I'd gain like twenty pounds. Not in my ass either, might I add."

"Girl, don't even start. Have you looked in the mirror? You're the ultimate hottie tamale!" Sliding into a chair across from her, I immediately dunked a salted lime chip into the guac. "As for my drink, don't knock it till you try it. This creation is legendary."

"You're a sugar maniac. Haven't you been getting migraines?"

Tylenol—glory be—was my only relief from those recent killer stress migraines.

"Marcy, my life has gone to the dogs. Sugar is the least of my problems." I took a big slurp of my drink. "Mmm, glucose." I offered her the cup as if it were the Holy Grail. "Take a sip. You're welcome."

She gulped down a single swallow and choked a little. Her hazel eyes widened.

"I know," I said cockily. "Evolutionary."

"No," she wheezed, pointing somewhere over my shoulder. *"Him."*

I spun around and my stomach plunged. David Star strolled into Manuel's dressed like a king among peasants. He wore a Gucci number (which I only knew because of Marcy's fashionista knowledge) paired with a leather jacket, which probably could have bought me a car that didn't stutter and groan every time I killed the ignition, and a pair of black aviator sunglasses.

David's granite features snapped in my direction. I quickly rotated back around.

"Kill me," I said.

"How did he find you?" Marcy asked.

"I don't know."

But I had an idea.

"Faith." The hair at the back of my neck stood on end. David stopped in front of our table. The whole restaurant had become silent, except for a few people whispering and stealing photos of David. Every muscle in my body tensed, ready to launch me into flight at any moment. "We need to talk."

Up close, everything about him was intoxicating, but I forced my pitiful self to look past his façade to see the jerk who had burned me today. "Um, no thanks."

He opened his mouth to reply, when Marcy came in hot. "She said no, *compadre*. Now take your hoity-toity fuckboy haircut and skedaddle, before I call my father. He's the sheriff in this town. Last time I checked, stalking is a criminal offense."

A smirk etched its way across David's lips. He tilted his head down to Marcy. "How rude of me." Slipping off his sunglasses, he tucked them into the pocket of his leather jacket and reached out a hand. "You must be Faith's garrulous best friend, Marcy. David Star."

She shook his hand numbly. Her mouth slowly fell open.

"Wow," was all she could muster. "You smell yummy."

"Marcy," I hissed and shook her tray. Startled, she blinked a few times, exiting dreamy mode. "He just *insulted* you, and we're *leaving*." I wrapped my tacos and stuffed them into my purse.

"Right," Marcy said, frowning. "Right, okay."

"Marcy." Her head snapped back to David. He flashed another charming smile, and my arms broke out into gooseflesh. I looked anxiously between him and her. "May I have a word alone with Faith? You have to use the bathroom."

"If you'll excuse me, I have a urinary urgency." She got up too fast for me to grab her, retreating to the restroom.

David turned his attention to me, and I jumped out of my chair, putting the table between us. "What the hell did you just do to her?"

"Don't make a scene," David said so low I had to read his lips.

"You've already done enough of that for the two of us!"

"Give me a chance to explain myself."

"There's nothing for you to explain." I inhaled a shaky breath, energy rushing through my veins. "Just go. Stay away from me."

He looked around at our audience, chuckling a little. Then he started to walk around the table. "I understand why you're upset. I have answers for you, but we can't talk in here."

"Do not come any closer." I whipped out my pepper spray and

aimed it at him. "It's not locked, and it's pointing away from me." I arched my brow. "Thanks for the tips."

Unfazed by my weapon, David slid on his sunglasses. "I'll be outside."

"That's nice. I'll be in here, calling the police." I increased my personal space and knocked into a couple sitting at a table. Muttering an apology, I reached into the back pocket of my jeans for my phone. Empty. *Seriously?* My eyes darted to my backpack, which was closer to David.

David and I stared each other down like cowboys dueling in a wild Western film. My fingers twitched at my side.

I lunged forward. At the last second, his hand shot out and fisted my backpack first. Grinning, he shouldered the bag and sauntered toward the exit.

"Hey! Hey, I need that—you—you *thief!*" He ignored my protests and shoved through the glass doors into the parking lot. Glancing around at the puzzled faces around me, I released a disgruntled curse. "Ever hear of the bystander effect, people?"

I raced after him.

"Give me back my backpack!" I demanded, feeling lame as hell as I jogged across the parking lot to David's retreating frame. "I'm talking to you!"

He pivoted sharply. I smacked into him. My vision filled with his handsome features and all thought suspended. "I'm not who you think I am."

"We've already established that," I said a bit breathlessly and lunged for my bag again. He lifted it out of reach, and I stopped myself before I jumped for it like a child. "We're both adults here, David. Give me the backpack."

"What I mean is," David said as he lowered the bag, "I'm not *him.*"

I had a heightened need to take a step back, so I did. "And by him, you mean . . . "

"The creature you were referencing today in my office. Death."

He clearly expected some sort of crazy reaction, and heck, I expected one too. When I didn't even flinch, he ran his thumb over his bottom lip and continued.

"Your car accident with Devin wasn't an accident. It was a planned intervention to protect you. If you want to know more, I can tell you everything right now. But if you choose to leave and go back to your friend, I won't track you down again. This is a onetime offer."

Deciding to throw caution to the wind, as I often found myself doing with David, I nodded. "Fine, I'm listening."

David tossed my backpack to me like it was a feather. I caught it with a grunt. *Freaking textbooks.*

"We knew about your existence a few weeks ago, tracked you down, and intercepted one of Death's encounters with you. That's what Devin and I do. Track down gifted people, with unusual circumstances like yours, and protect them."

Robotically, I slid my arms into the straps of my backpack. Somehow, I was able to formulate a sentence, so I did. "What kind of circumstance is mine?"

"You died, Faith. Before you could cross over to the other side, you were brought back to life. Now your soul is marked by *the Kiss of Death.*"

"The Kiss of Death," I said, laughing at the ridiculousness that was my life. "Let me get this straight. You're telling me, when an individual has an unusual situation like mine, such as the Kiss of Death, you and Devin are the ones who intervene?"

David crammed his hands into his pockets and scanned our surroundings. I watched him carefully for any nervous tics, but just like yesterday, he was a master at keeping a straight face. "That's exactly what I'm saying."

"And what proof do you have of this?"

"None I'm allowed to show you."

"How convenient!"

"Listen, I know how this looks. When this conversation is over, you can decide whether or not you believe me."

I regarded him skeptically. "Why are you doing this?"

David shifted in an uncomfortable way. "Because I care about you," he murmured. "I don't want to see you get hurt."

My heart fluttered. I repressed any nagging feelings and stared coolly at him. I could have been completely wrong about him; I'd jumped to conclusions with hardly any concrete evidence. Now was my chance to hear him out and make a decision afterward.

"Tell me everything."

"There are only a few beings left like Devin and me. We're called the Carrions. The Sixth Phylum of Angels. We accompany dark entities when they die and make sure their deaths are permanent. By dark entities, I'm referring to demons, vampires, ghouls, evil creatures that lurk in the night. We help keep your world at a balance between good and evil, so it isn't taken over by darkness."

I twisted the ring on my finger around and around. "Alrighty . . . "

"Devin is my boss, and my mentor. I consider him a father figure because I've known him for so long, but we're not related. He showed me the ropes when I was a rookie. My eyes are sensitive to bright light because I've spent more lifetimes than you can imagine tracking down night creatures in the dark. And the reason why I could take on that angel in my office is because I'm much stronger and faster than a human."

Jesus Christ. I tried to keep my cool after that second info dump, but my heart was pounding a mile a minute as I now mulled over a thousand racing thoughts.

"Lifetimes," I said finally. "You've spent *lifetimes* tracking down these creatures."

"Yes."

"Which would make you?"

"Much older than I appear," he conceded. "Existence-wise . . . I'm a couple centuries old."

I reached up and gripped the material of my flannel over my chest. "That's—that's not possible."

"I've aged impeccably well."

I waited for the laughter to kick in, for cameramen to jump out, for David to slip up and give me a sign he was lying. But he was unsmiling and grave. I could feel the weight of the truth behind his words.

Centuries. He'd been stuck at the same age for centuries. *Cool. I'm attracted to another immortal dinosaur.*

"If this is all true," I said, "then why would you lie to me yesterday?"

"I was warned to stay away from you."

"By who? Death?"

His gaze pierced through his sunglasses, answering my question. *Yes.* "I had a target on my back two days ago, and so did you. Angels have been dropping like flies in New York. Now we know why."

"Malphas," I muttered.

He nodded tightly. "I hope you didn't get close enough for an introduction."

I pulled up my sleeve, where the demon's bladelike talons had ripped into me. There was almost nothing visibly left of the gruesome wound. "Too close for comfort," I said.

"Malphas gave you that?"

"No, one of his demons did," I said, shoving down my sleeve to wrap my arms around myself. "I was attacked, and I would have died. Death . . . he saved my life."

David flexed his hands. I could tell he wanted to press more on the situation, but he didn't. "Has Death explained to you that Malphas is a demigod?"

"Oh, Death doesn't tell me anything. It's his thing."

"Malphas is the son of Hades and a mortal," David enlightened. "Hence, demigod. Two thousand years ago, he was destroyed by Death himself. Evidently, he's been resurrected. I suspect it was Hades's doing, or maybe his followers, since Malphas has worshippers, like any deity does. He is very, very dangerous, Faith. What you saw crash through my window was an archangel, a powerful guardian from the realm of Heaven that was infected by Malphas's venom. I recognized the guardian as one of my other mentors. I'm thinking the guardian was a decoy because those demons entered the D&S Tower as soon as I was distracted. They went after you, and they went after me too. That's why I couldn't help you in the alleyway."

"You're an angel," I stated, on the brink of a mental breakdown. But I promised myself I would wait until I got home, so I could wrap myself in a fuzzy blanket with my two good friends, Ben & Jerry, and have a proper nervous collapse.

"I'm a Carrion Angel," David said and bowed his head as if proclaiming the title was some sort of acknowledgment. "When we were notified that a dark entity had latched onto you, Devin and I tracked you down and tried to find a way to get closer to you."

"Thomas's party," I said.

"And the car crash with Devin," David said. "We needed to get closer to you and time was of the essence. When we realized what attached to you was the Angel of Death, things became a little . . . tricky. Death is virtually indestructible, unlike most of the dark entities we deal with. At first, Devin thought your situation was a mistake. A fluke in the system. Death has never latched onto a human before. And you seemed like a normal girl without any conceivable connection to the supernatural. Devin put you under my care to figure out what was so unique about you."

"You only took an interest in me because of Death." There was a painful lump in my throat. "The interview and the date were just a way to get information on me."

"I'll admit it may have started off that way, until I got to know you. You're funny, kind, intelligent, and beautiful. In every way, my type."

My heart drummed faster in my chest. "What about after we ate at the carnival?" I interrogated. Focusing on the details was the only way I could stay sane in this moment. "You were frozen. You weren't breathing or anything. Death froze time, and you were affected by his power. Why were you affected?"

He blew out a frustrated breath. "It was a fleeting spell. Death is known to have a few tricks up his sleeve. In retrospect, I shouldn't have taken you on that date, at least not without more reinforcements. I had no idea Death had communicated with you at the carnival, until you mentioned it to me yesterday. I wasn't thinking clearly, only focused on getting you to trust me."

When I didn't say anything, David continued, "Death is stronger than I am. His power is unparalleled." He didn't seem too thrilled about admitting that last part. "I can't interfere with his abilities because I'm a Light Angel. According to Seraph Law, Death takes precedence over Light Angels."

For some reason, I believed him, but I put on my best poker face and pretended my opinion of him remained the same. "Who the heck made that stupid rule?"

"They're called the Elders. The first Seraphs or angels to ever exist. Most of the rules they've created are outdated and unbreakable. Whenever they try to adjust these laws, the balance between good and evil has always tipped, and never in their favor. Even a being as merciless as Death serves a purpose for humanity."

"Merciless?"

"I've crossed paths with Death a few times, none of which were pleasant. Not only does he have a notorious disregard for human life, but like most Fallen Angels, he abhors anything good and holy, like the realm of Heaven."

"Did you—did you just say Death is a Fallen angel?"

"He is the Angel of Death, so yes," David said, and blood pulsed in my ears. "The good news is, Death isn't the one killing Light Angels for fun."

"But he does kill *humans* for fun," I speculated.

"Don't get me wrong, he'll torture mortals with their own fears just for kicks and giggles. But mostly he partakes in how they're supposed to die anyway and eats a small piece of their soul to satiate his death curse. Or so the legend says." David rubbed his clean-shaven jaw. "I digress, I have no sympathy for him. If you ask me, nobody made him become the monster he is today. He chose it. And he continues to choose it."

"That's not true," I said, and David's eyebrow arched. Even I was surprised I'd defended Death. "What I mean is, that *can't* be true. What kind of person voluntarily becomes a monster?"

"A psychopath? As much as I disagree with Death's methods, I've managed to stay out of his way. Until recently. He saw me with you at the carnival and threatened me last night." His jaw tightened, sharpening it. "Shortly after my encounter with him, I told Devin, and he ordered me to cut ties with you, said our investigation wasn't worth getting my head chopped off. I didn't feel like I had a choice today, Faith, but not for my sake. I couldn't risk *you* getting hurt because of me."

He loomed closer. "If Death really wanted to hurt you, he would have already. You being in the dark and unprotected feels riskier than telling you all of this. When you left my office earlier, it hit me how wrong it was to leave you defenseless. Haven't you always felt special, Faith? You have a unique soul, and Death wants to keep you because of it. Predators don't spare their prey unless they want to play with it. The moment he gets his hands on you, I worry he'll torture you like a lab rat and kill you. The point is, he's unpredictable. I don't know what the hell is running through that psychopath's mind. You must believe I'm on your side. I would never try to hurt you like he would. I want you safe."

As I listened to his side of the story, I saw how authentic and exposed he'd made himself. I wanted to believe him, but I had to be absolutely sure he wasn't lying.

"Give me your hand."

"My hand?"

I stuck out my hand between us. "You can't provide any physical evidence of who you are, and Death would never touch me." *Not after what happened at the warehouse.*

David edged closer. My body went static with fear. There wasn't even a heartbeat of hesitation before his long fingers gently gripped mine.

Nothing.

"Well, that was anticlimactic," I said, staring down at our intertwined hands. As if something would be triggered, I clutched his hand extra hard one last time and squeezed my eyes shut.

When I looked up at him, his mouth curved into an amused smile. "Satisfied?"

My face burned under his intense stare. "I have questions."

He released my hand and crossed his muscular arms over his chest. "Go."

"Why do you have the same ringtone as Death?"

"You're kidding," he said with a snicker. "You might not know this, but AC/DC is a popular band."

"Weak answer." My eyes narrowed. "Do you have wings?"

"All angels have wings."

"Even Fallen?"

"Yes."

Holy crud. My mind harked back to how Death had swooped down in the alleyway to save me. I hadn't seen his wings, but he'd flown. How had I missed *that* fact?

"Can I see yours?" I asked.

David rolled back his shoulders. "Wings can be considered an intimate part of angel's body. With you, it'd be the equivalent of showing you my dick."

Heat crawled up my neck. "Never mind." It was time to change the subject. "What else can you do? Can you read my mind?" *I sure hope not.*

"No," he said. "I can only control you slightly, like that trick I did earlier to Marcy. I tried to test the malleability of your mind during our interview, and it proved to be very difficult. "

"But if you really tried?"

"I should be able to influence you, yes."

"Try it right now."

Sighing, he lifted his sunglasses up. I watched the pupils of his eyes stutter. "Tell me a secret, Faith."

"I have two boxes of packaged cupcakes and my grandpa's old machete stored under my floorboards in case of a zombie apocalypse. First day of sophomore year, I wore this really pretty jumpsuit my aunt gave me as a gift. I drank way too much coffee that morning and had to go number two in the worst way. I rushed to the bathroom and into the stall. I almost made it. Bye, bye pretty jumpsuit."

David burst out laughing.

I snapped out of it, blinking fast. "How the hell did you do that?"

He wiped at his eyes under his sunglasses, crying from laughing so hard. "That time I got lucky. You told me two secrets instead of one. Coffee went right through you, huh?"

Mortified, I covered my face with both hands.

"What are your intentions now?" I asked, urgently trying to direct the conversation back to the point. "With me."

David pushed his jacket back to rest his hands on either side of his belt. "I want you to trust me, so I can protect you. There's a spare bedroom at my penthouse in the city and you could lay low there for a while. That way, you would be out of harm's way, while Devin and I find a way to thwart Death. Whatever connection Death has to you, it needs to be severed first and foremost. I have a feeling Malphas will back off then."

The day I was supposed to die, Death had seen something special in my soul. I couldn't explain why, or how, but I'd known all along he'd created an invisible bridge between us to come back to me. I hadn't seen the last of Death. He'd left his mark on my soul. There wasn't anything I could do about it on my own.

I looked down at my hands and curled my fingers into my palms. There was something inside of me, building, peaking at that very moment, and the migraine from earlier shoved through the Tylenol and hit me at full force.

"I meant what I said, about caring about you," David said, and there was a warm fluttering in my chest that seemed to reduce the headache. "Can you promise to keep this conversation between us?"

"Your secret is safe with me," I said, withdrawing back. "I have to get back to Marcy, and I need time to think about all of this. It's a lot to take in."

David nodded once in acceptance. "Take whatever time you need. Just know it may be of the essence. You know my number."

Without saying good-bye, we both turned our backs on each other and retreated. I entered Manuel's more confused and uncertain of the world than ever before.

XV

Marcy remembered she had to pick up her brother from soccer practice, so we parted ways from Manuel's around six. Now I was alone with my hectic thoughts.

I had tons of schoolwork, which meant I needed to stop in town to get me a vanilla latte to wake up, ASAP, before I risked passing out and falling behind again with my school assignments.

On the richer side of Pleasant Valley, there was a popular road called Station Street, the yellow brick road to my favorite coffee shop. I didn't visit Main Street often because it was always crowded and hard to park, but whenever I needed art supplies or a real good cup o' joe, I endured the social anxiety and headed into town.

Lined up on either side of Station Street were beautifully decorated stores. Each building stood apart from the other, colorful and unique, with window displays that made you stop and stare. This month's theme? Halloween, of course. As soon as I caught a glimpse of the decorations in the coffee shop, a sense of nostalgia brought a smile to my face. Aunt Sarah would always take me here around Christmas for new clothes. We'd check out all the festive holiday window displays and marvel at the strings of rainbow Christmas lights twinkling along streetlamps and stores.

As I approached the cozy shop, I felt like I'd made the right choice in coming here to reboot. I stopped for a moment to view the window display with various carved pumpkins and snapped a photo for Aunt Sarah. Satisfied, I started to walk away, when in the reflection of the window, a motionless figure standing across the street caught my eye.

I spun around and saw a man in all black. He stood apart from everyone else, dark hair, pale skin, beady black eyes. His sharp, unnatural features and malicious stare reminded me of Malphas's raven demons. I froze so stiffly that I couldn't breathe.

A bus rolled by, momentarily blocking my view of the man, and when it passed, he was gone.

A violent chill darted down my spine. Turning away from the coffee shop, I rushed down the sidewalk without a destination in mind. I'd parked my car too far away. I kept looking across the street, checking for the demon. I was so frantic, and neither I nor the person walking toward me on the sidewalk were paying attention to where we were going.

I smacked into a hard chest and a tiny bit of scalding hot liquid sloshed onto my flannel.

"Hot! Hot!" I pinched the wet fabric away from my skin.

"Shoot," a familiar voice mumbled. "I'm so—"

I locked eyes with Thomas Gregory.

"Sorry," Thomas finished with a sheepish smile. "Hey, Faith. What are the odds?"

"Even money," I said coldly. "I live in the same town as you."

Thomas laughed and scratched the back of his blond curls. "Listen, I um . . . "

I brushed past him. "See ya."

"Wait," he said, blocking my retreat. "I know you hate me. If it's any consolation at all, Marcy and I, we're just friends now."

"Do you think I'm stupid?"

He choked on his drink. "No, not at all. I just—"

"Is she your second choice or your thirtieth? I've seen you with other girls at school, and I saw you with Marcy at your party."

"What happened at the party was a mistake," he explained. "We were both drunk."

"I see right through you, Thomas. All you care about is yourself. You think you can toy with whatever girl you want without consequences, and if you think I'm going to let that happen to her again, you've got another thing coming, pool boy. Don't talk to her or me ever again. Got it? Good. Have a nice life."

He jogged to catch up to me. "Faith, hold on. Faith, wait—" I felt his hand grip my wrist, and my surroundings washed away.

I was elsewhere—standing on the sidewalk of Main Street, but in a different location, in front of a different store. Confused, I turned my head to the left, and I saw *myself* racing toward me down the sidewalk, dragging Thomas Gregory behind her. The two of them ran right through me, as if I were a ghost, before turning a corner past a popular sandwich shop. They headed to a patio with seating arrangements for a pizzeria and reached a dead end. An awful sensation settled in my gut, and I ran after them. When I reached the patio area and spotted them, chaos erupted. Ahead of them, two raven demons dropped down from the pizzeria and landed on the pavement.

I watched myself snap into action and grab Thomas by the arm, trying to tug him away from the demons. Terror washed over Thomas's face, but instead of escaping, he shunted me behind him, like he was protecting me. The smaller demon laughed in a chilling way and vanished. He reappeared right in front of Thomas and punched toward his chest. I couldn't see what had happened, until Thomas let out a wet gurgling noise and fell backward onto the pavement. The demon held a clump of bloody, gory flesh in his clawed hand. A heart. The one he'd ripped from Thomas's chest cavity . . .

I wrenched myself free from the vision.

"Oh my God!" Gasping for air, I gaped wide-eyed at Thomas Gregory. There was no wound on his chest. "Oh my God!"

I tore my hand free from his and rushed to the nearest trash can, retching my brains out. I was handed a napkin and cleaned myself off as best I could.

Thomas lightly touched my back. "Are you all right?"

"Stay back!" I gasped, stumbling away from him. It was dramatic, I knew, but the last thing I wanted to do was somehow make this situation worse. "Don't come near me!"

Thomas showed me his palms. "Whoa, chill out. Just making sure you're okay. I mean, shit, did I really make you physically ill?"

My mind surged with thoughts. He'd touched me, and I'd gone somewhere else, just like I had with Death. But this time, I'd been in the future. I'd seen him die. I'd seen those raven demons pursuing us. Thomas might have broken my best friend's heart, but I'd never hope for him or anyone else to die. Had I really seen the future? Was there a way to change his fate?

I had to act; I had to act *now*. My hands shook as I tried to dial David's number for help. Although it was impossible to reach his contact number on my cracked screen, I managed it by a miracle. The call went through, right as my luck ran out and my phone died.

"What's going on?" Thomas asked, finally figuring out I wasn't upset about him and Marcy.

I debated whether or not to tell him the truth. I had no way of proving that vision would even come true, but I'd seen what those demons were capable of outside of the D&S Tower. Telling him I had seen his death meant potentially dragging him into a world I wished I were oblivious to. Or it meant damning myself to the psych ward. Walking away after what I'd seen wasn't an option. If Thomas died because of those demons, and I didn't at least warn him, I would never forgive myself. I had the chance to save his life. That was the most important thing.

"Your life is in danger," I rushed out. "We have to go somewhere safe. *Right now.* They might have seen you with me." I pulled Thomas forward by the sleeve of his sweatshirt, but he resisted.

"What do you mean, my life is in danger?" He jerked away from my grasp, his expression a blend of *you've lost your marbles* and pure terror. "Who are *they*?"

Behind Thomas, a clearing opened up amongst people walking down the sidewalk. There, I saw a tall raven demon sauntering toward us with his hands in his pockets. If these demons could manifest like Death could, then running wouldn't help, but it was the only option I had at the moment.

Frantically, I turned back to Thomas. "I'll explain later, you have to trust me! Come on!" I yanked hard on his hand, and he finally obliged. "Across the street!"

The cars didn't move very fast on Station Street, but one nearly hit us. They swerved and laid on their horn as I hauled Thomas across the way and down the other sidewalk.

I turned over my shoulder and wished I hadn't. Two raven demons were close on our trail. And when I looked forward, another demon appeared directly in front of us. Thomas and I came to a halt. Suddenly two cloaked figures with shorter and smaller frames than Death emerged, dropping to the ground around us with blades in their hands. Seething, the demons both let out a frightening hiss.

"This way!" I yanked Thomas with me back across the street.

"What the fuck was that?" Thomas shouted.

No friggin' clue! "Just keep running!"

Creatures manifested ahead of us, crawling down the buildings and striking pedestrians to the ground. Thomas and I were forced to make another sharp turn, corralled into the very place I had been trying to avoid. The patio where I'd seen Thomas murdered.

Someone familiar was already there, waiting for us.

"Good evening, Faith," Malphas said.

He wore a sleek black shirt and silky black pants. Clean-shaven, his jaw was sharp and his cheeks were slightly hallowed in. Midnight hair twisted back into Viking braids, tied away from his face. He diffused a toxic type of attraction, as if I had no other choice but to consider him beautiful, and something about that feeling oddly reminded me of Death.

"If you come quietly, your friend will leave here unharmed," Malphas continued in that deep, hoarse voice. "If not, well . . . " He looked pointedly at Thomas, and then back at me. "One of you is disposable."

"All right, what is going on?" Thomas exclaimed. "Who is this creep, Faith?"

"Mind your business, *Chad*," Malphas seethed.

"I'm not going anywhere with you," I said, and the raven demigod switched his intense onyx eyes back to mine. I was pretty much done with this supernatural shit for today. I split my focus between Malphas's composed body language and the hyper, rabid-looking henchman demon standing beside him, who was focused on Thomas. He was the one I'd seen rip Thomas's heart out. "And if you're smart," I continued, discreetly wrapping my fingers around my pepper spray bottle in my pocket, "you'll leave both of us alone. Before Death arrives and rips you in half."

Malphas apparently didn't find Death too threatening since his only response was to lift a dark brow.

I acted fast, unleashing half the bottle of spray into the eyes of Malphas's henchman demon, who had been slowly advancing toward Thomas. Screeching, he dropped to his knees. Thomas and I watched in horror as the demon's face began to burn away beneath his fingers.

"Ouch," Thomas and I said in unison.

I turned the bottle on Malphas next, but suddenly my hand was empty, and the bottle was clutched in his dexterous fingers. "Smart girl." He laughed in a low way, inspecting the canister with black nails. "A pepper spray bottle filled with blessed water?"

"Five bucks on Amazon," I muttered, wishing I'd gotten the six-pack.

"Impressive." Malphas disposed of the container and grinned. "However, your little weapon would not have worked on me. I'm not a newborn demon. I'm a demigod." He glided toward me, and my thoughts darted around my skull. Where was he going to take me?

"Don't touch her!"

Surprised, Malphas switched his attention to Thomas. Thomas's chest heaved with adrenaline as he held out a glass bottle, which I suppose he'd found from the overflowing trash can at his side. Smashing the bottle's top, he threatened the raven demigod with the jagged edges. "Yeah, I'm talking to you, you ugly piece of shit. Ever hear of self-tanner?"

Malphas lifted his lip up in a snarl. "To think I almost spared you. Kill him. I don't want mortal blood on my Louis Vuittons." Two raven demons manifested behind Thomas. They grabbed him with their clawed hands.

"Get away from him!" I screamed.

Thomas writhed against the demons. "Get out of here, Faith!" I watched in horror as the demon's claws dug into his arms. "Go!"

"I'll go with you!" I cried to Malphas. Adrenaline spiked through my veins. Without warning, my fingertips were singed with fire, and

I winced from the violent migraine now hammering at my skull. "Just let him go!"

Malphas regarded me with a cold smile. "You'll leave with me either way." He gestured toward the demons to continue.

And I snapped.

"I said, *get away from him!*"

Out of instinct, I raised my hand toward Malphas's demons, and a surge of energy poured out of me like liquid fire racing down my arm. There was a flash of light, so blinding I had to turn my eyes away, and a noise that could only be described as a sonic boom. The stench of burning flesh filled the air, bringing tears to my eyes. Acid rose up my throat.

The light burned out. The migraine dissipated. Ashes piled thickly on the ground where Malphas's demons once stood. With an unsteady step backward, I gazed down at my hands and black splotches filled my vision. I stumbled, leaning against a patio table to keep myself up, my breathing shallow and quick. Panic made passing out that much more likely, so I tried to calm myself down. Through the gaps of consciousness, I saw Thomas. He had dropped to his knees in the ash, his entire body quaking as if he had an unending chill. Blood ran down both of his arms from the nails of those demons, mingled with a thick black substance.

He'd been poisoned, just like I'd been in the alleyway.

Thomas fell over on his side, his expression tightening into pure agony, and that's when I saw Malphas manifest ahead of me. He looked down at the piles of ash with a docile expression, then flicked those coal eyes back to me. I watched him make the decision to leave me or take me.

Malphas snatched Thomas by the varsity jacket instead and evaporated with him.

"NO!"

I stared at the now empty spot with widening eyes. Shadows danced across the ground from above. I forced myself to run, run far away from this never-ending nightmare. The world around me swirled. I stumbled, my fingers smacking against the pavement several times to keep myself from falling, until I regained control over my equilibrium and took off.

I ran as hard as I could, my will to survive fueling my body past every limit I thought I had. When I felt I'd run far enough, I hunkered down into a random store. The Crossroads was the name of the little shop, according to its Ouija board–looking sign at the front of the building. It had an antique door with various bells on strings hanging on the entryway that chimed when I entered. I slammed the door behind me, my ears popping like crazy, as if I'd entered a pressurized room.

Fatigue hit me hard. I collapsed behind a mannequin by a front display window. I tried to make sense of what had just happened, but there was too much to process. I'd turned those demons to ash. And *with what?* What the hell had come out of my hands? Those demons had been after me. *Me.* Not Thomas. He'd tried to sacrifice himself so I could get away. Why? Why had he done that for me? Now he was gone. I'd saved him from the terrible fate I'd foreseen, only for him to suffer a worse one. The slow, agonizing death that I'd once evaded. Was there a chance Thomas could survive? Was there a chance Malphas would let him go? I'd failed. I'd failed Thomas.

My chest felt heavy, constricted. Wrenching gasps for air turned to tears, then uncontrollable sobbing. Crying was the release my body needed to keep going.

I wiped at my eyes with my sleeves and observed my fingers again, flexing them. Forcing myself off the floor, I peered out behind the mannequin and looked out into the street. No demons or cloaked men in sight.

I had to call someone. What would I even tell the police? I couldn't endanger Marcy or my parents either. Marcy. How would I tell her what happened to Thomas? Could I? In my moment of fear, I'd called David. Now my mind was clearing up and that felt like a mistake. Relying on him was dangerous, especially considering I hadn't made up my mind about trusting him.

Maybe I'd call my dad, just to hear his voice and gain the confidence to go back to my car. I glanced around the Crossroads store. There was an empty cashier counter, which didn't have a phone, and tons of meditation trinkets and paraphernalia. After a few tries at turning on my cell, I gave up and decided to take a look around for an employee's help. It wasn't like I was about to go out *there*.

With wary steps, I walked through an archway ahead and my mouth went slack. Books were everywhere. Thousands and thousands of books. Old books on display in glass cases, thick books with stained bindings, books in various languages with leather covers. This place seemed to grow larger as I craned my neck to take in the towering shelves and the wooden staircases leading to different levels of balconies. A high ceiling curved with a glass dome at the top, arched above the spacious library. My Converse squeaked as I absorbed this quiet, magical place into memory. The more I wandered around, the more I forgot about why I'd entered the store to begin with, how my fingertips tingled from the remnants of that mysterious light, and how, for whatever reason, those demons hadn't followed me in here.

There was a sound not too far away, a door slamming. A spell shattered and my whole body went into alert mode. Behind a wall of bookshelves, I heard low voices.

With a hand clutching the front of my coffee-stained T-shirt beneath my flannel, I tracked the location of the voices. To my right was a display of pamphlets on a velvet table, advertising a psychic. I picked one up, studying the golden, upside-down palm with a violet eye at the center. A small whooshing sound drew my eyes to a set of thick curtains on the wall that I hadn't noticed before. The fabric swayed.

Trust me, the last thing I wanted to deal with was more paranormal crap right now. Nevertheless, I'd set my sights on getting to a phone, and this store had an indescribable lure that pulled me farther in. My fingers gripped the velvety fabric of the heavy curtains. Holding my breath, I yanked them open. Before me was yet another empty room. No axe murderer. My shoulders relaxed a little. At the center of the area sat a circular palm-reading table with a dimly lit, lavish chandelier suspended above it. A crystal ball sat on top of the table. It absorbed any and all light in the room and shimmered with radiance, as if directly beneath the sun.

With my curiosity piqued, I crept farther inside. The room was filled with candles melting at various stages and containers of spices that permeated the air. Jars packed with objects and coins, glass cases displaying lavish jewelry. Scattered here and there were leafy exotic greens, which I thought was odd because there wasn't any natural sunlight back here. Not that I knew anything about plants; I think I even killed my fake cactus.

I hovered around the ancient-looking artifacts dispersed throughout the room, pausing at a necklace, which gleamed as I glanced over it. The necklace hung on display in a tall, octangular glass box. I had never seen anything so small yet so detailed. It was a dainty gothic cross pendant with a blue gem at the center. The gem was so fascinating I almost didn't notice the black serpent coiled around the ornament.

Not exactly nunnery fashionwear.

Staring at this pendant, I brushed my fingers against my bare collarbone, where I always wore my communion cross my parents had given me. At the carnival, I'd foolishly thrown it at Death, and now it was never to be seen again. Although I only loosely practiced my Catholic religion, that cross always grounded me, reminding me of my morals and my family.

My family. They were completely in the dark about all of this. On second thought, maybe it was better I'd lost that necklace; it would have been a constant reminder of the secrets I was keeping from my loved ones. It made me physically ill to keep them in the dark, but I did not want to get them involved in any of this.

The air shifted, and I knew I was no longer alone.

XVI

DEATH

I manifested into my office and discarded my leather jacket. Shadows unfurled from my frame, crawling across the floor, the walls, and the tinted windows, until they plunged the room into complete darkness.

Lightning struck between my eyes in the form of a headache. I gripped my head with a growl and staggered as another bolt rocked my balance. My shin whacked into the coffee table. Inhaling a slow, steady breath, I straightened to my full height and drove my dress shoe down toward the culprit, shattering yet another glass coffee table with a violent stomp.

I dug hastily into the pocket of my pants for two cigarettes. My fingers shook so hard I dropped the damn things. I pinched the roll-ups between my lips, lit them both, and inhaled hard.

Falling back, I sagged into the couch with a satisfied groan and snapped my lighter closed. The temporary illusion over my skin began to fade away, evaporating into the air like smoke. I lifted my hand in front of my face. The false image of bare human fingers wavered like a mirage, until my black leather gloves emerged through the illusion.

"Forget to eat before your hot date?"

I didn't startle, but I did stiffen at the voice.

Here we go.

In my peripheral, a silhouette of a man sat in the shadows behind my large mahogany desk. His tan fingers steepled together, sapphire eyes daggering into mine.

"Lucifer." Smoke escaped my nostrils as I snubbed out my roll-ups in an ashtray beside the couch. "I can explain . . . "

"Have a seat." He gestured sharply to the chair in front of him.

Rising from the couch, I folded the sleeves of my dress shirt up my tattooed forearms and kept my affect cool. I strode to the desk to lower myself into the armchair. Devin Star leaned away from the shadows and into the light, his mouth curving in a deceivingly friendly manner. I prepared for the worst.

"Did you sleep with her?" His voice held a violent edge.

"Are you out of your mind?"

"I must be," Lucifer said. "I trusted you to handle this. *Carrion Angels*, eh? Never knew storytelling was your second calling. You should write a book."

I maintained a neutral expression. "You were watching us."

"I needed to see why you were prolonging our plans." Lucifer picked an imaginary piece of dust off his silken red dress shirt. "Imagine my surprise when I discovered you've been putting on a five-act fucking Shakespeare play for the girl."

My fingers tapped against the armrest. I scoped out the ceiling as I chose my words with careful precision. "In order for us to utilize her gift, she must be willing and trusting in me. Respectfully, I thought we were on the same page."

"The same page," Lucifer repeated, leaning forward in his seat.

"Tell me, kid, does being on the same page include you admitting your mistake today?"

"I don't make mistakes."

My phone went off from my pocket, blaring "Hells Bells." Lucifer placed his own phone flat on my desk, since he was the one who had called me, and ended it. "Subtle," he said.

I rubbed the back of my neck and silenced the device. *Damnit.* He knew about that too.

"Whatever, man. I broke things off with her as David. Got her all sad and vulnerable, just like you wanted, and yeah, I forgot to turn my ringer off. She put two and two together, so I had to save face with some bullshit story. Who cares?"

The temperature of the office rose to a sweltering level, enough to make my vision spin. I loosened the collar of my shirt with my finger, the heat in question coming from within me. Lucifer's glare sparked to flame with condemning rage.

"*You* care," he said suddenly, and there was a split second where I didn't know what to say back. "You *like* her."

An irritated smirk sliced across my mouth. "You have misconstrued my actions as affectionate. Faith is not my type—"

"You've lost your touch, kid—"

"Do *not* patronize me like I am a child," I snarled, my temper flaring with a whip of shadow in the air. "I've existed on this planet far too long to have crushes on mortals." My head tilted to one side as I lazed back into my chair again. "No offense . . . "

Lucifer lunged toward me, launching himself over the desk. His hand bit into my throat, pinning me immobile against the chair, and I just sat there, unafraid, indifferent.

"For centuries, I have treated you like you are my own son," Lucifer said, looming over me. "Together, we have lived a life of luxury and power, but *do not* forget how this alliance began."

"Take a joke, Lu," I said. "People will start to think you're getting sensitive in your prehistoric age—"

Lucifer wrung my neck in a vise grip. His power lapped across my skin like molten flames, searing a layer of my skin underneath my sleeves. I grinned like a masochist basking in the anguish, fangs clenched together and bared, daring him to do his worst. He squeezed my throat harder, and even though I didn't need to breathe, the innate mortal instinct snapped into place, and I could feel the sensation of suffocating. I clamped down on his forearm to try to tear him off me. It was useless. He was too strong. I conceded, albeit reluctantly, with an animalistic snarl.

"I'm sorry," I choked out. "I'm sorry, all right!"

Lucifer's hand released me at once. I quickly recovered to show no outward weakness, though I was humiliated and seething inside. He'd crushed my esophagus like a goddamn soda can with little effort. When was the last time I'd indulged on souls? I couldn't let myself get weak like this. Not around Lucifer.

Back behind my desk, Lucifer uncapped my bottle of "whiskey" and poured it into a glass. He took a sip and grimaced. "Iced tea. You're a little shit, you know that?"

I kept silent, still simmering with rage, my jaw wired shut to resist all the snarky, venomous comments rampant in my vindictive brain. Immortal or not, an archangel of Lucifer's age could tear my body limb from limb with ease and scatter my remains in all seven continents to slowly mend back together. Not that I'd personally tortured someone in that way . . .

"You and I, we have an understanding," Lucifer said. "Don't you want revenge? Don't you want freedom? Without her, you know I cannot lift your Seven Deadly Sins curse."

The grand illusion that our alliance was equal shattered centuries ago, after I'd struck a deal with the old Devil. I was twice cursed: my death curse, and the Seven Deadly Sins curse. In exchange for helping Lucifer secure a prophecy, he had promised to free me from the Seven Deadly Sins, which bound my soul to the realm of Heaven. It forced me to use my powers to collect all mortal souls and distribute them for the lucrative business of the afterlife.

Lucifer carved a shape on my desk with his talon. If I failed him, that single talon could cleave my entire body in half, black blood and gore pouring from the gash. He'd drag me to Hell and hang me up by my spine with my intestines spilling out. Where I'd stay, cursed, unable to feed and slowly mummifying, trapped in my own harrowing thoughts as I lost my mind. More than I already had.

"Bring me her soul by midnight tomorrow," Lucifer said. "On All Hallows' Eve."

"Your wish is my command, Your Majesty."

He vanished in a fit of flames.

Rage lengthened my fangs. I gripped my desk with one hand and chucked the whole fixture across the office with a menacing roar. It smashed into the television and blew a massive hole in the wall into the vacant office next door.

He'd hung my weakness over my head. He'd baited me like a fucking helpless child. I was no child. *I was two thousand years old.* Prowling back and forth, I tried to control my wrath before I tore this entire room apart and then took it to the streets. My talons had already extended from my fingertips, tearing through my gloves, and I could feel my *other side* purring to be let out.

I braced my hands on the wall and hung my head as I tried to calm myself. Faith's art portfolio lay open at my feet amongst a mess of files. My lip curled as I bent down to pick it up.

The painting of the willow tree.

There was too much on the line to let another deity take

advantage of her power. I could not let her get away. No matter how much she'd despise me once she found out the truth.

This is what you wanted.

I turned with her portfolio in hand and caught a glimpse of my reflection in the tinted windowpane. Sharp, cruel features repelling any signs of life, like cold marble. Hunger had hunted and killed the green hues in my mismatched eyes, draining them to an onyx black. It chilled me to the bone.

How I looked exactly like my father then.

The willow tree slipped from my fingertips, and I went back.

Back to my death.

I stood alone in the darkness of the corridors of the gladiator arena, torches flickering in the stale, humid space. Drums rolled out in a slow, rhythmic march. I felt no adrenaline. No fear. Nothing at all.

My hand clenched against the hilt of my sword, the familiar grip of my weapon giving me enough strength to trudge forward. Sunlight slanted into the corridor and chaos erupted, a roar of a crowd so blaringly loud, I swore the ground beneath my feet trembled. I sauntered down the corridor into the rowdy arena with a modest wave to the crowd.

Golden sunlight bounced off my armor, the shield down my right arm, and the designs along my helmet shifting color to black. I slashed my sword through the air and in a grand display of skill, spun the weapon around my body. The crowd's shrieking was deafening, having traveled from all over Rome to see the renowned "Dru the Beast" now in this arena.

I prowled to the center of the performance area and posed with a wide stance and a proud, erect posture. Then I feigned a smile at their heartless faces. The performance, the lively armor, it was all an act, an unwavering mask I'd worn for years as a slave to the game.

Once, in a moment of weakness, I'd *begged* those mortals, pleaded, for someone—anyone to see. See me for a human being. See the scars on my ankles and wrists. See how I'd tried to rise from this hell, and how my own father would pull me back down. What a waste, to beg humanity to save me. Mortals turned a blind eye to suffering for the sake of their own entertainment.

Today, my mask wavered. For beneath my hard-wearing exterior was a decimated soul so tortured it craved pain.

Unspeakable grief had stunned my heart into a complete state of numbness. For days, I'd wandered around Rome like an empty corpse. I'd lost *everything*. Everything, in a series of tribulations and deaths so sudden and swift they felt like cruel vanishing acts, leaving me questioning both my existence and the creators who had put me on my path.

Why me? I'd been torn limb from limb with everything still intact. I'd fallen to my knees, defeated by a power far out of my control, that left me with only the flicker of fading memories and the waning ghosts of people I should have held on to tighter. To be so shattered with grief you forget how to breathe. To live. Frightening is the man who has nothing left to lose.

"Dru the Beast! Dru the Beast! Dru the Beast!"

My insides churned with disgust at these sadistic people. They'd get their thrilling game today.

The drums rolled for the challenger.

My sorrow had ironically led me here. Back to the macabre games that had torn me from a normal childhood. Yes, this was where I planned to die, where I would coerce my opponent to take my life.

The challenger marched out from an opposite entrance. He ventured to the center of the elliptical area and faced off for battle.

This other gladiator, the challenger, stood a handful of inches shorter than my almost seven-foot height. Although he was slighter in stature and wore iron panels not as extravagantly detailed as mine, he held a certain confidence over my abilities. He didn't have bands around his ankles. He wore plain leather shoes. His obsidian cape, strewn into the armor on his shoulders, flogged the hot air with fine, thick material that seemed kingly.

The thunderous crowd roared on with eagerness for battle. A gate lifted into the arena and in came two midnight jaguars. Feeling their intense fear was a sixth sense that lifted the shackles of my awareness. They'd been taunted more than usual today.

The challenger did not seem fazed by the wild animals either. I played the part of my celebrity role and fell into a defensive position. The animals circled the perimeter of the arena at full sprint, clawing at the walls and howling, earning heckles from the crowd. Food was hurled into the pit, hitting the poor animals, and aggravating them further. Men with spears ran into the arena and corralled the jaguars to the center of the space. Petrified and riled up, the feline beasts turned their attention onto us, the fighters. They stalked closer to us, their heads lowered and ears flat.

I sank to the ground to mirror their movement, my golden plate guard scraping against old scar tissue over my heart. The remnants of three years before, when I'd tried to take my life in the river outside my home. As I reached my last moments, I'd thought better—I wanted to live, and I tried with all my might to surface from the water. The boulder I'd strapped to my back had done its job, and my feet slipped on the wet stones beneath the water. My mother had discovered my body later that day on the riverbank and made an ultimate sacrifice. She'd used the unpredictability of black magic to resurrect me by combining my heart with a cat's.

One of the jaguars charged across the arena toward me. I faced the animal as a predator myself, low to the ground and patient. I waited until the last second to bring up my sword, slashing the first jaguar with an explosion of thick ruby liquid and fur. The injury would satisfy the arena without killing the animal, an unspoken rule for most of the gladiators. Landing inelegantly, the jaguar rolled onto its feet and hurried away from me, blood trailing behind it. The injured feline was captured by the men with spears, chained, and hauled out of the arena alive.

The second cat stalked behind me, spring-loaded to pounce. I'd been distracted by my own thoughts, so I'd miscalculated its attack, and it knocked me hard to the ground. Its claws burrowed into the flesh of my shoulders and tried to rip apart tendons. As I was mauled, my challenger with the black cape made no move to help me, instead circling the scene with slow, calculated steps. I held open the animal's jaw with my bare bloodied hands and planned on wrestling the cat into exhaustion so it would be pulled out of the arena. The other competitor had plans of his own, as he stepped in and speared the animal through the top of its skull.

I staggered back in shock, hot blood running down my leg and into the sand. Edging toward the dying animal, I crouched down to comb my fingers through the animal's fur as it fought to live.

Turning my head away, I twisted my hands to break the animal's neck and end its pain. The competitor's boastful laugh grated down my spine.

I drew my sword and charged at the competitor at full force. Our massive blades crashed together. We shifted our weight as our weapons sliced through the air again, dodging each other at nearly equal skill levels. However, I had neither slept nor eaten enough to endure the physical demand of sword fighting, and the challenger's attacks were ceaseless and exhausting. He swung his blade out with inhuman speed, the blur of the weapon coming down hard as it carved a deeper wound into the claw-marked lesions I already had. My teeth grated as I clamped a hand over the wound, my vision strobing in and out.

When I looked up, the challenger vanished. I spun fast, and he was somehow standing behind me, his cape billowing out over the sun like a dark doom as he sprang toward me. He kicked out a foot and connected with my chest armor, hurling me back with a powerful force into the compacted sand. I landed hard on my injured shoulder with an agonizing scream, and the crowd swiftly switched their favor to the conquering gladiator with deafening cries.

The gladiator in the black cape turned toward the crowd, acknowledging their eruption of applause.

"What kind of man harms a helpless animal?" I shouted. "You are no *man* at all!"

Charging at him with my sword, we collided again. This time, I gained ground, negating each of his attacks, unleashing the full strength of my body into each hard blow.

The challenger bled from multiple small wounds, an oily black blood drenching the sand that I did not care to notice, and soon his weapon was knocked out of his hand. Tears blurred my vision as I carved the air with my entire body, slicing into his forearm between his armor sleeves. He buckled to the ground, clutching the space of skin where I'd cut him to the bone. One look at his injury, and his head went back. He'd fainted.

The crowd went crazy.

Energy pulsed in the air, retribution beckoning, raising the hair at my nape like a sixth sense. Slowly, I bent to pick up the challenger's sword. My shoulders stiffened, a powerful sensation washing over me from the moment my fingers clenched the handle. A key clicking into place inside a lock. My head tilted down and I dragged the rough pads of my fingers along the unusual engravings in the hilt and the metal of the weapon. As I did so, a dark whisper unfurled inside my mind.

The one you hate the most . . . must die.

Heat flushed my body with the rise of a lethal fever, and my fury amplified with it. I clenched the sword tighter and glared at the unconscious gladiator, imagining his veiled face was my father's. He had killed them. He'd killed them all. And now I'd kill *him*. Kill him for betraying us all, for all the abuse I'd suffered because of him!

"*DRU THE BEAST! DRU THE BEAST!*"

Sweat poured down the sides of my face, the world pulsing in hallucinations. They played out on the arena sand like ghosts on puppet strings. Sinister memories of my youth, my father's constant berating and abuse. His fist colliding with my small, boyish body and knocking me down. I'd blocked it out, blocked it all out, but now his wrongdoings were coming back to life, the fury of a childhood robbed fueling an uproar of retribution.

The mirage rippled, and I saw *myself* across the arena. False fabrications of me, as the full-grown man I was now, driving my sword through my father's heart. Mutilating his body until it was unrecognizable. The engraved sword grew hot and wavered in my hand as these thoughts spiraled out of control.

Your father destroyed your family, hissed a serpentine voice, *and you let him run away. Coward. You died in that room with your wife and unborn child. If anyone deserves to die, it's him. It's Malphas Cruscellio. Do it. Kill him, kill him now!*

I lifted the sword with a madman's intention, when my head turned, and in the reflection of the weapon, I saw my eyes. They were consumed in black with filaments branching outward like veins, and I recognized I was not myself. I threw down the weapon at once, feeling as though a vise had released my soul.

The sound of the arena warped back into full volume, and the sorrow tucked deep inside my heart exploded. My shoulders collapsed inward, a wheezed breath escaping me in a pained sob.

Weak, broken, pathetic. I'd never killed anyone before, and I'd never planned to. It was an oath I had made myself long ago.

I stared at the fallen sword, fear stricken at what it had done to me. Something vile, inherently evil had beckoned me from the blade, and how seamlessly it had sunk its fangs into my vulnerable mind. *And I liked it.*

Like a coward, I ran. Hurried toward the corridor to escape the arena. Faster, faster. The civilians in the stands became violent, boo-ing and heckling, throwing objects into the arena. Scorching heat rippled off the sand and their faces transformed, undulating between human and demented creatures. Creatures possessed by wrath.

It halted me in my tracks

Something was terribly wrong.

I turned to look over my shoulder. The silent challenger, who was very much awake, lifted his head. His injured arm mended back to normal, stretched out toward the ground. My heart hammered as the sinister engraved blade slid across the sand to him without any touch. The challenger rose from the ground as though in slow motion, his head lowered like a bull's before he kicked off, hurtling toward me in a blur.

I twisted fully around, reacting in a blur to his attack. Shock swept over my features. It happened so fast. My sword pierced clean through a gap in his armor to his heart. I freed the hilt of the blade, mortified. The veiled man fell back, his black cape sweeping out beneath him. The dark material transformed into a cloak, rippling against the sand like water as his body slammed into the ground, and his helmet came tumbling off.

I gazed into the challenger's endless black eyes and stumbled back, shock choking out my breath. "Father."

The one who had stolen everything from me. My heart pounded as I relived the tragedy in an instant. Him, standing over my dead mother, who lay in a broken heap on the floor. And my wife, and our child, who should have been born that night, unrecognizably torn apart in her birthing bed.

The blood dripping from the knife in my father's hand was the final blow. An unfathomable betrayal. I'd hurled myself toward him, but my father was a powerful demigod of manipulation. His power had brought me down to my knees, where I broke.

Inconsolable cries of grief had stretched out like a howl. Why? Why would he do this? I'd begged him to kill me too.

My father had placed his hand on my cheek, an ostensibly loving gesture I had never received from him. "My greatest offense is my most painful secret," he'd said. "A secret, which I must take to the grave."

Black eyes crueler and colder and emptier than ever before. And his words, those cryptic words. They stained my memory with unresolved mystery. I'd felt his power pour into me again, and my vision had faded to black.

When I'd awoken the next day, lying on the floor, the blood and the gore of the scene had been cleaned, but my loved ones remained dead, wrapped divinely in my mother's precious silk cloth. My father was gone. He'd left on horseback, leaving me to my own devices. Leaving me to bury these three precious souls, and my own heart, six feet underground.

Now I was here, in the arena, feeling as if I were separated from my body. My father, who I'd perceived as indestructible, dying, by *my* hand, *my* sword through his chest. And again, I asked the gods, *Why?* Why had he returned to fight me here? Why had he thrown himself at my sword? Why had he killed my family?

"Alexandru." His weak, raspy voice drew me to the present. The hard-hearted general, doling out edicts for his young soldier. This death should not have affected me. Malphas Cruscellio was no father. But he was always there, and now he would not be. I would be truly alone.

"Hurry, my son. Come closer . . . "

Tearing off my helmet, I collapsed to my knees. "I am here, Father. I am listening."

"In weeping, find strength in the root," he whispered. "How sharp, the willow's slender branch."

I leaned back to look at his face. His onyx eyes shone wet, and he was dead. Gone to the void of the afterlife, though his riddle lingered like a warning.

Blackness crawled from beneath his body. The hair at the back of my nape lifted, and I crawled backward as I tracked the large shadow slinking across the ground. It stretched along the sand, forming a dark apparition of a man as he rose to a looming height with thunderous laughter.

The draping hood of the cloak veiled all his face, except for the crescent smirk across his pale mouth. "Do you remember me, Alexandru?" the creature asked, mockery lacing his serpentine words. "Trapped in that mirror in the woods?"

Pressure broke at the center of my skull. I stood in an unhurried way, seized by fear.

"*Ahrimad,*" I said.

"Yes, it is I, my friend." He motioned with his hand, shadows spiraling in the air as a blade, the corrupted blade that had been in my father's hand, manifested into his. "I hunted Malphas down to latch to his tepid soul. To bring him here, for you. He put up a mighty fight, indeed."

My chest rose and fell with rapid breaths. "After all of these years . . . "

"Our deal remains."

"Does this mean . . . I have your power now?"

"I'm afraid not, child," Ahrimad answered. "For I am a deity and we do love our tricks. When we first encountered each other, I knew you were different. There was a greatness inside your soul, so much potential, you see. Had you killed your father of your own volition, then yes, I would be bound to this prophecy. This balance of good and evil my soul must abide, but I never had any intention of giving you my power. It is why I weaved Malphas's fate for you and *threw him onto your sword.*"

Thoughts swirled too fast to process it all. "I would have never—I would have never killed him."

"Everyone is capable of taking a life. You needed a push, my friend." Ahrimad's sinister grin widened, his teeth too sharp and too predatorial to be a man's. I could feel his shadowed eyes peering inside me, watching my soul wither from the inside out.

None of this could be real. How could it? I'd lost everything. I'd killed my own father. Now I was face-to-face with death.

The arena communicated their displeasure. The precious entertainment had paused. I tilted my head down to look at my father's vacant corpse, perspiration and tears dripping into the dry sand. My eyes squeezed shut as I reined in all feeling, all the pain crushing inside of me, and turned it into rage.

"You *fiend!*" I bellowed. "You trickster!"

"How I love the sound," Ahrimad said, shadows snapping over his shoulders like whips. "You should never have gone into those woods and released me from my prison." When he strode forward, I tried to retreat away, only my feet did not obey. "I bring only death and darkness to this crippled little realm. But you see, Alexandru, the world *needs* creatures like me. And I must thank you." He stopped to stand in front of me, my breaths sharp and quick with adrenaline. "For I lived in pure torment in the other world, unable to feed on the mortals, slowly mummifying. My vile heart would give anything for another meal—even risk my existence in equivalence for your help. I simply . . . could not resist another game. The temptation of ruining your pathetic, innocent life fueled my monster—

"Enough!" I shouted, my muscles straining as I finally tore myself from his hold and shuffled away. Ahrimad's head tilted, as though I'd caught him off guard. "Enough with your raging mania!" I fisted the hilt of my weapon and drew it with a slice of gleaming metal. "Draw your sword and fight me!"

"Foolish half-mortal. You *dare* challenge Death to a duel?" He laughed low in his throat and lifted his head. My sword wavered as sinister amber eyes blazed beneath the darkness of his hood. "It is a fight you will lose, child."

"You *forget*." I glided around Ahrimad, our footwork mirroring each other's. "I am no longer that naïve little boy you met in the woods. And you, my dear friend, forget, my mother was a powerful witch who'd practiced black magic, and I was her protégé." I planted my feet in a wide stance, gripping my sword tighter. "Draw your weapon."

Ahrimad kept his blade limp at his side. "Make your move, boy."

I charged toward him, though he disappeared in a black mist. The darkness he'd left behind hissed and twirled like a tornado and I was trapped at the eye. Within the shadow, I saw the dead bodies of my family, lying together in a gory, bloody mess. I wrenched free from the shadows with a panicked cry, Ahrimad's cruel laughter elevating over the crowd's screams of joy. Why weren't the mortals afraid? What had he done to them?

Ahrimad's blade came down in a skilled movement, and I felt off-kilter as I swung out to protect myself. My eyes widened as my weapon cracked beneath the blow.

Ahrimad lashed out, slamming a hurl of shadow into my body.

My body flew across the arena again and I landed hard, my shoulder dislocating as I rolled three times before landing in a broken heap. The arena exploded into applause, the sand blistering hot against my enraged cheek. Of course, they wanted me dead. The mortals were never on my side, and I was never one of them. They wanted blood. They wanted death—I thought I had wanted it too. Nonetheless, here I was, fighting to live. The ironic turn of events made me laugh, a lurid, insane cackle, blood oozing down my chin. I planted a foot on the ground and rose to my towering frame at the center of the arena.

"Such a sad, pitiful sight," Ahrimad said. "You have given these mortals your whole life, and your sanity. Still, they root against you."

Ahrimad threw out a hand, and my torso hunched inward as though I'd been punched in the stomach. I remained where I stood, paralyzed, as I felt an invisible force climb up my chest and grip within—his power clutching my soul.

"We will give them a show indeed," Ahrimad said, and then he lifted his palm.

Gasps of tight breaths left my lungs as my feet levitated off the ground. Now the arena had died down, the civilians stunned by the sight. My limbs locked in an inflexible position, my spine arching away from the ground as his power lifted me higher and higher. Dark clouds pummeled over the sky, creating an opaque cover over the sun as the blood rushed fast to my head.

Ahrimad's laughter bellowed over the mighty wind. His lean, cloaked frame strode upside down in my vision, his hand gripping the sword at his side like an executioner. The weapon glowed amber along the hilt and blade, the engravements forming an inverted picture. Coldness crawled over my skin. The etchings were weeping branches. Branches of a willow tree.

In weeping, find strength in the root.

My father's final words echoed as I remembered what led up to me freeing Ahrimad from the willow. How as a boy, I'd been drawn deep into the forest and discovered the ancient weapon buried in the ground. How it'd summoned *me* of all people, miles out from my home. The blade had rested perfectly in my small boyish palm, and I'd felt . . . unstoppable.

"Any last words, Alexandru?"

My vision dizzied as I tried to attain a deep breath, my spine still curved over the ground. I strained to free my uninjured arm from the tight position locked at my side. "I never imagined Death to be so short."

Ahrimad snarled and pulled his weapon behind him with the intention to sever my head, but I'd already freed my arm, my hand snapping out in the air. I knew not what I was doing, the sheer will of survival taking precedent over everything else. I imagined the blade in my hand instead of his. I willed it to happen with all my might and everything I had left. On the downward arc to my head, Ahrimad's features strained, his arms freezing in midair. The blade tore from his hand and landed in my vise grip.

His power released me at once, my body turning over in the air before I landed on all fours.

"Impossible," Ahrimad whispered, horror lacing his voice. "The blade has chosen *you* over me."

I rose to my towering height, the hurricane of violence in my head silencing doubt. Raw power breathed into me like a second chance, and I cast aside all thoughts but one: Death would not defeat me this time. I drove forward, slicing through shadow as it formed like a wall of darkness around Ahrimad. It grabbed onto my armor, hooking into my skin again with claws like knives to remind me of everything I'd lost. This time, I embraced it.

Ahrimad's body started to dissipate, waning away into a black mist, but the speed of my wrath was faster. I shoved through the shadow with all my might and thrust my blade forward. A battle cry exploded from my throat as I went down with Ahrimad, the shadows beneath his hood willowing away.

Picture my surprise when the deity of death's identity was not monstrous, and instead the face of an ordinary man. His dim amber eyes were lined with dark coal, olive-toned skin marked by branchy tattoos.

"Clever child," Ahrimad said. "You know not what you have done."

Then he grinned, slow and damning, revealing a mouthful of fangs like knives.

I stumbled to my feet, pure agony ripping across my body. Panicked, I gazed down at my armor and rapidly shrugged out of the heavy equipment. My skin had paled to that of a corpse. Directly over my heart, where that old, thick scar tissue lay, black filament veins pulsed outward.

"What is happening to me?"

"You have won our game, Alexandru. *Death* is what you hated the most. Take mine life, and with it, my wretched power. It is yours now, after all."

Pressure grew inside my head. Staggering to the side, I gripped my skull as if to keep the bone from exploding and crumbled to all fours. Pressing my forehead to the ground, I writhed against the earth screaming. Nails split open and extended into talons; muscles bulged and tautened in unbearable spasms. I lifted my head with a gulp of air, bloodied tears seeping into my dry mouth. I was thirsting for air now, begging my failing lungs to work. Suddenly, I stopped breathing altogether, but I was still conscious. Confusion knit my brows as I gazed down at my forearm, my skin color altering back to its normal bronze tan shade.

"I do not feel . . . the urge to breathe."

"Because you are dead," Ahrimad said weakly, as oily blood trickled out of the corners of his mouth. "Undead. Your body will painfully change. You will have an endless hunger in your stomach. *Nothing* will satisfy it. You will have to feed on mortals. An eternal monster of Hades unlike any other. Cursed to steal away the souls of the living." His breathing hitched, as he choked out, "Cursed . . . to *live*, Alexandru Cruscellio."

I gripped the sand with my hands and held on. A bellowing roar was unleashed from deep within me as the nightmare continued to unfurl, and I was reborn . . .

The memory dissipated in my mind as I flicked my lighter closed and inhaled from another rolled cigarette. I stepped up to the floor-to-ceiling windows and looked out into the modern labyrinth of New York City.

That was when I was alone against the world, and the world was not merciful. I was its pawn and it continued to beat me while I was down. I'd lost myself to the madness and became what I hated the most. Once, I was just a young man, unprepared for the cards I'd been dealt. I let fate grind me under its heel. Now I was a monster who held the deck. I could screw the whole world over and never look back. I felt nothing. How could I?

And yet . . .

My phone vibrated in my pocket.

One recent missed call from Faith. Five missed calls and a voicemail from one of my Fallen soldiers. "We were attacked by Malphas. Two of ours are dead. Faith encountered him and managed to get away. She ran into a bookstore in Pleasant Valley called the Crossroads. It's guarded by powerful wards and built on hallowed ground. We can't get close. Please advise."

Only one warlock recurrently opened up a bookshop under that title. He went by Ace, just Ace. A powerful clairvoyant and magic user. I hadn't seen that bastard in centuries. He'd opened up shop in Pleasant Valley, of all places.

Coincidences did not exist. Not with clairvoyants. Ace knew about Faith.

I crushed the phone in my hand.

Shadows curled around my shoulders and mended into my cloak. Lunging forward, I vanished into the dark and reappeared midsprint on the roof of the D&S Tower. My combat boot pushed off the concrete ledge, massive wings unfurling from my back as I dove down into the dusky city.

XVII

FAITH

"How'd you get into this room?"

I whirled around to find a short, angry woman. She looked a few years older than me with high cheekbones and bright-amber eyes that burned with a fire behind each iris. I hoped those were contacts. A mess of wild brown curls spiraled past a slim waist to the leather belt at her hips, where she kept two sheathed weapons.

"I-I was trying to find an employee to ask to use your phone. Mine's dead." I said, waving my cell. Now that I had to focus on coherent sentences, my mind felt hazy, like I'd been awoken from some sort of trance. "I have an emergency."

"An emergency?" Her voice was mellow, softer, not quite fitting her harsh appearance, so I had to conclude from her unwelcoming affect this was not the place to make a phone call. It was time to cut and run.

When I went to maneuver around her, she blocked my way. Her hand rested on the gun on her belt. I had to think up a way out of this, fast.

"Listen, I don't want any trouble," I said. "My friend is in danger. He'll die if I don't get help. I was looking for a phone in here, but I seem to have gotten . . . off-track."

Her eyes narrowed. In a flash, she slid a gun out of its holster and pointed it at me. "Sit down and shut up." She motioned the weapon toward the palm-reading table.

"Holy crap, okay!" I walked to the table, lowering myself into my seat. "Listen, I only have ten bucks in my wallet and a piece of gum that I found at the bottom of my backpack. The gum might be warm because I'm sitting on it." She continued to glare coldly at me. "Please don't kill me, I'm poor."

"Nobody is going to kill anyone, *ma chère*," announced a rich, French voice.

My eyes unglued from the end of the crazy woman's gun. On the opposite side of the room stood a young, strikingly handsome man. He leaned against a golden cane straight out of a storybook. It had a large octagon-shaped clear crystal at the top of it and carved foreign symbols down the shaft. The cane itself was mesmerizing, almost more so than the man that came with it. He wore a luxurious deep-purple suit and had shoulder-length stark white hair with a multitude of colors at the ends. Various ornaments and rings layered around his neck and his fingers, and he wore a top hat, which matched the color of his suit. It was tipped over his face, concealing his eyes.

"Do not blame yourself for your friend," continued the mysterious man. "The Fates work in mysterious ways. Thomas will survive and you will meet him again."

How could he possibly know about Thomas?

The man limped closer to me, favoring his left leg. I pressed back into the chair. Noticing my recoil, he stopped, and removed his hat, revealing abnormally bright violet eyes. Just like the eye on that mystic pamphlet. "On my honor, you have no reason to be afraid. Not here." He held his hat to his chest and bent low at the waist in a bow, and then placed it back on his head. "I've been expecting you."

"Expecting me?" I switched my attention back to the woman beside him and the barrel of the gun pointed at me. "For what? Target practice?"

Frenchy looked sharply at the amber-eyed woman. "Put the gun down, *ma moitié*! This girl is our guest!"

"She was snooping through your things," Crazy said. "Plus, she smells strange."

"I was not *snooping*. I was . . . browsing. As for your second comment . . . " I sniffed at my armpit. "I can't defend myself there. I've been running around a lot today and I nervous sweat."

"I told you a special guest was arriving today," Frenchy said to Crazy.

"You did not tell me that."

"I left you a Post-it."

"And you wonder why we have poor communication?"

I shifted awkwardly in my seat. Hearing these two loons bicker back and forth was the last thing I needed right now. As soon as I had an opening, I was gonna bolt.

Frenchy winced and transferred his weight to his other side, leaning differently on his cane. I wondered what sort of injury or disease he suffered from to need a cane at such a young age.

"Trixie is my security," he explained. "I own many valuable items, and we've had a few break-ins over the years. She can get a little overly cautious."

Crazy, now Trixie, tucked the weapon back into her belt. "Sorry."

"It's cool," I squeaked.

"Wonderful, now we can all start over," said the man. "You may call me Ace." Frenchy, now Ace, offered me a hand. I hesitantly reached to shake it and he kissed the back of my knuckles. The press of his lips burned, like a Totino's Pizza Roll straight out of the microwave. I wanted to sharply pull my hand back, when those electric violet eyes bore into mine, and I was held motionless. Every muscle in my body relaxed, all my worries and my guilt about Thomas sinking into a deep abyss.

"I already know who you are, Faith," Ace said with a mischievous smile. "I know why you've come here too. People can't hide much from me, you see."

"You're the psychic."

"The psychic title is for the money." He gently released my hand. "Have to make a living somehow, besides selling old books and crystals. To you, I am the warlock."

If the Angel of Death, demons, and Carrion Angels could exist, why couldn't a warlock?

"Where's your beard, wand, and pointy hat with stars on it?" I asked.

Trixie snickered. Since she'd laughed at my joke, I decided she wasn't a trigger-happy psychopath and had just been doing her job earlier.

Ace gave me a flat look. "Ha-ha. I'm not a wizard. Wizards don't exist." A smirk broke free on his stony face. "Although, I've worn a pointy hat with stars on it once or twice, but I was highly intoxicated." He lowered himself into the chair in front of me, removed his top hat, and raked his fingers through his colorful hair. "Let's begin. Trixie, *mon ange*, please wait outside."

She obediently left the room.

"Wait, begin what?"

Ace smiled like a fox. "Do not worry, *ma chère*. I am going to perform a reading and go from there."

"Um, hard pass. Thanks for the offer though."

"If you think you came here out of chance, you are wrong. Those who enter my shop enter for one reason and one reason only. They are at a crossroads." He leaned forward on his elbows, resting his ring-covered hands palm up on the table on either side of the crystal ball. An open invitation to put my hands over his. As oddly tempting as it was to accept, I kept my hands where they were, clasped tightly in my lap.

"A crossroads . . . " For all I knew, this guy was a con artist picking at straws. "Great pitch you got there. Can I borrow your phone?"

"Do you believe in a force greater than yourself, Faith?"

I let out a mirthless laugh. "At this point, I'd believe just about anything. But meeting a warlock who conveniently has all the answers I need is kind of a stretch for my mental tolerance."

"Non croyant de la magie," Ace said with a wry smile. "You doubt my power. Will you allow me to prove myself to you?"

"Fine." I shrugged. "Hit me with your best—" I cut my sentence short because my hair had whipped around my face from a gust of air and the candles surrounding us lit one by one.

"You've been attacked twice by demons," Ace said, looking me dead in the eye. "Just today, you've caught a glimpse of what makes you so exceptional. You're attempting to block it out because it terrifies you that you might not be as ordinary as you'd hoped. You fear for your loved ones' safety more than ever." He paused and rubbed his jaw, as if figuring out a crossword puzzle. "The Angel of Death has gotten in your head and vice versa, and now you feel him and others manipulating you in more ways than one. You don't know what to trust, including your instinct."

I stared at him, open-mouthed. "Whoa."

"Nonbelievers are my favorite to impress." He curled his fingers on the table, insinuating he wanted me to place my hands in his. "Shall we continue?"

Coming to terms with the fact that I was in front of yet another supernatural being, my heart started to pound in my chest. "Can you . . . can you give me a moment? I'm a little nauseous."

"You're nauseous because you're about to get your period." Ace scrunched up his face, grimacing. "I really wish I didn't know things like that. Perhaps we should discuss my payment before we jump into this?"

"Listen, man, I already told Lara Croft out there, I don't have any money."

Ace lifted his chin and his irises lightened from violet to lilac, like holographic foil. "I don't want your money, *ma chère*."

Then what the heck did he want?

Shadows danced over the warlock's handsome features and crazy-colored eyes. "What I require is . . . more important to me than money." His accent thickened as his voice dropped lower. "I seek a favor in return for my help. A trade. *Comercio*."

"A favor?" I leaned back in my seat. "What kind of favor?"

"I cannot disclose to you what the favor is. Though, it will not be illegal, sexual, or harm you or any of your loved ones in any way. I am not a man who is true to his word—I *am* my word. The choice is yours. One favor, and I will give you what you want most: answers. This is quite the barter, *Mademoiselle* Williams, especially considering my own personal information on the Angel of Death."

"You know him?"

"I've known Death since he was human." Those violet eyes darkened. "We were friends, once." Ace produced a small business card from the inside of his suit and flicked it into the air. It landed perfectly in front of me. An ace of spades. The surface shimmered, revealing his business and contact information in fancy cursive. "Although I understand your hesitation in trusting me, I feel you would be making a grave mistake leaving here without my help. Please, at least take my card."

I picked up the ace of spades, his warning echoing in my head. Perhaps all the answers were sitting right in front of me. If I didn't accept this help from Ace, I had a feeling, by the dread churning sourly in my gut, there would be consequences. Consequences I could not afford right now.

At this point, I had nothing left to lose.

"No need," I said, flattening the card on the table with my palm. "You have yourself a deal, Ace."

"*Fantastique, ma chère.* Once we begin, neither of us will be able to leave this room, no matter the circumstances. Not until the crystal has cleared. Breaking our connection could harm either one of us. Do you understand?"

"What if something goes horribly wrong?"

Ace pursed his lips. "Do you have good health insurance?"

"Let's do this," I said, shaking my head at the whole ludicrous situation. "I'm done thinking. Do your thing before I change my mind."

"Silence, please." Pulling my hands slightly closer to the center of the table, Ace bowed his head and shut his eyes. All I could hear was the crackle and flicker of the candles. He was quiet for a while, until he whispered foreign words under his breath.

He flinched. A candle blew out to my right.

"*L'esprits.*" The warlock's lids slowly opened, and he raised his head up. His irises had morphed from a bold violet to a coal black, and I stiffened. Then he spoke in a monotonous, dry voice unlike his own. "You have been given the Kiss of Death. There are consequences to this. A part of your soul has died, replaced by a fragment of Death's immortal one."

"Would that make me . . . immortal?"

"Not exactly." I couldn't remember the last time Ace had blinked. He was looking in my direction, but not quite into my eyes. It was as if he were torn between two worlds, interpreting what he was seeing to me in the *elsewhere*. "You are not immortal. You are not mortal either. You are . . . in-between."

Another candle blew out. *Okay. This was a bad idea.*

Ace flinched and his head snapped sharply to the side. His hands gripped mine tightly.

"What's happening?" I asked.

Ace remained locked in a rigid position, his breathing shallow for a few seconds, before he was able to turn his head back to me. "Hurry, look within the crystal. Tell me what you see."

Although I was shaking at this point, I did as he said. The liquid inside the crystal ball swirled around into obsidian smoke and my heart hammered in my chest.

"I see . . . darkness. Nothing."

"Impossible." Ace's voice was now bottomless, distant, as if he were searching for something deeper in that other world. "Your spiritual path is uncertain, which could mean—" His words were cut short, and as his breath hitched, three more candles extinguished. "There is no stopping the evil that is after you. The spirits are all talking at once. Chanting . . . They are chanting, *you are her*!"

"What do they mean I'm her? Who's *her*?"

"*Light.*" His eyes shifted back and forth, as if he were reading something fast. "A pure soul, a girl, wandering between Heaven and Earth, will be pardoned by Death himself, and with her resurrection will come a great power. She will bring with her a war unlike any other, the final fight between Heaven and Hell and the in-between. This evil, which is after you, is the most malicious of the rest. It thirsts for revenge. It cares not for your well-being, but for your purpose, for you will bring to it great power, and an ancient tome, called the *Book of the Dead*. If you do not bind yourself to the one who seeks this grimoire the most, he will kill everyone you love . . . "

"Who? Who will kill everyone I love? Death?"

"Death is but only one who desires your soul," Ace said cryptically.

Panic struck me hard as I tried to pull away from his grasp, but his fingers were like bent steel. One by one, the candles kept going out, as if switched off by a timer.

"Don't!" Ace exclaimed. "Breaking the connection now will hurt us both!"

I took a few harsh breaths. "Ask them how I can stop the Angel of Death."

"To have some power . . . over him . . . you must know his past, and you must know his true name." His hands began to grow limp in mine and the howling wind around us died down. "The link between our world and theirs is weakening. They want to warn you, before it is too late, but I cannot hear their words." Blood trickled from his nose.

"You're bleeding!"

"I'm fine, *mon chou*." Abruptly, the crystal ball in front of us burst into vibrant shades of blue and yellow.

The remaining candles began to flicker out. The crystal ball's swirling black smoke cleared.

A frown creased between Ace's brows. "The spirits tell me you share a similar ability to my clairvoyancy. With touch, you can see into the future and warp into the past through memories. If you can control this, you will be able to use this power without a physical connection. Before we part ways, they want to show you a different truth you seek. A memory of the Angel of Death's, which will help you at your crossroads. Let us channel your gift and see what you are made of."

Images instantly flashed before my eyes.

I fell into oblivion, plunging through darkness.

One by one, sparks of light appeared on a wall, candles hung

up in beautiful ornaments. I stood in a hot, stuffy corridor, a hallway carved from brown stone, crudely lit with torches and candles.
Ahead of me lay a metal gate.

Studying my surroundings, I saw one other person here with me
in this corridor. An enormously tall man, a gladiator. His shoulders
and arms were weapons of their own, yet his waist tapered down with
lean muscle. A gold military helmet curved around his skull, his face,
and a majority of the damp golden mane at the nape of his neck.
Lavish, intricately designed armor adorned his torso and carried
on down his right arm like a shield. The same armor also guarded
his legs. All of the gear was fastened together with brass hooks and
leather that clipped to a thick belt on his waist. The plate on his chest
appeared heavier than the other garments, a perfect sculpted cast of
what was, without a doubt, this man's actual chiseled abs.

Despite his ornate gear, the man's feet were bare. Around his ankles,
blisters and scars lingered, wounds from shackles. I happened to have
done a project about gladiators in honors history and presented a slide
show for a group project on Roman games. I'd learned that although
gladiators were pampered with banquets and massages before a fight
and after a victory, most gladiators were slaves to the death match.

Metal grated against metal up ahead, and the heavy gate lifted
away. Sunlight slanted in and chaos erupted, a roar of a crowd so
blaringly loud, I swore the ground beneath my feet trembled. Drums
rolled outside in a slow, rhythmic march. The gladiator clenched his
hands so hard that veins protruded. He sauntered down the corridor
into the rowdy arena with a modest wave to the crowd. I assumed, by
his grand introduction, he was not only a slave to the death match,
but one of the celebrity fighters.

The gladiator prowled to the center of the performance area and
the crowd's shrieking amplified.

In this place, I had no fear. Based on my experience with the first vision I had, I assumed I could not be seen or harmed, so I felt compelled to get closer to the gladiator. I walked down the corridor toward the arena, and the stone beneath my Converse turned to compacted sand with old bloodstains in various places. Everything about this moment felt real to my senses. The sweltering heat in the air, the humidity as it clung to my skin, the earsplitting noise of the crowd.

People of all ages gathered for the public spectacle, waving rags and other items of clothing in the air. A group of exceptionally giddy women in the front aristocrat area fawned over the gladiator. They jumped up and down with flushed faces, cupping their hands over their mouths to shout. I'd never seen so many people in one spot, sardined together in seating that extended all around the elliptical performance area. In unison, they started chanting the same foreign words over and over again. The longer it went on, the more the language slowly transformed, until I miraculously understood it.

"Dru the Beast! Dru the Beast! Dru the Beast!"

The gladiator, "Dru the Beast," ventured to the center of the elliptical area and faced off with his challenger, who wore a midnight-black riding cloak.

The fight began as a performance of great skill, but when the challenger ruthlessly mutilated a jaguar, Dru the Beast unleashed his fury, which ended with the challenger knocked to the ground.

Dru the Beast picked up his challenger's sword and I prepared for this to end gruesomely. To my astonishment, instead of finishing him off, Dru dropped the weapon with a shaking hand, pivoted, and made the choice to walk away. He didn't want to kill this man. People in the stands booed and heckled, hurling objects and food into the arena.

The fallen challenger, who was very much awake, held out his arm and his sword slid across the sand. He leapt off the ground and charged at Dru the Beast's back, his sword charging orange in a blaze of fire. *What the . . . ?*

Dru twisted around, reacting quickly as he thrust his ordinary-looking sword into the competitor's heart. I watched, paralyzed, as Dru the Beast freed the hilt of the blade. The competitor collapsed again, and this time, as his head hit the ground, his helmet was knocked off, unveiling his identity. Terror choked out my breath. The gladiator in the black cape was Malphas. The raven demigod. His black hair was cut shorter to his head, but he looked exactly the same now as he did in the current world.

"Dru the Beast" caught my eye as he wrenched his helmet off too. Shock and confusion slammed into me again, except this time with a force that almost brought me down to my knees. Suddenly, I was no longer detached from this memory. This was very, very personal. Although his features were much older than in the last memory I saw of him as a boy, I recognized Dru the Beast instantly.

Those mismatched green eyes were a dead giveaway.

The truth strangled my breath. "Dru" was short for "Alexandru." *He* was Death. The gladiator with the chain markings on his ankles. But he wasn't just Death; no, the betrayal cutting deep into my heart was for another reason. I struggled to understand what my eyes were capturing, what my brain was processing as the truth. How Death's identity in his past was all too familiar to me in the future.

Although Alexandru's hair was blond and his eyes were green, the similarities in his features revealed the undeniable. Alexandru was David Star. *Death* was David Star.

Ace was showing me some sort of battle centuries ago between Malphas and Alexandru. Alexandru had killed Malphas in a rage, but why? What had Malphas done to him? Alexandru knelt over Malphas's body, the words exchanged between them too soft for me to decipher. The raw, pained emotion on Alexandru's face as he bent over Malphas's body—it conveyed a deep, complicated grief. They must have known each other well.

I could feel this vision starting to dissolve away, but I held on. I had to know what was next. I had to understand the meaning of this memory.

Blackness crawled from beneath Malphas's body. The hair at the back of my nape lifted as I tracked the large shadows across the ground. They stretched along the sand, forming a dark apparition of a man as he rose to a looming height with thunderous laughter.

Ahrimad. From the willow tree memory. His face was shielded by the draping hood of his cloak, except for the crescent of an evil smirk across his pale mouth.

"Do you remember me, Alexandru?" Ahrimad asked. "Trapped in that mirror in the woods?"

I remembered him. I remembered the deal that was struck between this cruel god and young Alexandru under the willow tree. If Alexandru could kill the person he hated the most, he would have all of Ahrimad's power. Ahrimad had tried to trick Alexandru by throwing Malphas onto his sword, but what he hadn't expected was for *death* to be what Alexandru hated the most. I was rendered speechless as Alexandru got a hold of Ahrimad's sword and destroyed the death deity.

Of course, it was not without consequence. Soon after his sword pierced Ahrimad's heart, pure agony ripped across Alexandru's features. He rapidly shrugged out of the heavy equipment. His skin was riddled with lingering wounds, and directly over his heart lay a jagged line of thick scar tissue. He clutched at the area as black filament veins pulsed out from his heart, spreading across his chest.

The darkness spread up Alexandru's neck to his hair, strands of golden blond fading to jet-black from the roots down. Staggering, he gripped his skull.

With my heart in my throat, I took a step forward. Everything in me screamed to run to Death, despite how pointless it would be. Strange, how I gravitated toward him, even his past self. Seeing him suffer in this way broke my heart. It was too late, regardless. I saw the exact moment Alexandru lost the fight, as he crumpled to all fours.

He writhed against the earth screaming, bloodied tears pouring from his eyes. His lips and face purpled and I watched him die.

"You will have an endless hunger in your stomach. Nothing will satisfy it. You will have to feed on mortals. An eternal monster unlike any other. Damned to steal away the souls of the living. Damned . . . to live . . . Alexandru Cruscellio."

Alexandru gripped the sand with his hands and held on. He released a bellowing roar as redness poured from his gums, his teeth expelled from his mouth one by one. Bone like blades sprouted out from the empty roots in his gums. His already vertical pupils were rapidly dilating now, features sharpening and tightening abnormally against his facial structure. He laughed, a lurid, insane cackle, as blood oozed down his chin. Black filaments bulged in his face as he transformed. Transformed into the cloaked monster I'd known all along—

I was ripped back into Ace's room. The warlock seized in his chair.

"Ace!" I shrieked, lifting out of my seat. His hands held mine so tightly I thought my bones would break. "Oh, God, Ace! *Ace!*"

"Someone is overtaking my mind," he wheezed.

The sensation of coldness licking up my spine made me arch forward, as a sharp sting of pain pooled over the skin of my stomach. My memory snapped to an earlier moment when I'd experienced the same sensation. When I'd first met Death.

"Break the connection!" I shrieked. "It's him, Death is here!"

"His Fallen soldiers are trying to break through my ward," Ace gasped out, and his eyes rolled back in his head. "I don't know how long I can hold them. You can leave this room now, *ma chère*! Go! Through the back door!"

Ace freed my hands.

A blast of energy exploded from the table, knocking me backward. My skull banged against the floor, and my consciousness strobed in and out. Ace sat pinned in his seat; his head sat back at an odd angle that left his throat exposed. His body stiffened, mouth working through strangled words, as if he were fighting against something, *someone*.

Trixie sprinted into the room and froze.

"What's happening?" she asked Ace in hysterics. "What do I do?"

"Find a sacred . . . potion!" he gasped out.

Trixie snapped into action, rifling through various cabinets, knocking bottles all over the place. Without a second thought, I picked myself up and ran toward the door at the back of the room, which lead down a long hallway to another door. I barreled into the crisp night air. My mind was static. Past a back parking lot into a narrow alleyway lead me back to Main Street's sidewalk, where I clicked my key fob until I heard a beep.

I flung myself into my car, threw it into Drive, and sped home, fearing I'd opened Pandora's box.

XVIII

Nighttime closed in as I swung my car into the driveway. When I saw my dad's truck parked outside the garage, and my mother's silhouette in the warm glow of the kitchen window, I released the breath I'd been holding. My family was home safe.

I switched off the ignition and rested my forehead against the wheel, forcing myself to breathe in and out slowly. Adrenaline coursed through my veins like an anxious curse that never ended. I remained in the dark car until the heat from the vents ran out.

Gathering my things, I exited the vehicle and jogged to the front door.

"Look who decided to show up," my father said sternly, as I made my way into the house. He slid off his reading glasses and shut the book in his hands with a thud.

"Hey, Dad." I bolted the door closed and paused, mentally preparing myself for another web of lies. The overwhelming urge to tell my parents everything, or at least what happened to Thomas, ate away at me more than ever. Worried that my father would notice something was wrong, I headed to my room. "I, um, have a lot of homework."

"Wait a minute, young lady." I froze as Dad rose to his feet. "Where have you been? It's late."

"I'm so sorry," I muttered. "I hit traffic."

"Why didn't you call me and let me know? You always call or text when you're late. I called you three times."

"Phone died. Forgot my charger."

Dad analyzed my features with skepticism. "Is something wrong, Faith? You look like you've been crying."

"Nothing's wrong, Dad," I said, brightening up. "I'm just tired."

"Cupcake?"

I whirled around, and my mother stood directly behind me. I yelped, and so did she.

"Jesus on a pogo stick!" Mom exclaimed, putting an oven mitt to her chest. In her other hand, she held a strawberry frosted cupcake with black pumpkin-shaped sprinkles. "You almost gave me a heart attack! What's got you so jumpy?"

"I-I-I—"

"Where were you tonight?" Dad huffed, now standing on the other side of me. I knew I was just given a one-way ticket to the parental interrogation. "Were you with that boy? David Galaxy, or whatever his name is?"

A sinking feeling gripped my stomach. "No, I was studying, Dad."

"How is David anyway?" Mom beamed, wiping at the flour on her cheek. "Why didn't you ask him over? He would have loved these cupcakes! I read the funniest article in *Cosmopolitan* that said his favorite food is frosting."

I laughed in a stunted, nervous way. "That's great, Mom. Thanks for the cupcakes, but I'm not really in the mood for food right now. I'm feeling a little overwhelmed about this exam coming up. Now, if you'll both excuse me, I have to go bury myself in textbooks until dawn. Pray for Faith."

"Oh, no you don't," my dad said, blocking my path. He placed his hands on his hips, attempting an *I'm the man of this household* stance. Instead, he ended up looking like he was striking a Superman pose. "Lisa, your daughter is home three hours past her curfew, on a school night. She's clearly hiding something. Aren't you the least bit concerned?"

"Honey, Faith's eighteen," Mom said, rubbing his arm with an oven mitt. "She has to leave the nest, let her soar."

"I *am* letting her soar," Dad said stubbornly, as if they'd had this conversation plenty of times before. "Toward her *dreams* and her career goals. What I won't let her do is soar into the arms of some celebrity full-grown man who can't keep it in his pants—"

"Henry," Mom fumed, as I wordlessly shook my head in mortification. "Your daughter is mature for her age and responsible. David is nineteen. He's only one year older than her."

Give or take hundreds of years.

"That one-year age gap in boy time is equivalent to a lifetime of messing around with girls and figuring out how to con them," Dad said. "Trust me, Faith. Thirty years ago, I was his age, and in a college fraternity. This guy is a class act Casanova. He thinks with his *you-know-what.*"

Mom smacked Dad with her oven mitt.

"What? Am I wrong? Anyway, Faith knows she isn't allowed to date until she's married." In spite of his anger, Dad still managed to throw in that stale joke he'd used a thousand times before.

"Dad, seriously, I wasn't with David." I thought for sure I was going to have a mental breakdown at any second. "I hung out with

Marcy at Manuel's. We parted ways at around four and I sailed off to study. Had to stay longer than I thought . . . at the library."

"The library, huh?" Dad crossed his arms over his chest. "I see. And where's your backpack?"

I looked down at my small purse, realizing I'd either left my backpack in the car, or worse, abandoned it on Main Street to escape demons.

"Please, it's the twenty-first century. I studied on their online library. We don't read off stone tablets and tell time off of a stick in the sand anymore."

Mom gasped theatrically and pointed at Dad. "Burn!"

"Did you see that David punk or not?" Dad demanded, full-on scowling now. "I'm telling you, that boy is trouble. I can see it in his cocky smirk. Boys only want one thing, Faith."

"It's true," Mom agreed. She cupped her hand over the side of her mouth and thumbed toward Dad. "And it never changes . . . "

"Ew, ew, no. Guys, *please!*" I took a deep breath, splitting my attention between my parents. "For the last time, I was not with David. I grabbed food with Marcy and drove to the library to study! My phone died, and I lost track of time! I love you both and will you please let me go study?"

I maneuvered around my parents and hurried to my room.

My parents must've been shocked by my outburst, but I needed to be alone and fast, before I shattered into little pieces again.

Once in the privacy of my bedroom, I dropped my purse and double-checked my windows to make sure they were locked. I plugged my charger in with a trembling hand. The cracked screen lit up and a text from my Aunt Sarah popped up.

How's that Encyclopedia of Vampires book I gave you? Was it love at first
BITE? Laugh out loud! xoxoxoxoxoxoxoxoxoxo

Not in the right frame of mind to text her back, I set the phone back down, planning on replying later. Skittles strutted out from under my bed, rubbing against my shins and purring. I picked her up and gave her a quick kiss, then set her back on the floor. She gazed up at me with her big blue doe eyes.

"I'm okay, baby."

Deciding I needed to think this all over with a relaxing bath, I peeled off my clothes and headed to the bathroom. The shallow water was a little too hot as I lowered myself into it.

I tried to make sense of it all. Thomas's face would be all over town and maybe even on the news. And then there was Marcy. Marcy would be devastated . . .

The warlock, Ace, had told me Thomas would survive. He'd also proclaimed that horrifying fate for me, how I was given the Kiss of Death and shared a part of that monster's soul. He said I was *her*, and whoever *her* was, she had a prophesized power that everyone expected from me.

And David Star . . . Death. I'd watched that vivid memory through the warlock, seen a truth unravel itself. Visually, David Star looked almost exactly like Alexandru, Death's past self. Was David Star truly just a character that Death had created to fool the whole world? To fool me?

As I soaked in the tub, my eyes fell closed, and for a fleeting, blissful moment, my racing thoughts stopped. Until I thought of the deadly power that had shot out from my hands. How it had felt *good*. How it hadn't saved Thomas.

I leaned my head back against a rolled-up wet rag and wondered if there was a way for me to activate these powers on command. Maybe my blinding laser beam, or whatever it was, could come in handy the next time I faced off with Death.

Holding my breath, I sunk beneath the water. In the tranquility of complete silence, I squeezed my eyes shut, willing something to happen with my bizarre abilities. Vaguely, I remembered picturing Death.

Coldness washed down the back of my neck.

You're dead. A deep, velvety voice slid into my skull.

I came up for air with a gasp and turned my head to the side. Black shadows slinked beneath the door of the bathroom and crawled toward me. Snapping into alertness, I tried to lift myself up from the tub, but the shadows lurched at me. A force gripped my shoulders and shoved me down. The darkness held me beneath the water, gripping my skin like steel claws as I submerged to the bottom of the tub. My legs thrashed. Water was carried away, spilling over the rim of the bathtub and flooding the floor. Blindly reaching out, my hands sought one of the shadows and I latched onto it, wringing it out with my hand.

Images flashed in my mind. Ominous skies with a gaping hole at the center, where lightning struck, and clouds spun in a vicious vortex as if God were spitting back a monster into the world. A massive form split the sky, plummeting to the earth on fire and crashing into the black depths of an ocean. Beneath the murky water, the object uncoiled and revealed a body, a man with obsidian-colored markings paving every inch of his skin. Thick gashes marred his back in a gruesome V, where dark ribbons of blood surrounding him as the water swallowed him whole . . .

Yanked from the vision, my nails scraped the porcelain sides of the tub, and with one final heave, I resurfaced, gasping for air. I shoved my hands under the water and yanked the drain stopper free, rapidly scanning the bathroom as my breaths shot in and out. I was alone. The shadows were gone.

I don't know how long I sat there, gripping the sides of the tub, until the water drained completely. Death had sent his shadows to kill me, or this was a warning. Either way, I'd fought back and witnessed *another* forbidden piece to his past.

Yep. I was *so* dead.

Fear rattled in my bones. My parents.

I leapt from the tub and dashed across the tiled floor to my folded pajamas on the counter, almost slipping in the process. I yanked on a plain oversized navy sweatshirt and pajama pants with cartoon sheep.

When I sprinted into my bedroom, the small television next to my vanity was on at high volume. Skittles sat on my bed beside Mr. Wiggles, posed like a calm Egyptian feline goddess and fixated on a loose piece of string on my comforter.

I hurried into the hallway to peer into my parent's bedroom, instantly reassured to find them safe and sound asleep beneath their comforter.

My sopping wet hair dripped all over the floor as I paced the width of my bedroom back and forth. Unable to think straight with my whirling thoughts, I lunged to turn the TV off.

I could fix this. Maybe I just had to apologize to Death. No, what was I thinking? He wasn't the type to forgive, and I was not sorry for what I'd done. Which meant I'd have to stand up to him. All I knew was Ace had seemed to know more about Death and his limitations than I did, and I couldn't stay here. Not with my parents in harm's way. I had to go back to the warlock; I had to see if he could—

The television clicked back on by itself and displayed loud black-and-white static, and I nearly had a heart attack. As I watched the screen with widening eyes, it began rapidly changing channels, stopping on the 1978 version of *Halloween*. The final scene of panic and horror with Jamie Lee Curtis hiding in a closet and fighting off Michael Myers.

"It's just a scary coincidence," I said to myself. "It's just a scary coincidence."

Black-and-white static snow flashed over the screen again and the television blared a screeching noise.

Faith, the same unmistakable voice of Death purred through the static. *Come out and play, Faith.*

With my heart in my throat, I scrambled for the remote on my nightstand to turn the TV off. Outside, a blast of thunder crashed. The lights surged in and out with a hum. Armed with only the television remote, I pressed against the wall behind me, praying the power would stay on, but the room plunged into darkness. I remembered there was a tiny portable flashlight in my underwear drawer and tore open my dresser, fishing through it until I found it.

The flashlight illuminated a narrow beam. Skittles's eyes flashed under the light. She had hopped onto the edge of my bed, ears flat against her head, just like the frightened jaguars in the gladiator arena. She let out a startling hiss at nothing.

The flashlight's beam went in and out, in and out. "Come on, come *on!*" With shaking hands, I smacked the battery pack in an attempt to fix it. Skittles's fur brushed my pant leg as she weaved anxiously between my legs, and I almost screamed. The flashlight slipped from my fingers, clattered to the floor, and went out.

A bitter cold chill slid down my back. Across the bedroom, standing beside my window, stood a massive figure blacker than night.

The power came back on with a hum. The figure was gone.

The doorbell sounded.

"Ah, shoot."

Skittles's charm around her neck rattled as she skirted from the room. Breathing hard, I grabbed my old softball bat on the way out of my bedroom and crept down the hallway. I was fully aware that this was a scene straight out of a horror movie, but I was so tired of being afraid and helpless.

I held my palm out in front of my face, picturing the light, and curled my fingers into a fist. I would not go down without a fight.

Boom! I jumped a little at another crash of thunder and banged my hip into the corner of the kitchen counter with a wince. Okay, maybe cowering under the covers was a better option.

In my peripheral, the automatic porch light flicked on. Heavy, calculated footsteps creaked the old wooden boards of the front porch. *Death.* With my heart in my throat, I slinked closer to the door, peeking through the privacy window at the porch. Empty.

I've had enough of this. Clenching my teeth, I mustered up the courage to unbolt the lock, preparing to rip open the door and swing like a madwoman.

"Faith?" Dad asked.

The kitchen lights flicked on, and I sprang straight out of my skin for the umpteenth time that night.

Both of my parents stood behind me with their pajamas on. Mom held an unlit candle and wore an overnight face mask that made her look like a serial killer.

"Oh my God," I said, clutching my chest. "I almost peed my pants, bro!"

"Did someone really ring the doorbell this late?" Dad asked with a yawn and shut the front door. "And during a storm, nonetheless?"

"Maybe a Jehovah's Witness. They're relentless." Mom set down her candle and opened a kitchen drawer near me, probably to find a flashlight in case the power went out again. Looking up at me, she did a double take at the weapon in my hands. "Why do you have your softball bat, honey?"

"Raccoon," I said quickly. "Really big raccoon. I saw it eating one of the pumpkins on the porch steps, so I scared it off."

The doorbell went off again. I whirled toward the door, my fingers clutching the bat tighter.

"What's going on?" Dad didn't have his glasses on and squinted at me. "Who keeps ringing the doorbell? You better not be hiding anything from us, young lady."

"Nothing's going on, I swear." If Death was here, he was pissed, and I didn't want my parents to get in the middle of it. I dropped the bat to my side. "You guys should go back to sleep. You have to get up early for work."

Not buying it, Dad moved past me and peered through the peephole. When he pulled back, he was furious. "Doesn't look like *nothing*." He heaved the door open, and I stopped breathing.

David Star stood on my porch, untouched by the rain. Mom let out a small gasp over my shoulder. His athletic frame was illuminated like an angel under the halo of the porch light. He wore the same outfit he'd worn hours before at Manuel's: a Gucci suit with a black leather jacket. He had his hands clasped politely behind his back. I saw flashes of Alexandru in the arena, drenched in blood, transforming into that soul-eating monster.

"You must be Faith's father," David said. I noticed he didn't reach out his hand. "It's great to meet you, sir."

"I bet it is." Dad stood taller than usual and spoke in a deeper voice, as he often did to prove his authority. "It's late, starboy. If you're trying to sneak in a hookup with my daughter, think again."

Get him, Dad! Kick him to the curb!

"I can assure you, I have the utmost respect for your daughter," David said. He slid his eyes to me and there wasn't even a splinter of hostility in them. His expression remained blank, vacant of any emotion. "We're just friends." To my mother, he added charismatically, "And you must be Faith's . . . slightly older sister?"

Mom burst into giggles and snorts. "Oh, stop it!" She tucked a strand of hair behind her ear and fluttered her eyelashes in a way that left me horrified and cringing.

"I'm sorry to disturb your family at such a late hour," David said, "but Faith wasn't replying to my texts. I wanted to make sure she got home safe."

"Faith," my father began in his furious voice, "I thought you said you didn't see David tonight?"

I struggled to formulate another excuse.

"She didn't, sir," David answered smoothly. "I saw her a few days ago. My father and I have ongoing business with a corporate building in Pleasant Valley, so I happened to be in the area for a late meeting. When she didn't reply to my texts, I figured I'd swing by and make sure everything was okay."

Dad narrowed his eyes. I thanked the Lord he was suspicious of this ridiculously phony story. I mean really, why would he have a business meeting late at night, conveniently by our home? There was no way my father was buying this bull—

"You into football, David?" Dad asked.

What?

"I'm a huge Bears fan, sir."

"The Bears suck," my dad, a lifelong Giants fan, blurted out from habit. Any non-Giants fan would have gotten the same response from him.

"I lived in Chicago for a while. I know it's a been a cruel form of torture to follow them lately, but this is our year. Faith mentioned you two watch sports together. Giants fan?"

"Unfortunately, yes," Dad said sullenly. "Don't get me started."

"They're doing worse than the Jets this season," David said.

I could not *believe* this was happening!

"I'm safe at home!" I shouted, drawing David's dishonest eyes back to me. "Healthy as an ox. You can leave now. Bye. Good night. Drive safe. Don't let the front door hit you in the butt on your way out." I started to shut the door, when I felt a hurl of wind push against it.

David's mouth twitched a little as I resisted the wind.

"You left this in my car." He raised a tight fist and opened it. I shuffled a step backward, my fingers tightening on the doorjamb.

A religious cross dangled from his long fingers. *My communion cross.* The necklace I'd thrown at Death in the fun house in an attempt to thwart his efforts. Poof, went the tiniest sliver of doubt left in my mind that David wasn't Death.

It still hadn't made any logical sense why he would put on such a well-thought-out façade around me. But the look David gave me as I saw the necklace confirmed the truth. His eyes flashed with a frightening rage that sent a clear message. *You're dead.*

"You shouldn't have," I said tautly. "M'kay, bye." I tried with all my strength to shut the door again, but it wouldn't budge.

When I made no move to take the necklace from David, or invite him in, Mom reached out and took the necklace. "Aw, her communion cross! She wears this all the time. You must have been missing it, Faith. David, honey, it was so sweet of you to stop by and check on our daughter. What a gentleman." She put her hand to her heart and then ushered him in. "Come in! Stay for a little bit!"

"Yeah, man, at least until this storm lets up," Dad the Traitor said. I must have missed the part where he promoted David from "starboy" to "yeah, man."

David chuckled. "Oh, I don't want to inconvenience you. It's the dead of night."

I fought laboriously not to explode.

"I do have a *lot* of homework," I said, directing the statement at my mother, who was in total fangirl mode over David. "A mountain of it. So many tests and quizzes and projects due tomorrow! We should do this another time!"

It was pointless. Neither of my parents were listening. In fact, they appeared enraptured by David's presence, held under his influence.

"You're not an inconvenience at all!" Mom replied cheerfully, ignoring my protests. "Come on in, David, you must be freezing." She ventured into the kitchen. "Would you like a cupcake and coffee?"

"You had me at cupcake." Our eyes connected as David stepped into my home. The door clicked closed behind him without a touch. He took his sweet time raking his eyes over my pajamas. A string of expletives trailed through my mind as I desperately tried to think of a way out of this.

"It's so cute how both of you love cupcakes," Mom was ranting on in the background, while Dad worked the TV for the news channel. "Faith has loved cupcakes since she was a little girl with her little toy oven . . . "

I wedged myself between David and my home. "Get the hell off my property, or I'll bash your head in with this bat," I whispered.

David studied my weapon. When our eyes met again, a darkness spread outward from his pupils, consuming his chocolate-brown irises and a portion of the sclera. A slow, leering grin spread across his evil mouth. "Try," he dared.

Then he brushed past me with his hands in his pockets and struck up a conversation with my father about a recent Giants game.

My mother called me from the kitchen, so I withdrew to her, never taking my attention off David. The outer edges of my vision blurred. I was going to have a heart attack. What the hell was I supposed to do? Kill an immortal creature? Mom plated a cupcake and handed it to me.

"He's *lovely*, Faith." She performed a little dance in place. "Eeeek! Your first boyfriend, a Star. He's even more handsome in person. And he smells like a dream!" Her eyes fell on the bat still clutched in my hand. "Honey, please, enough with the bat. Put that thing away."

Looking at her numbly, I set the bat down on the counter and gripped the plate with white knuckles.

"Honey?" Mom asked, concern lacing her voice. "Faith, are you okay?"

I strained to smile. *Everything is marvelous, Mother, except the fact you invited a murderous, soul-sucking demonic parasite into our home, and he has a bone to pick with me.*

My father cackled at something David said, which drew my attention back to the monster in my house. Skittles rubbed against his calves, purring. She'd taken an unusual liking to him, considering she despised anyone outside of my family and Marcy. Still conversing with my father, David lowered to a crouch and ran his hand over Skittles's snowy-white fur. She bowed her head in submission as though to worship him. Then she rolled over and purred obscenely.

Perfect. Even my cat was charmed by him.

David turned his head. Our eyes connected again. This time, he winked.

I stormed toward him, tossing the plate and cupcake to the side. His spine straightened as I fisted the warm sleeve of his leather jacket. "This is between you and me, psycho," I grated between my teeth. "We need to talk. In *private.*"

I hadn't even noticed there was background noise until every sound in the house smothered to a complete hush. I looked at my father, to find him unmoving, perched mid–football throw. I looked back over my shoulder at my mom, who was mid–hair flip.

When I turned back to David, he glared down at my hand on his jacket. "Yes," he said, clipping the word. "Let's talk."

White-hot pain ricocheted up the hand touching him like an electric current, traveling to a place over my stomach, where the ghost of a bullet wound lingered like an eternal scar. I released his arm and lurched back, clutching at my gut. A flicker of pleasure burned wickedly in his gaze as he watched me hyperventilate.

"I warned you not to touch me," he purred.

In a moment of clarity, I reached back, grabbed the bat on the kitchen table, and swung hard at David's head. Like a scene straight of a movie, he snatched the bat at the last second before it pulverized his face. His head tilted. On the side of the bat was a big dollop of strawberry-pink frosting from one of the cupcakes. Keeping his intense stare on me, his tongue darted out and licked all the icing off, before his fingers crushed the aluminum barrel to a pulp as if it were a can. He tore the bat easily from my hand and cast it aside.

"Now, that wasn't very nice," he growled and bared a mouthful of serrated teeth.

Stumbling out of the kitchen with a scream, I ran into the hallway. I struggled to focus on "David" as my whole body felt inhibited by pain. Thunder rumbled through the hallway and the lights surged on and off. He pursued me with a lazy, unhurried swagger, shadows peeling off the walls on either side of him like stripped paint. They latched onto his shoulders, forming a regal cape, which then reshaped into a cloak as he leisurely blended into the darkness.

"You should have left my business alone, Faith."

His voice was deepening, altering, an unmarked accent rhythmically purring out the words. A horrific look of wrath carved into his features. Bones shifted in his face, forming something sharper, angular, as beautiful as poison. He cracked his head sharply to the side and light-colored markings danced beneath his skin, spreading like a wildfire. They climbed up his neck, curved alongside his face, and blackened into tattoos.

"Nobody cheats Death."

Boom! I jerked as another rumble of thunder was unleashed

outside. The hallway light stuttered wildly over his features, and I screamed as his image distorted to the wicked, green-eyed creature I'd watched Alexandru turn into. The lights surged on for the last time, before finally going out altogether. I took off through our one-story house, sprinting into my room in the direction of the window and . . .

Crashed into a hard cloaked frame.

"Especially you, *cupcake*."

"Jesus!"

"Wrong." Death snatched me around the throat with his massive gloved hand. My bedroom door slammed shut and he pinned me against it. His hooded face crowded my vision. The alluring aroma of leather, cherries, and cologne. "Sexy sheep pajamas. I would have never expected those."

"Get your hand off me!" I gasped.

"I know you struck a deal with the warlock to get information on me," he snarled. "You have until zero to tell me everything he told you." His mouth lingered at my neck, and I envisioned those hidden razor sharp fangs ripping into my throat. "Ten."

"Screw you!"

He laughed. A low, chilling sound. "Rain check. Nine."

"Because of you, my friend is dead!" I snarled.

"You only have one friend. She's alive. *Eight*."

"Thomas was my friend. I can't tell anyone about what I saw, or how he was taken. He was innocent! He had nothing to do with this!"

"*Seven,*" he growled. "I warned you that you needed my protection. Learn from your mistakes."

"Learn from my mistakes?" In a moment of clarity, I brought my knee up to his crotch and slammed into hard muscle.

He released a low hiss. "Great aim, Bruce Lee. That was my thigh—"

"Hiya!" I connected with softer flesh.

Death bent over with a grunt. I ripped free from his hold, maneuvering swiftly under his arm. He straightened to his full height, and I was breathless for a moment at the sight of his looming cloaked frame. His head nearly touched the *ceiling*.

"You'll pay for that." From the strain in Death's voice, it seemed not even the Grim Reaper could recover fast from a hard knee to the jewels.

"Add it to my tab." Now that his raging muscle wasn't trapping me, I aspired to bash his nose in with my knuckles and raised my fists to my face. "You let Malphas take Thomas, didn't you? You didn't come help us because you wanted me to be afraid!"

"I'm not your guardian angel," he sneered. "My Fallen were ambushed and your *friend* was taken because of your own stubbornness. This could have all been avoided if you had listened to me from the beginning."

"Don't you *dare* blame me," I said with a tremor. "You're a heartless monster!"

"Projecting your grief onto me is a waste of energy. Thomas's life holds no value to me."

Tears brimmed my eyes. "Get out of my house!"

"Make me." Death took a step forward, and the floor groaned beneath his combat boot. Everything about him oozed dominance. "Leave it to *you* to wander like a ditz into town and enter a warlock's store. His building is on hallowed ground. Do you have any idea how difficult it was for me to reach you? He could have . . . " Death stopped himself, breathing raggedly as his baritone voice slipped into something velvety and otherworldly. "He could have imprisoned you there for the rest of your life, and no one would have ever been able to find you."

"You wouldn't give me answers. You've lied and kept *everything* from me."

"I don't owe you anything," he said maliciously. "I never said I was the good guy."

"You never said you were the bad guy either! Yet, here you are, trying to store me away for your own personal use!"

The hair on my nape lifted at his soul-chilling, bestial growl. "You have no idea the lengths I've gone to protect you."

"Protect me? You were never protecting me. You try to keep me in one piece, so I'm still valuable to you!"

He took another step forward. This time, I didn't back away, and every inch of my skin was charged by his proximity. "What a whiny little race, mortals. You fool, *fate* is your only injustice, not I."

Tension crackled between us. The air felt thick, so excruciating it painfully blocked my lungs. He was a live wire and the closer we came together, the closer we approached something unpredictable. We were both quiet for a while, looking at one another. I stared into the never-ending void of his face, searching for any sight of Alexandru. For the man, and not the monster.

"You look different without all that makeup around your eyes," he said in an oddly quiet voice.

"At least I show my face," I snapped, insecure if what he'd said had been a compliment or not.

His demeanor turned cynical again. "I'd watch how you speak to me. That way, when I punish you for what you've done tonight, I'll go easier on you. Tell me what you learned at the Crossroads."

"He showed me the truth about you," I said, since there was no point in keeping it all to myself. "I watched you . . . change. Ahrimad gave you his power because you killed him in the arena. You killed the person you hated the most. You killed Malphas, too, but you were devastated after what you'd done, you were grieving him like you'd made a mistake—"

"I didn't ask for your analysis." He towered over me, scary and unstable. The moonlight curved through the window as if storm clouds had shifted past the moon, outlining Death's menacing black silhouette even more. "There are parts of my past you will never see, parts you would *never* understand. If you think I owe you my life story, Faith Williams, you are sorely mistaken."

"You lied to me," I said hoarsely. "Why lie to me to such a degree? Why take me on a date? What was the point of it all, Death? Why do you hide behind that cloak?"

He didn't respond. I hated when he said nothing. At least he'd chosen not to lie.

I thought of my parents, how they were probably still frozen in the kitchen. Running for my life right now was out of the question. I'd seen how fast he could move. I was trapped. But that didn't mean he wasn't either.

"You owe me an explanation," I said, forcing back a surge of emotion in my throat. "For once, just tell me the truth!"

He tilted his head to the side, and I could feel his hidden gaze skimming my furious features. "I haven't shown a mortal my identity for centuries. Not until the moment I take their soul."

"Why?"

"Your kind is not worthy of my beauty, for one."

I laughed in a humorless way, although on the inside I pitifully agreed with him. I could barely get used to his smooth, velvety, accented voice. His voice alone unarmed me in a frightening way. If he still looked anything like Alexandru, he would be deliciously attractive, a Roman god, and his effect on me would only get worse.

Regardless, his answer was shady. I knew there was more to the hood, more to him and why he hid from me still, or maybe keeping me in the dark was all part of his twisted little game.

"Only a heartless monster would do what you did to me," I said, and I wanted to shout it a second time at the top of my lungs. "But

I'll admit it, you're damn good at manipulating. A real pro. Really fooled me with the Carrion Angel story. Is that what your massive ego wanted to hear? Leave. I want you gone. Get out of my house!" My hands smacked into his chest to push him back, but it was like punching an impenetrable wall. "I *hate* you!"

"You don't hate me," he murmured. "You only wish you did."

I glowered at him, teeth clenched tight. "Don't flatter yourself. The only reason you've tried to get closer to me was either to gain my trust, or just mindfuck me. Those aren't exactly attractive qualities in a man I'd check off on a crush quiz in a magazine."

"I need to know what else was exchanged between you and the warlock," Death said in a gravelly tone. "Either you're going to tell me everything you've seen from my past, including the pieces from the warehouse, or I'm going to tear it out of you."

"I know why your eyes are sensitive to light," I said.

"I think you should get your hearing checked."

"Only after *you* see a therapist."

He released another growl, reminding me of the frightening creature he was. Whenever he made that noise, I fought the innate urge to run and cower behind something. Once again, I tried to picture the monster beneath the hood, questioning if he even resembled a human anymore.

"Take a peek, princess," he purred. The hairs at the back of my neck stood up. Had he read my mind again?

I inhaled as deep of a breath as I could and stood my ground. "A wild animal injured your eye all those years ago." Cautiously, I started walking around him. He tracked me like a hawk, his shoulders rigid as if he were prepared for anything. "That's why you wear the hood, isn't it? That's why "David Star" has to wear sunglasses. Because *you* suffer from chronic photophobia. You even have a scar over your lighter green eye to prove the permanent damage . . . " I traced the skin on my eyebrow to my cheekbone. "I saw it in your memories twice. Painted it on my canvases too. Your younger self said a wild animal damaged it." Silent, Death watched me under his shadowed veil.

"I first noticed your slipups when David made a mistake in his office. Even though I told him I left the carnival because I was nauseous, when I saw him the next day, he asked me how my head was. He didn't know I hit my head. But you, *you knew*, because you're the one who caused it! And then there's the most obvious slipup, your ringtone. Real smooth with that one, Grimmy."

Death flexed his hands, leather creaking. "I appreciate this little act," he said silkily, never taking his concealed eyes off me. "Circling me as if we've swapped roles . . . "

"You think you have me under your thumb, don't you?" I asked, my chest heaving from the peak of adrenaline his closeness caused. "I'm learning more about you and your intentions day by day. You said you went to great lengths to protect me? I'll go a further distance to protect my family. I will go back to Ace again for answers, even if it means risking everything. And there's nothing you can do to stop me." I took a stunted breath. "Because I know your true name."

The temperature in the room plummeted.

"What did you just say?" His voice rumbled stronger than pending thunder in the horizon.

"You heard me." I paused, arming myself with the name that felt deadly to say out loud. "Your name . . . is Alexandru Cruscellio."

"What did you offer the warlock?" I could tell by his stiff posture he was struggling to keep his fury at bay. "If he touched you . . . " Whatever threat hung on the end of that was never completed and also not directed at me. My face scorched a deep crimson.

"No—*no*, it's not like that," I said, flustered and talking too fast. "He said I owed him a favor in the future. Not that it's any of your business—"

"You *are* my business," Death snarled, his accent thickening now with rage. "You're mine. Mine to protect!"

My stomach flip-flopped. "Well, you're mine too. I know your full name. I have power over you."

Death lunged at me in a blur, and I rolled over onto my back on the mattress, curling up my knees at the sight of his looming figure at the head of my bed. He was a thing out of nightmares with the heavy cloak and the endlessly black space where his face should have been. All the shadows in the room slinked toward him, until an aura of darkness surrounded his frame, stretching out from his back in the form of massive wings. I drew back farther on the comforter in blank horror.

"I could eat you from your toes all the way up to your smart tongue," Death purred. More shadows collected at the edges of the bed, swarming toward me like spiders and snakes. "If you even utter that name out loud again, it'll be the last two words you ever say. And I will take my sweet fucking time making sure of it. Understand?"

All I could do was gape at his shadows, trembling so hard that I shook the bed with me.

"*Do you understand?*" he snarled vehemently, his voice on the edge of monstrous.

"I understand!" The shadows recoiled away from me. I scrambled off the bed, peering fearfully up at Death as he remained where he was, his hooded head aimed in my direction.

I could still feel his wicked eyes drilling into me. "Don't look at me like that. If you'd done exactly as I said from the beginning, we would not have any issues between us. You'd be a good, obedient human, and I wouldn't have to discipline you tonight."

"I really think you should try therapy. Or a giant Xanax."

Another low growl came from his hood. "I've just about had enough of that mouth of yours."

He maneuvered around the bed and prowled closer. I legit heard *Jaws* music in my head. I wanted to dive over the bed Michael Phelps–style, put *something* between us, but I couldn't, or maybe I didn't want to.

My feet were nailed to the ground. After a few seconds I snapped out of it, backpedaling until my butt hit the wall. Now I was wedged between a nightstand and a canvas. Sweat trickled down my spine as I peered up at Death's looming frame, sinking into the overlay of darkness across his features. Without touch, his power beckoned me closer. I resisted the urge to obey with all my might and pressed further against the wall, but the pull between us remained undeniable. We were like two opposite ends of magnets, hovering inches away from each other. A part of me desperately wanted to test this attraction, give in, lean into the monster. See what would happen.

"Frustrating, isn't it?" He cocked his head to the side again, an animal playing with its prey. "Nothing can smother my sheer allure. It's a curse." I could sense his provocative grin, feel his dark delight like a caress against my lips. "Although, I get the sense all those silly little feelings that flutter in your stomach when I come around have nothing to do with my allure, cupcake. That's all *you*."

"You smug bastard," I gritted out. "The only true feeling I have toward you is this: disgust. You make me sick."

He pinched a strand of my damp hair and slid his fingers down, releasing a droplet of water from the end. "I can see the truth in your eyes, in the way you look at me."

"I'm looking at you the same way I've always looked at you," I whispered. "Like you're a—"

"Monster?" He reached past me and picked up a clean paint-brush. "A part of you is scared of me, sure, but you always look at me like you want to understand me." He swept the paintbrush down my nose and skimmed my lips. My nerve endings ignited, even as

I aggressively flinched away. He flattened his palm beside my head with a snicker, leaning into me. "Tell me I'm lying."

"You took advantage of me," I said. "You manipulated my emotions—"

"I wore only an illusion," he said. "There's an aura about you that limits my power, so I had to affect you in other mundane ways. Deep down, you know the truth." His voice was husky, sensual. If he was trying to have an effect on me, it was working. "It wouldn't be a challenge to seduce you. You want me, and you always have."

"Sounds like you're trying to validate something."

Death laughed, a low sultry sound. "You're not ready for me to validate anything, Virgin Girl."

"Do you want to know what I think?" I leaned in closer to his face, daring to touch demise. He pulled back faintly, but his gloved hand remained on the wall, caging us both in. "I think deep down— and I'm talking Grand Canyon deep—you care about me. It scares you."

"As if I'd care about a girl as prude and inexperienced as you." I could imagine the nasty, condescending grin he wore.

My gut twisted. "I wasn't asking you to confirm it for my benefit. I wanted you to admit it for yourself. You know what your problem is? You're too much of a control freak to admit it wasn't *all* a lie. Or maybe it bothers you so much that I outsmarted you, you refuse to see what's really going on here."

"Don't be pathetic, Faith. You fell in love with an idea, and now you're trying to summon a ghost."

"I know what you're trying to do, Death. It's not working. I know you feel, I know you're not heartless, or else you wouldn't have gone out of your way to save me in the alleyway and in the warehouse. You wouldn't have gone out of your way to be here, with me."

The room blackened around him until the outline of my room was smothered completely from the moonlight. I remained untouched by the darkness.

"Do you want to know why I kept things from you? Why I've lied to you and pretended to be someone I'm not?" He was so close that my bare feet touched the toe of his leather combat boot, and I could taste the trace of cherries and mint lingering on his breath. "Because I *can*. Ever since you entered my mind, I've had to put much more effort into guarding myself from you. It was all worth it though. Now I know everything that makes you tick. You think you know yourself? I know you better. I've become your worst fear, I've *plagued* you, and now you will never escape me, unless I show you how. I own you, Faith. Mind, body, and soul. If I wanted you to leave with me right now, you would. If I wanted you to kneel between my legs for the rest of your pathetic mortal life, you would."

"Then what's stopping you?" I demanded fiercely.

Our mouths crashed together.

His lips slanted sinfully over mine, stubble scraping against my sensitive skin like delicious thorns. My brain signaled this was a lethal embrace. His kiss held a magnetic decree of night. A claim that would stain my lips forever. If I didn't stop this now, he would ruin all other valiant attempts.

We tore apart, an afterthought of hesitation. Panting together in silence, the gravity of this moment felt like a sucker punch to the face. This was wrong. Neither of us trusted each other. He scared me; I annoyed him. Predator and prey orbiting around each other in a dangerous push-and-pull dance of forbidden attraction. That's how we worked. That's how we *coexisted*.

And yet . . .

All the times I avoided going out to parties to hook up, all the dates Marcy set up for me that I was too nervous to attend, and all my insecurities about never being kissed felt like silly hiccups in a path that was destined to lead me here. I thought my first kiss would be unsure, but this I was certain. Death had awoken a piece of my soul that craved the dark. I wanted more. I wanted him. *To hell with the consequences.*

Reaching for him again, my fingers traced the sinewy outline of his cloaked arms. He stood surprisingly still, looming over me as I stretched onto my toes. I dragged my hands up his broad shoulders, drew the monster closer like a possessed enchantress. He smelled just like he tasted. Lethal. Intoxicating. Dried cherries from rolled cigarettes, leather, and a masculine cologne bursting with clean citrus, a leafy forest, cedar, and him, in all of his intensity.

When I grasped the edges of his hood, he came to life again as his gloved hands seized my waist to flatten me against the wall. Our bodies molded together seamlessly.

"No touching," he said coarsely.

My arms rose lazily above my head, his shadows twirling around my wrists like silk and pinning me to the wall. Only then did Death's mouth finally dip down for slow seconds. I melted, drank in his venomous lips as my own naturally parted in an invitation. Death released a guttural growl, hotly prodding his tongue into my mouth. The low drone of it vibrated in his throat like a purr, rousing a sense of urgency between us. His kisses became rougher, unrestrained—he knew I wouldn't break easily. He lifted me up to his height and hooked my legs around his waist. Leather-gloved fingers dug into the backs of my thighs, my heart pounding with a newfangled desire for deadly touches.

I wanted to wrap my hands around his neck, grip his hair, except my wrists remained locked cruelly in place. My teeth had a mind of their own and pulled at his bottom lip. He let out another bestial noise of approval and ground his hips into mine. The swell of my breasts crushed against the solid wall of his chest, his power seeping into my skin like warm oil and sending delicious tremors throughout my body. I drowned in the euphoria of his enticing shadows, submerged in his night.

Faltering against his lips with a hard shudder, an unusual jolt of heat darted down my arms. The sensation was similar to the feeling I had right before I'd unleashed that powerful light onto the demons. It ignited me to the core, tingles of electricity surging through my veins as warmth seared my palms . . .

I was a bomb about to go off.

Death must have known it too because he stepped back fast. My arms released from the wall, and I dropped clumsily to my feet.

"Your hands," he rasped.

My fingers quivered violently, ice-blue fire licking up the lengths of them. I watched in both awe and horror as the fire lifted, twirling in my hands in spirals until the entire room was illuminated by the hue of the flames. I couldn't control the surge. A blast shot out from my fingertips, straightening both my arms outward from the sheer thrust of the energy. As the fire abandoned my hands, it transformed into a blinding white light, which nailed the Grim Reaper in the chest. His whole body jolted, as if he'd been struck by lightning. The light climbed up the shadows of his frame, curling around his body, and unfurling around him in a brilliant aura. An aura that electrified the shadowy exoskeleton of two ginormous, once invisible limbs that protruded from his back. *Black wings.*

Death took a wavering stride backward and rocked on his feet. His body tipped and the rest was left to gravity. He crashed hard into the ground with a cringe-worthy thud and clatter of metal. The floorboards shook with such force that a framed picture of my family at the beach tumbled off my nightstand and shattered.

I gaped at his unmoving frame with my mouth wide open.

"Death?" Cautiously, I maneuvered around him and gave his head a little kick. Nothing happened. I nudged his arm with my toe, then his head again. Reaching down, I lifted his gloved hand. It was a dead weight and smacked on the ground when I let go.

"Ah, shit. I killed him." Then, panicked, as it fully hit me: "I killed the Grim Reaper!"

Pacing the floor, I swiped my thumb over my raw swollen lips and contemplated what to do next. His body blocked my way to the bedroom door. I couldn't just leave him here with my parents in the house.

How would I explain this to them? Were my parents still "paused" by Death's power? Would they be stuck like that forever? Where would I store his body? Could I go to jail for this? Was there a supernatural prison for instances like this, where I'd be locked in a cell with another mythical being, like a bloodthirsty vampire? Were vampires hot and spicy like they were in romance novels? I shook myself.

He couldn't be dead. Cautiously, I lowered to my knees and cowered back as I reached my fingers underneath his sleeve to get to his wrist. Pressing two fingers into his skin felt like I was petting a deadly rattlesnake. I couldn't feel a heartbeat, but his skin was scorching hot. *How the hell do I check if this dude is alive?*

I took a deep breath and moved my fingers toward his shadowy neck to check his pulse again. My fingers disappeared beneath the darkness of his hood, as if I'd pressed through a thick fog, the empty black slate where a nose, eyes, and mouth should be. Curiously, I darted my hand in and out of the shadow and wiggled my invisible fingers. "Now, that is freaky . . . "

I'll admit my heart stuttered when my fingertips accidentally touched his cheek. Truth be told, it was a little anticlimactic. He felt . . . normal. And Death hadn't jumped at me and ripped me apart, nor did my hand catch on fire, or rapidly dissolve away with decay like I'd imagined it would so many times.

Feeling like a madwoman, I caressed the coarse hair of short stubble on his jaw. Heat burned up my neck as I recalled the way those hairs had rubbed against my skin. Gliding to his cheekbones, I imagined the strong jaw on Alexandru, his chiseled, handsome features. I wandered to the raised skin of the scar above his right eye. The damaged tissue was thicker toward the top, as if his eyebrow had split open from the inflicted wound.

Must have hurt.

Slowly, I skimmed over a few smaller raised areas of scar tissue scattered around his sculpted features. I reached his lips, velvety soft and a little pouty. The cold metal of the piercing in his bottom lip made my skin prickle, in response to the memory of our kiss. He had another piercing in his eyebrow, the one with the scar.

Realizing I was cradling his face, I sharply pulled back and a spell shattered. *Good God, what is wrong with you?!*

Sitting back on my heels, I glanced back at my empty canvas, recalling a time I'd painted him over and over again, the eyes that had marked their territory on all those off-white linen boards. I'd never forget the haunting soul engraved within them, the vicious, raging storm.

When I looked down at Death again, I noticed his cloak was not only parted, but he was *shirtless* underneath it. His skin held a golden-bronze tan, and I could tell his lower stomach rippled with deep muscle. What shocked me the most (since I already knew he was ripped and fine as hell. Not that I thought about that often. Or that I cared.) were the black, intricate markings and symbols spreading across his exposed skin. They were exotic, mesmerizing, unlike anything I'd ever seen before.

"Don't do it, Faith . . . " I warned myself.

With my heart in my throat, I avoided touching his skin and parted the lapel of his cloak. I followed the visible trail of intricate tattoos up his torso to his chest, where branchy lines grouped together into a formation of foreign symbols. They told a secret story, like cryptic puzzle pieces of his past were engraved into his skin like reminders. Suddenly his large gloved hand shot out and clamped down on my wrist. I froze. Death could have snapped my arm right then and there, but he didn't.

Instead, he vanished in an explosion of black mist, and I knew he'd been awake the entire time.

XIX

After Death evaporated, I stood alone in the dark to collect myself. Then I found my flashlight and hurried to check on my parents. They were no longer frozen in the kitchen by Death's power and were back in bed asleep, so I gently shut their door and headed back into my bedroom.

David Star was Death. The world's youngest, most famous multi-conglomerate business protégé was the Grim Reaper, and I'd *kissed* him!

My fingers lifted to my lips, tracing the memory of our hot and heavy moment. I couldn't believe I'd let *Death* himself have my first smacker. Not that I was complaining—the kiss was not to be forgotten. He'd known exactly what he was doing, and he'd done it exceptionally well.

Jerk.

For the second time in the same day, I'd unleashed an unexplainable force from my hands. The two-hundred-and-forty-pound shredded Jerkules had been knocked flat on his back by whatever shot out of my hands.

Who the hell am I? WHAT am I? Could I really be this prophesized entity who would start wars, just like Ace had predicted?

Skittles purred as she rubbed her fur against my bed curtain, drawing my attention to the magazines featuring David and "Mystery Girl" that my mother had bought at the airport. They were stacked chaotically under my bed, and when I slid one out, the glossy image of David Star's brown eyes unsettled me. They now appeared lifeless, empty, merely a mask concealing the monster behind them.

Death posed as a celebrity seemingly for sport, slipped on a façade so everyone worshiped him. It was irredeemably evil. How did he reap the souls of the dead while being David anyway? Did he have help? There was no way one person could collect all those souls at once.

I gulped a breath. *Could* he be in multiple places at once? The last thing I needed to worry about was twenty thousand Deaths wandering around the planet. I already had enough trouble sleeping at the thought of one of him.

Another idea presented itself as I riffled through the pages of a second magazine. If David Star was Death himself, then what was the D&S Tower? Who the hell was Devin Star? My skin tingled as I reached a page of David and Devin posed together. Gorgeous, the picturesque duo that all of New York and beyond was obsessed with, but now that I knew the truth about David, it was clear all aspects of the Star family were fabricated. I sat back on the floor, shining the beam of light from the flashlight onto Devin Star.

I recalled my first encounter with Devin. He was charming, and so handsome it was almost agonizing to look at him. My thumb crept onto the magazine page and covered the *n* in his name. *Devi.*

I slid my thumb away from the page, horror spreading through me, as I filled in the missing letter with another. *Devil.* I shook my head, voicing my denial with a repeated "No."

"There's no way I got in a car accident with the Devil," I said, and laughed, since talking to myself had become the norm. "I mean, come on."

Devin is my boss, and my mentor, David had told me outside of Manuel's taco shack. *He showed me the ropes when I was a rookie.*

I quickly shoved the magazines back under the bed. How could I have been so blind? Death and the Devil controlled the D&S Tower. I already rode one yellow bus to hell my first three years of high school. Now I would be riding a one-way train to Satan's *actual* everlasting torture chamber.

Sighing, I climbed to my feet to make a chamomile tea. When I stood up, my vision swam with dizziness. I fell back, thankfully against my mattress. Having almost fainted, I yanked myself up onto the bed and gripped the comforter in dazed confusion. My mind raced, but my heart slowed. Something wasn't right.

When I got my wisdom teeth removed, they drugged me and counted back from ten as I drifted into oblivion. I hadn't been able control the plunge, and this felt the same way. A mighty wave of fatigue sucked every last ounce of energy from me, and my eyes fluttered shut.

The nightmares began a few weeks before I met Death at Thomas's house. Fragments of the same vague images would terrorize me all night long. Just before I'd wake up, a massive shadow would always approach me, and I'd be unable to move. These night terrors had gotten stronger since meeting Death, until I discovered he was the shadow all along.

Now the same paralyzing sensation of the nightmare overcame my body, but the dream itself was altered. This time, I was in the alleyway near the D&S Tower. The figure approaching me was not Death.

"Hello, Faith," the Raven demigod rasped in his bone-chilling voice. "We meet again."

The last time I'd seen Malphas, he'd taken Thomas with him on Main Street. He'd also died in Death's Roman gladiator memory.

I should have been afraid. Here, I didn't feel much of anything. "Why am I here? I was asleep."

"And in sleep you remain. This is called a demonic projection. I thought perhaps you'd feel more comfortable if we met alone, on your terms. If you want to leave, all you have to do is wake up."

I felt torn between two decisions. One part of me desperately wanted to say, *Later, ho,* and make haste like the Road Runner— whereas the other part of me just couldn't leave.

"What do you want?" I asked.

"To help you."

"Uh-huh . . . " Looking Malphas directly in the eyes felt like a dare to touch the tip of a scorpion's tail. "Haven't really been getting that vibe from you. You know, when one of your helpers slashed my arm in the alleyway and I almost died? Or when you kidnapped and murdered Thomas?"

"It was never my intention to harm you, Faith." Malphas leaned against the shadowy wall beside him and put his hands in his pockets—the only human mannerism I'd seen from him. I wondered how old he was. Visually, he looked to be in his early thirties. There was a distinct lilt to his voice, too, which resembled Death's untraceable accent. It even made my blood run cold in a similar way. "My subordinates were severely punished for what they did to you outside the D&S Tower. As for your friend Thomas, I can assure you he is not dead."

My heart skipped a beat. "Prove it."

"Thomas will prove it for you soon. You'll see." He smirked, and I imagined he was incredibly handsome, once. His entrancing, blazing coal eyes bore into mine, until my head felt heavy. "You took shelter in the Crossroads today. Tell me, has a revelation unfolded?"

"He killed you," I said. "He killed you in the arena."

His smile tightened.

"Who are you, Malphas? To Death?"

"A ghost," he replied.

My shoulders tensed up as he approached me. All thoughts about Thomas strangely lifted away, as a crushing weight built up in my chest. Certain details about Malphas disturbed me up close, like how his eyes were onyx black with no visible pupils, or how his skin appeared so pale I could see some of the veins beneath it.

Malphas raised a clawed finger. "Death lied to you, didn't he?"

All I could do was stand static, numb to fear. The air shifted, rippled, as if his power were edging closer to me.

"Don't you see what he really wants is control over you?" Malphas circled me, strobing in and out of focus like a broken camera lens. "Don't be naïve, Faith. He wants you to obey his every command. Like a good pet."

Ultimately Death's intentions with me were unclear, but if there was one thing that man enjoyed more than anything, it was controlling everything around him. My mind harked back to every encounter with Death, how he asserted his authority over me in every possible aspect, from the interview, to the date, to the fable about him being a Carrion Angel, and then finally, his unwelcome visit to my home. Every move he'd made had been a deliberate, calculated decision to maintain a power position.

"You poor girl, you had to discover the truth about him for yourself. You haven't even seen the worst parts." Malphas moved his fingers in a small motion. I could have sworn something akin to a claw scraped lightly against the inside of my skull.

"Remember when you were hurting, and he kept hurting you?" Those obsidian eyes held me in place, two scary bottomless pits skimming over my features as if he were reading a book. "You can feel it, can't you? His power over you. It lingers in your veins, awaiting his next command. You were afraid to let him in. You have dreams, *aspirations*. Too many girls your age get swept up in temporary relationships, just like your friend Marcy. And Death . . . he knew this from the beginning. He knew you wouldn't be easy to break, unlike other mortals. That's why he hid his true intentions from you. You were a conquest to him, a mouse for the cat to play with. Death *knew* you were developing feelings for him, and he knew you were hesitant to let anyone in. He took advantage of this. He put you in danger. Now he's put your family in danger. He doesn't care about *you*. He only wants your soul, his property as he sees it, and everything else is inconsequential."

At the mention of my family, my face turned ashen. I couldn't allow my parents to fall into this mess.

I imagined my date with David at the carnival, and all the distance he'd put between us whenever I tried to understand him, which I was sure was by design. How was I supposed to put my trust in someone that I only knew through fragmented memories and fabricated alter egos?

The demigod leaned in closer, drawing my attention to his alien yet attractive features. "Aren't you the least bit curious why he came to your house, darling?" Malphas asked. "He didn't have to interact with your parents at all. What point do you think he was trying to make there?"

That he was powerful, and if I didn't do exactly as he said, both my Mom's and Dad's lives would be in danger. With merely a glance, Death had put both my parents under his spell. It would take even less effort for him to kill them.

"How do you know all of this?" I asked Malphas, fighting past a fuzziness blurring my vision again.

"I voice an echo of what you already know in your heart. Death may claim to protect you, but you know it is out of selfishness. Look at his actions, Faith. Not his words. Only I can stop him." A chilling smirk curled his sinister mouth. Malphas stepped back, fading into a growing darkness behind him. "Summon me in your darkest hour. I am yours."

I woke up in a cold sweat. Morning light streamed in through slight gaps in the blinds, cutting across my eyes and making me wince and roll onto my side. Nausea clawed my throat and when I lifted my forearm, it throbbed where the demon had injured me in the alleyway. Jolting up, I swung my legs off the bed and bolted to the bathroom. I barely made it to the toilet as I dropped to my knees and retched.

With white knuckles I gripped the porcelain seat, dripping sweat, acid, and suppressed tears into the water. My muscles were weak and overworked, as if I'd run a marathon the day before. I practically had. I flushed the toilet and dragged my feet to the sink to rinse my mouth out several times, then two more times with mouthwash. As I brushed my teeth, I wrestled with the depressing thought that there was no way out. I was hopeless in my situation now.

"Let's recap," I told my reflection. "You're prophesied to start a war between Heaven and Hell and who knows what other realms. Every evil creature and their mother are after you. You've developed the ability to see into the past and the future, not to mention an uncontrollable lantern power that affects evil beings. If you don't do as Death wishes, he'll massacre your entire family. Oh, and you still have to go to school."

School. Sprinting out of the bathroom, I lunged for my alarm clock on my nightstand and read the time. The screen was black. Probably broken from Death's light show with our electricity the

night before. I growled and checked my shattered phone screen. I
was three hours late for school!

My bedroom door blew open, hitting the wall with a crack.

"SURPRISE!"

"Jesus!" I screamed, grabbing my chest. I took in the thirtysomething-
year-old woman with poker-straight blond hair and a glowing smile
that could brighten up anybody's day. "Aunt Sarah?"

She crossed the room in a few excited leaps and squeezed me
tightly against her bulky pumpkin sweater. "Happy Halloween! I
was going to surprise you in the kitchen, but I just couldn't wait!"
She held me at arm's length, her crystal blue eyes identical to my
mother's. "You get more and more gorgeous every time I see you."

"I literally just saw you," I laughed out. "What are you doing
here? I have school today." A wave of panic hit me as I remembered
the time. "And I'm late!"

Aunt Sarah blocked my path. "Are you kidding? You better *not*
be going to school, missy! Your mom told me this morning on the
phone you've been stressed and she was going to let you sleep in. I'm
off today. Figured I'd stop by and take you out to cheer you up."

"You're kidnapping me?"

"Well, duh. Playing hooky was my specialty in high school. As
far as Pleasant Valley knows, you've had these terrible on-and-off
migraines the past few days, and it's best for you to do something
spooky fun today." She jumped a little in excitement, and so did
I, although less enthusiastically. Unbeknownst to her, I *had* been
getting terrible migraines. "Mom called you in sick at school! Play
along, kid, I'm breaking you out of jail!"

Once Aunt Sarah left my room to let me get changed, I paced
my bedroom floor, reconsidering this whole thing. Going out felt
like another demon incident waiting to happen and staying home or
going to school could be just as damning.

Death knew where I lived. Hell, he could find me anywhere I went. Hiding under a blanket in my closet wouldn't protect me. The last thing I wanted to do was stay cooped up in the house all day, terrified of what would happen next. Maybe going out with my aunt was just what I needed.

I wore a pair of medium wash ripped jeans with black fishnets underneath and my old "Batman's Wife" T-shirt to be festive for Halloween. Then I brushed my long black hair until it was bone straight and shiny, laced up my Converse, and quickly applied mascara, eyeliner, and burgundy lipstick.

On my vanity mirror hung my communion cross, which my mother must have snuck into my room while I was sleeping. I clasped the dainty cross around my neck, so it hung close to my throat.

I inhaled a slow breath.

"You're a normal girl," I told myself. "You are a *normal girl.*" I grabbed a zip-up hoodie and headed out of my bedroom. "Who shoots light beams from her hands."

I spent the car ride venting to Aunt Sarah about art school options and potential majors that interested me. Before entering *The Twilight Zone*, starring Death, college had been my number one stressor. Funny, when actual life-threatening problems enter your life, the other trivial issues you had before then, which had felt like the end of the world, vanish into thin air.

Happiness to me was to be immersed in art for the rest of my life, embraced by the magic of color and creating. Realistically, I knew I might have to settle on being an art teacher or some variation of that, since art studies and fashion design were so competitive. I wasn't the type of person to settle on anything less than what I truly wanted though. Not until I'd exhausted every other option to get to it. "David Star" helped me see that strength within myself.

The radio was on low in the background, and Aunt Sarah turned it up to hear it.

"The crime rate in New York City has snowballed, leaving citizens frazzled," said a male broadcaster, "after a man was found dead outside the Empire State Building. Witnesses have referred to him as the 'Man with Wings.' Before investigators could arrive to the scene, it is claimed the mystery man 'vanished into thin air.' Video footage has turned up of this 'Man with Wings' lying on the sidewalk. Some believe this bizarre incident is real, while others say it's a Halloween prank, or a publicity stunt. An eyewitness has come forward with disturbing details about the supposed dead man, claiming, 'His eyes were pecked out of his head, and he had massive white wings, like an angel.'"

"He was alive for a while," a staticky recording of a male voice said, who I assumed was the eyewitness. "He spoke to me. There was this blinding light, and he just went 'poof.' Gone. Like one of those Las Vegas magicians. Something ain't right about this city anymore."

"You can say that again," I muttered.

"Witnesses have reported that in the man's final moments, he warned of a 'great evil coming.'"

My blood turned to ice. The angel that had crashed through David Star's office had said those same words. With a bitter tang in my mouth, I remembered the bloody mess and the gory pits where the angel's eyes once were. Had another angel been attacked by Malphas and his underlings? What kind of message was he trying to get across to Death?

Aunt Sarah switched off the radio. "A stuntman with fake wings is found dead and now the whole city is freaking out like it's the apocalypse. Classic NYC."

I felt ashamed for feeling concerned about Death's safety. A part of me wanted to call him, confirm he was all right, and tell him about the demonic projection with Malphas. Then I remembered who he truly was. Remembered how he'd hurt me. How he'd come to my house the night before and made me feel exposed and helpless. How we'd kissed, and somehow, that was the cruelest part of all because none of it was real. The man I wanted to kiss wasn't real. He was a character, a persona that went up in flames at the strike of a match, exposing the wicked creature standing behind a curtain of fire.

I clutched my phone with white knuckles, staring but not seeing the passing scenery outside the car. *Then why did I kiss him back?*

"In other news," Aunt Sarah said. "Faith, is it true you're dating David Star? Your mom sent me a picture of you and him in a magazine."

It crossed my mind that she should have seen those magazines at her bookstore. If she'd checked any of her social media, she would have known too.

"We're acquaintances through mutual friends," I replied. "It's a small world."

We pulled into a picturesque farm with a freshly painted red barn, apple trees, pumpkin patches, and corn lined up in neat rows. Sunny Haven's farm, where Pleasant Valley went to enjoy all their favorite fall festivities. Normally, Mom and Dad took me pumpkin and apple picking every year here, but the past two years we hadn't gone. I missed our Halloween traditions, so I planned on bringing Mom home plenty of apples to bake apple pie with her and picking the biggest pumpkin in the patch to carve a jack-o'-lantern with Dad. He wouldn't care if we did it the day after Halloween.

I spent the next few hours pretending it was any other day. The two of us went on a hayride to go pumpkin picking, ventured back to the car to drop off our harvest, and then rode another hayride for apple picking. It didn't look like it had rained here on the farm last night, even though the drive was only twenty minutes from my house. I wondered if Death had brought that nasty storm with him, like the force of nature that he was.

"When you were a little squirt," Aunt Sarah began, as we carried our wooden buckets of apples down an endless aisle of trees, "we used to get you a bunch of those little mini pumpkins they sell at the barn. You loved painting them. And chucking them at your dad."

"That's too much," I laughed.

"No really, you used to do this thing where you'd toss the pumpkins at your father. You'd never really hit him, but he'd pretend to be hurt and say 'ouch!' so that you'd giggle hysterically."

"Sounds like I was a sadistic child."

"The most adorable, always smiling, sadistic child."

RAWK!

I nearly dropped the wooden basket in my hand as a raven landed on a high branch above us. All of a sudden, the bird nose-dived toward me, but I ducked down, so it crossed over to another tree. Quickly jerking its head side to side, the raven stared down at me with beady black eyes. As the dark bird opened its mouth and continued its throaty squawk, Aunt Sarah did the unthinkable and hurled an apple at it. She would have hit it, too, had it not taken flight at the last second.

"Nice throw," I said unsteadily. The phantom mark on my forearm stung again, like claws scraping at my skin from the inside. I pressed my hand against the pain until the sensation went away. I was in too deep with this supernatural stuff to dismiss the bird as a coincidence, but I couldn't bring myself to ruin another day just yet. "Now I know where I got my softball skills from."

The whole hayride back I was on edge, watching the skies for crazed ravens. By the time the ride stopped by the main entrance without a single bird or demon in sight, I'd convinced myself the raven really was just a coincidence this time.

"So," Aunt Sarah said, as we hopped off the wagon. "What's up with your celebrity boyfriend? You kinda blew me off before and your mom is convinced you're dating him."

"David's not my boyfriend," I said, kicking gravel as we walked. "Turns out he's as fake as I initially thought he was."

Aunt Sarah placed her hand on my shoulder with a serious expression, stopping us both. "I had no idea. I'm so sorry you're hurting."

"I thought I would see this coming, but I was blindsided. Now I feel stupid. I wasted so much energy on someone who wasn't even real."

"Aw, sweetheart . . . " Aunt Sarah hugged me in a firm embrace and emotion tightened my throat. "You are not stupid, Faith. When you're in a new relationship it's fun and exciting. It can be hard to see the warning signs that things might not work out." She pulled me back at arm's length. "Listen, life will not always work out as planned, and it shouldn't. When things don't work out, when we're disappointed by love, or life, we learn the most about ourselves. Heartbreak is part of growing up and figuring out who you are. Who you are to me is intelligent, kind, brave, and so worthy of love. You're allowed to be upset because it's disappointing, but don't put yourself down. Look at how much you've learned instead."

I braved a smile. "Thank you. I really needed to hear that."

"Anytime, kiddo." She looked toward the various food trucks parked to the right of us in a compacted dirt area. "You hungry? Don't know about you, but I'm in the mood for fried chicken."

I laughed, since she didn't eat meat. I hadn't eaten since tacos with Marcy yesterday, and the morning vomit session had left me incredibly shaky. Before I could respond, a familiar cold sensation pricked at the back of my neck.

Death was here.

I scanned my surroundings and couldn't see him anywhere. *What could he possibly want with me now?*

"Is something wrong, Faith?"

I gazed back at Aunt Sarah, to find her staring at me with an odd expression on her face.

"Nope, I'm just starving," I said with an authenticity that put Oscar nominees to shame. "Let's go eat—"

Someone bumped into me as they walked past us, nearly knocking me to the ground.

I whirled around to glower at the clobbering idiot as the cold sensation hit me again. The wide back, broad shoulders, and overall massive frame of the man walking away from us was unmistakably Death. Clad in black jeans and a hoodie with a leather jacket over it, collar up, he managed to blend in with the people around us. At my stare, in almost slow motion, he looked back over his shoulder, revealing a shadowy area where his features should have been.

Death took one last drag from his cigarette, flicked it to the side, and then stuffed his hands into his pockets. He headed in the direction of the big red barn, and as I watched him stalk away, his deep voice invaded my skull. *We need to talk. Meet me in the barn.*

My heart pounded incessantly in my ears.

Aunt Sarah tilted her chin up, as if she were about to shout something crude to Death, but then her brows scrunched together, and her eyes narrowed.

"What a jerk," she said. Glancing back at Death again, Aunt Sarah grabbed my shoulder, steering me toward the Sunny Haven's food trucks for guests. "Come on, time to eat all the fries."

Feeling drained of energy, I decided to eat before Death

ultimately sought me out. Besides feeling betrayed and angry, I was also a little scared to be alone with him again.

I ordered a huge tray of cheese fries and a slice of pepperoni pizza at one of the grease trucks, then popped a squat at a wooden picnic table. Aunt Sarah stood in a ridiculously long line at another truck to buy her veggie burger.

I'll admit it, I didn't wait for my aunt and attacked my large carton of cheese fries with the restraint of a ferociously hungry wildebeest. Can you blame me? I was starving. I couldn't remember the last time I'd had the ability to eat without feeling sick from nerves.

I finished half my fries and pizza in record time. Glancing back at my aunt, who was *still* in line for her veggie burger, I shook the ice at the bottom of my soda and crushed the cardboard container, stacking it on top of my empty french fry container and paper plate.

I swung my leg out from the picnic table and leaned toward the garbage can nearby to toss my trash. Since my aunt notoriously never locked her car, I figured I'd put my apples away while I waited for her. I lifted the wooden basket beside me and headed to the back of the lot, following a family lugging their pumpkins to their car—a mom, a dad, and a little girl skipping in between them. As they crossed the dirt lot and I approached Aunt Sarah's car, the little girl glanced back at me. Half of her face was painted like a skull.

A car honked, and I lurched back as a purple Jeep came flying past to pull haphazardly into the spot right next to Aunt Sarah's Toyota. Pleasant Valley's golden boy linebacker, Brody McCormick, hopped out of the car, along with Nicole Hawkins and her two clones. Brody had painted gruesome zombie makeup on his face and the three girls were dressed as cats.

"Hey, Wednesday Addams!" Nicole greeted with a sugary sweet fake smile. "Lose your sidekick again, freak?"

"Who, Marcy?" Brody asked, chewing a piece of gum like a cow.

He inspected an imaginary spot on his car and rubbed at it with his varsity jacket. "That slut's probably getting tested for the clap as we speak."

"I heard she hooked up with Tommy at his party and now he's sick," Nicole added, twirling a strand of her glossy honey hair. "Wanna bet he got it from her?"

"Sure didn't get it from this freak," Brody said, thumbing toward me. "Unless he's got a hard-on for ugly goth chicks."

"Aren't you a little young to have a receding hairline, Brody?" I blurted before I could stop myself. "Don't worry, I'm sure you have enough butt hair to solve the issue."

The one cheerleader giggled, suppressing it with her palm as Nicole gave her a sharp look. Brody reddened, his zombie-painted features tightening. He raised his arm, and I flinched, thinking he might hit me. Instead, he swatted my crate with a fake severed human hand, spilling apples all over the ground. "Watch your mouth, you ugly bitch."

My hand tightened around my mace in my pocket, ready to use it. Brody backed off and strode away. The girls trailed behind him, now laughing at my expense. Pleasant Valley. The irony kills me.

Growling, I bent down to pick up my apples, when an icy chill ran down the back of my neck.

"Happy Halloween."

Straightening at that deep, velvety voice, I jerked my head to the side. And there he was.

"Death," I breathed.

"The man, the myth, the legend," he said dryly. "Sexy, aren't I?" The last time we were together, he'd been knocked unconscious by my crazy light beam, and my treacherous little fingers had investigated him like I was Nancy Drew. Now he was leaning against Brody's Jeep, his tall frame angled toward me. I replayed our encounter from the night before and tried not to seek out the bulky muscles beneath his leather jacket, or the menacing shadow over his face, and instead focused lamely on the center of his chest.

"Have you any concept of time?" Death asked, when I couldn't find the courage to speak. "I gave you explicit instructions to meet me at the barn. It's been an hour of you futzing around." Then he took a knife out from underneath his jacket and slashed Brody's tire with it.

"Dude, what the heck!"

"He's lucky it's not his face."

As the tire hissed out, Death prowled past me to the annihilate the next tire, when I grabbed his leather-clad shoulder. "Can you *stop?*"

"*Little Brody* was one smart remark away from getting his head lopped off," Death said, twirling the blade around his gloved fingers in a dangerous dance. "He knows damn well you're beautiful."

I was so stunned by the compliment that I almost overlooked the whole lop-his-head-off thing.

Feeling as though someone was listening in, I glanced back at the picnic tables, to find my aunt approaching the table with her food. I turned back to Death, playing with the cross around my neck. His head dipped down, and I could feel his shadowed eyes track the movement.

"This might come as a surprise to your enormous ego," I said at last, "but I don't need you to defend me." I proceeded to fix the bottom of the apple basket by wedging a broken piece of wood into the circular frame. Then I bent down to pick up the apples on the grass, gingerly placing them into the basket. "Don't you have anything better to do than stalk me all the time? Like, oh, I don't know, do your *job* and collect souls?"

"Thanks for the concern, but I've already surpassed my quota. Why don't you worry about upgrading your pants situation?"

"They're called ripped jeans." I stood up with the basket, all sass. "Calvin Klein's. Didn't *David Star* do a campaign for them? I expect an employee discount."

Death slinked closer to me, broad shoulders rolling in that delicious leather jacket and long powerful legs working a hell of a pair of dark jeans. He gestured to my T-shirt. "Hello, wife. Should I have worn my 'I'm Batman' shirt today?"

"Charming." A sear of heat crept up my neck. I bent down again to pick up the rest of the apples to hide the flush he'd triggered. "Do me a huge favor? Perform your vanishing act and never return. It'll be your best trick yet, I promise!"

"You're mad about the kiss," Death speculated in an amused voice, and my fingers paused on the skin of a McIntosh. "I'll make it easy for you, forget it happened. It was a mistake."

My stomach sank. As much as I didn't want to admit it now, the kiss had meant something to me. "You must be dense in the head if you think *your kiss* was my biggest takeaway of last night. You betrayed me, and you lied to me."

"Go on," he said with an encouraging wave of a gloved hand. Like I was *complimenting* him.

Oooh, he just made me *so* . . .

"What the hell's the matter with you? This isn't a joke. I'm not upset about the kiss, although it was the most disappointing portion of the night!"

He had the nerve to snicker. "You're a horrible liar."

"Good thing I have you around to give me plenty of pointers."

"Don't act like you didn't enjoy kissing me, Faith," Death purred, in a way that thickened his untraceable accent. "You loved it. It just shouldn't have happened."

"Always trying to validate something. Could there be confidence issues beneath his overbearing personality and veiled shadow?"

Death freed a growl. "Nothing to validate, sweetheart. In all my existence, a woman has never clung to my arms as desperately as you did last night." He was a master at getting under my skin because I was already seething like a rabid dog from his taunting.

"If I was touching your arms, which I don't recall doing, I was trying to push you away." *As if I could ever forget those sculpted biceps.*

"Right, you don't recall," he said silkily. I hated how he could manipulate his voice like that. It did things to me. "Just like you won't remember moaning into my mouth."

"Okay, that's enough of you."

I could *feel* his provocative grin. "Is it?"

"If you're so hot and glorious like you claim you are, why don't you take off that stupid hood and show me what the big deal is?"

"Because you couldn't handle all of me, *cupcake.*" His voice was a mere purr again. "I'm doing you a favor."

I couldn't challenge that. To be honest, at the thought of him showing me his face, I started to get nervous. If he was as frighteningly hot as I believed, it would only make resisting him even more difficult.

"Last night, I tried to tell you to stop," I insisted, continuing our cat and mouse game. "The last thing I wanted was your lying, two-faced, dead—"

"Undead," he corrected.

"*Undead* breath in my mouth!" I finished with a huff.

"Your tongue had a funny way of showing it."

"I-I don't remember that either," I stammered. Thinking about his wicked tongue fueled my corrupted imagination in ways that made my reckless hormones perform enthusiastic backflips. Poker-faced, but burning all over, I tilted my chin up. "Next, you're going to tell me I kissed you first, right?"

"That goes without saying."

I barked out a laugh. "Good joke!"

He stole an apple from my basket and raised it to his shadowy mouth. A few crunches, and the whole apple, including the core, was polished off. *Well, that was unnecessary.*

Death braced a powerful hand on the roof of Aunt Sarah's car, like a composed predator. "You got on your tippy-toes. All doe-eyed and awkward. I felt bad, so I let it happen. The end."

"We kissed at the exact same time," I said, fuming over this.

"Sure about that?"

I looked off into space, second-guessing myself. "No!" I shouted, pointing a finger at him as I placed the basket of apples on the ground. "No, no, *no*! You're screwing with me again! It was at the same time! Might I add, I distinctly recall your hands grabbing my ass! And my thighs!" Shouting these things at him made that night somehow more real. "Which means you—you were into it, too!"

"Gaining your memory back, I see?" I could hear him grinning. "Now do you remember the moaning?"

"I thought you didn't like me," I fired back.

"I *don't*," he seethed, his voice slipping back into that preternatural growl. "You are, without a shadow of a doubt, the most annoying person to ever exist." He leaned into me. "But I won't deny that last night was . . . surprising. Your body felt perfect against mine. You have a great ass too. I love an ass I can get a nice handful of."

Burn. Everything was burning inside me. "You need help. Serious therapy, dude. Padded room, straitjacket, meds, the whole nine yards! We are *never* talking about this again. I'm so serious. Never again. It never happened."

"Fine by me."

"Good," I panted out. I had gotten so worked up that I'd barely been breathing. "Because I'd like to pretend my first wasn't with death personified, thank you very much."

He didn't say anything for a moment. "Your *first*? I was your first kiss?"

I wanted to push my hair in front of my face and hide like Cousin Itt. "You knew I was a virgin, but you didn't know I'd never kissed before?"

"The virgin part was obvious. You wore slacks to the interview."

"That doesn't make any sense."

"Says the virgin. Lucky you, having me as your first. The mortal boys would have drooled into your mouth like a faucet. Me? I pride myself on my flawless tongue technique." He lowered his voice as he leaned into me. "It's all about the teasing and the flicking."

I crossed my arms over my chest, boiling again over the clear underlying innuendo in his sensual voice. My attempt at an intimidating pose didn't do much, considering the virtual bulldozer before me, and that only made me angrier.

"That's it! Back up!" I jabbed at the air in front of me, and as if I had popped a bubble of sexual tension between us, heat rolled from Death's body and sank into my sweatshirt to my bare skin. *What the hell?* "Give me space. You always loom over me like a skyscraper. I get it, you're big."

He snickered at the back of his throat. "Damn right, sunshine."

"And the whole game you play with your body and how you present yourself," I continued now that I was on a roll. "Do you think I don't notice how you always make that little growl at me?"

"Well," Death began, lighting a cigarette, "maybe if you'd play with me more and gave me love and affection, I wouldn't growl so much—"

"I'm not falling for this new playful act. We have one make-out session and suddenly you're making the moves on me? What, did you buy catnip on the way over here and now you're frisky?"

"The irresistible don't need moves," he said, exhaling cherry-scented smoke. "And FYI, catnip makes me sleepy. Souls on the other hand, now, they perk me right up."

"You don't actually eat people?"

"No, I'm vegan."

My eyes widened. "You *consume* souls?"

"Yes, Faith, the stereotype of consuming souls does in fact align with my pseudonym and my entire existence," Death said. "Don't look at me like that, I don't eat the whole thing. The soul is not destroyed. I trim off some pieces for a snack." He made a quick slicing motion in the air. "Then I send the little shit off."

He had a way with words. "Do you collect all the souls on this entire planet?"

"Yep." He popped the *p*. He sounded bored of conversation.

"By *yourself?*"

"Along with my seven *reapers.*"

Reapers? Were there more of his kind?

I tried to wrap my mind around this. "There's no way that you and seven reapers . . . or whatever, could reap all the souls in the world. Especially while you're constantly out gallivanting around with hot models and celebrities as David Star."

Death reclined lazily against Aunt Sarah's car again, angling himself toward me with a dark laugh. "Jealousy is a delicious look on you, but you should know the only girl I've been gallivanting around with is you."

I felt a mild fluttering in my chest. "Just tell me how you do it. How you . . . *collect* so many souls."

"I'm a monster of many talents. It's simple, really." Suddenly, I felt a presence behind me. "I can multiply," he whispered into my ear.

Startled, I whirled around. Death stood *behind* me, snickering. I snapped around, to find him lazily inclined against the sports car on the other side of me too. Looking back and forth between the two Deaths, I struggled to process what I was seeing. He could *multiply*.

Now, this . . . this was *not* good. One Death I could handle. Barely. But two? *Hundreds?* Fantastic—now my dirty mind imagined multiple Deaths kissing me at the same time.

"Oh my G*od*, this is so not okay," I said. "How many times can you freaking copy and paste yourself?"

"Thousands," said Death One.

"When I have the energy," Death Two added, flicking a strand of my hair into my face with his gloved finger, before exploding into a black mist.

"The duplicates only last a few minutes," the remaining Death explained. "I send them out to do their job, and then they dissipate and the energy they collected from the mortal soul returns back to me. It's taken years of practice. My mind can exist in layers like this. It's a trick. Magic. As with any magic, there are consequences that directly affect me so that I do not overreach my . . . limitations as the Grim Reaper."

"Checks and balances."

"Exactly," he said. "Duplicating, stopping time, it can all deplete me fast if I'm not careful." He rolled back his one shoulder, as though he were uncomfortable. "Then it gets complicated."

"I'm following just fine," I said softly.

"In essence, energy from a mortal's life is my incentive to keep working. The soul keeps me temporarily satiated. It's all part of my punishment."

"Punishment for what?"

Death stared down at me for a beat before continuing. "Long story short, after I was cursed as Death, Heaven recruited me to become an angel. To use my ability to see into people's souls for good. Let's just say I broke a few rules up there and they didn't take kindly to it. Now I'm

Fallen on top of whatever *else* I already was, and my soul is still bound to Heaven. And as punishment for being a bad boy, I'm twice cursed. Cursed as a death creature and cursed to reap souls and distribute them to both Heaven and Hell, for all eternity."

Damn.

"So don't worry your pretty little innocent, moral head, cupcake," Death continued, shifting back to his teasing mood. "I only eat the parts of a mortal's soul I'm supposed to have." I could feel him grinning like a piranha. "Unless, of course, a poor soul meets me on a bad day . . . "

I loosed a shaky breath, wondering if he had more bad days than good ones.

"What about human food?" I asked, taking advantage of the fact that we were having a normal-ish discussion. If *normal* was the word to describe chatting with the Angel of Death.

"I tolerate it, when I'm starving." He sounded uninterested again, or maybe he hated that he'd become the main topic of conversation. "I lost my palate for mortal food a long time ago. Sugar and meat have always been an exception though."

No wonder he loves frosting. "What happens if you don't eat at all? Reap human souls, I mean."

His head slanted down to me, and the air plunged a few degrees colder. "We're talking too much. Time to come with me." He inclined a gloved finger to himself. "Now, if you will."

"Not happening. Especially after you reminded me my soul is a Happy Meal for you."

The huskiness of his laugh was like a hot caress against my skin. "Every moment you remain exposed, you put yourself and your loved ones in danger. You will only attract more creatures to your essence. Do I need to tattoo these words on the palm of your hand for you to finally grasp them?"

With great restraint, I bit down on my tongue to hold back a sarcastic response, something I probably should have done a lot more often. I hated how superior he considered himself. My eyes raked from his combat boots, up his massive frame, to stare into the hidden eyes of the creature beneath the hood. Shadows twisted around his cloak, coiling in the air like phantom snakes. When we kissed, that darkness had embraced me. I'd been engulfed by his shadows and kissed by them, as if they were also a part of him. As my brain roved over dirty thoughts of Death's shadows—of all things—I could feel the monster himself silently watching me from beneath his veil.

I had to stop thinking about that damn kiss and remember whom I was dealing with.

"I'm not going," I said firmly, as heat surged down my arms. "I'm not leaving my loved ones alone and exposed to you, and I won't let you use me anymore. I'd rather die."

He released a baritone growl that rattled at the back of his throat. It was impossible not to recoil. When I did, my foot tripped over the basket of apples. His strong gloved hand shot out and clasped my wrist before I fell. Death pulled me forward and to the side, pinning me to the Toyota.

"Be careful what you wish for," he purred against my throbbing pulse. "I can take a life just as quickly as I can spare one." He lowered his head to the crook of my neck. I let him, succumbing to the madness. "You're different than the other mortals. That's unfortunate for you, because I find the most unusual things in this world are the tastiest."

Out of instinct, or maybe out of pure insanity, my hands reached out to fist the warm T-shirt beneath his leather jacket. Layers of carved muscles tightened just beyond a thin layer of cotton. "Do *not*. Threaten me."

"It wasn't a threat." Death pressed his lips to my neck. A jolt of heat slid down my spine, coiling in the very place he'd roused the night before. All of my senses shut down, except for touch. My eyes fluttered closed as his cruel gloved hands drifted down the outline of my ribs, my waist, my hips. When he brushed a small patch of exposed skin on the upper leg of my ripped jeans, he slid a finger inside, grazing the bare flesh of my thigh and my fishnets with leather. I could not breathe. With a low laugh, his tongue stroked a wicked path up the column of my throat in a leisurely caress. "It was a promise."

Rather than disappearing into a black mist, he pushed off the Toyota and prowled away into the parking lot. Looked like he'd be hanging around.

"Boo!" Aunt Sarah shouted from behind me. I was a miracle I hadn't peed myself.

"Why do people keep doing that to me?" I lashed out, slapping a hand over my neck, where moments ago Death's tongue had been.

"I'm sorry, sweetheart," she said, taken aback by my outburst. "I was trying to be funny."

"I know." I removed my fingers from my neck in shame and raked them through my hair. "I know, I'm sorry."

"Who were you talking to?" Aunt Sarah asked.

It took a humiliating amount of effort to focus on an answer. "Just a friend from class." The phantom trace of Death's caress tingled on my neck, mocking my lie. "He had a question about our homework."

Her shaped eyebrows bowed inward, the incredulity in her expression making me nervous. "You'd tell me if it was something else, right?"

"There's nothing else. Honest." I smiled convincingly.

"Good . . . Well, let me help you with that before your arms fall off." Brightening, she took the crate of apples from me and placed them on the towels in the backseat of her Toyota.

"What do you think about you and me hanging out at that cute coffee shop in the barn house until the sun goes down?" Aunt Sarah asked, once she closed the door. In a theatrical movement, she flashed a set of haunted hayride tickets in front of my face. "Since I got these bad boys!"

XX

My initial reaction was to say no. After meeting with Death, I wanted to go home to my safe ground. But maybe that was exactly what he wanted, and I was sick and tired of living in fear.

"Hey, *chicas*!" I turned, just in time to unexpectedly catch Marcy running full force into me. "Fancy seeing you two gorgeous gals here!" She bumped the sides of her hips with mine and Aunt Sarah's. "You know, Faith, part of playing hooky is picking the prime day to skip. It was an early dismissal today and Principal Mallory handed out candy in homeroom. Should have just come in, ya boob."

"My fault," Aunt Sarah said with a laugh. "I'm the one who kidnapped her."

"What's up, Auntie?" Marcy lifted her fist to bump knuckles with my aunt. "Did you get your hair done? Looks fab."

"Really? You like it?" Aunt Sarah gushed, fluffing her blond hair. "Went a little darker blond this time. It's supposed to make me look less old, according to *Cosmo*."

"Old?" Marcy jerked back. "Excuse me, I will not accept such negativity in my presence. You could literally pass for a superhot college girl. The color is a total vibe."

Marcy and Aunt Sarah caught up, while I stood in silence. The shock and panic of *two* of my loved ones here with Death lurking around settled sourly in my gut.

"This is Nathan, by the way." Marcy motioned to the handsome boy approaching us with a funnel cake in his hand. With his surfer boy blond hair and twinkling blue eyes, I instantly compared him to Thomas, which made me even more sick to my stomach as I harked back to Thomas being taken away with Malphas. "Faith, you know Nathan, right? He's on the basketball team and lives down the street from me."

She gave me a knowing look to play along, and I bit back a laugh. Ever since Marcy witnessed Nathan washing down his truck last summer with his shirt off, she'd had huge heart eyes for him. Nathan's knack for hitting three-pointers was legendary in Pleasant Valley. The kid was smart too. He was in a few of my AP classes.

"Sure, I know Nathan," I said with my best *I'm friendly and outgoing* smile. Fake it till you make it, right? "Congratulations, by the way. Word in the hallways is you already have a full ride to the University of Kentucky."

"Thank you," he said with a bashful smile. "I'm excited for November, gonna make Coach proud my last season. You should come out and see us when we're home." He smiled at Marcy. "It'd be cool to see both of you in the stands."

"We would love to!" I enthused.

Nathan seemed kind and down-to-earth.

"So," Marcy said, stealing some of Nathan's funnel cake, "you guys going on the haunted hayride later?"

Our hayride shone vibrant neon green in the night, decorated with glow-in-the-dark pumpkin signs with spooky faces.

"Woo-hoo!" Aunt Sarah bounced up and down on her stack of hay. She shook my shoulder playfully. "Aren't you excited?"

"Excited as hypothermia will allow." I pulled the ends of my sweatshirt sleeves over my hands and fisted the fabric closed in my palms. Had I known it would be this cold at night, I would have packed a parka. And a space heater. Better yet, I would have stayed in bed.

The freezing temperature wasn't the only reason for my foul mood. Aunt Sarah and I sat all the way in the back of the second cart with Marcy and Nathan. In the first cart, attached to ours by a few questionable rusty bolts and chains, were a few more teenagers from our high school and a man dressed in all black with his back to us. I scowled. Instead of a cloak, Death wore the same hoodie and leather jacket with the popped collar that he sported earlier. He had appeared out of nowhere, of course, but only I seemed to notice.

I glanced over at Marcy and Nathan. Catching my eye, Marcy jabbed a finger discreetly at Nathan's crotch and raised both her eyebrows with wide eyes. Then she winked with a sly smile. I laughed, immediately understanding.

Apparently, she anticipated Nathan had a nice you-know-what.

"What are you two giggling at?" Nathan asked in a joking tone.

"Nothing," Marcy and I said at the same time, laughing harder.

"Weirdos." Nathan rolled his eyes and stretched his arm behind Marcy. She cuddled into his side, and I thought they'd make a great couple. She seemed genuinely happy with him, which made me happy.

There were a few stops along the ride and a few corn mazes to choose from. The cart jerked to a halt at the easiest maze, near the beginning.

"Meet you at the other corn maze?" Marcy asked, offering me a stick of gum as she popped one into her mouth and stood up. "This one's supposed to be less scary."

I threw up a peace sign. "Text if you need me."

"Kay-kay."

They got off the hayride.

Aunt Sarah laughed. "They're finding somewhere to hook up, aren't they?"

"Oh, one hundred percent."

The hayride trudged up a hill past a shadowy pumpkin patch. I did a double take. In the first cart, ahead of us, Death gave a dramatic yawn and lounged with his long legs up on the barrels of hay beside him, so that he hogged all the seats. It bothered me beyond belief that he was following me around. I knew in a way it shouldn't, since he *had* saved my life and all, twice, but that didn't change the fact that the guy was an egotistical a-hole who'd lied to me. He'd made it clear his protection wasn't offered entirely out of kindness too.

Death lit up a cigarette and took a drag, letting out a lazy puff of smoke, which hit Aunt Sarah and I directly in the face.

"Pretty sure you aren't supposed to smoke on a *hay*ride, buddy!" I hollered.

Aunt Sarah smacked my arm. "Stop it," she hissed. "He could be crazy."

She had no idea.

Spiderweb-tangled lanterns hung from the branchy trees, casting the path in an eerie light. The hayride passed a sign that hung over us marked in crooked red letters: WELCOME TO HELL.

Evil laughter erupted from the trees. The bumpy cart slowed at a graveyard, which smelled of a barbecue, blanketed by a layer of creepy fog. Loud organ music played through static speakers and spasmodic bursts of fire shot out from torches.

"You have met your death!" announced a booming voice. Out came a lanky man dressed as the Grim Reaper. The costume was meant to be serious, but the cloak looked more like a silky spa robe than the cape of an evil entity. In his hand he held a ridiculously small plastic scythe. If it were any smaller, it'd be a gardening tool in one of those mini toy Zen gardens. "Thou shall not pass! I want your soul! Arrrgghh!" The man lifted his skinny arms to the sky and people hidden poorly in camouflage banged garbage can lids for the effect of thunder.

Deep, hearty laughter exploded from the hayride. My eyes darted to Death as he slow clapped. "Fantastic interpretation," he mocked. "Such realism. It's like looking in the mirror!"

The cart wobbled forward. The stereotypical scary music continued, and the tractor rolled to a stop in front of a small stage, cutting its engine. The stage was set up to look like a little girl's room, with a small bed, a bubblegum-pink comforter and pink-lemonade walls. Painted a darker shade of pink, a prominent closet door was nestled in a corner of the bedroom.

Lying on the bed was a girl around my age, modeled after a little girl. Her golden-blond hair was up in pigtails with wire that kept them up in a wacky U shape against her pillow. She wore a frilly magenta dress that went to her knees and high socks, and in her hands, she clutched a teddy bear that resembled my own childhood bear, Mr. Wiggles.

As I observed the stage, a solid knock came from the girl's closet door. "Momma, is that you?" the actress promptly asked. A masculine cackle of a laugh replied. Visibly afraid, the girl squeezed the bear tighter to her chest. "Papa! Papa! Help me! The clown is here again!"

Hell no.

Papa, aka a brawny guy with a beer gut, threw open the girl's bedroom door.

"What's the matter this time, Little Sophie!" he bellowed, follcwed by a belch that made our whole cart laugh.

"The monster is back!" Sophie shouted back, clutching the teddy bear even harder. "It knocked on the door again! I'm not lying, Papa!"

"Yeah, yeah, whatever! I'll check again, if it will get you to finally sleep." The dad stomped across the stage like a drunk T. rex and threw open the closet door, sticking his head in to look around. "See? No monster."

"I heard it knock," the girl insisted.

The dad walked toward her daughter's bed, shaking his head theatrically as he placed his hands on his hips. "What am I going to do with you, Sophie?"

A guy in a terrifying clown mask stuck his head out of the open closet door, covered his mouth with a white-gloved hand, and shook with silent laughter. I gripped the railing of the hayride with white knuckles as the clown held out a knife, bringing it back as if to stab the father.

The girl shrieked. "Behind you!"

The father spun around, but the clown had already ducked back into the darkness.

With a growl, the dad closed the closet door and turned to look over to the daughter. "There, are you satisfied now?"

With a menacing giggle, the clown came charging out of the closet with a large knife, stabbing the father over and over. Fake blood and gore exploded from the father's clothes. As the clown lunged for the daughter and dragged her across the stage screaming, the lights went off. The music went off. Then it was silent, besides a hurl of frigid air, which made my teeth chatter.

I found myself looking over at Death in the other wagon. His hooded head was already turned toward me, and he watched me from underneath his shadows with his arms spread out on either side of the railing. He inclined his head toward himself, as if to tell me, *If you're scared, angel, come over here.*

I shook my head once. *Drop dead.*

He snickered out loud. He'd heard me.

Despite a few glimpses into his past, I knew very little about Death. I found myself increasingly curious about him. The countless souls he'd collected over the centuries. The people who had died at his hand. How did someone cope with everything he'd been through? How many friendships had he broken, and enemies had he made? How many times had he fallen in love, had he married? Did he have kids? How many women had he kissed? How many women had he—? Dang, I really didn't want to think about *that*, but there was no way to unthink it now. Did he enjoy being the Grim Reaper? Did he know God? *Gods?* Elvis?

No, Death said. I assumed that was the answer to knowing Elvis, but I was too mortified to care. He'd read my thoughts again. Now I had to promptly bury my head in the sand like an ostrich.

"He-he-he!" a voice exclaimed from behind me. I whirled around to find the clown from the stage right in my face. With the loudest shriek I could muster, I catapulted across the wagon and fell onto another stack of hay, plastered against the wooden rails parallel to the other wagon.

"Sure you don't want to hop over into this cart?" asked the velvety voice of my supernatural stalker. I swiveled around, coming face-to-darkness with Death on the front wagon. He leaned over the railing toward me, his voice dropping to a husky murmur. "I'll keep those pesky clowns away."

"Your personality does tend to repel everything with and without a pulse."

"Ouch." He tapped his gloved fingers against the wooden railing. "And to think I was going to let you sit on my lap."

"Stay away from my niece," Aunt Sarah snapped, and suddenly I was yanked back from the edge of the wagon and disposed onto another haystack, landing inelegantly in the process. My mouth gaped in utter confusion, as she now stood fearlessly between Death and me. "Leave us alone. You're not welcome here."

Death freed a stunted laugh and looked away from us. "Way to kill the mood."

"You can see him too?" I asked.

"I asked nicely," Aunt Sarah continued, her focus locked on the Grim Reaper. She snatched an ancient-looking cross from the back of her jeans and held it up. "Next time, I'll cast you straight back to Hell with Lucifer, where you belong."

"I'd rip your throat out two words into that spell," Death said.

An awful sensation rotted in my gut as I looked between the two of them in puzzlement.

"What's going on here?" I demanded. When both of them played the quiet game, I looked pleadingly at my aunt. "Aunt Sarah?" I gestured at the ancient cross in her hand. "Do you have something to tell me?"

The tractor came to a halt in front of a large sign that read HAUNTED CORN MAZE in neon lights. The small group of teenagers on the ride poured out of Death's cart, screaming and giggling.

Aunt Sarah clenched her jaw. "I'm a demon hunter, Faith."

"A *slayer*? Like . . . *Buffy*? I thought you owned a bookstore!"

"It's kind of a side hustle."

I could not believe what I was hearing. "How long have you been hiding this?"

"There's a lot we have to talk about, Faith."

"*Clearly!* You know, at this point, nothing really surprises me!

Angel of Death, this is my Aunt Sarah, demon hunter. Aunt Sarah, this is the Angel of Death."

"Hi," Death said, then cleared his throat. "I mean, *yo*."

I faced Aunt Sarah. "He's a psychopath."

"It's an art, like anything else," Death said.

"I was under the impression he was just an asshole," Aunt Sarah quipped.

"You two spoil me with compliments." Death tipped his head back over the railing behind him, lounging without a care. "Faith, your aunt and I already know each other. She and Lucifer crossed paths once or twice—"

"Shut up," my aunt snapped at him. "Shut your mouth, or I'll stick this cross so far up your ass—"

She stopped midsentence, as Death picked himself up and rose to his incredible height. He raised a huge boot to the railing at the back of his cart, then the other, and balanced impossibly on the edge like a cat. His leather jacket had evaporated into darkness, shadows billowing out from his frame into a long regal cloak, which whipped around in the night. At the sight of his looming frame, Aunt Sarah backpedaled a few steps, and me with her. With a sinister laugh, Death took a single long stride, stepping over the gap between our carts. He jumped down in front of us, metal clinking underneath his cloak as the cart shuddered from his weight.

"If you think I feel threatened by a little pocket cross," he growled in that deep, lilted voice, "you're *gravely* mistaken." With a slight swish of a gloved hand, his enormous scythe appeared at his side, gleaming in the night.

Aunt Sarah gripped the cross tighter, and I could see her fingers were trembling. "I'm not afraid of you. I have the power of the Ancients by my side."

Death cocked his head. "I was wondering what that smell was."

"Lucifer knows better than to send you to harm a hunter of the Guild," Aunt Sarah said. "The Elders will find out, and who knows, maybe this will be the last straw. Maybe you'll get your wings sliced off again. Unless you want the flight of a penguin, I suggest you leave us alone and go prey on someone else."

"You're clearly out of the loop." Death weighed the staff of his scythe in his gloved hands. "I'm not here for you. I'm here for *her*."

Aunt Sarah looked at me in quiet horror. "What?"

"Faith died, I spared her life with a deal," Death explained, "and now she owes me. It's time for me to collect what is mine: her soul . . . and *her*. Attempt to break this arrangement, and you will only be damaging your niece in the process."

Aunt Sarah kept her attention daggered to Death, like he might attack her at any moment. "Why didn't you tell me about this, Faith?"

"Because I prefer my bedroom over padded cell walls? How was I supposed to know you were so well acquainted with the supernatural world?"

"I'm so sorry you had to find out this way," she said. "I can't tell anyone what I am. Not even my own sister. As for you, Fallen, my niece and I are getting off this ride. If you follow us, I *will* condemn you to Hell."

"By all means, go for it," Death dared. "It's a little nippy outside anyway."

"If you're after the book, you're wasting your time," she added. "Faith knows nothing about it, and she doesn't know where it is. Nobody does."

"A book," I echoed, suddenly recalling what Ace had told me in his séance room about me leading those who sought the book. "The *Book of the Dead*," I said, recalling the name. "You're talking about the *Book of the Dead*."

Shouldn't have said that out loud.

Panic filled Aunt Sarah's expression. "Who told you about the *Book of the Dead?*"

"If I had to guess, she learned about it from a warlock, Ace," Death answered, sounding entertained by my aunt's panic. He maneuvered his scythe in a skilled movement and rested it on the back of his shoulders with his arms draped over the pole.

"I don't understand," Aunt Sarah said. "What do you want from Faith?"

"All you need to know is I need my property, unscathed. I will not leave here tonight without her. Faith's already attracted creatures to her essence, it's only a matter of time before she gets herself killed. Doesn't help that she acts impulsively and trips over particles of dust."

I narrowed my eyes at him.

"She doesn't belong to you," Aunt Sarah seethed, "and she certainly doesn't belong to *him!*"

"I'm afraid you can't make claim to her anymore." I could hear the cruel smirk hidden beneath Death's black veil and blood pulsed in my ears in anticipation of his next words. "Only I control the Order of the Kiss of Death. See how my name is in the title? If Faith will not conform to me, then she will never see you, or her family, ever again. She would be officially rescinding our agreement, my *merciful* act of life, and she would therefore fall dead to the ground. That is my law, not Lucifer's. And there is nothing you, nor any god or holy object, can do about it."

I sucked in an unfulfilling breath. I would die if I didn't go with him?

"When exactly were you going to tell me *that?*" I shouted at Death.

Death maneuvered his menacing scythe again so that it stood at his side. With a wave of his hand, the weapon evaporated away. "Surely you didn't think you'd deny my right to your soul, and then be sent on your merry way?"

"Your trustworthiness grows by the minute," I spat.

"As does your attitude, little mortal," he purred. "Maybe you should consider the fragile state of your soul and pay me some respect."

"You'll get my respect when you deserve it. So never."

Death released a low hiss in my direction, and then his hooded head snapped toward my aunt. He made a small gesture with his gloved fingers. Dark wisps of matter wrapped around her hand and made her palm snap back, revealing a bottle clutched tight in her fingers.

My heart leapt to my throat as Aunt Sarah visibly strained against Death's power. He snatched the bottle from her fingers and analyzed its contents.

"Well, well. You really were going to condemn me back to Hell." He clucked his tongue disapprovingly and dropped the bottle to the ground, crushing it underneath his heel. "Sarah, since you have made it abundantly clear you won't be cooperating and will continue to get in my way, you'll understand why I will now drag *you* to Hell. Feel free to take up your dissatisfaction of my methods with Lucifer. I'm sure he'd love to reconnect with an ex."

Before I could process that *last part*, a shadow dropped from the trees around us, and then another. I could see the outline of their huge bodies as they slinked toward us on all fours. I pressed against the railing as they approached the ride. There were two of them, brawny creatures with wide hunches and enormous clawed paws. Iridescent eyes with striking shades of red, orange, and yellow, which flickered like flames in their irises. Their lips peeled back into snarls, long, ivory fangs like a wolf's.

"Hell hounds," Aunt Sarah said with horror, clutching my hand.

"Those are definitely *not* dogs." I backed away from the rail, reeling over what would happen to her if she were taken, what they would do to her in Hell. "Death, don't do this. Please, if you have any compassion left in you—"

"I don't," he said, the tails of his cloak flogging the air as the wind kicked up. "Unless . . ."

I looked to Aunt Sarah, and there wasn't a flicker of fear in her face. I could see her mulling her options over, until she came to the same conclusion as mine. Slowly, she shook her head at me. "No."

"I can stop this," I said, squeezing her hand.

"No, *no*, you don't understand, Faith." Desperation misted her eyes. "You don't know what you're agreeing to—"

"*Argh!*" A bird plunged into the night and attacked Death, fluttered its wings violently around him. The raven from before. Aunt Sarah and I huddled together, attuned to the massive hell hounds outside of the hayride, which had begun howling. With a terrifying snarl that was more intimidating than the hounds, Death made a lunge for the bird, but it moved with an unnatural speed and darted out of the way and rocketed toward the trees. Death snapped his head toward the retreating path of the animal and vanished into a black mist.

My aunt ripped her hand free from mine, her gaze set on the hell hounds. Her fingers curled into her palms, and now I had an overwhelming urge to stop her from doing whatever it was she was about to do.

"Run!" she shouted at me. "Get out of here! Now!"

Panic struck me hard, and I briefly locked eyes with one of the massive creatures below us. Fire ignited within its pupils like two endless pits.

"I can hold them off with magic!" Aunt Sarah threw out her hand, and with a single foreign command, the hell hounds fell to the ground whining and writhing in obvious agony. I stared at her in shock, my chest heaving up and down.

"This is all my fault, Faith," she said. Her color had drained to the point that she looked visibly fatigued, and I put two and two together and realized it had been from that spell. "I lied to protect you and your mother, but I've put you in danger. You have to run. You have to *fight him*. I'll come find you, I promise."

"I'm not leaving you!" I cried.

"Put your name to good use tonight, kiddo." She released me and jumped off the hayride, sprinting back down the path from where the hayride had come. The hounds broke free from whatever spell they were under and scrambled after her as she screamed, *"Run!"*

My brain spiraled. I tried the gate of the hayride, but it wouldn't unlock. With my heart in my throat, I jumped off the side of the cart and winced as my ankles took the weight of my body when I hit the ground. I took off, running into the haunted corn maze brightly lit by floodlights.

The truth was I still didn't know what kind of creature I was dealing with. Death was unpredictable and unstable, but I knew I had to keep fighting.

Moving fast around a corner, I crashed into a body.

"Faith?"

"Marcy!" I could have cried in relief and instead pulled her into a hug. Her normally sun goddess tan skin had washed away to a milky white, and every inch of her trembled so hard her teeth chattered. Had she seen one of the hell hounds? Or worse, had she seen Death?

"What's wrong?" I asked. "What happened?"

"Nathan and I, we were hooking up," Marcy began shakily, casting a look behind her. "We heard this rustling and growling, so started running. When I looked back, Nathan was gone. I followed the hayride path to here and when I got to the entrance of your maze, Thomas was there." She pushed a strand of hair out of her face. "He went into the maze, so I-I followed him. He didn't look right, Faith. Like he was really sick, or on drugs, or . . . "

"Or none of the above," Thomas said.

Marcy's eyes went wide as my heart slammed into overdrive. Slowly, I turned. Thomas Gregory stood on the path. His skin had lost any trace of its usual tan, his cheeks slightly hallowed in, and the bones in his face too sharp, too angled. His blond curls were now jet-black, and his once vibrant blue eyes had dimmed to a bottomless ocean. I probably wouldn't have recognized him had he not been wearing his usual black-and-silver varsity jacket.

"Thomas," I said, prying the name from my tight throat.

He moved toward us, and I couldn't move. There was no way we could both outrun him.

"My body accepted the demon mark," Thomas said, as if to clear the air, "so they gave me two choices. I chose to live." His laugh was short, sarcastic. "If you can call this *living*, I guess."

Guilt wrenched me apart all over again. I'd failed him.

"I need you to do me a favor, Faith," Thomas continued, prying the words out like they were painful. "I-I've been terrible to both of you, but you're the only two I can rely on."

"Can somebody tell me what the hell is going on?" Marcy asked. "I feel like I'm missing something here."

Thomas ran a frustrated hand through his hair. "I can't go back to my old life. I can't ever see my family or my friends ever again. It's not safe for me to be around anyone right now."

"What do you mean, you can't go back?" I could see the raw denial and confusion in Marcy's face as she tried to comprehend the situation. "What happened? Your mother is worried sick!"

Thomas grimaced at the mention of his mother. He clutched at his head and winced. All at once, the darkness swallowed the whiteness out of Thomas's eyes, suffocating the blue eyes of our childhood friend.

"*Fuck!* Stay back!" Thomas stretched out his jaw and roared gutturally, and his once charming smile held a mouthful of fangs. Fangs that dripped a black substance that matched the endless void of his eyes.

Marcy edged away from Thomas in fear. I could see myself in her reaction as she rapidly tried to make sense of what she'd just seen. In that moment, Thomas had looked otherworldly. Demonic. She cast a frightful look in my direction, and I silently confirmed it.

"Please, don't run," Thomas panted once he regained his bearings. He spat dark liquid to the ground like it disgusted him. "I'm not going to hurt you, I swear." When he looked up at us, oily black tears were leaking from his eyes, and my heart clenched.

"What do you need?" I asked softly.

"My mom, she's not going to handle me being gone well," he said, swiping under his eyes to erase any trace of emotion. "She'll blame herself. I need you to tell her it's not her fault. Can you do that for me?"

"Thomas, you're scaring me," Marcy whispered, hugging her arms to her chest. "Whatever's going on, whatever trouble you're in, let us help you." She took a wavering step forward, reaching for him. "I can talk to my father. He has connections, he can get you help."

"*You don't understand!*" Thomas exploded as his pupils expanded over the width of his eyes again. He'd lost enough control that his demon had slipped through, so I lunged forward to pull Marcy back. Thomas somehow remained in control and covered his face in shame. "I need you to give my mom that message. Please. Please . . ."

"I will." I had to be strong and help him. "I'll tell her."

"Thank you." When Thomas removed his hands from his face, his expression was pained, vulnerable, a ghost of his humanity still intact. "Marcy, I'm so sorry. For everything. I took advantage of you."

He bowed his head and rubbed the back of his neck. "You deserve so much better than what I could give you. Which is why I'm letting you go. For good."

There was a tightness at the back of my throat as Thomas retreated away from us. If only I hadn't gone to Main Street that day, if only I'd gotten far, far away from Thomas the moment I had that vision of his death. Then, maybe, he wouldn't have had to suffer this way.

"Thomas? Tommy, wait!" Marcy ran after him, but Thomas moved in a blur and vanished into the cornstalks. She stopped at the edge of the path, hyperventilating. "Tommy!"

"Marcy?" It was Nathan, Marcy's date for tonight. He cut through the cornstalks and caught Marcy in his arms. There were bloody scratches all over his face.

"Thank God you're okay," Nathan said and hugged her tight. "There're these *things* in the corn maze. Rabid dogs as big as wolves. Everyone is freaking out. I was looking all over for you."

Marcy swayed as he released her, a blank expression of shock on her face as Nathan encouraged her to leave with him. It killed me to leave her like this, without explaining everything I knew. The adrenaline shooting through my system told me it was time to keep moving. I had to separate myself from Marcy and Nathan. Thomas had said good-bye to protect the people he loved and now I had to do the same. My heart couldn't bear anybody else dying tonight. Not after what had happened to Thomas.

As Nathan looped an arm around Marcy's shoulders to help steer her down the path, I stepped deeper into the cornstalks and hid until they left. Marcy would be okay. She didn't need me to protect her. Once the coast was clear, I guardedly made my way back from which I came, to the beginning of the labyrinth. I had to find Death. If I could talk to him alone, I could convince him to spare my aunt.

Maybe I could appeal to him to see if there was anything he could do to save Thomas too. *Yeah, as if Death would care.*

Fear shackled my feet to the ground. The entrance to the maze was gone. In its place stood cornstalks I knew weren't there before.

Freaking out at this point, I pushed through the wall of cornstalks to try to find the entrance of the maze, but the cornstalks never ended and became too tough to climb through. The stalks cut my skin and I smacked at the occasional sensation of a bug biting my arms, until I found my way back to the dirt path in the maze. The path of broken cornstalks seemed to go on forever.

With only the sounds of my breathing and a backdrop of crickets, I edged forward.

A train whistle blasted in my ears, and I jumped a foot into the air. It was just a speaker in the haunted maze, but it was enough to get me going again. I sprinted down a narrow path to my left with the crazed effort of a madwoman, until my throat started to burn. There were no signs. No people jumping out to scare me. Just me, alone, in the corn maze, like some re-created nightmare. By the time I reached a fork in the path, I nearly fell to the ground from exhaustion.

"Have some hearts, my precious!" shouted a witch who leapt from the stalks. She held a rubber, bloody organ in her hands. I released a scream as another, taller person jumped into the path dressed as Jason Voorhees from the Friday the 13th series. He waved around a chain saw without the blade, while the witch held the most ridiculous expression, refusing to let me past as she cackled.

"I get it, I get it!" I shouted. "I really don't have time for this!" I pushed her to the side and ducked beneath the guy's chain saw, racing down the path.

ALMOST THERE! read a wooden sign attached to a pole on my right. Then I passed another one that read JUST KIDDING! and hit a dead end.

"This can't be happening," I gasped.

Whispering, along with the faint noise of footsteps behind me, sent me whirling around. Nobody was there.

A headache pounded against my forehead. I gripped both sides of my skull. Sweat pooled at the back of my neck and slid down my spine, my breaths mere gasps of air. I shut my eyes, willing my thoughts to relax. I couldn't black out. I wouldn't.

Faith. Death's silky voice slithered into my skull. He was furious.

My eyes burst open, and I looked around once more. For a moment, the world was slightly fuzzy, like a dream. When I pinched myself, I felt the pain fully. I looked around and realized the haze was a thin gray glittering fog pouring into the path. I thought it was from a fog machine, except it smelled peppery, like an herb of some sort. As I inspected the sparkling mist in bewilderment, my vision blurred, and my head felt droopy on my neck.

To my left, a shadow slinked through the cornstalks.

"Thomas?"

Rustling. Deep, psychotic laughter. My spine straightened. Frozen in fear, I told myself they were only workers on the farm hidden in the maze. Then animal noises growled behind me, and I thought otherwise.

I turned, stunned to find David Star's receptionist standing in the center of the path. Tiara. She wore a tight all-black business outfit, her striking red hair the color of summer cherries beneath the bright football stadium floodlights. I gazed down at her fingers. Blood dripped down the lengths of them, and her nails were unnaturally long, like talons.

She strutted toward me, red stiletto heels carefully balancing on the compacted ground. I retreated against the cornstalks. Her image wavered for a sliver of a second into something else, something monstrous, and it was too fast to process.

A small, hostile smile lined her red painted lips. "Hello, Faith."

"Why are you here?" I asked, fighting to focus on her face as she grew closer. "What . . . what is that fog?"

"What, this fog?" Tiara lifted her closed hand. With a sharp exhale, she blew a puff of gray glitter fog into my face. I inhaled the contents out of reflex, and it burned all the way up my nostrils and down my throat. Thrown into a coughing fit, I doubled over. She started to cackle, her high-pitched giggling hitting me like knives jabbing into my brain.

"Look at you," she said, her voice distorted. The cornstalks shifted colors from purples and blues to neon green and pink, tripping me out. "A pathetic girl, drooling over a *man*. Don't you see what you really are? You're nothing, *nothing* to him. All he's doing is using you, playing with you like all his other pets. Like the insignificant, wretched little whore you are."

Any other night, her words would have cut me deep. "You know, I'm a nice person, but just because my name is Faith doesn't mean I'm a pacifist." I rolled up the ends of my sleeves. "Kicking your ass is long overdue."

I wound back a fist and connected with Tiara's sculpted cheek. She shuffled back, clutching her face in astonishment. I came at her again, but Tiara disappeared in a blur. A clawed hand grabbed me from behind, drawing blood. I kicked out, nailing her in the leg and twisted around to backhand her across the face.

Tiara recovered fast and struck back, much harder, landing a blow to my stomach that knocked the wind right out of me. She got a hold of my shirt with those talon-like nails and shoved me to the unforgiving ground with an inhuman force.

"You stupid bitch, you don't deserve him! He's a prince, a *god*!" Black swallowed the whites of her eyes as her face altered, sharpening into an unrecognizable creature with ruby irises. "I'll be damned if I let *you* take him away from me!" Tiara moved toward me like a snake, but abruptly stopped. She scanned our surroundings. "Ah, I thought they were never going to show up."

My whole body ached as I tried to get a deep breath. "They?"

"My friends," Tiara said with a spiteful grin. "Death can't know it was me who killed you. No hard feelings, I hope. I don't share."

She turned and darted into the corn.

"That's what I thought!" I shouted, shaking a wounded fist in the air. "You better run away!"

"Do you know where the Bad Man is?"

My skin prickled.

I had not been left alone.

Straight ahead was a little blond-haired girl with two French braids. She stood with her back to me and sang under her breath. My eyes locked on the blood soaking her shirt, the teddy bear clutched tightly in her pale hand by her side.

"What the . . . ?"

"*He wants your blood, he wants your flesh,*" the little girl sang. "*Your soul is gone, your brain is dead. Don't you see? His eyes, they hunt. His mouth, it bites, his nails, they cut. Blood. Blood. Blood.*"

I found the courage to stand up and slowly tiptoed the opposite way. "Can't say I've heard that nursery rhyme before, but I'll take your word for it."

"Please, don't leave me." The girl's head bowed, and she started to sob into her hands. "The Bad Man is coming!"

I halted. Her voice sounded so familiar. "Who are you?"

"I'm you!" the little girl sobbed.

I staggered back.

The girl's eyes were identical to mine, her facial features identical to mine as a kid, except her skin was suctioned to her face like a skeleton, and her lips were purpling.

"You're not me." This was a figment of my imagination. It had to be. "You're not real."

Her smile was two rows of rotted teeth. "Of course, I'm you, dummy! I'm you after you died!" As she approached, the bones in her legs shook like delicate pins threatening to snap. A piece of her skin slowly slid off her cheek. "You don't remember me, do you? I remember you, and I remember him too. Death. He said his name was Death. *Blood. Blood. Blood.*"

A violent chill overtook my body. I shut my eyes, willing the hallucination to go away.

"Why won't you look at me? Look at what you would have been!"

"Leave me alone!"

"I'll haunt you forever, Faith! You'll never be normal, you *died!*" I opened my eyes as the girl cackled, blood seeping from her rotten teeth. My face fell as her image distorted again, into an ugly creature with scaly gray skin and cloudy eyes that bore into mine. When I tried to get away, my feet chugged at a sluggish pace, like running in a dream. I tried to call out, but I couldn't, as a heaviness overtook my limbs. Nothing felt real. A screeching noise that resembled a shriek resounded through the field, followed by a thunderous roar. The creature before me ceased any movement, snapping its head toward the direction of the sounds, and I felt ripped free from an invisible hold on me.

I took off, staggering and zigzagging at first in a drunken state. It took a few moments for the fuzziness in my vision to dissipate enough for me to gain speed. When I did, I thought for sure I would collapse. Grasping my second wind by the throat, I burst with energy and gained enough strength to finally run at full speed again.

"Faith! Faith, where are you?"

My aunt's voice. She sounded so far away.

"Here!" I wheezed out, coming out onto a path and turning

down another maze route. Her voice came from all directions. Unable to amplify my voice, I continued to cough as loud as I could, expelling some of that gray fog from my mouth. "I'm right here! I'm in the maze!"

ALMOST THERE! mocked the same wooden sign I'd seen earlier. I'd gone in circles.

"Help," I panted out, wiping at my bleary, tear-soaked eyes. "Help! Aunt Sarah, I need you!" I couldn't catch my breath, the constant sensation that someone was watching me beckoning a panic attack as I scanned the cornstalks on either side of me.

A man emerged into the pathway. Alexandru Cruscellio.

He wore his gladiator uniform, the one with various intricate designs carved into lavish armor, held together with brass hooks and leather. He was enormous, almost filling the width of the path with rippling, sun-kissed muscle. He appeared exactly as he did in Death's memory.

He stalked closer with a leopard-like grace, and I couldn't move. His face was so alike David's, but even more perfect—a sculpture chiseled from stone, angular cheekbones, skin unlined by wrinkles or imperfections. A strong Roman nose, and full, sinfully pouty lips, curved into a sly smile. His unusual eyes were two lustrous shades of green with vertical slits for pupils. The irises altered underneath the stadium lights, like metamorphosing kaleidoscopes, flickering between mint and lime in the one iris, and emerald and moss in the other. Despite his wicked features, I found him magnetic—unequivocally beautiful.

He stopped in front of me and just stood there, staring at me in a curious way. I gulped, and my mouth became cotton. I tasted bitter acid which made me long for something to drink, anything to quench my thirst.

"No more running, Faith," Alexandru said. The voice was

recognizably Death's, but the intonation didn't sound quite right. I couldn't put my finger on it.

"This is impossible," I said, retreating back. The closer he got, the more detailed he became, down to the slave bands around his ankles. His feet left imprints in the ground.

"In my world, nothing is impossible." He held out his hand like an offering. His fingers were long and calloused, his palms large and masculine. I pictured Death's leather gloves and knew they'd fit perfectly over those powerful hands.

"I feel . . . strange." I kept my arms locked at my sides, straining to concentrate on his face as the cornstalks shifted colors again.

"Don't you find me attractive, Faith?" Now he was standing right next to me like a jump cut.

My mouth felt bone dry, my lips cracking from the frigid air. "I don't understand. I watched you change, in the arena. You're not this man anymore."

His head cocked. "I'm anyone you want me to be."

"Am I dreaming?"

"Don't you want to touch me?" His voice was a low purr, as his lips hovered over my cheek. The instant he touched my skin, I was drowsy again, leaning into him. His fingers lingered on the zipper of my sweatshirt. The bare skin of my arms hit the frigid air as he slipped my jacket off. "I want you, Faith. Take your clothes off."

I drowned in his exotic eyes, itched to touch his smooth skin. I pressed my hand against the plate on his chest. The metal wasn't cold, as I'd expected it to be. In fact, it didn't feel like much of anything, if that even made sense. This little puzzlement sobered me up.

"You're not real," I said, coming fully to the realization.

"I'm not real?" He grinned, ran the tip of his tongue over the edges of his top teeth. "Of course, I'm real, *cupcake*."

His voice. His voice was what triggered it. A spell broke. Clarity hit me at full force, and the small hairs on the nape of my neck lifted. I shunted him away. "Your voice," I said, pointing at him with accusation. "You don't have his accent. You're not him." Coughing, I clutched at my T-shirt and reeled backward. Smoke expelled from my lungs, as tears forcefully streamed down my face. "Show me— *show me what's true!*"

Alexandru blinked, and his eyes clouded. Like a mirage, his image shimmered away, and his face altered, transforming into a frightening thin creature with pale skin and yellow teeth. The creature had various tics and twitches, as if it couldn't stand still. A terrifying grin was permanently engraved into its features, as if its lips were pulled up by invisible fishhooks. I knew it was male from its bared genitals.

"What a clever girl!" it shouted with glee. "You found my fault!"

An identical creature materialized beside the first monster. This one was narrower and possibly female. "You were amazing, baby." She approached the other creature and they started to kiss in a graphic PDA of lizard-like tongues, groping, and saliva. Then they broke apart and looked at me at the same time.

The male transformed back into to the image of Alexandru. "Dinner is served, my love," he said.

The hideous female started toward me.

"Don't forget your appetizer, bitch!" Aunt Sarah sprang into the path and hurled herself into the one creature, knocking it to the ground. She was saturated in blood, most of which wasn't her own, with two deep lacerations cut into her bicep. She was weak, profusely sweating. Still, she was able to bury a dagger into the female's throat, ripping through cords of muscle and tendons, severing its head. Fake Alexandru released a snarl and lunged for my aunt, tossing her damaged body like a rag doll farther down the path.

My eyes bulged out of my head. "Don't touch her!"

Its attention swiveled to me. The Alexandru clone moved in a flash, jumping right in front of me as he released a heinous screech. "Fine, I'll eat you first! After all, *you're* the prize!" The creature clutched my throat with bony fingers and opened its nasty mouth. I felt paralyzed as its jaw dislocated to become unnaturally wide, so I could see down its putrid throat. Needlelike teeth lengthened from rotted gums, and—

Suddenly, a curved blade cut upward through its middle, and the creature gurgled a strangled noise. Rotten skin crackled and burned.

Death's cloaked frame rose behind the creature in a whirl of shadows, his gloved hand gripping the curved weapon penetrating the creature. "Fun's over," he hissed. "I don't like to be imitated."

He removed the blade and sliced the air again. The creature rippled, transforming from Alexandru back into its true form. With a hand still clutching my neck, the demon crumpled, and I with it. The creature's ugly head slid off its wrinkly body before hitting the ground in a slop of flesh. I held back a scream.

Another hideous creature identical to the others pounced into the pathway, hunched low and jaws wide open. It took one look at Death and its violent expression fell away in disbelief.

Dropping to its knees, the creature gasped with a forked tongue, "Your Highnesss. We didn't mean to interfere with your . . . dinner?"

Death stalked in the direction of the kneeling beast. "Tell me who sent you," he commanded like thunder.

"Who sent us?" The creature laughed anxiously. "Nobody, my lord. We were well within our hunting grounds—"

Death kept coming at him.

"Please, please, don't!" shouted the creature. "I'll do anything you want! Have mercy! No, *no*—!"

I turned away, squeezing my eyes shut as Death lashed out. A sickening wet noise followed by crackles like embers from a fire cut through the air. Boots lumbered against the compacted ground.

"Are you all right?" Death asked. I knew it was bad when he genuinely sounded concerned.

All I could do was focus down at the ground, to avoid looking into the eyes of the beheaded male creature in front of me. My chest tightened, like I needed to scream to release the terror locked inside me.

Death clenched the hilt of the knife at his side so hard the thick leather of his gloves creaked. I had a feeling he wanted to keep ruthlessly stabbing these things. Instead, he withheld his monster and gestured with his hand. The corpses around us burst into flames that licked at my skin, until a bed of ash lay beneath my fingertips.

He spoke again. I tuned him out. Tuned everything out. A buzzing filled my ears, a sweet, blissful tune detaching me from the rest of the world.

A hand clamped down on my shoulder.

"Faith," Death said in a sharp tone. "Answer me."

"How do I know you're real?" I mumbled at the ground.

"Illusions always have a fault. Once you control your fear and focus, they shatter." His pause hung in the air as he lowered to the ground beside me. "Look at me."

I tilted my head upward, gradually sliding up the length of Death's cloak to his shadowy face. He was his usual scary self, all right. I focused on his clothing, the shadows snaking around his body, and concluded that it was really him.

"How did they find me?" I croaked.

"Same way I found you. Your soul attracts our kind. Its innate purity stands out amongst the other mortals'." He methodically cleaned the bloody, jagged knife with a cloth. The way he'd easily grouped himself with those creatures, his kind, made me sick to my stomach.

Realizing I had forgotten about my aunt, I tore my gaze ahead to the path, where her body once lay.

"Where's my aunt?"

"Don't worry about her." He twirled the clean blade between his fingers and tilted his head down at me. "She's alive."

And in Hell, he didn't have to add. My insides crumbled in fear that I would never see her again, but I knew Death well enough at this point to know I wouldn't get much more out of him. "What were those things?"

"Wraiths, or Tricksters." He sheathed the weapon in his belt and stepped closer, the edge of his cloak and his leather combat boots in my line of vision. "Wraiths are a species of demon who feed on human fears. They use herbs and a hallucinogenic fog that expels from their mouths to guide their prey to a state of delusion. Then they mimic their prey's darkest fears, and occasionally, their deepest desires, until they go insane. It's their favorite playtime. You missed the grand finale—where they tear you limb from limb and crack open your skull to get to your brain. Fear makes the brain taste sweeter. Luckily for you, I didn't pack any popcorn, so I cut your grand finale short."

"Did you know this was their hunting ground?" I demanded through tight teeth.

"No, I did not know," he said with a solemn voice. "Wraiths are senseless slobs and tend to leave behind a mess. I highly doubt they would be offered a farm like this to hunt. Especially on Halloween, with kids frequenting the area." He paused. "Why are you holding your arm like that?"

As I became aware of my sore arm, I thought back to Tiara. I bridged the connection between her and this attack, and it dawned on me that she might not have been a Trickster.

"Oh my God," I choked out. "She tried to kill me! Your insane gargoyle receptionist tried to *kill* me!"

"What are you talking about?"

"Tiara Reid!" I shouted. "Tiara was here, and she tried to kill me! She must have bribed those creatures to do it!"

"Not possible. Wraiths are slaves to their master."

"Then Tiara made some deal with their master! I'm telling you, she was *here*, Death. She told me that the moment she met me, she wanted to get rid of me, but she didn't want you to—"

"Nothing you saw in this maze was real, until a few minutes ago," he said. "You're in shock."

A sudden onset of anger pierced through the numbness within me. "Are you kidding me right now? I know what I saw! She wasn't like the rest of the Wraiths. She was different. She was *here*. So were Marcy, Nathan, and . . . *Thomas* . . . "

Death said nothing as he prowled around the open space.

"Why won't you believe me?" I felt childish, like I needed the validation of him being on my side, as if that would suddenly make this night a little less insane.

"Your mind was altered by hallucinogens," Death said in a dismissive, apathetic tone. I could tell his patience was wearing thin. "We don't have time to keep chatting. You are not safe here. We need to leave."

"Unbelievable." I shook my head with disdain. "You're taking Tiara's side. Why, because she's been your slam piece for a couple hundred years—?"

"*Enough!*"

My vision blurred with tears. I tore my gaze away from him and gripped the ash beneath my hands. "Am I supposed to thank you? One monster killing another to avenge his property? You're my savior. My *hero!*"

"Get up. You're acting like a child." When I didn't move, Death grabbed me roughly by the back of the shirt and lifted me off the ground. I tossed a handful of ash into his veiled face, making him free me at once with a curse.

Screw him. I was already too far away to hear what he shouted after me. I tore into the corn and avoided the trail altogether. Death was never on my side. He was a deceiving creature just like the rest of them, whose disregard and hatred for mortals was imbedded deep in his veins. His dismissal of my aunt's life did not go unnoticed either. For all I knew, this twisted fuck was toying with me again, and she was already dead.

In a moment of weakness and raw fear, I thought of the only person left who could help me. I summoned his name in my mind, and the air grew colder. "Malphas!"

The leaves of the corn cut through my flesh as sharp as blades, leaving behind thin cuts on my hands, face, and the skin exposed from the rips in my jeans. Reaching an end of the crop, my Converse hit compacted ground and I entered an open space in the maze. Twirling in a circle, Death's laughter rumbled from all around me, and my skin erupted into gooseflesh.

"Did you really think you could escape me?"

I whirled around, to find Death standing a mere foot from me. "Christ!"

"Wrong." Death looked taller and more menacing, if that was even possible. I backpedaled away from him. "Maybe you haven't noticed," he continued in a gravelly manner, blackness swirling around his frame as he fully manifested, "but I'm everywhere. Pull a stunt like that again, and I'll make sure you never forget it."

The wind kicked up. He stalked around me with a pantherine grace, the lapels of his cloak billowing out and revealing the muscular frame of the creature clad in black underneath. If he wasn't my villain, I would have admired the peep show. Right now, I was trying not to soil myself. He circled me again, like a jungle cat analyzing its favorite meal and making sure it was unmarked by any other predator.

Once he was satisfied with whatever he was inspecting, he came to a halt in front of me. We stared at each other in silence. Every breath I took was labored.

"Cupcake," he said.

"Death."

He prowled closer. Too close. A part of me wanted to run the other way with my tail between my legs, and another part of me betrayed any logic and wanted to continue what we'd started the night before.

"You don't want me as an enemy, Faith. End this. Come with me."

Deep down, I knew those Wraiths paled in comparison to what Death could do to me. Everything about him was lethal. His build, his voice, his touch.

"I never wanted you to be my enemy," I said, clutching at my chest as my body quaked uncontrollably. "I never wanted . . . *any* of this. I've never felt so alone and isolated in my life. And you . . . you wanted me to feel this way. You toyed with me, like the manipulating creature you are!"

"Choose your next words wisely."

"Maybe you gave me a second chance at life because there's some good in you," I found myself saying. "It doesn't have to be like this. Maybe we could come to another agreement. Maybe . . . maybe . . . "

"We could be friends?" His laughter had a sinister edge, and he began circling me again. "Don't hold your breath. We're well past friends, don't you think?"

His power skimmed my neck, a phantom caress that was dangerously enticing. The feeling snuck up the column of my neck in calculated, tantalizing kisses. Although I fought to hide my reaction, his concealed eyes clung to my every movement, intensifying the effect on me. My mouth parted. I gave in to him, and the slow burn of his influence sank hotly into my skin as if it belonged there.

Coming to my senses, I fled to a different spot in the clearing and wiped my neck with disgust, trying to pretend my entire body wasn't quaking with desire.

"Don't do that *ever* again," I hissed.

A low, sultry snicker. "Why must you fight me?" In sync, we moved clockwise, changing positions in a dangerous dance, while remaining on opposite sides of the clearing. "Take a hard look at the past few weeks. See any rainbows or unicorns? Wake up. Nothing will ever be the same. You belong in my world."

"I pity you, Death." A single tear slid down my face, and I wouldn't let him see a single more. "I wish I didn't, but I do. I pity you and all the tragedies you've been through that have made you this way."

"You think I didn't choose to be what I am today?" His voice was stark, cold, cruel. "You think life forced me to become *this*? Was I dealt a bad hand, Faith, like all the villains you mortals fabricate?" The void between us closed. "Do you have any idea the sins a man has to commit to spend an eternity cursed as a monster? Would you like to know how many people I've killed? How many times I've devoured your kind, watched the light drain from their eyes? How many times I've *loved* it? I've simply lost count. But don't be mistaken, I chose to be this way."

Our stares bored painfully into each other's, until he turned his back sharply on me. I couldn't breathe. I'd accessed a part of him he kept tucked away in the darkest corner of his mind.

"It is a choice we all must face," Death said, and his voice vibrated with conviction. "A crossroads. There will come a time in your life when you have to decide if you are the person you want to be, and if not, you have the power to change. If you don't make that change, then you risk losing who you're meant to be. Look at me closely. And tell me, is being a monster such a terrible thing? Because I find who I am now far superior to who I was."

I was rendered speechless, reeling over his profound words.

"I don't think you're a monster," I said. "You've forgotten you're not alone. Hiding your pain behind a mask just means you're human."

In what seemed like an instant, everything changed. A force heaved into me, and the earth groaned as my feet slid across the ground like I was skating on ice. Red circles and various designs emerged from the dirt in front of me. Death stood rigid at the center of the clearing, right in the middle of the intricate pattern on the ground.

"What's going on?" I exclaimed.

"It's a sigil," he growled with a curse, his head moving as if he were reading a message on the ground. "I'm imprisoned. The lines are immaculate." He lifted his hooded head and bellowed a thundering roar. My eyes widened at the shadows crawling out of the cornstalks, how they barreled toward the sigil and tried to break through it.

Feathers rustled and the shadows dissipated.

"Looks like the cat is caged this time," said a mocking, cultured voice. I whipped my head to my right, and a scream caught in my throat. Malphas, the raven demigod, materialized outside the sigil.

A thousand thoughts rattled my brain. Malphas had his hands clasped behind his back, a position of calm authority, as if he had full command of this situation. And his eyes were black as coal, unpredictable.

"Father," Death said, a speckle of panic in his menacing voice.

I looked between both men. *Father?*

"I told you, Faith," Malphas said with a venomous smirk. "I am the only one capable of stopping Death. He is my son, after all."

My gut plummeted. Physically, Malphas appeared young enough to be Death's older brother. I questioned whether this was another game from the Wraiths, like I so desperately wanted it to be, but I knew in my gut this was real. Which meant Death had killed his own father in the gladiator arena.

"Whoa," I said. *Talk about some serious family issues.*

I stood rooted in my spot, reliving the horror show in the alleyway. The demons chasing Thomas and I down Main Street, crawling down the buildings in hordes, with their beady black eyes and porcelain skin. All of it because of a vendetta between a father and son.

"I never imagined I'd trap the Prince of Darkness," Malphas continued. "It was a risk indeed, but all thanks to you, an easy task, lovely Faith Williams."

A monstrous noise arose from Death. "Touch her, and I'll rip your head off! You have two fucking seconds to break the sigil!"

"Oh, how I've been waiting for this moment," Malphas said with a fiendish, evil smirk. "I knew it would only be a matter of time before you screwed up. Honestly, all your power, and a *girl* is your undoing? It's quite pathetic, son. Dare I say, cliché."

"You don't have to do this," Death said, and I could hear the tremor in his deep voice. "Killing her won't change what I did."

"Do not lecture me about morality when you stand in the gray. For *two thousand years*, my soul was imprisoned in the Underworld. You could not fathom the pain and suffering I endured. All while you paraded around with Lucifer, all while you were treated like *celebrity* amongst the mortals!"

Our surroundings pulsed with electric currents as Malphas's anger amplified to a wrathful roar. His ravens soared high above us, circling the floodlights like vultures.

"The long wait was worth it, though," he continued, calming himself with graceful precision. "It seems I couldn't have arrived at a better time to stir up the balance between good and evil."

His ominous words rattled me to the bone.

"I was a *child*!" Death thundered. "I was a child and a slave to those Roman games you put me through. Ahrimad took advantage of my innocence—"

"You made your choice," Malphas said coldly. "*Your* words, not mine."

"I have no remorse for you," Death snarled, each word like poison in his mouth. "You took . . . everything I loved and destroyed it. You should have stayed dead."

Malphas's face tightened with rage. He began uttering a chant, the words amplifying as he lifted his arms toward the night. The sigil pulsed to a violent rhythm with scarlet flames. Death stiffened, the shadows lingering around his frame pressing against their unyielding confinements.

"You'll find I am not the only one who won't stay dead," Malphas said. "There is another who hungers to be freed. To free him, I will need to borrow your scythe. Hope you don't mind."

With a menacing roar unlike any animal I'd ever heard, Death thrashed in the circle, hurling himself into an invisible barrier. He dropped forcefully to one knee, then the other.

Anxiety squeezed at my heart. Death would die because of me, because I called on Malphas. I had to do something. I *had* to intervene.

"Stop!" I exclaimed. "Please, stop! I didn't want this! I didn't want you to hurt him!"

Malphas wouldn't listen.

"Come on, come *on!*" I shook out my fingers and flexed them as if it would charge the mysterious power within me. *"Do something!"*

With no luck, I barreled into the sigil, and I heard Malphas's shout from the outside. Pain crippled me instantly, coiled and twisted as if I was being torn apart from the inside. Deeper into the lines of magic, pressure crushed against my skull, but my will was stronger. I reached a shuddering hand toward Death, just beyond the barrier of magic containing him at the center.

"Take my hand!" Tears surged down my face as my fingertips

flickered to life with light, slowly burning an opening into the center sigil. "You're not dying on me. Not tonight!"

Death's gloves tore and talons slid out. With one last heave of strength, he slashed at the barriers remaining between us. The inner sigil exploded, and I was flung out of the lines with a blast of painful jolts up my legs and spine. I knew Death had saved my life again as the whole sigil spewed out ferocious red flames.

Death's shoulders slumped; his movements turned lethargic. The beast beneath the cloak stirred, growling and hissing.

Death weakly lifted his head, hands gripping the earth. Our eyes connected through the darkness concealing his features, and in that painful moment, I knew this was good-bye.

A strangled cry ripped free from Death's throat, as an orb of light ripped out from his body. The glow hovered in the air as bright as a blue flare, and then flung itself into the night. The shadow of Death's face waned away as he collapsed forward, hitting the ground at a dead weight.

"DEATH!" I lurched to my feet to run into the sigil again and was jolted once more. Malphas's once onyx-black eyes blazed the same shade of scarlet as the sigil's lines. When I tried to escape the clearing, he pointed at me with a casual outstretched hand and suddenly I was consumed by a crushing, clawing pain from inside my skull. I screamed as it only amplified, my vision strobing in and out, before the sensations expired, and I hit the ground in utter exhaustion.

A grin spread over Malphas's mouth. A tormentor proud of the pain he'd inflicted. "Not so fast, girl," he tsked. "You and I are not done here." Wind swept over the clearing and smothered the red flames to smoke, as Malphas strolled into the sigil and squatted down, reaching toward Death's head.

"No!" I cried out at the top of my lungs. My limbs were like dead weights as I tried to get off the ground. Tears rushed from my eyes. "Please, don't, Malphas! Don't hurt him anymore! He's your son!"

The Raven God seemed to pause.

Moving my mouth, I forced myself to speak. "I didn't want this. I didn't want you to hurt him."

"This is exactly what you wanted, darling," Malphas said in his composed, raspy voice. "Remember, you called to me. You wanted freedom." Malphas reached around Death's body and grabbed his fallen scythe. His expression flinched, the corners of his eyes tightening with rage. The branches of the willow tree along the staff and the blade seemed to illuminate briefly against his touch.

In a dazed blur, my eyes drifted to Death and his lifeless body at the center of the sigil. I imagined this was all pretend. Any second now, he would get back up. He'd become my unlikely savior again and remain the unstoppable force I'd painted him as.

But he was so still, and I felt so cold.

It's cruel when we listen to our hearts only after we lose someone forever. All the things I couldn't say surfaced and ripped me apart from the inside out. Through the manipulation, the games, and trauma Death had caused me—whether it was right or wrong—I had fallen hopelessly in love with the monster beneath the hood. I was in love with the Grim Reaper.

Now he was gone. He was dead. And it was all my fault.

"The great darkness is coming." Malphas stood over me with Death's scythe clenched in his hands, rain trickling down his stony face. His eyes were dead black, vacant . . . possessed. "Ahrimad shall rise again."

My vision tunneled as the world shuttered to black like the end of a film roll.

EPILOGUE

DEATH

I awoke in a confused state of panic, choking, clutching my throat as my lungs failed to pull in air. Lurching into an upward position, I remembered what I was. Undead. I didn't need oxygen.

I shut off my lungs and heart. Breathing from time to time was a force of habit, an odd occasional comfort that shadowed me into immortality.

It took a moment to get my bearings straight. I'd been in the corn maze, and now I was sitting in the heart of Times Square, but the world was drained of color. The flashy HD advertisements and vibrant billboards stretching across the lengths of the buildings like light show collages were all blank. No blaring horns, no pedestrians rushing to get from place to place.

But there were souls. The corporeal ones moved sluggishly all around me, zombies, eyes sunken in, skin pale and translucent. Some of them wore clothes from hundreds of years ago. None of them spoke a word, only an occasional grunt or sob. My head tilted heavenward. Dark-gray gusts of energy swirled around the sky, shrieking and moaning as they whirled through the realm.

I leapt to my feet and violently swore.

Limbo. I was in *Limbo*, a realm between Heaven and Hell, where memories and lost souls wandered.

I'd been so close. *So close* to bringing Faith voluntarily back to Hell for Lucifer, and then Malphas interfered. He'd taken the perfect opportunity to draw magic into the ground and trap me in the corn maze. The next thing I knew, he'd used Latin to separate my soul from my body. I was completely debilitated inside of the sigil.

Although I'd known Malphas had been having me shadowed by his underlings, I hadn't expected him to be so bold as to attack me all alone. This begged for a war from Hell, and he didn't have the soldiers to fight Lucifer's legion.

There was more to this plan of my father's. It was written all over Faith Williams's expression. As my soul ripped from my corpse, I'd seen the guilt in her eyes. She blamed herself for what'd happened to me, which meant she'd been in on it. Malphas must have found a way to communicate with Faith without my knowledge, perhaps through the slash on her forearm from the attack in the alleyway.

Maybe he seduced her.

The twisted thought set me off. I unleashed a thunderous roar, and a stabbing sensation cleaved the center of my chest. I clutched at my shirt; it was soaked, sticky with blood. I ripped the clothing over my head, uncovering an intricate pattern of deep puncture wounds around my heart in the exact design of the sigil Malphas had drawn. I recognized the pattern of symbols. A wandering spell, which trapped anyone or anything in Purgatory.

"I should have taken her the moment we met in that pool house," I raged out loud. "I should have thrown her ass over my shoulder, kidnapped her, and forced her into complacency. To hell with the rules, I'd kill anyone in my way. That would have been fun. But *no*! That would have been too *easy*!"

I hurled my torn shirt to the side, a complete meltdown in my wake. Fangs lengthened in my mouth. Pure rage rippled through me at the thought of my cloak being gone. My scythe was gone too. Actual steam expelled from my bare skin as my temper flared against the cool, damp weather of this realm.

"I had to get curious and get to know her! I had to start worrying about her safety and *feel* things, like a weak, pathetic mortal!" I gripped both sides of my skull and squeezed. "And it turns out she doesn't even like normal, or behaved! She likes *me*!"

Another snarl tore out of my throat. Energy pulsed through my veins, limitless and unpredictable.

Faith Williams had betrayed me. For my father.

My nostrils flared. She was *so* dead.

"GLENN!" I bellowed. All I heard was the groans of the lost souls around me. It was driving me insane. "Glenn, I summon you!"

Nothing.

Worthless worm.

I looked down at my empty hands. My scythe. Malphas had my scythe. My scythe allowed me to travel between Earth, Limbo, and Hell. Lucifer knew the routes between the realms like the back of his hand, but not me. Now I regretted my extreme lack of care in not memorizing the paths myself.

You'll find I am not the only one who won't stay dead.

My eyes widened as it hit me. "No . . . "

Surely, my father hadn't meant Ahrimad. The original death god who had cursed me. I'd destroyed him. Then again, I was certain my father was gone forever, and he'd weaseled his way out of the graveyard aviary. Damn. Ahrimad would sure be one spiteful bastard because of the whole *you wrecked my ass in the arena two thousand years ago* thing.

My mind harked back to all the Light Angels Malphas had killed. How had I not seen this coming? He'd taken their eyes. And he'd kept them. Trinkets of sacrifices. Depending on how many angels he'd killed, he could probably fuel a resurrection spell. Because my soul was no longer within my corpse, my body was up for grabs for any soul. Was it *possible* Ahrimad's soul had somehow survived that fateful fight?

If that were the case, Malphas could use my corpse as a conduit for Ahrimad's soul. Or worse, Ahrimad could take control of another body and control my corpse like a puppet. Ahrimad would be temporarily, or maybe even permanently, freed. Lucifer would not get Faith's soul by midnight either.

And I would be here.

Trapped.

This was an unmitigated disaster, to say the least.

I'd thought I was in control. I'd thought I had *everything* under control, but I'd been wrong. This wasn't just a small miscalculation on my part—it was an impending cataclysm of epic proportions.

Adrenaline propelled me to finally move. I paced in fierce strides, gripping the sides of my skull again to concentrate. I tried to search through every book, every memory I had read and encountered about Purgatory, but my thoughts were too chaotic, like J-walking across a six-lane highway at rush hour.

I stood in front of the display window of an abandoned store. There, I found my reflection. An exotic creature with mismatched, slitted eyes glared back at me. My lips peeled back in a feral grin.

Bingo.

Holding my bare hands out, I carved into the glass with my nails and murmured an enchantment. The only way to communicate from Purgatory to Earth was to create an enchantment in a mirror, or, in this case, a reflection in a window.

A display of numbers and letters floated onto the glass pane. I selected English as my preferred language and the state of New York as my last residency. *Hello! Welcome to Purgatory. Please insert three quarters*, the screen promptly read.

".Oh, come on!" I heard footsteps and pivoted on my heel. A lost soul with a hoodie strode by me. Barreling toward the soul, I snatched him by the nape. I rummaged through his pockets, coming away with one condom and a handful of change.

I glanced at the condom package and snickered.

The lost soul stared blankly at me, hunched forward.

"Thanks for the change." I wanted nothing more than to take my anger out on this man. Too bad he was only a soul, and I couldn't do much damage at this point. "With a bankroll of eighty-five cents, I doubt you'll be needing the condom."

The lost soul held the same blank, uninterested expression.

I scowled and pocketed the condom. Bullying wasn't fun when my victim was silent. Unless it was Glenn, my everlasting demon servant.

"Get the hell out of my sight. You're freaking me out."

The lost soul continued to wander down the block.

Cracking my neck from side to side, I returned to the enchantment and inserted three quarters. Then I impatiently tapped the screen in hopes of moving things faster along. "Come on, baby," I sweet-talked the enchantment. "Get Daddy out of this shithole."

"Hello, and thank for using Limbo to Earth Communication Services!" the enchantment said in a female automated electronic voice. "If you wish to leave Limbo, please press one—"

I smashed my finger into the button, twitching all over.

"If you seek reexamination of your situation through appointment, please press one. If you seek penance, press two. If you would like to speak to a representative in respect to selling your soul, press six-six-six."

Rolling my eyes, I grudgingly dialed six-six-six. The moment I told him where I was, Lucifer would burn the skin and flesh off my bones until I looked like a top Google search of the Grim Reaper. Better than being stuck here.

"One moment, please, as we process your entry."

I propped a leg on the enchantment, tapping my talons against the glass as I glowered at the lost souls of this parallel universe. My energy was depleting, fast. Hunger gnawed at my insides, and I shuddered. Being stuck in Limbo meant being surrounded by a scrumptious buffet of souls that I was unable to devour. Each wandering soul had a small tattoo beneath their ear, indicating their spirit was claimed by Purgatory. The last thing I needed on top of everything was a vicious lawsuit from the in-between.

Normally I had thousands of duplicates of myself feeding off human souls, plus my reapers pitching in. Now that I was in here, stuck in another realm, I had nothing. No source of energy. Zip. Nada. Which was exactly why I never stayed long in Purgatory.

Only in passing did I visit here. When I had the patience to guide a lost soul through the afterlife to their forever home. It happened more often with adults and the elderly, depending on how they died. But rarely with children, like when I met little Faith. Her soul had wandered in the in-between, and I could sense she'd needed guidance. When a young, deceased soul leaned toward good, guardian angels would often help their charges pass into the realm of Heaven. For some reason, little Faith had not been assigned. I'd intended to send little Faith off to Heaven myself. As impersonal as my job had begun to feel centuries ago, allowing a child to walk through Purgatory alone was a cruel and unusual punishment I did not agree with.

Faith was no longer that innocent child. She was a woman, and she'd made a drastic decision to turn against me tonight. The mere thought of the backstabbing bitch sent my blood pressure through the roof. I didn't even *have* blood pressure.

When I was done with her, she'd be begging for forgiveness. Just the thought of Faith on her knees with her cosmic blue eyes all red and tear-filled reduced my anger. Oh yeah, I would have the last laugh.

The thought of punishing her sent my hormones straight down Horny Street, to a forbidden place—when I'd kissed her in her bedroom. Her soft lips, her hands on my body, the push and pull of that undeniable attraction . . .

Blood. Kill. Murder. Ridding myself of any of *those* illicit thoughts, I worked my jaw and seethed with evil intentions.

A dial tone hummed from within the enchantment.

"Hello, my name is Ron, and I'm a trusted representative at Limbo," Lucifer answered.

Ron? Really?

"It's me," I rushed out. "Malphas has Faith—"

"You've reached Extension 666," Lucifer's voice added. The pause in his words had been a small break in the line.

Wi-Fi wasn't exactly easy to come by in Limbo.

"I'm unavailable at this time," the recording continued. Claws sprung from my fingertips, destroying yet another pair of leather gloves. "However, if you leave your name, age, cause of death, and social security number, I will get back to you as soon as possible."

I ended the call with a monstrous hiss. I knew damn well he never checked his voicemails. Gripping the sides of the enchantment, I proceeded to bang my skull repeatedly against the glass. The fissures it formed in the windowpane rapidly mended together. "And you tell me I don't know how to use a phone, old man?"

"You have two remaining calls," the enchantment said. "If you would like to contact a specific person, please insert one dollar and fifty cents."

Spinning around, I limbered up my shoulders, bulleted forward, and slashed my talons into the steel of a street trash can. I tore straight through the webbed structure of the bin and sent the trash can flying thousands of feet, smashing into a window at the upper floor of a skyscraper. As if I was trapped in a video game simulation, the building restored itself instantly and the bin returned to its original place on the curb, unmarked.

None of the wandering souls seemed to notice this outburst. *Figures.*

Once I simmered down from wrath to moderate irritation again, I pickpocketed six wandering souls to get enough change for the enchantment. Scraping my talons down the short hairs along my jaw, I paced back and forth like a caged animal in the zoo. I ticked through a list of names to call in my head.

It was a short list. I didn't trust any of them enough with my existence.

Wow, I really have nobody.

"Call Glenn," I bit out.

Glenn's face popped up on the screen. He held an armful of papers and was rushing around my office to organize various folders.

"Glenn." I noticed he wore headphones and raised my voice. "Glenn, over here!"

Glenn bopped his hips, singing an off-key Britney Spears song as he watered two indoor snake plants by my television and the devil's ivy behind my desk.

"Glenn!" I barked.

Glenn shrieked and wrenched his headphones from his ears. Papers went flying in a hazardous rain of impending paper cuts. "My lord?" He glanced skittishly around the room. "Wh-wh-where are you?"

"You have sixty seconds remaining for this call," the enchantment said.

Limbo was officially on my hit list. "Glenn, this is urgent. I'm in the mirror."

Glenn's eyes locked onto mine as he found the only mirror in the room. His eyes bulged. "My lord, why are you . . . "

"I'm trapped in Limbo. I need you to tell Lucifer I'm here. Tell him I don't have my scythe. Malphas trapped me here with a wandering spell, which means my corpse is unattended." I didn't even want to think about what that could entail. "Also, tell him Faith Williams . . . " I grated my fangs together. "She's with my father, and he'll want to hurt her. I can't escape Limbo alone. I need some sort of guide, or map from Lucifer. I don't know the pathways between these worlds well enough to sift through them."

"Does anyone else know you're trapped?"

I blinked. "No?"

Glenn bit back a laugh. "Oh, this is gold. This is *gold*."

I bared my teeth in a snarl. "I'd watch your just-grown-back tongue, Glenn. I could make a smoothie out of you and drink you down with one of those quirkily shaped colorful straws. Remember who you work for."

"I'm afraid you've mistaken me for somebody else. I no longer work for anybody." Glenn kicked at the papers on the ground and fired middle fingers at them. He loosened his tie. "Seems like my boss went on vacation and won't be coming back!"

"*Excuse me?*"

Glenn fell into uneasy laughter. "Let me get this straight. You expected my help to escape Limbo, when nobody knows where you are?" Glenn balled up his hands into fists. "After everything you've put me through, you really think I would help you of my own free will? You know, I wet the bed once because of you!"

"Call will terminate in twenty-five seconds," the enchantment said.

I worked my jaw several times, and then attempted to sound as pleasant as inhumanly possible. "Glenn, listen to me, buddy. I know you hate me. There's nothing I can say in twenty seconds to change that. Just think of her. Faith. She's a good girl. You've heard about Malphas, you know what he's capable of. This isn't about me, Glenn."

For a demon, Glenn was about as evil as a newborn puppy. He was a low-class demon, which meant his sins before death were only slightly above normal. I thought he would change his mind and be sensitive to the girl's safety.

"It's always about you, Death," Glenn said. "You—you *deserve* this!"

The call went dead.

"*Glenn!*" I pounded on the glass. "I'm going to slice you into cubes and stew you in a Crock-Pot!" I went off in another language as a deafening crash of thunder shook the ground and lightning shattered the sky in spiderlike white fractures. Limbo was known for its melodramatic, shitty-ass weather. My mood made it worse.

"You have one remaining call," the enchantment said.

I speared my fingers through my hair and called my last resort.

The line picked up.

"*Bonsoir*, my old friend." Ace's thick French accent slid out of the enchantment. He stood before a mirror, having anticipated the call. Clearly, he'd received one of his premonitions. "You have gotten yourself in quite the dilemma on this mystical night." He spoke in a cruel, condescending way, enjoying every moment of this. "Another ghost from your past has perhaps awakened, and you are *there*. Imprisoned. Unable to feed, deteriorating. And poor Faith, *votre amour* . . . "

My fangs shot forward with a hiss. "I want out, Ace. What do you want in return?"

A slow, wicked grin twisted the warlock's mouth. "The *Book of the Dead*."

ACKNOWLEDGMENTS

I wrote the first draft of *Death is My BFF* when I was just fourteen years old. I am now twenty-seven, and it would be an understatement (and perhaps a bad pun) to say this book has a piece of my soul in it. In elementary and early middle school, I was bullied and had a lot of anxiety. I didn't have many friends either. Reading books had always been a magical form of escapism for me, so it was no surprise that writing stories quickly became my remedy to navigate difficult emotions. Looking back, I created Faith as a role model of resiliency and courage, so that I could overcome my own fears, and discover my own "light" within myself. My hope is that I have now given this gift to others through Faith Williams.

All of this frames me thanking my family. Thank you, Mom, for helping me discover my passion for storytelling. At fourteen years old, you are the one who sat me down and encouraged me to channel my emotions and imagination into writing. That day changed my life forever. Dad, thank you for always helping me with witty lines and being the best manager and father in the whole world. A true Super Dad (with great hair!), you're always ready to save the day, and I appreciate all the advice you've given me over the years that has gotten me here. Christina, my little sis, my best friend, and my twin, thank you for being my rock and my number one fan. Thank you for reading my manuscript as I wrote it (sometimes out loud in character) and giving me feedback that helped create a book that we would want to read. I love you guys so much!

I have to acknowledge my powerhouse literary agent, Elaine

Spencer. Elaine, thank you for always being there and always knowing what to do! You rock! Thank you to Deanna McFadden for your editorial guidance. If not for you, I wouldn't have added MORE Death perspective, which made such a massive difference in the final product. The entire team at Wattpad Books have been incredible to work with, and I appreciate all their hard work on *Death is My BFF*.

This book would not be in your hands if not for my Wattpad readers. To the Wattpad readers who beta read the old drafts, sent me fan art and messages of support, left me comments, and voted on my chapters, and even to the quiet reader who was always there: Thank you so much, cupcakes!

Lastly, I am so grateful for YOU, reader. Thank you for reading *Death is My BFF*. It is a dream come true to finally get my novel physically in the hands of readers, and I hope you are enjoying Faith and Death's journey.

More to come soon!

All my love,
Katarina E. Tonks

ABOUT THE AUTHOR

Katarina E. Tonks is an award-winning author who began her career on the Wattpad platform. Since then, she has amassed nearly half a million followers—or "cupcakes" and "reapers" as she calls them—who she loves to interact with in forums where "Death" will sometimes jump in and respond himself. She has over 100 million reads collectively on the early drafts of her Death Chronicles and the Vendetta series, and she is considered one of Wattpad's most influential writers.

Kat has been creating stories since she was old enough to hold a crayon. Never one to color between the lines, her books are often dark romance with morally gray love interests. She graduated from Fairleigh Dickinson University with a bachelor's degree in creative writing and is pursuing her master's degree in clinical mental health counseling. Kat is a Jersey Girl and lives with her family and many pets.

Get updates on Kat on her social media!

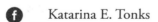

Katarina E. Tonks

@katrocks247

Turn the page for a preview of book two in
THE DEATH CHRONICLES

Death is My Ride or Die

Coming soon from Wattpad Books!

I

FAITH

When I opened my eyes, the illusion that I was safe evaporated.

Across the way, Malphas sat regally on a Victorian-style red velvet couch. He was dressed in silk. His lustrous raven-black hair was tied neatly back and woven together into warrior braids. Bathed in soft lighting, the room was bare except for a large Persian rug, a rather ornate coffee table, and the couches where we sat opposite of each other.

I pictured Death's motionless corpse in the sigil. The painful howls of a man I'd thought was unstoppable. The heaviness in my heart anchored me to the image of him dying. I wanted to believe he was alive. That he was a force of nature and nothing could take him away from this world, but deep inside I knew this was real.

I'd wanted nothing more to do with Death. He'd played me from the beginning. And yet, he also saved my life time and time again. No matter how I tried to rationalize it, I felt guilty. The cold-hearted monster who claimed I was only a possession, yet kissed me with a passion like I was his saving grace, was gone. I'd killed him.

"Not gone," Malphas said with a sinister smirk. "I sent his soul to a different realm, temporarily."

My whole body trembled as I fought back a surge of emotion. I desperately wanted to believe him.

"Where did you send him?" I demanded.

"He's in Limbo. Or perhaps you are more familiar with its other name, Purgatory." Malphas smoothed down a wrinkle in the fabric covering his forearm. I could have sworn I felt his touch on the invisible scar left by his underling on my own forearm. "There are other worlds besides the human one. They are mostly abandoned and filled with darkness and other things . . . things that wander into the mortal realm and go bump in the night. Limbo is a complex realm that parallels what you see as earth. A place for wandering and forgotten souls. That is where Death's soul lies."

"So, Death's soul is trapped in Limbo. But what about his body?"

Malphas grinned in an enigmatic way. "Inaccessible at the moment."

My fingers curled against the cushion beneath me. I had no idea what Malphas was capable of, so I knew I had to tread carefully and keep quiet.

"Your aunt is rumored to have possession of an object," Malphas continued, his abrasive, sandpapery voice sending chills down my spine, "a book that Ahrimad will require once he rises. Torturing her over it would have been a waste of energy. Hunters like her wear jewelry and engrave tattoos into their bodies that limit my power. So, I waited. I waited for the right moment." He reached out to touch an object standing on the coffee table in between the couches. The small device began to tick like a metronome. "Your essence is so peculiar, I knew right away you were the girl. The one he *spared*. You, my dear girl, are a treasure."

"You can save the 'join me' evil villain speech. I'm not helping you with whatever twisted plan you have up your sleeve."

Tick-tock. The ticking of the device reverberated in my ears, vibrating my vision, pulsing with an intense pressure as Malphas's image blurred. I craned my neck to the side and winced. The sensations left me at once as the ticking became background noise again.

"Either you are with me or you are against me," Malphas said. "No matter which option you choose, our paths will cross again. I always get what I want, one way or another."

"You don't scare me," I said, my voice trembling so hard I had to tighten my muscles to speak. "You sick, heartless creature."

"You called for me in your hour of need, and I answered. I was the weapon, but you pulled the trigger."

"It was a mistake!" I exclaimed. "A moment of weakness, not need. I was scared, and I should have never relied on you. Only a monster does what you did to your son."

The raven demon's coal eyes burned with wrath as he lifted his chin. "Alexandru is hardly my son. He never appreciated the sacrifices I made for him."

"You *abused* him."

Something flinched a little in his marble features. "He was never meant for a delicate mortal hand."

"You act like being human is a disease."

"Because it *is* a disease. I was mortal once. I've lived it."

Despite my utter distain for him, he captured my attention. "Just curious, how does one become immortal?"

"It's easy. First, you have to die in battle. It helps if there's a practicing dark magic witch nearby to combine your lifeless heart with that of a loitering raven, who happened to be perched on your corpse." A sly smirk lined the raven demon's mouth. "And if you're happy with your resurrection, you might even marry the witch and raise an ungrateful, vindictive son."

My gaze drifted over the contours of his pallid face. "Your

humanity," I said, drawing a shaky breath, "is it completely gone now?"

The raven demigod morphed into an explosion of birds, and I flinched back against the couch. Feathers caved inward in the churning chaos of ravens hurling around the room, imploding back into a mass of dismantled bodies and feathers. The mass quickly molded back into flesh and the shape of a man, the gruesome transformation almost instantaneous. In a matter of seconds, I was staring into Malphas's onyx eyes again.

"What do you think?" he asked with a grin.

Well, that was horrifying . . .

"Alexandru had my demigod blood in his veins," Malphas explained. "As I mentioned, his mother was a powerful witch and certain gifts were passed on genetically there as well. You see, Alexandru was the first of his kind, a lethal, unpredictable creature even before he became death itself. I did what I had to do so he could reach his full potential."

Tick-tock. Tick-tock. My eyes were now trapped on the metronome on the coffee table. I thought it was strange to have one there, but then it vanished into thin air. When I looked up at Malphas again, he was watching me intently. My eyelids felt oddly heavy.

"Even as a small boy," Malphas continued, "his inner animal drove him to hunt and kill. I started training him as soon as he understood he was different. If not for my guidance, Alexandru would have never learned discipline over himself. He would have never been a prodigy—a celebrity fighter admired by all of Rome."

I pictured the little boy from Death's memories. How he was mistreated and forced by his father to become a gladiator. When he was older, he had scars and sores around his ankles and wrists as if he were a prisoner, just like the lions that the fighters were forced to fight in the arena. Although, I'd never forget the haunting look of confliction in Alexandru's eyes as he knelt over Malphas' dead body in the arena. Whatever had happened between them, it was complicated, and there was so much more I didn't know. But what I did know was the fragments of Death's life that I had seen told a very different tale than what his father was telling me now.

I catapulted to my feet. "That was a nice little contrived, fictional story you spun. Forgive me if I don't buy a single word."

Malphas stood up as well. The violence in his expression made my body go rigid. "You know nothing of our world. You are just a scared little girl with fear in your eyes and a fate you can't escape. I'm finished with my part in this game, Miss Williams. I'm the least of your worries now." The room came to a hush as my vision tunneled. "Once Alexandru returns from Limbo, he will be weak. You're the only one who can get close enough to him to complete this task."

Malphas snapped his fingers and the metronome stopped.

My head slumped forward, my eyes closed.

"I'm going to hand you something. You believe it to be an ordinary bottle of hand lotion." Malphas reached into his pocket. "Open your eyes and look at the item in front of you. What is it?"

My eyes cracked open and analyzed the blade pinched between his black fingertips. "An ordinary bottle of lotion."

"Close your eyes again," Malphas instructed. "I'm giving you a dagger laced with poison. You see, Faith, we can help one another. You want to escape the consequences of the Kiss of Death, and I—I want Death out of my way. Open your eyes." As I did, I saw the murderous edge to Malphas's lifeless gaze. "All you have to do is nick Death with this blade once he returns from Limbo. It will paralyze him for a few hours. I expect he'll be back just in time for the D&S Tower event, where he'll go to find Lucifer."

My blinks were slow. "What happens once he's paralyzed?"

"You let me worry about that." When Malphas's hand pressed

onto my shoulder, a claw scratched its way into my skull and skimmed my brain. I stared deep into his onyx eyes, sinking as his power whirled in my head. When I mentally shoved him away, he didn't seem to notice. But I did. I pushed against that sensation with all my might, and the scraping sensation subsided. Malphas released my shoulder. I feared he'd noticed.

"You foolish girl," he chided. "You feel so deeply for Death, and he'll never love you back. He's incapable of it." He paused and handed me the dagger. "A little advice, Faith. The trick to life is not to let the imitation of what was once there fool you into believing it lives on in the present. Beyond the shallow depths of any façade, there's always the truth." As he stepped back, his features shimmered into a dreadful creature with translucent skin and bluish-black fangs. "You just need to peel away the mask."

He vanished, and suddenly I was in my bedroom.

I exhaled the breath I'd been holding and stared at the spot where Malphas had once been, a frown knit between my eyebrows. I clenched the dagger in my hand.

As soon as Malphas was gone, my ponytail flew forward. A blustery blast of air swirled through the room from my open bedroom window.

"Bonjour, *mon ange*."

I turned to my left and found a familiar lively, handsome warlock with bright violet eyes. My mind felt dreamlike, too delirious to comprehend why he was here. He wore a deep purple satin suit jacket with an ornate Victorian vest made of tapestry fabric beneath. Luxurious black velvet lapels and metal buttons down the center decorated the vest. His pants matched the lavish obsidian fabric lining the collar of the jacket.

"Ace!"

He bowed theatrically and twisted his hand in a fast gesture, producing a black rose from thin air. "*Votre sourire est un don.* Your smile is a gift."

"What—what are you doing here?" I timidly held the flower and inhaled the fragrance of its petals, which then blossomed to life in my hand and altered to a passionate red.

Instead of answering, Ace checked his watch.

"Oh, *là là.* We are going to be late! We should leave as soon as possible. *Dès que possible.*" Those colorful eyes drifted over my corn maze–attacked clothes. "I will certainly need to cook you up something creative to wear—" he tapped my knee playfully with the large octagon-shaped crystal at the head of his golden cane "—since I'm your dashing date for tonight!"

Ace twirled his cane with a laugh as shimmering smoke gathered around us.